Tangier, A Novel

To Midori

Enjoy,

Diane Ponasik

To order additional copies, please contact us.
BookSurge, LLC
www.booksurge.com
1-866-308-6235
orders@booksurge.com

DIANE
SKELLY PONASIK

TANGIER,
A NOVEL

2005

Tangier, A Novel

TANGIER, a novel
Diane Skelly Ponasik

**

This novel is set in Tangier in the late 19th and early 20th centuries. It is the story of Lili, a Moroccan girl raised by the American Minister (Ambassador) in Tangier. Lili struggles between her adopted American identity and her Moroccan origins. Although she falls in love with Tariq, a noble from the High Atlas, she chooses to marry an American diplomat, believing she will be happier and more free as an American woman. But fate will bring the two together as they are caught in a rebellion against the young Sultan. It is also the story of Lili's stepbrother, Ted, who marries a young Tangier Jew, Meriam. Meriam is caught in a vicious Anti-Semitic attack during the rebellion and decides to leave Morocco, but Ted, whose profession as a reporter is dependent on his contacts in Morocco, is not ready to leave the country he grew up in.

**

Cover photograph of the American Legation in Tangier courtesy of Thor Kuniholm, director of the Legation. Painting of the Woman is by James McBey, The man is a portrait by Ian Peridcaris called Groom with horse. Both are excerpts of larger paintings and are courtesy of the American Legation in Tangier

ACKNOWLEDGEMENTS

So many people have helped me in the course of writing this book. My first 'outside reader', Ann Hauge, was wonderful in encouraging me to continue and giving valuable feedback on language and characters. She has continued to read newer versions and I am very grateful for her advice. Friends who read various early versions of this included Susan Dichter and Susan Schaeffer Davis, both knowledgeable about Morocco. Susan Gilson Miller was kind enough to give me several books and articles on Jewish life in Tangier before the Protectorate. Judith Bunker gave me many helpful suggestions on setting. Douglas Porch, whose book, The *Conquest of Morocco,* inspired me to begin this task, provided me with bibiliographic references for the battle with Bou Hamara. Winifred Mulligan proofread my final draft and gave many appreciated corrections in grammar and punctuation. Linda Cashden provided professional editing and wonderful ideas. My writers' group, most particularly Phil Kurata and Nadine Siak, added valuable insights about character development. Kathy and Ahmed Morabet caught some important errors. My husband, Gerald Ponasik, and my daughter, Amal Disparte, read several versions and were unstinting in their support and encouragement, for which I am very grateful.

This book was inspired by Douglas Porch's historical account of the French takeover of Morocco. Many other books contributed greatly to my general knowledge of Morocco, particularly Rosita Forbes, *Sultan of the Mountains*; Walter Harris, *Morocco That Was;* Gavin Maxwell, *Lords of the Atlas;* William Hoisington, Jr. *Lyautey and the French Conquest of Morocco;* Edith Wharton, *In Morocco;* and many others too numerous to name. Nevertheless, I have taken some liberties, most specifically in placing Lyautey in Algeria in June when he did not in fact arrive there until that September.

There are two direct quotes which I used vertbatim, as they really couldn't be improved upon. One is the welcome speech that Al-Glaoui gives to Sultan Hassan when he is stranded in the High Atlas mountains. This is taken from Gavin Maxwell's *Lords of the Atlas.* The second one, which I translated from French to English, are the words uttered by Abdel Aziz to the Cooper assassin when he passed judgment on him. This speech was taken from *Au temps du Mehalla* , Louis Arnaud, a fascinating book setting down the memories of a Moroccan soldier who served under Menebbhi.

CHARACTERS
(Those marked * are recorded in history)

Rulers
*Sultan Moulay Hassan: died in 1894
*Sultan Moulay Abdul Aziz IV: ruled from 1894-1908
*Sultan Moulay Hafid: ruled from 1908-1912
Moulay Ali ben Hassan: younger son of Hassan
*Ba Ahmed: Chamberlain to Sultan Hassan, and then regent for Abdul Aziz, died 1900

Prominent Moroccans
*Abdul Karim Ben Slimane: Minister of Foreign Affairs
*Madani al Glaoui: A Lord of the Atlas near Marrakesh
*Fadoul al Gharnit: Chamberlain (Prime Minister) to Abdul Aziz
*Tayyib Al Goundafi: a Lord of the Atlas
*Omar al Tazi: Minister of the Army
*Mohammed Ghebbas: Succeeded el Menebbhi as Minister of War
*Mehdi al Mennebhi: Minister of War ('allam) until 1903
*Abdel Malik al Mtouggi : A Lord of the Atlas
*Bou Hamara: Pretender to the Throne
*Sidi Abdurrahman: Qaid of Tangier
*Ahmed al Raisuni: A Sherif from Tetouan
Mohammed al Matari: A Sherif from Matar
Kassim al Matari: an adopted son of the Sherif of Matar

Tariq ash-Sherif: Cousin of al-Menebbhi; general in Moroccan Army

Americans
Matthew Shields: American Minister to Morocco
*Samuel Grummere: American Minister to Morocco
Lili Shields Crampton: Adopted daughter of Matthew Shields
Arthur Crampton: Husband of Lili Shields and U.S.diplomat
*Ian Perdicaris: Resident in Tangier from about 1865—1904
Alice Watson: Wife of the *Sherif* of Matar

British
*Sir Arthur Nicholson: British Minister to Morocco
*David Cooper: Missionary
*Sir Walter Harris: Resident in Tangier and journalist
Amelia Hastings: married to Matthew Shields
Ted Hastings: Amelia's son
*Qaid Harry Maclean: Commander of the Moroccan Army
*Ellen Varley:Wife of Ian Perdicaris
Rosemary Higgins: governess to the Moroccan nobility

French
*Georges St. Rene Taillandier: French Minister to Morocco
*Conte de St. Aulaire: French diplomat in Morocco
*Eugene Regnault: succeeded Taillandier as French Minister in Tangier
*Theophile Delcassé: French Foreign Minister

*Marechal Louis-Hubert Lyautey: France's first Resident General in Morocco

Jewish Population
Brahim Ben Simon: Chief agent for American Legation
Leah Ben Simon: Brahim's wife
Meriam Ben Simon: Brahim and Leah's daughter
Gabriel Ben Simon: Brahim and Leah's daughter
Rachel Cohen: Leah's sister
Israel Cohen: Rachel's husband

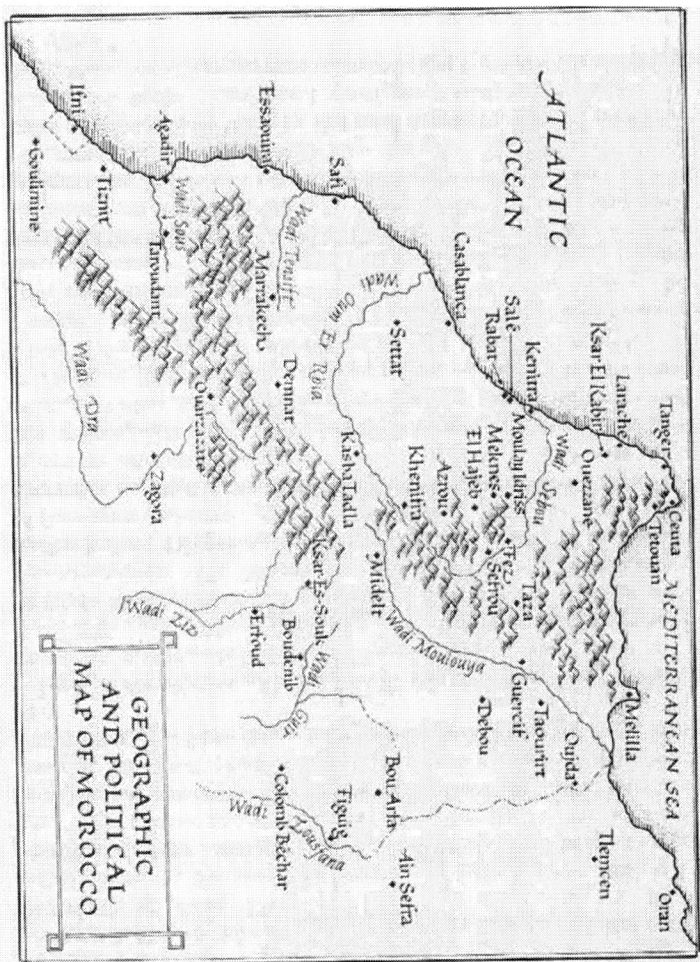

GEOGRAPHIC
AND POLITICAL
MAP OF MOROCCO

ATLANTIC
OCEAN

MEDITERRANEAN SEA

CHAPTER ONE
1882

Matt Shields picked his way down the shadowy labyrinth that formed the Tangier Kasbah, following the beam of his manservant, Hamoud's, lantern.

The call to prayer floated over the streets and Matt realized it must be close to three a.m. He hadn't noticed how late it was when he left the house where he and some of his bachelor friends had been playing poker. Matt cursed softly as he stumbled over a cat searching the garbage piled along a house wall. Would Tangier ever install gaslights like those he had seen in San Francisco? Not in this century, he guessed. Matt breathed in deeply, hoping to clear the whiskey from his head, and coughed as he inhaled the fumes of decayed food, mixed with the tangy smell of the nearby sea. He was nearing the American Legation, his office and his home as Minister of the United States, when Hamoud's cautioning arm brought him to a standstill.

A woman's screams filled the silence. Peering into the murky distance, Matt noted a bend in the alley just ahead. Adrenaline instantly cleared away the alcohol. Were they about to be robbed? He touched his pocket where he always kept his pistol ready. Ignoring Hamoud's warning he pushed forward. A small group of men in short gray *djellabah*s scattered at his approach. Hamoud lifted his lantern. The light fell across the body of a young woman.

"May Allah curse you and your mothers. What will I do now? You've taken my money. Oh Allah, what will happen to me?"

Matt hadn't anticipated finding a female as a victim. He leaned over her. "What happened? Did those sons of sin hurt you?" he asked in fluent Arabic. "Can I help you?"

The girl's face was partly obscured by a red and white shawl. Glossy black braids escaped from her scarf. She lay sprawled on the ground. Her embroidered slippers had fallen from her feet, their location marking her attempted flight from the attackers. She had a bad scratch on her face, and blood running down her cheek.

"Can you walk?" Matt realized he reeked of alcohol and cigars, not the most comforting smells.

She rose unsteadily to her feet, only to double over as her ankle gave way.

Matt could feel Hamoud's hesitation. It was unseemly for men to address Moroccan women. It was also rare to find a young girl who, judging by her clothes and beautifully tattooed hands and feet, was from a respectable family, on the streets by herself at night. He conferred with Hamoud.

"Well," Matt said, "You look poorly and it's late. We'd best get you to my house, which is only a few steps away."

The young woman was barely able to stand. He offered her his arm. When he saw that would not be enough he shrugged his shoulders at tradition and scooped her up in his arms.

The door opened to the colorfully tiled courtyard of his official residence. In a small room off the gallery, Matt gently deposited the half-conscious girl on one of the many couches.

"Call Aisha," he instructed Hamoud, hoping his housekeeper had not yet gone to bed and would know what to do with this unexpected guest.

Within minutes Aisha appeared, fully clothed in her long caftan, the sleeves tucked up in their elastic guards, her hair severely pulled out of view under an immaculate white cotton scarf tied turban-style around her head.

"Oh, *Si* Matt, who is this?" Aisha addressed him with the respectful title women always used with men in Morocco.

Matt explained briefly and then decided to disappear. This was not the appropriate time for questions. The morning would be early enough to supply answers and see what had to be done next.

***

Matt's diplomatic duties, which dealt mainly with tax problems of American ships entering or leaving the Mediterranean, or facilitating exports of grain and wool, left him plenty of time to explore the background of the young woman. He and the few other diplomats in Tangier, mostly Spanish and British, enjoyed a leisurely life style for the most part. He had plenty of spare time to get to know his guest.

The girl's name was Mina.

"*Ya sidi*," (Matt was amused that she spoke to him the same way she might have addressed the Sultan), "I have dishonored my family." The first day or so, this was as far as Matt could get before she dissolved in tears and Aisha shooed him from the room. Then, little by little, he and Aisha coaxed the rest of the story from her.

"When my *baba* (father) found out I was pregnant, his brothers told him he must kill me. The dishonor was too great. I was so frightened, *ya sidi*. I thought they would let us marry. But our families are from different tribes and there is a feud between us."

Matt urged her to continue.

3

"One night they were all gathered with my father, talking about me. I heard shouting and arguing. My mother came to me. She said I must leave right away because they were getting ready to do something. She was shaking and crying, *ya sidi*. She gave me her gold bracelets, tied up in a little bundle, and some bread and sugar. She found me a mule and told me I must come here to Tangier and find the White Ladies, who would help me. It was terrible! I didn't know the way. And I was afraid to ask. So I just followed the paths, but I hid whenever I saw men because I knew they would wonder what a girl was doing on the road by herself." She shuddered.

"When I got here, it was already dark. So I asked a boy selling charcoal. I got down from my mule to talk to him and when I turned around, *ya* Allah, the mule was gone! And the boy didn't know about any White Ladies. What to do, what to do, I was so frightened! Suddenly, there were men all around me, looking right into my face, even touching my clothes! It was terrible, *Si* Matt!

"These men told me they would take me to the White Ladies. And that's how you found me, *ya sidi*. They took me into the city. *Ya harami*—who knows what they were going to do! May Allah punish them and their evil ways. But I got suspicious and started to cry and struggle. *Alhamdu'llah*, (Praise God), you heard me."

Matt wasn't sure what to do. But he had a big household, with plenty of female servants. One more girl wouldn't make any difference. And what were her chances outside his custody? Maybe the sisters of the Holy Spirit, her White Ladies, would take her in, but for how long? And then what would happen to her? Selfishly he also thought he could improve his knowledge of Berber by talking to her a little each day.

He guessed Mina's age at about 14. She was delicate, small,

hardly more than a child herself. She had broken her ankle in that struggle and had to be confined to her bed. When her leg healed they would see what to do.

Mina fit into the spacious American Legation easily. Matt had been delighted on returning to Tangier in 1875, when the former U.S. Minister took him to the beautiful old palace and told him that it would be his home as well as his working quarters. Located very near the walls of the city, in the Jewish quarter, the Legation covered several hectares of land. There had been an American Minister in Tangier ever since the United States had declared its independence. Once the Barbary pirates had been tamed, in the 19th century, there had been no pressing need for American representation in this Islamic kingdom, which did not welcome foreigners in its interior, but the U.S. had stayed on, to look over its commercial interests, and to honor the relationship with the Sultan, who had been the first head of State to recognize it. The British and Spanish had long had representation here, too, and just recently a French delegation had arrived.

Sprawling on both sides of the narrow alley that bisected it, the Legation's family living quarters had originally been a harem where a rich Arab could keep his four wives, with plenty of space for children. Since he wasn't planning to ever have that big a family, Matt had turned this area over to his household staff. He had never really counted all the rooms in this Legation, but he guessed there were at least thirty. There was certainly room for one small Berber girl.

Matt gradually came to know Mina well. Although Aisha had seen to it that she was quickly packed off and installed in the former harem, now the servants' quarters, during the day they carried her out to the main courtyard of the building to sit in the sun, so she wouldn't be lonely while the women went about their chores. This way, they could chat with her and also tend to her needs without having to run back to the other part of the house. As all were naturally gregarious and used to being together, to leave her alone was unthinkable. And Mina could spin and card wool for them, or work on a piece of the beautiful Fezzi style embroidery her mother had shown her how to do. Her cheerful, sunny personality completely won them over, and soon not only Aisha, but Latifa and Habiba, the kitchen girls, were close friends with her, constantly putting their heads together to giggle over some antic or tease the doorman, Hamoud.

As the months lengthened into fall, and finally winter, Aisha had Mina moved into one of the antechambers where Matt usually ate lunch in the cold weather. There was a cheerful fire there, and it was on the way to the kitchen, so there was plenty of coming and going to keep her company. Matt would stop work around noon and quickly settle down to talk to Mina before lunch arrived. Timid and unused to talking to men, Mina was obviously amused and flattered that this tall handsome foreigner kept asking her questions in stumbling, but recognizable, Berber.

"How old are you?"

"I don't know, *ya sidi*. My mother told me I was born a little after the Spanish came to Tetouan."

"How far is it from here to Chaouen? We foreigners aren't allowed to go there, you know."

"It takes three days by mule. My village is very beautiful, but not as big as Tanja."

"Is your father a landholder?"

"Everyone has land, *ya sidi*. Isn't that true for you, too? Our tribes own land and we share it according to our need."

"What was your life like in Chaouen? How did you spend your time?"

"When I was able to stand on my feet, I began watching my Mama and her sisters weaving. For a long time I could only help with scarves and plain things, and I wanted so much to make rugs with them. But the knife is so dangerous. You could cut off a finger just like that." She snapped her fingers. "One of my aunts was missing the first knuckle of her hand, this one," she showed him her index finger. "It was ugly and made it hard for her to embroider. So when I started, I was so careful with that knife. I was afraid, really. But I felt like a big girl when I got to sit on the bench with my aunts and sisters."

"What else did you like to do?" Matt asked.

"Ramadan is my favorite time." Mina was talking about the Islamic month when all Muslims go without food and drink all day, breaking their fast at sundown. "We spent the whole day cooking, making *harira*, (a spicy lentil soup), and my mama has the best recipe in the village. She has some secrets I promised never to tell anyone. And she is famous for her *shebakiya* all tied in knots, dipped in sesame, and dripping with honey. Umm, it makes me hungry just thinking about it."

Mina giggled as she related stories of learning to dance and how she and the other girls would dance for each other at the women's parties. "I started dancing as soon as I could stand. I watched the other girls; of course, there were no boys or men there, so we could do as we pleased. I'm a good dancer, but not now with this leg, I guess." She looked down at her wrapped ankle. "It doesn't hurt too much any more. Maybe one day I can dance for you!

"And every so often we have *moussems* to celebrate saints' birthdays. Oh, *Si* Matt, it is so fun! There are vendors selling all kinds of beautiful things, wonderful cottons from abroad which are so much nicer to wear than the scratchy wool we usually have! And many story tellers, although we girls have

to hide behind our fathers or brothers if we want to hear. Then
in the afternoons we unmarried girls stand all in a line, and
the young men face us in a line and we sing. We make up
poems as we go along; it is wonderful! Sometimes, if one boy
particularly likes a young girl," she blushed, "he makes up a
verse especially for her, and then she has to answer it, and we
have a contest, to see who can make up the best ones, and think
the fastest." She fell silent with her memories as she finished
this tale.

Matt quickly intervened, to take her mind away from this
sadness. "Who watches the sheep? Is it only the boys?"

"Mostly boys, unless a family is unlucky enough to only
have girls. Then sometimes they do, too. It's not good for girls
to tend the sheep though. They can get in trouble that way,"
Mina nodded her head wisely, as though repeating something
she had often heard from her mother. "But now, *Si* Matt,
there are problems with taxes. I heard my *baba* talking with
my uncles about demands made by the *qaid* (tribal leader), on
the part of the *makhsen* (government). Every year they ask for
more and more. It seems the Sultan owes the Spanish money,
may God have mercy on him, because of some big war we had
before I was born. Usually my father pays these taxes with the
wool, but now there are Jews, who work for *nisrani* (foreigners)
like you, who come to Chaouen, and they also want this wool.
I think they offer more money to my father.

Mina's talks with Matt pinpointed a growing problem
in Morocco. As European powers increasingly realized the
commercial value of Morocco as a supplier, not only of wheat,
but of the wool needed to feed the growing weaving and cloth
industries of the north, they sought special trading relationships
with merchants, like Mina's own father, who would sell their
entire supply to them. This deprived the Sultan of the tax

money he relied on. Morocco was falling more deeply into debt with the Europeans and tribes and merchants were placed in a vise by the demands upon them from the sultan for taxes to pay his debts.

As Mina gained courage through their daily conversations, she could no longer restrain her curiosity about *Amrika*. "How far is it from here? Can you walk there?"

"It takes many days on a big ship to get to New York," Matt told her.

"By water! But how can such a big *babour* stay up on that water? And don't you get hungry?"

Matt promised that when her ankle was healed, he would take her to the harbor to see the huge sea-going vessels, and maybe even visit one of them.

"But why are you here? How can you live in such a big house without a wife or a family?"

Matt laughed, "Maybe some day I'll get around to marrying, but I'm happy right now as I am, young lady!"

Another time as they were sitting quietly, she burst out, "How come you always sit on that funny chair? Don't you find it uncomfortable to have your legs dangling down like that?"

"On the contrary," Matt said, "I don't see how you folk can sit cross-legged on the floor for hours. If I do that, I fall down when I try to get up."

Mina saw a tall, gangly man, maybe in his early 40s. He was fair, like some of the Berbers she knew, with light brown hair which tended to hang down over his eyes, which were a curious shade of brown, almost green in some lights. He wore spectacles, like some of the old men who visited her father. Although Matt put on a woolen *djellabah* when he stopped working, he wore clothes very different from Berber men, preferring those tight uncomfortable looking pantaloons, which made his legs look so long, and waist coats in a shiny fabric with a gold watch linked by a chain into his pocket, and long buttoned up jackets. Mina wondered why any one would choose to wear such constricting, tight and somewhat immodest clothes instead of the billowing loose Turkish trousers (*serwal*) both men and women in her world wore, covered by loose flowing woolen or silk robes, depending on the time of year. But she was proud of Matt and the progress he had made in Berber, thanks to her.

Once she asked, "What is in all those books? I didn't know so much was written about Islam." She was amazed to find that none of these books was about Islam, and the wide range of topics they covered fascinated her. Matt was a good story teller, and, as his Berber improved, he drew parallels from her own *Thousand and One Nights*, as well as from Dickens and Victor Hugo.

***

In December Matt reckoned Mina was about to give birth. One day after lunch, Matt asked her about her plans. When she responded, Matt realized she had been doing a lot of thinking.

"*Si* Matt, can a Berber become an American?"

"Um, anyone can become an American. But Mina, Morocco is a good country, too."

"Yes, *Si* Matt, that is true. But my father was not able to be kind to me. His love could not overcome his anger at my impurity. My tradition does not offer me salvation or forgiveness. I want to become an American and I want my child to be one, Allah willing. I want it to be like you. You showed me compassion and did not judge me only on my faults. I will never forget that."

Matt thought Mina looked unusually wan; her dark eyes were huge in a thinner, more drawn face. A pallor had replaced the fresh rosiness of her cheeks.

"Mina, maybe we should bring a nurse to see you."

"Good, *Si* Matt. If you think so." Mina closed her eyes and appeared to be sleeping.

That evening there was a knock on the door and when Hamoud opened it, he was confronted with a pair of nuns.

"Take us to your master, my good man."

"Yes, sisters, this way."

He led them to the study, where Matt was smoking a cigar and hard at work on his accounts, due in Washington at the end of the month. Bookkeeping was not his favorite task, and the figures never seemed to add up. Washington had been after him for some time for a reckoning.

"You are Matthew Shields, U.S. Minister here in Tangier? The man who sent us the note earlier today?"

"Yes?" It wasn't until he saw the nuns that he remembered summoning them.

"How does this young woman come under your protection?" The older of the two asked him.

Realizing how things might appear to an outsider, he quickly explained the situation. The nuns' reserve softened slightly, but skepticism still lingered. He knew they were familiar with the habit of picking pretty young Moroccan girls to warm the beds of unattached bachelors, and guessed they had catered to these cast-out mistresses during unwanted pregnancies more times than they could count.

"Let me take you to see Mina. Frankly, I'm a tad concerned about her health and it was only today I realized she was looking peaked. My housekeeper and the other women have been looking after her and I just left them to it." He led the way to the small room where they had made a daybed for Mina.

The room was cozy, illuminated by a fire and several kerosene lamps and filled with the aroma of *sheba*, a tea made from anise, which a maid poured out of a silver tea pot into delicate gold embossed glasses that she offered to the party.

Mina struggled to sit up and greeted the sisters. "Oh, the White Ladies. My mother told me you would help me. Now I hope you can help my child, too, in case I die."

Matt started. No one had mentioned dying. He saw her eyes fill with tears.

"I am sorry to tell you that this child seems very unfit," the nun told him later in his study.

"I doubt she's strong enough to give birth. Girls this age usually miscarry earlier in their term, and it's probably a blessing because their bodies aren't really ready for children. Perhaps the months of rest forced on her by the broken ankle preserved her baby better than nature intended. I don't think there really was much you could do," the Sister reassured Matt.

"You sheltered her, fed her well, and protected her from the streets, from what she tells me. You may comfort yourself that she has been well looked after. Now the best thing is to keep her happy and comfortable. I would guess that she's due in a week or so, maybe at Christmas. We'll come every day to care for her."

Matt wandered restlessly around the Legation, worrying about Mina. What if the child survived and she did not? Finally, he raised this with her.

"*Si* Matt, you have been so kind to me. You have been better than my father and like a father to me. If I die, could you make my child an American, and raise it as your own?"

He, raise a child? How could he do this? But it was true that an illegitimate baby would not have many options. It could probably go to the Sisters, but what would its future be? If it was a girl, she might at best become a nun herself, regardless of whether she had any vocation. And if she did not, she would be an outcast, a fatherless child with no dowry, nothing to make her marriageable. And a boy wouldn't fare much better; in fact, probably wouldn't be able to stay with the nuns very long. And then what?

But did he want to saddle himself with a new responsibility? He wasn't even married. He loved his work, sports, exploring Morocco. Probably some day he'd find a wife but there wasn't any rush.

On Christmas Eve Aisha came to tell him Mina had gone into labor.

"*Ya sidi*, it doesn't look good for her. The midwife is here and Sister Theresa is coming, but Mina is weak. It is too hard for her!"

Matt waited through the long day and a half it took for Mina to deliver, affected by her cries, wondering again and again how it was that women underwent this agony all the time. Then from his study, he heard her cries getting weaker. Then it was quiet. Aisha knocked on his door, red-eyed from weeping and exhausted from her eighteen-hour vigil.

"*Si* Matt, can you come? I think it is almost the end. Mina needs to talk to you."

He entered the overly heated room where his eyes were quickly drawn to the bed. At first he didn't even recognize the pale, tiny figure lying so still with her eyes closed.

He turned to Aisha, "You didn't tell me. Is she, has she gone?"

Mina opened her eyes. "No, *Si* Matt. Not without saying good-bye and thanking you for everything." She beckoned him closer.

"*Si* Matt. Here is my daughter. Please be her father. Be as kind to her as you were to me. I trust you with her. May Allah bless you for your generosity."

Matt leaned over Mina's bed, stroking her forehead with his rough hand.

"Mina, don't worry. God bless you and bless this child. We'll look after her. I will miss you very much. You brightened my life."

But as he spoke he saw Mina was gone. She gave a final sigh, closed her eyes, and released her grip on Matt's hand.

CHAPTER TWO
1888-1890

Tangier sparkled in the morning sunshine. From its wide Mediterranean harbor which had made it so popular with the pirates of the Barbary Coast, the city rose steeply up the cliffs, spreading out on the plateau above in a series of flat-topped white houses. A sprinkling of green-tiled roofs marked out the homes of the rich, while church steeples competed with peaked minarets in this polyglot city which, although technically part of Morocco, was a free port and one of a handful of coastal cities where Christians, Muslims and Jews could live together and trade.

Lili and Hamoud were at the fish market, where she was helping the butler pick out red snappers for the wedding party that evening.

"Lili, always look at their eyes, to make sure they're very bright, like yours, *habibti*! And there, touch the fish. It shouldn't be slimy. Be careful, though. Don't prick your finger!" Hamoud turned away from the child to bargain with the vendor.

"What? Fifty *rials* for this tiny fish? *Ya khoya*, my brother, twenty would be a favor to you, only because you're my mother's brother's son." He settled down and called for a glass of mint tea.

Lili wandered off, knowing Hamoud would keep her in his sight and that she was safe in this area, as she was on a first-name basis with most of the vendors. The fishermen were busy unloading their catches. Nets filled the cobble-stoned street; vendors of the pungent coriander and parsley needed to cook this seafood wove in and out, hawking their wares; seagulls swirled overhead, occasionally swooping down to steal a fish from an unwary vendor; piles of lemons and spring onions filled the empty spaces. She glanced up the sharp incline leading back to the Legation. From here if you stretched as high as you could on tiptoe you could also see off to the right the Detroit, the Portuguese fort at the very top of the Kasbah, with its huge searchlight illuminating the bay at night, to keep sailing vessels from breaking up on the rocks in the dangerous harbor. Papa had taken her up there. And on a clear day if you looked very hard and shaded your eyes, sometimes you could see *Jebel Tariq*, or Gibraltar, as he called it.

It was fun to look at all the different people in the market and see if she could figure out where they came from. Many were Spanish, she knew, from Papa, although probably the majority of the population was Jewish or Arab. The Jews, many of whom had lived in Morocco since the Diaspora, plus those who had come when they were expelled from Spain during the Spanish Inquisition, were the merchants, although increasing numbers were working for the foreign legations now. The Arabs in Tangier were mainly officials of the Sultan's government. She had often heard Papa remark on what a motley crew the Spanish were, just ruffians and ne'er-do-wells who couldn't make a living in their own country, he said, and came down here to see what trouble they could get up to. This, of course, did not refer to his own lovely mother, now deceased, whose Spanish family had run a coffee shop in Tangier.

Sometimes she even saw Sister Theresa, who had kept a friendly eye on her since her birth. She had heard Aisha and the other maids giggling one day in the kitchen about some new Spanish nuns who had recently arrived.

"*Ya*, a Muslim man can have only four wives, but that Spanish priest, he has at least six of those sisters with him."

When she repeated this to Sister Theresa, the nun just sniffed and said, "Ignorant people; don't pay them any mind".

She ran back to Hamoud. The vendor's perspiring and flushed face showed that Hamoud had gotten his price.

"*Yallah*, Lili. We'd better get back to the Legation and make sure those lazy girls have made the bread," he said.

"Oh Uncle Hamoud, can't we go to Souk al Barra first? Aisha will look after the bread." Hamoud and Lili loved the lively souk, or market, in front of the main gate to the *medina*, or walled city, where they all lived.

"Well, we do need some vegetables and we're running low on tea and sugar. "Here." He hailed a passing porter and gave him instructions to deliver the fish to the American Legation, with dire threats should it not arrive fresh and in the same condition it now was. He hoisted Lili up in front of him on his mule and they slowly made their way up the hill, along the stone walls of the city until they reached the marketplace.

"Oh look, there must be at least five storytellers here today!" Lili pointed to the large circles of country men grouped around entertainers from all over, who were recounting her beloved Arabian Nights, or telling news of far-away towns like Marrakesh and Fez. She squealed with pleasure as she sighted the red-and-black-robed acrobats from the South, "Let's go watch them." She never tired of watching the jugglers and contortionists who made three and four-man-high pyramids, holding each other, it seemed, with just a finger. Her eye was attracted then by a strangely quiet crowd of men. She pushed her way through the sea of legs and scratchy *djellabahs*, just in time to see a raggedy man, holding a long snake, stick its head in his mouth and crunch down. She and the whole crowd gasped, as he pulled the headless body out of his mouth to show his deed, and then proceeded to chew and swallow until he had fully consumed the head. Hamoud caught up with his charge at that moment and pulled her gently away.

"Leave this, *habibti*. Such a sight will give you bad dreams." He tossed the charmer a handful of coins, then perched the child on his shoulders, from where she continued to watch as the charmer slowly ate the rest of the still-wriggling body.

From her lofty perch, Lili could survey the entire souk. In front of her was the gate to the city, and all around it were circles of peasants and townspeople. In one corner drumming and jingling announced the Ganawa, the African dancers dressed in black and white, who wore special hats trimmed in cowry shells which they could set spinning to the rhythms of their drums. It was rumored that these men were famous magicians, but Sister Theresa always cautioned her that magic was the devil's work, and Lili should stay far away from them.

She dug her heels into Hamoud's back, "Look, Uncle Hamoud, there's a pickpocket over there!" She watched in fascination as a country man, entranced by a shell game in progress in front of him, was unaware of the thief stealthily cutting away his long fringed purse. Suddenly sensing something, the peasant jerked around and grabbed at the pickpocket, who darted away in the crowd.

The sun was high in the sky by the time they made their purchases. Lili gave a sudden squeak, "Oh Uncle Hamoud, I forgot. I'm going to the *hammam* today with Aisha and Latifa to help Habiba get ready for her wedding. Maybe we should hurry."

***

Matt was giving a wedding feast for Habiba, one of the maids in the Legation. Wonderful smells emerged as the women chopped coriander and parsley, diced onions and garlic, ground cumin and paprika, and plucked chickens to prepare the essential three dishes needed to honor the bride. In the back courtyard, men were skinning a newly-slaughtered sheep that they would barbecue over an open spit, and others were plucking pigeons to be served in a flaky cinnamon pie called *bastilla* as the first course of the wedding feast. Elsewhere young girls were squatting over bowls of semolina, rolling the grains in their hands with flour to prepare couscous for the final plate of the banquet.

Lili ran through the rooms to the servants' quarter, where Habiba was resting. She lay down next to her, cuddling up close. She loved this young country girl who was always full of pranks and jokes.

"Habiba, are you asleep?"

Habiba yawned, and hugged her: "Not any more, *hyati*. Where have you been all morning?"

Lili told her about all the sights and experiences of the souk. "But Habiba, you look sad. What's wrong?"

"*Habibti*, tonight I will leave you to go live with a stranger. Who knows what he will be like? Maybe his mother will be mean and beat me if I don't work hard enough! Allah, I wish I could stay here!" Tears filled her eyes.

"But aren't you happy to be getting married?"

"Well, it will be fun to have my own children, especially if they're as sweet and lively as you! *Si* Mohammed's sisters seem nice enough and they promise he's kind. But who knows? I wish I had a cousin of my own, so I wouldn't have to marry a stranger." She started to cry again.

Aisha came in. "Now, let's not have any of these nerves.

You're lucky to be marrying into such a fine family. I hear *Si* Mohammed is young and handsome, and has a good future ahead of him working with his father to raise vegetables for the townspeople. Now, let's get you ready for the wedding night!"

They gathered up their black tarry soap and scrubbing pads, towels, combs, putting them in the round-handled copper buckets reserved for the *hammam*. Lili held Habiba's hand tightly to comfort her.

They stooped down to enter the semi-underground caverns, and having paid their few douros to the bath keeper, entered the first of three rooms, where cries of children echoed off the walls, and the scrape of the *hammam* buckets clanging against the tiled floors filled Lili's ears. Aisha sat her down on a bench, unwrapped the scarf that covered her hair, and undid her braids. She removed her ankle length dress, three more layers of petticoats and dresses, and finally her Turkish-style trousers. Lili loved this moment of being entirely free of the many layers of binding clothes and stretched luxuriously, waiting for the other women to disrobe.

In the next room a large pool at one end stored hot water. They dipped their buckets into the pool and brought them to where they sat. Through the steam, Lili could make out many of Habiba's friends, there to help her get ready. Habiba was led off into a separate cubbyhole, where her friends would use the taffy-like *helwa* to remove all her body hair and make her beautiful for the wedding night. Aisha held the curious child back, "No, young lady, that's not for you, yet! "

Sitting her down firmly on the floor, she pulled out a string-covered pad and began slowly scrubbing away at the child's body, waiting as the steam opened her body pores and loosened the outer layer of skin which the scrubbing would remove, leaving her pink and tingling. Lili looked down between her legs and wondered when she would have hair there, like the big girls. Everywhere she looked women were rubbing each others' backs, while children crawled around in the dark, occasionally upsetting someone's bucket, producing screams and squeals which reverberated against the walls. Lili dreaded the occasional fights that broke out here, where women would throw the *hammam* buckets at each other and people would slip, sometimes hurting themselves seriously on the tiled floors.

Luckily, today was a good day; everyone was happy for the bride, who emerged from her cubbyhole to join the others. Lili helped comb her long curly hair and wash it with *ghasoul*, the earthy looking shampoo Aisha bought at the *souk*, which made hair soft and easy to comb. Friends had helped apply henna to Habiba's hair last night, and she had spent the whole day with it wrapped in cloth, as shown by the trickles of the red dye running down her neck. They had also painted intricate designs that closely resembled cross-stitch embroidery on Habiba's hands and feet. If applied properly and held over fire to dry, these designs would last as long as a month to mark her special status as a bride. Lili was determined to keep a small design on the front of her hand as long as she could.

As they were sitting in the second, cooler room, resting and letting their bodies return to normal heat, the bath-keeper tapped on the door to let them know Hamoud was outside to escort them home.

Hours later, the bridal mistress settled Habiba on a large brass tray and paraded her around the room. Her eyes were heavily outlined in kohl, and small red dots sprinkled on her cheeks; a green and gold taffeta headdress covered her hair, with ropes of pearls hanging to her shoulders from either side. Her brocaded caftan was covered with heavy silver jewelry, and a metal belt encircled her waist.

Habiba took her seat on a couch decorated with flowers and brocade, and the women guests began a ululating trill to express their approval. The women who had dressed her led a lively singing ceremony in which they urged the guests to contribute generously to wedding gifts for the young couple, as well as tips for themselves.

Lili ran back and forth between the women's and men's parties. While the women were so pretty, dancing for each other, making jokes, and singing, the men were dressed somberly in fine white woolen and silk *djellabahs*, red fezzes covering their heads. They sat quietly listening to a group of musicians play classical Andalusian music, talking very little, sipping tea, and smoking the water pipe.

Aisha beckoned her back to the women, "Come, *habibti*, sit by me." She then continued her conversation with her neighbor, Leila, one of Habiba's new sisters-in-law. "Yes, Lili is a pretty girl, but I don't know what will happen to her when she grows up."

"Oh," replied Leila, "such a sweet little thing, and so lively. She won't have any trouble finding a good match."

"Yes, but you forget that she's a *nisraniya*, a foreigner. Where she'll find a man in our world, I've no idea."

"What? How is she a *nisraniya*? Wasn't her mother a Moroccan, like us? And her father, too?"

"Yes, by Allah," Aisha said. "But her mama, who loved this little baby with all her heart, even before she was born, made *Si* Matt promise that he would bring Lili up as a foreigner. I heard her with my own ears, Allah have mercy on her soul, when she lay dying. Bless her heart; she thought it would give Lili a better life." Aisha hugged the little girl as she recounted her tale.

Leila said, "Won't *Si* Matt find a husband for her?"

"I don't know. He makes no signs of marrying that I know of. And he's no domestic one, that one. Oh, he's very fond of Lili, right enough, but not very practical. Without a woman to arrange these things, who knows how it will turn out."

Lili was just opening her mouth to ask some questions about this new piece of information, when three women streamed into the crowded room bearing huge platters. One was piled high with golden chicken dotted with bits of marinated lemons and rosy mesallah olives, sitting in juices flavored with butter, ginger and saffron. Another had chunks of braised lamb, decorated with browned almonds and prunes, in a sauce flavored with honey and sesame. A third dish featured the huge red snapper Hamoud had bought that morning, sitting on a bed of sliced potatoes, marinated in coriander, parsley, onions, garlic, lemons and tomatoes.

Small plates of salads were put on each table: grated carrots mixed with oranges and mint, covered with powdered sugar and flavored with orange-blossom water; green peppers and tomatoes minced fine and cooked until very soft with cumin and paprika, coriander and lemon; cucumbers and mint flavored with rose water; Lili's favorite was *zaalouk*, with eggplants, tomatoes, summer squash, cooked with cumin and paprika.

Bread, still warm from the oven, was carried in and arranged around the numerous small round tables, and the women gathered round, sitting cross-legged on small cushions. Lili and a few of the other young girls ran to get the silver basins and ewers filled with warm water. Looping embroidered towels over their shoulders, the girls passed among the guests, allowing all to wash in preparation for eating with their hands.

Lili's mouth had been watering for the fragrant roast

lamb, juicy and flavored with cumin, but it was not offered to the ladies. The men got first choice of everything but she had been hoping there would be enough to offer to the women. She knew that the plates now being served in their room were left over from the men's room, although they had been fixed so skillfully that they didn't really look like leftovers. She stood on one foot and then the other, debating which table to join. Finally, she squeezed herself in at the table with the fish. Of course, she had been well trained by Aisha, so she patiently fingered little pieces of bread and dipped them in the sauce and vegetables, greedily eyeing the fish but knowing until the word was given by the senior woman at the table, she couldn't touch it. She took great care to eat only in front of her, gradually carving out a little round indentation, as did all the others, till she was more than half full from the bread.

Finally someone said, "Help yourselves to the fish," and she was able to stick her fingers daintily into the firm flesh and pull out several good bites. She was glad she wasn't sitting near the head, and in fact, had carefully positioned herself near the center of the fish, since the eyeballs, cheeks and other head parts held no appeal for her.

Lili stole quietly up to Habiba with a tidbit of the fish, "Habiba, can't you eat just a little piece of this delicious fish?"

But Habiba just looked at her mournfully and a tear ran down her cheek, "Oh, I couldn't, Lili. I'm too scared."

Lili continued to be puzzled. This was the second time today Habiba had mentioned fear. Prior to the wedding, she had been very excited, humming and singing at her work, and even bragging a little to the other girls about her soon-to-change status.

Heaping bowls of couscous appeared, garnished with alternating bands of cinnamon and powdered sugar and sprinkled with toasted almonds. Digging down into the bowls with their hands, the women encountered juicy bits of lamb, which they expertly molded into tight mouth-size balls of couscous.

Aisha took a drum from one of the couches and started tapping out a rhythm; many of the young girls had finished eating and a few rose to begin dancing for the bride. Soon women in brilliant silk dresses and floating chiffon overdresses were undulating in the center, repeating the thrusting motions of the pelvis which were the basics of the Moroccan belly dance and beckoning with their arms as though entreating suitors of their own.

Satiated from the enormous meal, the women, began gossiping and telling stories about their own wedding nights, and as the evening progressed, the stories got more and more bawdy, "I tell you, the third time around," one laughed, while another, lowering her voice slightly was talking about "…him coming up from back of me," while the women shrieked with laughter. Lili saw that Habiba was both repelled and fascinated as she listened spellbound to some of the juicier tales. It was time for the night prayer. The women's voices lowered, children's eyelids drooped.

A loud knock came at the door. "Prepare the bride."

"Who is there?" cried the women.

"Her husband awaits," came the answer.

Lili was prodded awake. "Come, say goodbye to Habiba. She's going to her husband now."

She stared drowsily at Habiba, who was being helped to rise from her place of honor. The men were at the door and Lili caught a glimpse of *Si* Mohammed, the groom. His sisters escorted Habiba out of the Legation, helping her onto a waiting horse.

Soon Lili was tucked up in bed, nestled close to Aisha. She had a lot to think about. Why had Habiba been so unhappy? Even more strange, why did Aisha think she would never find a husband? On the other hand, who wanted to get married? Habiba didn't want to. Papa seemed perfectly content, and he didn't have a wife. And if he did get married, what did that have to do with her finding a husband? And what exactly was a foreigner, anyway?

***

Matt carved out a bachelor's niche in Tangier, reveling in the wild boar hunts, the races along the beach, polo and almost nightly poker games. His business alliances with wealthy Jewish traders, merchants and landowners gave him influence and power locally and made him a man to be reckoned with, a man who could get things done without too many questions asked. As the diplomatic community began to grow, especially the British and French Legations, he was the convenient 'extra man' at many evening soirées where political talk flourished. Although the United States had little strategic interest in Morocco, it became clear to Matt, as the personnel of the British diplomatic mission grew, that they were more than a little interested in acquiring this country, so strategically located at the tip of the Mediterranean and almost a stone's throw from Gibraltar. It would safeguard British travel through the newly-opened Suez Canal and on to India. The French, too, were increasing their representation in the country, and Matt understood that since they had added neighboring Algeria to their empire in the 1830s, in fact making it officially a part of their country, they would feel more comfortable if its neighbor, Morocco, also fell under their influence. Interesting times, he thought, as speculations about the fate of Morocco were voiced freely over glasses of port, and many pulled him aside for private chats, knowing his discretion could be trusted. Everyone knew America had no real strategic interest in Morocco, aside from trade, mostly in raw Moroccan wool and skins.

***

Matt set out on foot from the Legation, heading out of the walled city and up a steep hill to El Minza, the private home of a glamorous but unconventional young couple who had arrived in Tangier in the late 70s. Ian Perdicaris was a wealthy American in his early forties, like Matt. Ellen Varley, who accompanied him, had caused quite a stir in Tangier when it became known that she had deserted a husband in England in favor of this stocky and unprepossessing Greek-American who offered her the exciting life and riches her middle-class engineer spouse was unable to provide. Matt, less concerned with convention than most Tangerinos, had been friendly to this couple at the beginning of their stay, but within a few months, the rest of the foreigners were flocking to their luxurious house, wooed by their lavish parties.

This evening Matt was not disappointed. As he neared the house, he could hear strains of Viennese waltzes coming from an orchestra set up in their large open courtyard. He handed his hat to a servant dressed in white caftan and red fez, and looked expectantly through the crowd, searching for Ian Perdicaris. Soon he spotted the plump, slightly balding host, who came to meet him, arms outstretched. "Ah, our American Minister, welcome!"

"Good to see you, Ian. Got a poker game going yet?"

Ian slapped him on the back. "Hell, yes. It's in the back parlor. You know the way."

Matt moved through the crowd, greeting friends. He

entered a room that was thick with cigar smoke, took off his jacket and rolled up his sleeves. Now this was more like it. Two hours later, with Matt down fifty dollars, a gong announced supper. Reluctantly, the men put down their cards. "Damnation, I was just beginning to recoup my losses," Matt complained.

"Never mind, after supper, you'll have another chance," his victor assured him.

They returned to the spacious black and white marble hall. Ellen Varley took Matt's arm as he was about to go downstairs to the dining room. "Matt, dear, may I introduce you to Amelia Hastings. Would you mind taking her into dinner?"

Matt bowed and turned to an attractive brown-haired woman, who blushed slightly as she held out her gloved hand. "How kind of you," she said.

"Delighted. Now how come I haven't met you before? Are you new to Tangier?"

The Perdicaris dining room, on the lower level of their house, looked out on one side to the Tangier Bay, while its interior opened to a spacious tiled courtyard. A long table was set with place cards and Matt found their seats, in the middle of the room. He held out the chair for Amelia, who settled her pale violet satin train around her. She turned to talk to her other neighbor, a man Matt knew slightly. Matt eyed her softly rounded shoulders for a moment, and then addressed himself to the Spanish Minister's wife. He looked to see Ian talking to Budgett Meakin, editor of the Tangier Times and to his surprise, heard Ian say, "Matt does a lot of favors for people who can help him." As he was processing this, Amelia turned toward Matt, "Actually, I've seen you before. I work for The Tangier Times, doing their bookkeeping. I've lived here for ten years, but I don't get out too much, since I have a little boy."

"From your accent I guess you're British. What does your husband do here?" Matt said.

"He died several years ago, of malaria. In fact, I'm only recently out of mourning," she said, indicating the lavender color of her dress. "But I know he would not want me to become a recluse. He was a wonderful man, a writer, and he loved Tangier so much. He made me promise to try and stay here and make a new life for myself, and I'm determined to do so."

"That's a tough assignment for a single woman with a child," Matt said.

"Well, people have been very kind. And it's so exciting here, don't you think?" Amelia said.

Matt laughed, "I sure do, but that's the first time I've heard a woman say so."

Amelia was a year or two younger than Matt. She was very fair, with light brown hair, which always seemed to be escaping from its upsweep and curling gently around her face. She had wide intelligent blue eyes that sparkled when she laughed. She spoke with a soft English accent. Matt couldn't imagine a young woman like Amelia surviving on her own without a husband. He thought he'd never met such a courageous young lady.

By the end of supper, Matt had forgotten about his poker game and was trying to figure out how he could see Mrs. Hastings again.

***

In the nearby mountain town of Zinat a disheveled young woman rushed into the house of the local *Sherif*. Throwing herself at the feet of the young noble, she cried, "Please, my lord. Give me vengeance."

Sherif al-Raisuni, tall, slender and handsome in his twentieth year, helped the woman to her feet. "What has happened, my sister?"

"Thieves, my lord," she gasped. "They broke into our house today, this morning. My husband and my son," she broke into tears. "They are dead, murdered by those sons of sin. And everything we had is gone. They emptied our house, our wheat, wool, gold. My life is over. You must help me."

Al-Raisuni questioned the woman closely. Then he clapped his hands and called for his horse. "You will lead me to your house. With Allah's help we will have retribution for you."

Twenty men and slaves rode with the young lord. As they neared the house the woman pointed out, "There is one of the men. There, in our orchard."

Al-Raisuni lifted his rifle and shot the man dead. "Quickly, men, spread out and catch the others."

They found two more bandits lounging nearby, just finishing a meal. They stood these men in front of the young widow, "Are these all the men?" al-Raisuni asked.

"Yes, ya *Sherif*, these are the sons of sin who killed my family. May they rot in Hell," she said.

"May Allah treat them as they treated you, *ya lalla*," al-Raisuni replied. "Shoot them," he commanded his men.

＊＊＊

At a Queen's Birthday Party hosted by Sir John Drummond Hay, the British Minister in Tangier, Matt stood uncomfortably in the large salon, nodding politely at friends, trying to find someone to bring him a neat whiskey. Then he heard a familiar laugh from the dining room and made his way there, finding Amelia seated at the head of the table, dressed in white and pink, her cheeks scarlet from the heat of the samovar as she poured tea.

He steeled himself to push through the crowd of women clustered around Amelia and approached her. "Good afternoon, Mrs. Hastings."

Amelia smiled back, cheeks becoming slightly more flushed. "Oh Mr. Shields. How wonderful to see you. I shall soon be finished with my turn serving tea. Will you still be here?"

The party had suddenly become much less dull. Matt hovered near the table, content to watch Amelia as she poured. Later, after another British wife replaced her, Matt suggested they take a stroll in the beautiful gardens of Ravensrock, the British Residence.

"I wonder how they keep their roses so healthy," Amelia remarked, fanning herself.

"Lots of sweat, I would imagine," Matt replied, "but I really have to give the Drummond Hays credit for keeping this garden up. I miss these grounds."

"Oh," Amelia said. "How many years have you been coming here? Do you know something about its history?"

"Oh yes," Matt chuckled. "I guess I do. I grew up in this house."

"Really? But I thought you were from California?"

"Well, yes and no. Fact is, I was born here. Guess that's why I like it so much. My Pa was an Irish sailor who billeted here for a spell back around 1820 and he met a beautiful young senorita whose family had been living here for a long time. They fell in love, married here and had me. My Pa later became the honorary British Consul here, but they're both gone now, God bless 'em."

"How did you get all the way to California?"

"Well, like a lot of young men, I got restless here. You know, there's not that much to do here now, and back in 1855, when I was just a young whippersnapper, this seemed like the dullest place in the world. I was just hanging around, mostly getting into trouble. My Pa gave me my reins, in fact, encouraged me to go."

"How wise."

"Yes, I reckon he was. So I signed on one of the ships passing through here and worked my way across to America. When I landed there I heard talk of gold being discovered in California, so I found another ship, one of them clipper ships, and worked my way around South America until I got to San Francisco. I spent three happy years out there in the gold fields of Calaveras County. And I did pretty well, too. I was lucky."

"Then did you come back to Tangier?"

"Not directly. I went down to San Francisco and invested in some land, played around some there in the real estate market. Made a lot of good friends out there in San Francisco. But then the War Between the States broke out and well, heck, I was still a young man, so I decided to enlist. Figured I could ride a horse and shoot as well as the next man, and maybe I owed something to that country. It was pretty good to me. California was raising a regiment, so I signed up."

"I hadn't realized the west of the United States had been involved in the war."

"Well, there's lots of people don't know that, I reckon. We were kind of a token. The settlers out in California wanted to support the Union, even if it was just one regiment. They sent us back east. And we saw plenty of action there, too, I can tell you!"

"My, what a varied life you've had," Amelia said. "So many people here in Tangier seem like you. They've had so many adventures."

"I don't know about that," Matt said. "I just put my hand at whatever came up, and I've been pretty lucky so far. And then after the war I had myself a good rank and a lot of friends in California, and I got involved some in politics. Then, before I knew it, the Democrats were looking to put a couple of

Californians in some diplomatic posts, and my name came up, and I thought how nice it would be to go back to Tangier, now that I'd seen the world. So, here I am."

"Surely it was more than just luck," Amelia said. "You're being far too modest."

"Maybe yes, and maybe no," Matt replied. "Anyway, I know I feel a lot luckier since I've met you, Mrs. Hastings. And I hope we'll be seeing more of each other."

Now it was Amelia's turn to blush. She hadn't been expecting such a direct compliment from this shy man. "I would enjoy that, too, Mr. Shields."

Amelia was even more reticent about herself than Matt, but over time he learned more of Amelia's history. Amelia's father was a parson in Gloucestershire, the second son of a baronet. She and her two sisters had been raised quietly with a governess, rarely leaving the county. But Amelia's mother had an eccentric sister who had eloped with a poet and traveled all over the world with him, living in Egypt, China, France. Periodically, Aunt Lizzy would descend upon their quiet parsonage, bringing gifts, shimmering silks from China, alabaster plates from Egypt, exotic scents, and best of all, stories and stories about distant lands, exciting people, adventure. Amelia had always begged for more, until it had become a joke in her family that she was 'the traveler,' even though it was just from an armchair.

When Amelia was eighteen and engaged to be married to Roger, Aunt Lizzy died and surprised them all by leaving Amelia a small legacy with instructions that it was to be spent only in foreign lands, so that she could experience the pleasures of travel first-hand. That, plus Roger's investments, had made it possible for her to stay on after her husband's death.

Over the next few years Amelia and Matt gradually fell

into the habit of each other's company. Matt escorted her to many of the social events that formed the calendar of life in Tangier, and Sundays became their special day, when Matt would often arrive with a second horse to take Amelia riding, or they would take Ted and Lili and pack a big picnic lunch to eat up on the mountain slopes that towered over the city. Matt and Amelia both enjoyed tennis and often made up a party with some of the other young couples of Tangier. Matt had always avoided the company of women, finding them too demanding and too prim. But Amelia was different; she was fun to be with, a good listener; he found himself looking forward to their outings.

The more Matt saw of Amelia, the more he found himself relying on her. He discovered that parties, rather than being an unpleasant diplomatic obligation, could be relaxed and pleasurable when Amelia organized them. Matt enjoyed spending time at her home, where Amelia saw to it that he was comfortable and well looked after. Contrary to his expectations, she even allowed him to smoke.

***

Amelia Hastings lived in a small villa with her son, Ted. Their house was located in the newly developing European section of Tangier called the Marjan, behind the Portuguese Fortress.

Amelia invited Matt and Lili for Sunday lunch, along with Matt's Jewish agent, Brahim, his wife Leah, her sister Rebecca, and their two children, Meriam and Gabriel. Other guests included Budgett Meakin, the lively 24 year-old son of the Tangier Times publisher, and Rosemary Higgins, an English woman who was a governess in Tangier. Walter Harris, a young aristocrat and sometime contributor to the London Times, and

Georges St René Taillandier, the French Minister in Tangier, joined them.

Teddy, Amelia's son, raced off with Gabriel to inspect the ducks at the back of the house, while Lili and Meriam went to the kitchen to get some lemonade. As her guests sipped refreshments, Amelia turned to Rosemary, having carefully informed herself in advance of this woman's interests and background.

"Rosemary, I've heard you're teaching the children of the *Sherif* of Matar. I suppose his wife, Alice, suggested that. How do you like it?"

"It's quite a challenge. You know, it's not just his children. I also have one of the Sultan's children, Ali, as well as Tariq Ash-Sherif, a cousin of the Glaoui, who is the head of an important tribe below Marrakesh. So altogether there are three boys, who so far have only learned the Koran by heart, how to write Arabic verses, and some elementary mathematics. There's a difference in ages, too. Ali is the youngest at eight, and Kassim, a child the *Sherif* has taken in, is about the same age as your Ted; he's ten, isn't he? Tariq is twelve. At the moment, I've decided to start by teaching them some English. I thought once they got more familiar with the language, I could then get into geography and literature. But it's very difficult, since they think English is just a game, and always speak Arabic among themselves."

"I can see that," Amelia said. "I have the same problem learning Arabic; I spend too much time with English and French speakers."

"I was discussing this the other day with the *Sherif* and Alice, and he suggested that I see if there might be an English-speaking boy in Tangier who would like to join these children for their lessons." Rosemary's eyes brightened. "Do you think

Teddy would be interested? It would be an unusual and interesting opportunity for him, as well as for the Moroccans. They'd have a chance to practice their English, but it would be a wonderful opportunity for these young Arabs, all of whom will soon have positions of the highest responsibility, to widen their horizons and learn more about the West. And of course, an English boy would have the chance of a lifetime to learn first-hand how these Arab princes think and maybe to become their friend."

"I'd have to think this over with Teddy," Amelia said. "Personally, I think it's quite intriguing. It could make a significant difference in Ted's future. If he plans to keep Morocco as his home, I can't think of a better opportunity. He could learn so much from these boys: about Islam, the Arabic language, and Arab attitudes towards life. But where would they study?"

Rosemary said, "Probably we would spend some time here, some in Marrakesh at the Sultan's palace, and some time in Matar at the *Sherif*'s home."

Amelia looked toward Matt who was talking with the French Minister and Budgett Meakin. What a wonderful opportunity for Teddy to live with a *Sherif*, who was a type of Arab noble, claiming direct descent from the Prophet and considered to have special healing powers, as well as being the Sultan's leading mediator. This would be like going to live with a powerful earl in Britain. And the boys Teddy would study with could be valuable friends later on.

"You know," Taillandier said to Matt, "now that we have pacified Alger, we worry that *les tribus* within Morocco will interfere with our efforts to establish farms and French homes there. After fifty years, many *Français* consider Alger as home, and some of the *Algeriens* are even converting, especially *les*

Berbères. Probablement they were Christian long before they were *Muselmans* in any case."

Matt and Budgett exchanged glances. The French romance with the blond, blue-eyed Berbers was a subject of amusement to the Anglo community, who felt the French were beguiled by this ethnic minority, placing a rather naive trust in their apparent fidelity to the colonial power.

"*Franchement,*" Taillandier said, "it is clear that this country is going nowhere as it now is. *C'est difficile* to believe it is almost the 20th century. *Les paysans* are living in *la misère*; disease is appalling. They should not live in such ignorance and misery. And the Court," he raised his shoulders in a typical Gallic shrug, "They seem *pas motivé* to address this situation.

"The worst," he continued, "is *la dette*. We do not like to have such a situation so close to Alger. We have made many loans to Sultan Hassan. And this when we have not recuperated from the Prussian war. I shudder to think what might happen should the Sultan default. Why can these people not just settle down to their farming and herding, and produce what is needed to pay us back?"

Amelia was a firm believer that religion, politics and finances did not lead to good digestion. She signaled her butler, Mohammed, to announce lunch, hoping to change the subject, and they made their way into the dining room for roast beef and Yorkshire pudding.

"Rebecca, I believe congratulations are in order on your recent engagement?" Amelia said. Leah's younger sister blushed in confusion.

Brahim came to the rescue, "Yes, about a month ago Ruth and Shimeon, Leah's mother and father, came from Fez to visit us. They discussed with us the possibility for Rebecca to become engaged to Israel Rabine, a distant cousin."

"Well, Rebecca, that's very exciting. Tell us about Israel."

Sixteen year-old Rebecca smiled shyly at Amelia. "He's a merchant living in Taza, although his family is from Fez, like ours. He's not too old; I think about twenty-five."

"And how do you feel about leaving Leah and moving to Taza?" asked Rosemary.

"That's the hardest part," Rebecca said. "I hate to think of leaving Leah. I've enjoyed living in Tangier."

Taza was a small town, about two days ride east from Fez, on the road to Oran, in Algeria. Although she knew it had a sizable Jewish population, which should make it easier for Rebecca to find friends, Amelia doubted it would be easy for this fun-loving, outgoing girl to adjust to life in a backwater town, now that she was used to Tangier. Tangier Jews prided themselves on living like the French, in comfortable houses with modern conveniences, books, and enjoyed attending lectures, concerts and musical events. Even though the foreign women frequently complained about the lack of things to do in Tangier, life in Taza would be primitive in comparison.

"Rebecca has been taking some cultural classes for women at the Alliance Israelite," Brahim said. "She's been studying Hebrew and has made friends here. We will all miss her, but I hope she won't have to leave for a while. Maybe at least six months."

The ladies withdrew, leaving the men to their cigars and port. The men settled comfortably around the table and Matt passed the decanter. The French Minister offered cigars. "A new protégé of mine gets these from Havana. He just gave me a case, in thanks for saving him hundreds of douros in taxes."

The protégé system was widely used by the diplomatic community in Tangier, who were allowed to take agents under their protection. The agents were drawn almost exclusively from the sizeable Jewish minority. The Jews who had come down from the north, usually referred to as Andalusian Jews, were well educated Spanish speakers and had settled in Morocco's cities, where they served as merchants and jewelers. Many of the more ancient group of Jews, often uneducated and less cultured, lived in the countryside, some working as farm labor, since they were not permitted to own land, others as blacksmiths and small traders. Since the Muslim Arabs considered both Christians and Jews unclean and preferred to deal with them as little as possible, the merchant class of Jews had long been consigned the task of trading with all foreigners, and over the centuries this task had evolved into handling any import or export of commodities. The Jews paid a heavy tax to the Sultan on such transactions, contributing substantially to the royal coffers.

As the Western powers increased their trade, they gradually took on these Jews as their agents in Morocco, since they were already well-connected to producers and could travel freely in the country, something foreigners were not allowed to do. The agents, known as protégés, were protected by the foreigners, since they were representing them, and by the nineteenth century, the foreign legations offered their agents citizenship in their countries, and therefore exemption from all local taxes and laws. The diplomats could send these agents, mostly Jewish, into the interior to represent the foreign nation, negotiating business arrangements, buying wool and cereal, even land, for their protectors.

Sir Walter Harris, who fancied himself a serious student of Moroccan culture, said, "It's an interesting point, isn't it? I should guess that the very reason why the Sultan has always entrusted the Jews with foreign commerce is because he can hold them hostage by imposing heavy taxes on them when they start to get too independent. But now we foreigners have unbalanced his system and deprived him of a valuable source of income."

Matt glanced at Brahim, "Well, Brahim here is the best agent a man could have. But so far the best I've gotten from any of my protégés is a brace of ducks."

***

Lili and Meriam, Brahim's daughter, were curled up like two kittens in the living room.

"Mama gave me this new doll for Hanukah," Meriam said. "Look, it opens and closes its eyes."

"Oh," Lili touched it reverently. "Its clothes are beautiful."

Meriam handed the doll to her. "Why don't you keep it until I come over to play. We can share it."

***

Amelia knocked on Matt's office door at the Legation. "Matt, I hope you don't mind my bothering you at your office, but I wanted to get your opinion on something that's been troubling me."

"Heck no! It gives me a good excuse to forget about these pesky papers for a while." Matt stood, removing a pile of ledgers from the nearest chair to make room for her. He waved ineffectually at the air, thick with the smoke of a thousand cigars. "This room's a mess. Here, take a seat. I'll open this window. Sorry about all this smoke. I can't think without my cigar." He made a few feeble attempts to move papers around and finally gave up, settling down on a chair near Amelia. "The bookkeepers from Washington are driving me to drink. They always seem to have some question about some expense, want receipts for everything. Receipts, can you imagine, here in Tangier?"

Amelia settled down in her chair and smiled soothingly at Matt, "Could I help you with any of that? I'm not a bad clerk, you know."

"Oh, I wasn't hinting at that. I know you have work of your own. Here, I'm forgetting my manners. Let me get us some tea."

Matt rang for tea. He leaned back in his chair, "It sure is a pleasure to see you here. What can I do for you?"

"Well, I have a little nest egg saved up, and I was hoping you could advise me on how to invest it. I was thinking maybe I should buy the house I'm living in."

"The town is booming," Matt said. "Real estate's probably a good idea. But if Ted's going off to join those Moroccan boys, will you need all that room?"

"Probably not. Or I might even consider taking a boarder."

Matt shifted a bit in his chair. "I'm real pleased that you would come to me for advice. Matter of fact, I've been wanting to talk to you, but never seemed to find just the right moment."

Amelia gazed earnestly at Matt, "Yes, Matt?"

"I, well, I'm forty-six now and successful enough, so seeing as how you're alone here and we seem to get along fine, why don't you and I get married? What do you think?" He stared at her, maybe realizing too late that his proposal was a bit abrupt.

Amelia said smiling, "Yes Matt, I would like that very much."

"Well, hurrah, that's grand!" He picked her up and whirled her around, setting her down long enough to plant a big kiss on her lips. "I'm a lucky man."

***

Matt and Amelia were married at the Episcopal Church in Tangier. Lili and Teddy served as flower boy and girl at the ceremony.

When Matt first broke the news to Lili that he was going to be married, she wondered what this would mean for her. She wasn't sure she wanted to share Papa with anyone. But as soon as Amelia and Ted moved into the Legation, Lili found instead she had two more friends. Amelia immediately insisted she call her Mama. Instead of hanging around the kitchen all day with Aisha, who was often busy, Lili started having breakfast with Amelia and Ted every morning. Amelia always had a list of things the three of them could do and endless questions for her.

The first morning after Amelia moved in, she came into Lili's room and gave her a kiss. She smoothed Lili's hair, or tried to. "Lili, sweetheart, why are you wearing that scarf over your beautiful hair?"

Lili said, "Aisha puts it on me when I go to the *hammam*."

"When was that, dear?"

"Last Thursday, Mama. She braids my hair after she washes it and then she puts on the scarf, to keep it clean. You know, girls shouldn't show their hair."

"Um hum. Well, my dear, I think we will change that. In the West we girls don't cover our hair; in fact, we call it our crowning glory."

Lili's hair was matted and dull when Amelia pulled off the scarf. It had been four or five days since she had been to the baths and it had not been rebraided or combed in any way since then.

"This morning we will wash your hair here and maybe we'll try a new hairdo. Would you like that?"

Lili nodded, although she was fearful. "You won't cut it all off, though, will you?"

Amelia laughed. "No, of course not, but I think it's time to pretty you up a little. Now, let me look at your clothes."

Lili was wearing baggy Turkish pants, very comfortable for sitting cross-legged on the floor. Over this she wore a long belted dress that buttoned all the way to the ground, and over it was another long-sleeved floor length dress that was open at the sides from the waist down. The dress was made of satin lined with flannel, for winter, but to be sure Lili was warm, Aisha had added two cotton undershirts under the dresses. Her feet were bare, since she was inside.

"Sweetheart, maybe we should find you some Western clothes, unless you particularly wish to continue dressing like a Moroccan?"

Lili had really never thought about her clothes. Aisha provided them, and Papa had never commented on them. "But everyone dresses like this, Mama!"

"Other European and American girls don't dress that way, dear. Nor does Meriam. By dressing that way, people will assume you're a Moroccan."

Lili put great store by her American citizenship. "Yes, Mama, in that case I would like to change my dress."

The eight-year-old soon found herself in crinolines and pinafores, long stockings on her feet and high button shoes. On the whole she didn't mind, although she found the tight waists constricting. The hardest part was getting used to the laced shoes which pinched Lili's feet and made her feel she might loose her balance. She was used to running barefoot in the house and wearing heelless slippers outside. Once she got used to the shoes, though, Lili admitted that she could actually run faster, since she didn't have to worry about stepping on anything, or stubbing her toe. Her glossy black hair was still braided, but these now hung down and had bows, rather than being wound around her head and covered with a scarf. On special occasions, Amelia tied her hair at night in rags to make long curls. This produced admiring looks from Ted and prompted Matt to declare, "Well, it looks like we have a young beauty in our house!" producing blushes and giggles from Lili.

At their first dinner together, Lili picked up her soup bowl and drank from it. The second course was chicken, mashed potatoes and carrots. Lili picked up the chicken in her hands and ate the potatoes and carrots using bread to pick them up. Amelia watched in horror. "Lili, my dear, you must use your knife and fork."

Lili looked down at her lap. "I don't know how, Mama."

Lili motioned to Hamoud to bring her water to wash off her hands. Amelia handed her a napkin. "If you use a knife and fork, my dear, your hands are not so dirty and can be wiped on this. It's easier."

When Amelia mentioned Lili's lack of table manners to Matt in private, he responded a bit defensively, "Well, you know I wasn't around for that many meals and Lili spent a lot of every day with Aisha and the girls in the kitchen. I guess I just never thought much about that kind of thing."

"Never mind," she assured him. "No harm done. But Lili is such a lovely intelligent young girl. It's not too late to take her in hand."

Lili loved it. At first the meals were a challenge. Every bite she took received criticism from Amelia. "Keep your mouth closed, dear, when you chew. Use your napkin to wipe, so nothing drips down your chin. No elbows on the table." She thought she would never learn to use the knife and fork properly. On her first try, she pushed the knife too hard and her meat shot off her plate and on to Ted's shirt. Lili sat there, shocked; then Ted started to laugh.

"Thanks, little sister. That looked like a better piece than mine, anyway," he said, popping it into his mouth.

Lili took a sip of water. Amelia corrected her gently, "You see, my dear. There's a greasy stain on the glass now. That would be embarrassing if you were at a dinner party. So take care to wipe your mouth before you take a drink." So many rules. Sometimes Lili sneaked back to the kitchen, where she could sit on the floor and eat, properly, but with Moroccan rules. She tried but found she couldn't sit comfortably on the floor in her new clothes. It was confusing.

Lili was convinced that what Amelia taught her was for her own good. She knew she needed to become an American, since this was where her future lay. She became aware of many things she hadn't really thought about; differences between herself and other Moroccan girls. She could read and talk in English, Arabic and French; she had always spent time with Papa reading and talking; she knew Arab girls didn't do these things but stayed with their mothers in the harem, or women's part of the house. She began to notice more similarities between herself and Meriam, in terms of the way they lived and the values of their parents and to recognize that these were European ways of behavior.

Meriam, too, noticed the changes in her, "You are different."

"I'm wearing *nisrani* clothes. Mama says I should become more Western, since I'm not a Moroccan. She says I should dress more like you, instead of like Aisha."

"It pleases me. And now we can exchange! That will be *amusant*!"

"Maybe it will help me find a husband," Lili said.

"A husband! You want to marry? Why do you think of that?" said Meriam, wrinkling her nose in disgust.

"I heard Aisha talking when Habiba got married, and she said I'd never get married as long as I didn't have a mother, because I'm not a Muslim, and Papa wouldn't be able to find a husband for me. So now I have a mother and I mustn't look or act like a Moroccan anymore," Lili explained.

Leah was in the adjoining room and she laughed when she overheard Lili. "Well, bless your heart! You do have a point, my dear. But you don't have to worry about that for a long time. You know, Westerners do not marry as young as Muslims. And their parents do not arrange it. Still, I do like the way you look now; it is more modern. And you look more like the rest of your family."

Lili took this very seriously. When Amelia and Matt suggested that she go to boarding school in America, Lili accepted enthusiastically. This would ensure that she learn Western ways. Matt and Amelia proposed to go to Washington as part of their honeymoon, where Matt would try to straighten out his books. They left after Ted had departed for his schooling with the Arab boys, and Lili went with them all the way to California, where Matt still had friends and knew of a good convent boarding school.

CHAPTER THREE
1890-1897

Lili and Ted spent the next six years preparing for their lives. The education that Ted Hastings, Amelia's son, would receive provided him with a life-long friend; Lili's school left her prepared to be a perfect diplomat's spouse.

As Ted prepared for this adventure and wondered about his new classmates, they, too, were full of questions about him. Tariq ash-Sherif was the most curious, since he had never met any Westerners, male or female. Tariq had joined the other Moroccan boys earlier that year, when he was about twelve. He didn't really know how old he was, since no one registered births, but his cousin, Mehdi, said that was approximately his age, since he had been born about two years before the Sultan's oldest son, Abdul Aziz.

Tariq hadn't had a choice in joining the other boys in Matar. He was the oldest boy of a large Berber family. His father had died in a tribal clash when Tariq was about eight and since then he had been the head of the household. Despite his youth, Tariq had worked for his cousin, Mehdi al-Menebbhi, as one of his soldiers or bodyguards. He had participated in dozens of tribal skirmishes, defending the honor of his clan, grabbing what spoils he could, be they horses, sheep, carpets, jewelry, to ensure his mother and younger siblings were provided for. Tariq understood the laws of feuds and vengeance perfectly, but Mehdi had spotted higher qualities in him and had decreed that he go to Matar, learn English, and receive a Western education. What his cousin, Mehdi, ordered, Tariq did.

The *zawiya*, or sanctuary, of Matar was located not far from Tariq's own village in the High Atlas Mountains below Marrakesh. But Matar was a gray stone city, unlike his village, where all the houses were four and five stories high, built of brownish mud bricks, dark inside with small windows and high stairs.

Tariq was older than his two school mates. The ten year old, olive-skinned boy was Kassim, he soon learned, and although he went by the name of Matari, he was not actually related to the *Sherif*, but the son of a distant impoverished relative. From his quickness to respond to the *Sherif* of Matar, the family head, Tariq guessed that Kassim wanted very much to belong to this family.

Ali, son of a junior wife of the Sultan, was only eight when he began their classes. From his chubbiness and childish friendliness, Tariq guessed Ali had been living in the *harem* with his mother and the other ladies, who had been spoiling him with sweets and soft words. But little Ali outshone both the older boys at their classes, quickly picking up English.

None of the three boys had any formal education, although they had all learned to recite the Koran, whether sitting on the dirt floor in a small local mosque, like Tariq, or on a tiled court in the palace, in Ali's case. There they sat cross-legged on the floor in front of a grey-bearded *fquih*, or religious scholar, each with his own writing board and pen. The *fquih* recited a verse to them and they recited it back, gradually also learning to write it down. Every mistake was punished by a blow or a pinch from the *fquih*.

The first day of classes in Matar, Tariq entered a sunny room carrying his writing board and pen. To his puzzlement he saw three small tables with benches sitting side by side. In front was a big black board. Kassim snickered at Tariq's obvious confusion. Then Ali bounced up to him and took his hand, leading him to one of the tables, "We each get our own table and a bench to sit at. No more sitting on the cold floor."

Tariq perched gingerly on the bench, which he found uncomfortable. He didn't like the feeling of his legs dangling down. But he was determined to do as the other boys did. Then their governess, Rosemary Higgins, entered the room. Her face was uncovered, as well as her auburn hair, which was piled on top of her head. Before coming to Matar the only women Tariq had seen with face and hair exposed were his mother and sisters. Her clothes, too, were strange, and all pinched in at the waist. He wondered why she would want to be so constricted and thought it must be hard to breathe. Then Miss Higgins began speaking to the boys. Tariq couldn't understand a single word. He already knew *Shilha* and Arabic, but hadn't realized people spoke other languages. He couldn't imagine why he needed this clickety language with funny vowel sounds, spoken only by Christians, but his cousin, Mehdi, insisted that he learn it, promising him that he would thank him later.

The *Sherif*'s American wife, Alice Watson, was also very different from his own mother, who spent most of her day spinning wool, weaving rugs with her friends, or cooking. Every time he saw her she was reading. Allah, he thought, even women wear glasses! She wore shoes all the time, even inside. Both she and Miss Higgins smelled like flowers.

Miss Higgins had to tell her students more than once that they must look at her when they spoke. This confused Tariq since polite Arab boys learned early in life that, unless it was your mother or sister, you did not look at women if you had to address them, and preferably you didn't talk directly to them either, but asked some male relative anything you needed to know from the woman.

***

Located across the bay from San Francisco in Marin County, Lili's school was a white Victorian building set on spacious grounds planted with fragrant eucalyptus and oleander shrubs. The softly rounded golden peaks of Mount Tamalpais made Lili ache with homesickness for the mountains surrounding Tangier.

When she first went to the convent with Matt and Amelia, they were shown into the parlor by a nun, who bowed, whispering that she would return with the Mother Superior. Lili looked around the room in curiosity. She had never seen wood as flooring before. It smelled funny, like petrol, which later she learned was used to clean it. The floor was so shiny she could see her face in it.

Then Mother Mary Margaret came in. Lili thought she looked a little like her beloved Sister Theresa, although her dress was different. This nun had a starched white and black headdress that stood out from her head in an arc, and the rest of her habit (as she learned to call it), was white. In some ways, Lili decided, it wasn't that different from Moroccan clothing, since it had an underdress and a floating white panel on top. Mother Mary Margaret smiled at Lili and said, "Now you must say good-bye to your Mama and Papa. It will be a while before you see them again, but I'm sure you will be very happy here."

Lili hadn't thought about actually being separated from Matt and Amelia. Her eyes filled with tears. So did Matt's, she saw. They hugged, with promises to write often and to see each other the next summer, and before she knew it, she was alone with Mother Mary Margaret.

"Come along, Lili." The nun took her hand. "You will soon get used to our convent and you will make friends among the girls. You must think of us as your parents." Lili nodded, tears running down her face. She couldn't imagine that these nuns would ever feel that way to her. They went upstairs to a large dormitory which was divided into cell-like rooms by partitions that went halfway to the ceiling on two sides. At the front was a curtain that could be drawn across for privacy. A small iron bed and a dresser furnished the alcove. This was so different from her spacious room in the Legation, with its wool-stuffed mattress and silk hangings that she found it hard to think of as a room.

Mother Mary Margaret indicated the dresser. "The top drawer is for your handkerchiefs, and gloves. In the second drawer you will put your stockings. The third drawer is for undergarments. The fourth and fifth drawers may be used for scarves, sweaters. On the top you may put your comb and brush and a trinket box, if you like." There was a small locker next to the dresser. "This is for your uniforms," Mother Mary Margaret advised her. Lili had already had uniforms made, with Amelia's help. Lili had two midcalf-length dresses of black serge with a white cotton pinafore for winter, and two similar lighter dresses for summer. For Sundays they changed to organdy pinafores.

A girl with curly red hair poked her head through the curtains as she sat on the bed, wiping her tears with her sleeve.

"We're not allowed to sit on our beds, ever. Here, sit on this chair, and I'll bring mine, too, so we can talk. I'm Sheila. It's not so bad here. You'll see. Where are you from?" She was whispering.

Lili started telling her story and within a few seconds,

another nun, Sister Louise, appeared. "Young ladies, we do not speak in loud voices here. I know you are new, Lili, so I will excuse you this once, but please remember in the future to use well-modulated, tones and speak genteelly."

Used as she was to the hustle and bustle of a Moroccan household, Lili struggled to accustom herself to the customs of the convent. The next morning, she was awakened by a bell, and Sheila, who was in the next alcove, came and whispered to her, "Now we wash and get dressed quickly for Mass."

Wash, Lili thought with surprise. Just like Mama said. Dutifully she followed the other girls to the lavatory and splashed cold water on her face. She sat through the Mass, stomach rumbling, and fell asleep once, only to be awakened by a nun tapping her on the shoulder. At the end, Lili skipped out of the chapel and started running toward the refectory. She was starving. Quickly Sister Louise caught her by the arm. "Young ladies do not run, my dear. Walk properly, like your classmates."

***

Miss Higgins told the three Moroccan boys at Matar that an English boy would be joining them. "Ted Hastings will feel very strange here, so far from his people and his way of life," she warned them, "so try to make him feel welcome and comfortable." This piqued Tariq's curiosity; what could be so different here for an English boy? They had plenty of room, servants to help them, horses to ride, good food. Surely the English must have the same.

Tariq and his schoolmates ran to the front courtyard to get a glimpse of their new classmate. They saw a gangly boy with red hair parted on the side and brushed flat, dressed in short wool pants, high socks and brown shoes, like Miss Higgins', only with lower heels, a white shirt tucked into his pants and a wool jacket. The Moroccan boys, with shaven heads, wearing short wool *djellabahs*, and *baboushes*, donned only for outside, were partly hiding behind the *Sherif* and his wife, Alice. They dissolved in giggles and whisperings at Ted's appearance, until a frown from Alice, and a warning cuff from the *Sherif*, made it clear that they were to be silent.

Ted descended from the mule he'd been riding, and approached the *Sherif*. Politely, he took the *Sherif's* hand and laid it on his head, answering the *Sherif's* welcome in good dialectical Arabic, "*Ya sidi*, I thank you for your hospitality and hope that you will be as a father to me, and your sons will be as my brothers."

Well, Tariq thought, he may look strange, but at least he has good manners. He and Ali took Ted across the tiled open courtyard and entered a vast garden behind the mosque that was an integral part of the property. Delicate white pavilions were scattered around a garden blooming with roses and orange trees. There was plenty of room to house the pilgrims and tribesmen who routinely came here seeking assistance and advice from the *Sherif*. The boys brought Ted to a building that opened into a courtyard with a splashing fountain, surrounded by arabesque arches framing several rooms. This looked so much like the Legation that Ted relaxed. Each room was sparsely furnished with couches covered in hand woven blankets, and cushions at the back to provide protection from the cold plaster. Tariq indicated a painted trunk in one room, "You can put your things there." Tariq stood while Ted unpacked. He counted ten white shirts, three sweaters, many pairs of stockings, three, no four pairs of those tight wool shorts.

"Why so many clothes, *ya* Ted?" he asked, unable to contain himself. Tariq had one change of clothes, and even Ali had the same.

"I dunno," Ted said, scratching his head. "My mother packed."

***

Kassim went out early to the stables. "From now on," he told the stable boy, "I will choose the horses for riding, and I will saddle them. You do not need to help."

***

Tariq noticed Ted straining to sit cross-legged in his short pants. After lunch he took him aside, "*Ya* Ted, can I speak to you as a brother?"

Ted nodded.

"Why do you wear those short tight pants? It is embarrassing the men to see you sitting in them when we eat. Can you think of wearing our *serwal* instead?" Tariq was referring to the baggy Turkish pants Moroccans wore, whose crotch came down to the knees with wide legs gathered in at the ankles. "By Allah, you will be more comfortable for eating and also for horse riding."

***

Lili adapted fast to her school, as she desired above all to fit in with these American girls. She grew ultra sensitive to any reference that she was foreign. One day they were practicing deportment, and learning to glide beautifully across a room. When Lili's turn came, she heard one of the older girls laugh and say to her neighbor, "She should do well at this, since she probably used to carry water on her head like all those natives."

Lili's eyes stung at this, but she was determined not to let it show. She couldn't think of any way to respond, so she picked up several books and put them on her head. As she glided across the room, she announced, "I think of these as trays. The kind my maid used to bring from the kitchen to the dining room in the morning." This was silly, of course, since Aisha and the other women did no such thing, but there were fewer comments after that, especially since Lili learned quickly and was popular with her schoolmates. Soon the sisters were commenting on her exquisite manners, as well as her speed in learning them. Whenever she detected that a phrase or an element of her behavior or deportment brought raised eyebrows, she carefully studied the others and she learned to blend in, severely disciplining her own nature, restraining her impulsiveness.

***

Ted sat down to dinner in his new Turkish trousers. Tariq was right, it was easier to sit cross-legged in them. He waited politely until the *Sherif* offered him a piece of bread. He reached across and took something from Tariq's portion. Tariq immediately offered it to him, "Please, *ya* Ted, take this morsel. You will like it." After several similar incidents, Ted realized he should only eat what was in front of him.

***

Breakfast. At least, Lili thought, Mama had prepared her for this. But no, almost immediately after she picked up her knife and fork and attacked her eggs, Sister Louise was at her side, "Left hand in your lap, dear. Sit up straight. Lift the fork when conveying food to the mouth, not the head to the fork." Lili reached for the bread, which had been passed to her. She took a bite of the toast. "No, Lili, break the bread into small pieces. Then eat it." In the name of Allah, Lili thought, will they ever leave me in peace? The bell rang again. Sheila whispered, "Now we have class."

At noon they went back to the dormitory to wash up for lunch. In her alcove Lili found all her bedding on the floor. Looking on her dresser, covered by a white runner, she saw a note. "There are three hairs on the runner, plus many in your brush. Please clean your brush and make your bed neatly, with no wrinkles. Do not let this happen again or you will be issued demerits." Demerits, Lili would learn, if accumulated, could prevent a trip to the opera or some other nice outing.

Sister Louise poked her head through the curtains at the front of the cubicle. "You must make your bed properly, young lady."

"But, Sister, I don't know how."

"Obviously. Here, we will do it together. Even though you will always have servants to do this for you, you must know how it should be done so that you can supervise them."

***

They were having lamb with wild artichokes in Matar. Ted ate several of the long stems; they were delicious. Then Kassim leaned toward him, a dripping morsel in his hand. "Here, Ted, you will enjoy this."

The *Sherif* smiled, looking proud of his protégé's manners.

Ted took what Kassim offered; it was an eyeball. He popped it in his mouth and chewed thoroughly, willing his stomach to cooperate. "Delicious, *ya* Kassim. Many thanks."

The *Sherif* looked thoughtfully at Ted and nodded to himself. Kassim watched the *Sherif* and clenched his fists. At the next meal the *Sherif* patted the space next to him, "*Ya* Ted, sit next to me. I would like to learn more about the West."

***

"That is wise, I think," Tariq said, nodding. "We will all have enemies in our lives sooner or later. It is good to be wary and not trust until we know men. Men of power attract hatred. My father taught me that when I was young. It is good to know this."

***

Despite Tariq's private warning to him, Ted agreed to go out hawking with Kassim. Ted loved flying the hawks. The thrill of casting these huge birds into the air and watching them dip and sway floating on currents of air never failed to move him. The boys went quite far, following the birds, climbing into territory unknown to Ted. Engrossed in the flight of the hawks, Ted neglected to notice what the path was like and his horse stumbled. Ted had been riding a much gentler horse since his first experience, but the horse he had been given today was the oldest one in the stables and probably not really strong enough for the trip they had taken.

He got down to examine the horse and saw that the injury was serious. "Crikes!" he said to Kassim. "I think this is bad. I won't be able to ride her back with this injury. What shall we do now?"

Kassim gave the horse's leg a cursory inspection and confirmed that the horse was too lame to carry Ted. "I'll go back and get help." Catching the lame horse by the bridle, he turned towards Matar, saying to Ted, "Just wait for me here."

Ted sat by the side of the path, cursing himself for his stupidity in not insisting on returning with Kassim. He hadn't had a chance to think before Kassim rode off. Ted had never taken *Sherif* Mohammed's attentions that seriously. Now, he asked himself bitterly, what price would he pay? He wondered if Kassim would come back at all, refusing to believe he could cold-heartedly abandon him on this desolate mountain track.

***

Lili noticed a line of Chinese mothers and children assembled behind the school kitchen. She went closer and saw two nuns, their sleeves rolled up, were dishing out soup to the women. Intrigued, she later asked Sister Louise about this.

"My dear, these unfortunate women have lost their husbands, who worked for the railroad. They are stranded here in California, with little money and no way to earn a living. We try to do what we can for them."

"Can I help, Sister?" Lili asked.

"Of course, my dear. Why don't you join me on Saturday morning? We have a little clinic for the children."

That Saturday after breakfast Lili found Sister Louise holding a tiny baby on her lap. She was dipping her finger in a bowl and dripping liquid into its mouth. When she saw Lili she said, "Here, dear heart. Take this baby and keep doing what I'm doing. Just keep putting this sweet water in its mouth."

Gingerly, Lili took the infant and sat down. "Is this a special treat for the baby?"

"No, Lili. This little child is very ill. It has diarrhea and has lost too much fluid. We will do what we can to put that fluid back."

Lili worked with the baby all morning and managed to empty most of the bowl into it. She was intrigued, as she saw color come back to the infant's face and it began to move its legs and arms more forcefully. The next Saturday she was back as early as the school allowed. "Sister Louise, teach me what you know. I like doing this."

***

It turned very cold and the *djellabah* Ted was wearing soon became inadequate. He had no idea where he was or even the direction to follow back. If he started walking, he could easily go astray and if a search party did come for him, it would be even harder for them to find him.

Ted found some dry rocks that might serve as a flint. He managed to light a small fire using some dry bushes to kindle the flame. He sat huddled over the heat, trying to keep it going, occasionally falling asleep. Then, shortly before dawn, he heard riders in the distance. He stood up, waving his arms, and saw Tariq and Mohammed coming towards him led by one of the *Sherif*'s hunting dogs.

Tariq reached him first. "Ted, we were worried. Kassim told us you decided to stay by yourself and not to fret. Then when it got late, we realized something had happened and decided to come and search for you. *Al Hamdu'llah*, we had this dog to track you."

Ted said, "Yes, my horse went lame and got away and then I didn't know which way to go. So I reckoned the best thing to do was stay put and wait for someone to find me."

He and Tariq exchanged glances. Mohammed uttered a few religious phrases, giving thanks for Ted's rescue, and helped him onto his horse. But later that day, Mohammed sent for Tariq and questioned him more thoroughly about the incident.

"*Ya* Tariq, what happened, truly? Did Kassim leave Ted there alone?"

Tariq looked uncomfortable and said, "Ted told me he decided to stay behind and then his horse bolted."

Mohammed said, "I saw that horse in the stables. With Allah's help it found its way back alone and no one wondered where Ted was."

Tariq said nothing.

***

Tariq found Kassim alone, near the stables. "What are you playing at with Ted?" he asked.

Kassim opened his eyes wide. "I don't know what you mean." He turned to leave.

Tariq grabbed his arm, "Leaving Ted out there was deliberate. He could have died."

"So what? He's just an infidel anyway. Who would care?"

"Ted is a schoolmate and a guest here. Does that not mean anything to you?"

"No, not really," Kassim said, eyes narrowed.

"By Allah, consider this a warning from me, *ya* Kassim. I will be watching you at all times. What you do to Ted, you do to me. Do not forget this." Kassim struggled to get free.

"You be careful, too. A curse on both of you." Kassim ran off.

***

The summer of 1894 Lili and Ted discovered they could be friends. One hot evening they were sitting on the terrace of the Legation, playing cards in a desultory fashion, when Lili said, "Ted, what do you do in the evenings in Tangier, when your friends are here?"

"Sometimes we go to coffee houses and just sit there, watching people. And sometimes we go where there are dancing girls. You should see them, Lili. They can really dance."

"Oh, Ted," interrupted Lili, "Let's go! I haven't seen any dancing for a long time, and it sounds like fun!"

"But girls can't go to things like that! It's not proper."

"But I'm bored! And it sounds exciting! Can't you smuggle me in somehow? Could I dress up like a boy? Come on, Ted. Don't be so dull. I want to see!" Little by little, Lili coaxed him. "Look, I can hide all my hair in a turban, and I'll put on a *djellabah*, and no one will know at all. And I'll keep my voice low; it's not that different from a young boy's anyway. Come on, Ted, it'll be good fun. You won't be sorry!"

"I guess it would be all right. But Tariq might be coming by. He said something about that."

"Oh bother Tariq. Come on, Ted. Let's go."

Lili went to get ready, enlisting a protesting Aisha into her plans. She presented herself to Ted, pirouetting around in the courtyard. "You see, Ted, you really can't tell I'm a girl." Just as Ted was congratulating her, Tariq came in.

"*Salaam*, Ted. Do you still want to go out tonight?"

"Oh, hullo, Tariq. Welcome. Yes, I was just thinking about it."

Lili nudged him.

"Oh, this is my friend, Li…uh, Larabi."

Lili offered her hand, "*Ahlen, ya* Tariq." She kept her eyes down and stood somewhat in the shadows.

Ted offered Tariq a seat and called for some tea. "Uh, Tariq, I have some unfinished business with Larabi. Would you excuse us a minute?" Ted hustled Lili out of the room.

"Lili, we can't go through with this. Tariq will catch on."

"Well, I don't give a fig if he does. It's not the end of the world, is it? Isn't he your good friend? I'll be very unobtrusive and quiet and he probably won't notice anything. After all, he's not expecting me to be a girl, is he?"

Reluctantly, Ted agreed, and the three left for the Sokko Chico, where the coffee houses were located. Tariq led them to a dark smoky coffee house, where they were served hot coffee spiced with pepper and chick peas. They called for water pipes, and settled back on the banquettes to watch the girls dance.

Not wanting to call attention to herself by refusing the water pipe, Lili carefully watched as the two boys went through the preparations to be sure the charcoal was well lit and the pipe was drawing well, then taking a few contented pulls on the long pipe and listening to the gurgling as the water bubbled in the lower container, cooling the tobacco as it passed through the hose to their mouths. It looked fairly easily, so she cautiously took a puff, and then sputtered and coughed as the acrid smoke burned through her throat and lungs.

"Careful, *ya* Larabi," cautioned Tariq, pounding her on the back. "Is this your first time with the water pipe?"

Lili waved him away. "No, it's fine, just a different type of tobacco. Maybe I'll lay off the pipe for tonight." She wiped her eyes and took a few sips of coffee, moving back into the shadows to recover. Fortunately, a dancing girl entered the room just at that time and drew Tariq's attention away from her.

The dancing girl looked about her age. She was heavily made up, with kohl on her eyes, and rouged cheeks and lips. Unlike the women Lili had seen at parties when she was younger, much of this girl's body was visible through her gauzy clothes. Lili drew her breath in surprise and Tariq turned to look at her lazily, "*Ya* Larabi, is this your first time to see a dancing girl, too?" He looked at her rather closely this time, and Lili lowered her eyes quickly.

Ted said, "Larabi comes from Larache so he hasn't been to our coffee houses before."

The dancer twirled and swayed to the beat of the drummers behind her, and the crowd egged her on with suggestive comments. Some of the men pushed forward to paste money to her chest or tuck it into her low hip band. These men received special attentions from the girl, who gyrated her hips more suggestively toward them, sometimes allowing their hands to linger caressingly over her breasts or buttocks for a moment.

Lili was almost hypnotized. She had never imagined this

when she used to dance as a little girl, and despite herself, she felt her own body respond to the deliberate movements and repetitive drumming. One girl was replaced by two who danced together. Then some acrobats, similar to those Lili had loved to watch when she was young, performed. They were followed by a man and a woman together, at which point Ted stood up.

"Well," he said to Tariq, "I'd better be taking my young friend back. It's getting late."

"The fun is just starting," Tariq said. "Don't you want to stay a while and get to know some of these girls?" he inquired, stretching himself like a cat and casting a glance toward Lili to include her in the conversation.

Lili blushed deep crimson. "No," she responded in what she hoped was a gruff voice. "I think I've seen enough for one night."

Ted said, "You stay, Tariq. We'll just go on back. See you tomorrow, *insh'allah*."

"*Insh'allah*. Will Larabi be there tomorrow, too?"

Ted said, "I think Larabi is leaving in the morning."

"Well," said Tariq, taking Lili's hand, "It has been an honor to meet you, Larabi. I hope you enjoyed our Tangier night life."

Ted and Lili escaped into the hot night, exploding with laughter and the relief of having finished the escapade without discovery. They raced their mules back to the Legation, laughing and joking and snuck in, cajoling Hamoud and a very disapproving Aisha into protecting their secret from their parents, who were still out at their party.

"That was marvelous, Ted. I loved it! Half the fun was being in disguise. Do you think Tariq was suspicious? I thought at the end he looked too long at my hands, and I realized I should have cut my nails or done something to make them rough."

"I don't know," Ted admitted. "It was a jolly crazy thing to do, though. What if something had happened? It really wasn't a proper place for a young girl."

Aisha clucked her tongue in vigorous agreement with him.

"Oh bother, Aisha!" Lili said. "Nothing happened. It was such fun to be like a thief in the night, seeing things young ladies don't usually get to see."

***

In the coldest month of the year, Sultan Hassan led his army through the high mountain pass of Tisn-Tishka, near Marrakesh. His men were starving, their horses being slaughtered for food. The snow was knee-high, and the royal army of five thousand was foundering. From his fortress at the top of the mountain, the young tribal *sheikh* Madani al-Glaoui received a message that the Sultan was nearby. His brother, T'Hami, sat with him, "If we strike now, we could overcome him and seize all his riches."

"That is so, my brother, but what would it gain us? We have no contender to suggest as his replacement. No, we will use this as an opportunity to glorify our family," Madani said. He called for his tribal council and issued quick orders; all horses, mules, sheep, cattle, chickens in the area were to be confiscated and brought immediately to his palace. Then he arrayed himself in his best, and he and his brother, accompanied by their warriors, went out to meet the Sultan.

Madani knelt down before the starving Sultan, and repeated the formula of submission," Lord of all, be pleased to rest with us a while; Lord of all, accept our humble homage;

Lord of all, be pleased to accept what little your slave can offer; Lord of all, be gracious, and with your illustrious presence lighten the darkness of my Kasbah; Lord of all, bestow the favor that I may feed your harka (progress); Lord of all, bestow your blessing upon my will to be your slave; Lord of all, tell me how I may serve you."

Sultan Hassan and all his army sat at table all night, feasting upon food they had not seen for months. Madani al-Glaoui gifted the Sultan with enough horses and mules to reprovision the army.

When the royal cortege left, refreshed after three days with al-Glaoui, the Sultan named the *sheikh* representative of all the tribes between the High Atlas and the Sahara. He also presented him with modern arms and ammunition, including a Krupp cannon, the only one in Morocco not owned by the Sultan.

***

Tariq and Ted grew closer. One day, as they were packing to go down to Marrakesh, Ted brought this up directly with his friend. "*Ya* Tariq, I owe so much to you, probably my life, in fact. I don't know how to repay you."

Tariq started to utter an Arabic proverb, "No thanks are needed for an obligation."

"No, Tariq, there must be something I could do for you, too. I know! I could help you lots more with English. Would you like that?"

Tariq nodded. "Yes, my cousin Mehdi is not happy with my progress. You could help, indeed."

"Fine, from now on you and I will only speak English. It'll be hard at first, but it should help you a lot."

***

Ted was in Tangier for a school break. He ran down to the market in the Socco Chico and bought a bunch of pale pink roses, which he directed the seller to wrap with a red ribbon he had bought for that purpose. That afternoon he rang Brahim's doorbell. Leah answered, looking surprised, "Why young Ted. How are you? Did you want to see Gabriel? I'll see if he's here."

Ted looked at his shoes, then cleared his throat, "Uh, Auntie Leah, I brought these roses for Miss Meriam. Is she home?"

Meriam came running, "Is that you, Ted?" She stopped and clapped her hands when she saw the roses. "For me? Why Ted, no one has ever brought me flowers before. *Merci.*"

***

Ian Perdicaris sat in Budgett Meakin's office at the Tangier Times. "Damn it, Meakin, that Matt Shields is going too far. I have it on good authority that he's selling the right to be a protégé to rich Jews."

Budgett sipped his tea, "Why would a chap like Matt do that, Ian? I've never heard a word against him before."

Perdicaris leaned forward to speak confidentially, "You know, I wouldn't be surprised if he's fiddling his books at the Legation. There are auditors out here all the time. He has a lot of gambling debts, as I have reason to know. So maybe he's hard up."

Meakin raised an eyebrow, "Possibly, but I find it hard to believe he'd go so far as to sell those privileges. That's breaking the law. You'd better have good proof before you make any accusations."

***

As his English improved, Tariq began to benefit more from Miss Higgins' lessons. He was particularly impressed with her classes on English and French history. "Tell us again about the French Revolution," he would beg.

She would comply, and then Tariq was full of questions, "So now are the French all the same? How do they rule without a Sultan?"

"They have a constitution with rules and a Parliament that enforces these."

"And the people, they follow these rules willingly?"

"Well, there is force, if they don't obey. They will go to jail if they break the law. But, yes, generally in Britain, as well as France, and in America, too, the citizens understand that the rules are good for them."

"By Allah, how do they know this?"

"Well, they know that although it's unpleasant to pay taxes, they receive services from that money, for example."

Tariq persisted, "But what if they pay the taxes and then they do not get the services?"

Miss Higgins laughed, "Such a lot of questions, Tariq. Well, if they don't get the services, they can vote their representative out of office and elect someone else, who will honor his commitment."

Tariq asked Ted many more questions about this type of government. Ted knew some things from Tangier, which was run more like a European city, with a Sanitary Board, but had to admit that, since he had spent almost no time in Britain, he, too, was ignorant. "But, it is interesting, *ya* Tariq. My stepfather is on that Board. And I know they started it because Tangier was so dirty and people were getting sick. So they set up rules about collecting and disposing of garbage, protecting the water supply, and people did understand that it would keep them healthier."

***

Sultan Hassan's army set out from Marrakesh to put down a rebellion north of the city. Two days out, the Sultan died. His Chamberlain, Ba Ahmed, called together a few trusted slaves, "My boys, *Sidna*, (our Lord), has died. Should the tribes around here hear of this, they could attack us and create an uprising. We must keep this a secret among ourselves until we can proclaim a new King."

That night, contrary to custom, Ba Ahmed announced that the Sultan would not hold his usual audiences, as he was resting. In the morning, camp was broken early and the army traveled north, stopping only once, so that tea and breakfast could be carried into the Sultan's tent. When camp was made, Ba Ahmed took papers into the Sultan's tent and came out later, looking satisfied that his ruler had signed certain documents.

The masquerade was carried on for two days, while express riders galloped to Rabat, where they announced that young prince Abdel Aziz would inherit his father's crown. Since the prince was only twelve years old, Ba Ahmed, the Chamberlain, would be his regent.

***

The boys' schooling fell into a pattern; spring was spent in Matar, summer contained a short break during the hottest part of the season and then they recommenced in Tangier, where the boys could have recourse to the beach when the heat overwhelmed them. In the fall they traveled to Marrakesh to spend winter at the court. Tariq loved Marrakesh. His cousin Mehdi was there, and their relative, Ba Ahmed, the Royal Chamberlain, now Regent. He liked having close relatives around, even though they were too busy to pay him much attention. Marrakesh was huge compared to Tangier, although Tariq thought this impression might partly be due to its setting, since Marrakesh was set in a lush oasis, with palm trees and low red clay buildings, laid out on a spacious plain, while Tangier was hilly, situated on a cliff sloping to the sea. And of course, the weather in Marrakesh was dry and hot, scented with orange blossoms, not to be compared with the cold salty air of the north.

The palace was a sprawling, two story building, made of whitewashed, plastered mud bricks. It was tiled throughout, in the colorful mosaics made famous by the builders of the Alhambra, and had a sparkling green tiled roof. The young prince, Ali, pointed out to the other boys that this palace had inspired that Spanish version. The warm semi-tropical climate of the city allowed for fragrant gardens enclosed within the palace walls, where orange trees blossomed, and gilded cages filled with exotic birds hung suspended from their branches.

The day the boys arrived in Marrakesh they entered the palace through huge bronze gates that led into a large courtyard. Two steps in, Ted was knocked down by a bicycle. He looked up indignantly, saying, "Bastard! Look where you're going, why don't you!" Suddenly the twenty bicyclers, involved in some intricate slalom-type race, weaving through packed boxes and around abandoned carriages, all came to a halt and there was absolute quiet. Tariq, standing next to Ted, knelt down quickly in front of the young bicyclist, and kissed his hand. "*Sidna*, my lord, this is Ted Hastings, our English friend. He did not know who you were. May Allah pardon him."

Then the young Prince, who had hit Ted, got off his bike and started laughing. "Well, I'm not a bastard. I'm sure about that! But sorry to have knocked you down. *Allah isemmah*, may God forgive it." He held out his hand to pull Ted up, "I am

Prince Abdel Aziz, but my friends call me Aziz. So you are the English boy studying with Ali and Tariq. *Ahlen wa sahlen,* welcome. They tell me I cannot study with you because affairs of state are too pressing, but I want to learn English. You are all right, are you not?" He turned to Tariq and embraced him. "It is such a pleasure to see you again, my friend. We will have some good times here now. Come on, take a bicycle and join us. It is fun. We are seeing who can make it around all these boxes and things fastest, without falling off. *Qaid* Maclean, over there, is timing us to see who will be fastest, but I assure you, I will win!"

Tariq laughed, too, and pulled Ted towards a large packing crate that was full of shiny new bikes. Soon they were all tearing around the courtyard after a wobbly start, since even Ted had never been on a bicycle, hardly practical in the hilly cobblestone streets of Tangier. Ali had the most trouble, pedaling too slowly and continually losing his balance. Then he lost control of his machine, going down a few stairs and crashing into an alabaster fountain, reducing his bike to a twisted mess. He looked aghast at Abdel Aziz. "Sorry, brother. I didn't know how to stop."

Aziz kicked the broken vehicle aside, "Never mind. There are salesmen here every day from Europe and they have lots of these. The important thing is to have fun. Come on," he said as he pedaled away, leading the group into the palace corridors, whooping as he went.

***

Ian Perdicaris rode out to a village north east of Tangier. The village *sheikh* was expecting him and had prepared a banquet. As they sat there, watching heavily-made up boy dancers perform, Perdicaris said to the chief, "I can put your village under my protection and save these boys from having to go into the army."

"*Ya sidi*, it would be a blessing from Allah if we could be spared paying our taxes. They are too high for a poor village like ours."

"You can become my protégés and in return I will take ownership of this village and its land."

"*Insh'allah*," the *sheikh* replied.

***

The boys settled happily into the comfortable, orange blossom-scented quarters in the huge mass of buildings, which housed at least 3,000 people. Abdel Aziz never became proficient in English, but he was quick to learn tennis and soccer from Ted, and after the bicycle tires were all punctured and the bikes themselves broken, they had regular tennis matches every afternoon.

Tariq introduced the others to the *medina* of Marrakesh. Because of his royal status, Ali was not as free to wander here as he was in Tangier and Matar; but Tariq, Kassim and Ted quickly fell into a pattern of exploring the city during their free hours, much as they had hunted in Matar. They would saddle up their horses and wander the streets, praying in the centuries-old mosques, spending hours watching the wool dyers or leather workers. One day they came upon the slave market. Ted wanted to go in. Kassim and Tariq wrinkled their noses, "Come on, Ted, this is disgusting. Why would you want to see this? It's dirty and the slaves stink."

But Ted couldn't take his eyes away, "How can you justify offering these human beings for sale, as though they were animals?" He was watching a young black woman being brought out. She looked about Meriam's age. She appeared dazed as she was led into the light by the slave dealer, and then as she stood on the sale block, the dealer tore off her simple cotton shift, leaving her naked before the crowd of about twenty-five men.

The girl attempted to cover her breasts and pubic area, but the men surged around her, stroking her skin, forcing her mouth open to examine her teeth. One man grasped one of her firm young breasts and stroked its nipple, as a tear slid down her cheek. Ted started forward, but Tariq held his arm and spoke to him, "Ted, my brother, this is not your affair. I know you British do not approve of slavery, but now you are in Morocco. You think this is cruel but this young girl will go to a life of comfort in the harem of one of these men. She is healthy and beautiful. She will give pleasure to her master, and if she pleases him by bearing a child, she will be freed, to live as a free woman in his home."

"But how can they treat her like this in front of everyone?" Ted said

"She has no honor. She does not belong to any family. She is just a slave. What is the harm?" Kassim said. He looked quite interested in the girl, Tariq noticed.

Tariq added, "You see, Ted, men will pay many silver douros for a young woman in good health and without blemish. They look at her teeth to see if there is any rot that would cause bad breath and be offensive. They touch and stroke to see the healthy skin and nipples that would provide plentiful milk to a child. A young virgin like this could go for as much as 2,500 *douros* today."

At Ted's questioning look Tariq added, "Yes, they will be sure she is a virgin. No man would care to spend so much money and not be sure her issue was truly his. After all, her son could become his heir."

Ted shook his head, "I can't argue with your logic. But it doesn't seem right to me."

Tariq was silent for a while and then said, "Have we not read in one of your Thomas Hardy novels that in England there are maids in great houses who become pregnant by the master and are then cast out into the streets? And are there not other poor young girls who lead lives of great hardship and are abused by the wealthy without legal protection? Are we not more honest and fairer in our practices?"

Ted said, "Yes, in some ways, I should have to agree. There is less hypocrisy here. But on the other hand, this girl doesn't have a choice, does she? She was probably captured in Africa somewhere, against her will, and brought up to Morocco in a filthy caravan where she was badly treated. I'm sure no one ever asked her if she wanted to become a concubine."

"True, *ya* Ted," Kassim said, "but life as a concubine is better than the life she might have led as a wife in Africa, where I believe wives labor in the fields all day and are still forced to submit to their husbands. This girl will live in luxury, not expected to exert herself in work." Kassim strolled off.

"You'll never convince me that slavery is right," Ted said, "but I do see that nothing is quite as simple as it seems at first glance."

Tariq watched Kassim talking to the auctioneer. "Maybe he has decided to acquire a slave of his own. He is old enough, I suppose. But Allah protect the girl, *meskina (*poor thing*)*. I would not want to be owned by Kassim."

Ted turned his head away as Kassim casually felt the girl's buttocks, putting his hands in her most intimate places. "This is disgusting," he said to Tariq.

Evidently satisfied, Kassim turned to the slave dealer and began bargaining. While Ted and Tariq stood on the sidelines, Kassim concluded the deal and shook hands with the auctioneer. They threw a caftan over the girl, with a veil for her face, and Kassim joined them, leading her by the hand. She was shaking with fear. Ted blurted out, "She's very young, Kassim. Be gentle to her."

Kassim just leered and tugged on her arm, leading her down a street. Tariq knew he had some relatives in a house near there and supposed he would take her there. After that, Kassim spent less time with them outside of school hours, for which they were grateful, but they wondered occasionally how the young slave was faring.

***

The summer Lili was fourteen and Ted sixteen, she cajoled Ted into taking her to the *moussem*, a fair celebrating a local saint. "Who will know the difference, anyway?" she asked. "It's just the two of us. And I have so much fun when I don't have to be a proper lady."

They arrived on the huge dusty plain at mid-day. Lili and Ted pushed through the crowd of peasants from the Rif with their brown and white striped ankle-length *djellabahs* and crocheted skullcaps. The red-and-white woven shawls of the Rifi women shimmered in the summer heat, shade provided only by their wide-brimmed straw hats trimmed with crimson wool. Lili breathed in the pungent odors of fresh manure, sweat, and unwashed clothes, competing with sharper hints of the tangy henna and cloves the women used in their hair, smiling in her relief to be out of the house and into the action.

Weaving through the vendors and their mules laden with vegetables and fruit, Ted led the way towards the area of the fairgrounds where ragged white tents were set up to cater to the crowd. On a more remote side of the area, Lili could make out black Berber tents housing distinguished guests. She and Ted headed in that direction to set up their picnic. As they struggled through the crowd, a voice boomed out, "Ted, my brother, what brings you here?"

Out of one of the tents Tariq emerged. Lili shrank into her *djellabah*, freezing her face into a mask. Tariq approached them and clapped Ted on the back. Then he grasped him on the shoulders and they exchanged kisses on the cheeks, Moroccan-style.

"You and your friend must come and watch the festivities in our tent."

Of course, Lili thought. Tariq's family would be among the dignitaries presiding over this *moussem*, and it was just their luck to run into him. There was no way they could refuse Ted's closest friend without a serious insult.

Tariq turned to Lili, "Isn't this Larabi, who was with you at the coffee house a few years ago?" He extended his hand, and they greeted each other, Lili remembering to look him straight in the eye without flinching, like a boy.

She couldn't help noting that Tariq, in a sleeveless white silk *djellabah*, was tall and, she supposed, some would think he was handsome. Personally, she thought he was too conceited and sure of himself to be attractive. She calculated that he must be about eighteen, as she knew he was two years older than Ted.

It was Lili's first time in a tent, although she could see that Ted was comfortable under the huge black awning where at least fifteen people sat. They left their slippers at the edge of the tent. Her bare feet settled with appreciation into the rich red rugs that completely covered the dusty ground. Straw mats embroidered with wool stood against the walls of the tent to reinforce them. Lili had heard somewhere that the black was intended to repel heat, but here the warmth seemed captive, motionless, baking the black wool of the tent so it gave off a faint odor of scorched lanolin.

Tariq waved them towards some plump wool-stuffed cushions and they sat down together in the hot shade. She scrunched down, trying to hide herself in the shadows, bemoaning her stubbornness in insisting on this stupid disguise. Now she was even less free to roam around because of the fear of discovery and humiliation. Ted was lucky, she thought. He always dressed like a Moroccan, ever since he started studying with those boys, and of course his Arabic was perfect, maybe even better than hers. Looking at him, she thought, you really couldn't tell he wasn't a Rifi Berber, since so many of them also had red hair, freckles, and pale skin.

Stretching forward, Lili peeked out of the tent. She'd heard so much about the festivities surrounding the tomb of this local saint, which was the reason for today's fair. Would she get to see anything? Noticing this, Tariq said, "*Ya* Larabi, do you want to walk around and look while we wait for lunch? There are some Aissawa, holy men, dancing around the tomb. Shall we take a look?"

Lili accepted, forgetting the implications of her skimpy disguise in her desire to escape the tent and see what was going on. Then she realized it was going to be hard to fool Tariq up close. She cast a pleading glance at Ted, but he was talking to some other people. He was not going to be able to save her. So she rose to her feet and left the tent with Tariq.

They walked through the animal market, dodging the cattle being offered for sale, then passing the wares laid out on the ground for medicinal cures, where dried lizards and rats were displayed alongside various leaves and mysterious powders. Finally they emerged on the other side of the fair, closer to the tomb. In a wide clearing a group of men in white *djellabahs* were holding hands and repeating, "Allah, Allah," as they slowly moved together in the circle. The chanters were going into a hypnotic trance and Lili stepped closer to see. She was immersed in a crowd of scratchy djallabahs and stood on tiptoes, craning her neck. Noticing this, Tariq navigated Lili to the front, gently pushing her forward till she was only a few feet away from the dancers.

The men gradually let go of each other's hands and began to twirl in a state of religious ecstasy. Their short robes puffed out around them as they closed their eyes, raising their hands and chanting the ritual phrases of their brotherhood. Some spun as long as fifteen minutes before succumbing to faintness and moving to the edge of the circle to recover. Lili watched in horror as a snake wrapped around one of the men's necks struck several times at his skull, drawing blood, but the man seemed not to notice.

She wondered where they had come from; then, looking down she saw a half-open basket, reptiles writhing, no more than three feet from where they were standing. Without thinking, she clutched at Tariq's arm, pointing to the basket. "Tariq, look!"

Turning in the direction she had pointed, Tariq laughed. Stretching down, he picked up a small snake that had escaped from its container and brought it closer to Lili. She shrank back and despite herself felt tears rising in her eyes. She put her hands up, protectively. Tariq looked at her, and then his expression changed to one of annoyance. He carefully put the snake back and took her arm roughly, steering her out of the crowd. Lili barely had time to think where they were going; she was so relieved to remove herself from the snakes. Tariq was moving purposefully, almost dragging her along. She tried to shake herself free. This was more than just going to another part of the fair. Finally, he pulled her behind some of the vendor tents, in an area where people had left their mules. He stared at her angrily, and then he reached up and pulled off her turban. Her long black curls fell down all around her face.

"Lili! What is this?"

"Oh, Tariq, be quiet," Lili said, furious at being discovered and still shaken from the close encounter with the snake. "I just wanted to see the moussem. You men have all the fun and we girls never get to see anything. But you didn't have to go waving that snake right in my face. Here, give me back my turban." She grabbed it out of his hands.

He slapped her hard, on her cheek. "How could you be so stupid? Do you not know this is dangerous for girls? What if some one else, Allah forbid, had noticed you were a girl? These holy men could be dangerous, if they sensed such an insult."

Lili's eyes filled with tears at the unexpected slap. She pushed him back. "You had no right to do that. Just leave me alone. It's none of your business, anyway. It's boring to be a girl and not get to do anything."

Tariq stood there watching while she wrapped the cloth around her head again, stuffing her hair back up into it.

"You didn't recognize me before when we met at the café last summer!" Lili said.

He said, "Allah, so that was you. You were a pretty boy." Tariq shrugged. "You can find your own way back." He stalked off hardly waiting to see if Lili was behind him, and went back to the tent, where lunch was being served.

***

When Ted was sixteen, on his fourth visit to Marrakesh, Prince Abdel Aziz called him out of his classes one day. He was fiddling with a large gold object when Ted came in. "Look this way, my brother."

Ted looked up, startled, and Abdel Aziz pushed a button. "There, I have a picture of you. Is this not amazing?"

Ted examined the camera the young prince handed him. It was completed encased in gold and had precious stones for buttons. "Is this solid gold, *ya sidi?*"

Abdel Aziz took it back carelessly. "It is amusing. I have two. Would you like one?"

"*Sidna*, that is too kind." Ted berated himself for forgetting he should never praise anything directly. It always resulted in being offered it as a gift. What would he do with a stupid gold camera? Then he brightened, he could give it to Meriam.

"*Ya*, Ted, my brother, can you help me with a meeting? We are considering allowing a vice consul from your country to take residence here in Marrakesh, and some of his people are here now, conferring with Ba Ahmed. I would like to talk to one of those men, but I need an interpreter."

"Oh, jolly good! I mean," Ted quickly correctly himself as Abdel Aziz looked puzzled, "I would be honored, *sidna*." Ted had long dreamed of undertaking such a service, but he had not expected an opportunity to arise for at least several more years.

He donned a linen suit that he had brought with him from Tangier and presented himself in one of the minor reception rooms, arriving in advance. The room, which opened at one end to a quiet tiled courtyard with a fountain playing down onto pots of vivid geraniums, was light and airy, and furnished with elaborate red velvet-upholstered gilt furniture, in honor of the Western visitor.

On a gilt table a silver tray had been laid with a dozen small tea glasses heavily embossed in gold. Silver pots with large chunks of sugar and freshly cut mint lay nearby, along with a silver hammer to break the sugar into smaller pieces.

A servant sat cross-legged waiting to be of service. The walls had several portraits of the late *Moulay* Hassan, Abdel Aziz's father, and one of his grandfather as well. Ted supposed these were painted from description rather than life, as portraits were quite a recent and daring introduction in this conservative Muslim household, which did not generally believe in realistic representation of the human figure. There were also three grandfather clocks, all of which showed different times, and an elaborate porcelain table clock which chimed every fifteen minutes, ejecting a small boy and girl who pirouetted three times before being spun back into the clock.

Ted was bent over this clock examining it when Abdel Aziz entered. He was dressed regally in a long white silk and wool *djellabah* with a hood pulled over his red fez, and he carried silver worry beads in his hand. He smelled strongly of rose water, which Ted suspected he had just smoothed over his close-cropped hair.

"By Allah, Ted," he exclaimed, "you look just like a foreigner!"

"Well, Your Highness," Ted responded. "I thought if I were to play the role of your interpreter, perhaps it would look more official if I were recognizable as a British subject."

"By Allah, I had thought you would be dressed like us. But it is all right; you look official," said the prince. "I think I hear them coming now."

A youngish English man entered the room escorted by two royal guards elegantly attired in white *djellabahs* with black felt cloaks flung back over their shoulders and attached with gold cords. Woven gold belts encircled their waists from which hung curved daggers in gold-embroidered sheaths. The two guards came to attention near the door of the room and the visitor stepped forward, extending his hand.

"Your Highness, I'm Frank Coggins, from the London Times."

Abdel Aziz cocked his head toward Ted, who translated, causing Coggins to notice him.

"Oh, you're a surprise!"

Ted modestly and quickly introduced himself, not wishing to detract from the purpose of the meeting. Abdel Aziz let him give the basics about himself and then interrupted, urging his visitor to be seated, and clapping his hands for servants to bring hot water and make tea.

Although only fourteen years old, Abdel Aziz, Ted thought, was amazingly poised for this meeting. He put the reporter at his ease with some chit chat, explaining more about Ted's status. Coggins was fascinated by this novel idea of some Moroccan notables' children learning English, and asked Abdel Aziz why he hadn't joined in.

"Well," answered Abdel Aziz carefully in English, "I am study with they when they are in Marrakesh. But, *ya* Ted…help me," he finished in Arabic, unable to explain about security and why it would be difficult for him to move about as freely as the others.

As the servant in the corner discretely made them tea, pouring the frothy green liquid back and forth from the pot to the glasses to ensure that the sugar was well mixed and distributed, they moved to the reporter's real questions.

"Tell me, your Highness, why does Morocco refuse to have foreign diplomats in the interior, restricting everyone only to Tangier, Casablanca and other coastal cities?"

"You must understand, Mr. Coggins, that we are a tribal country. We are not in control of all the country all the time. Most of our people do not trust Christians and might do them injury, which we would not be able to prevent. By limiting them to areas where people are more cosmopolitan and where there are more Christians, we protect them," Ted translated.

"But surely," responded Coggins, "it would be to the benefit of Morocco to have Europeans understand you better, as does Ted here. Wouldn't it lead to fewer misunderstandings and bring Morocco closer to its European neighbors?"

Ted knew this reporter was heading into difficult diplomatic waters. Morocco did not really want to be closer to its European neighbors, since it perceived them mainly as wishing to exploit Morocco for its resources and possibly even to annex it. He knew France already had accomplished this in Algeria and Britain seemed well on its way to dominating Egypt.

Abdel Aziz responded simply. "As you know, we have several European advisors here in Marrakesh. *Qaid* Maclean, whom I believe you know as Harry Maclean, has been at court since before I was born and trains our army. We receive other diplomatic missions frequently. But to be frank, Mr. Coggins, these missions deal primarily with sad tales of foreign consuls defending their Jewish agents who are under their protection. We hear stories that they have thrown Moroccans into jail for non-payment of debts. Many of our poor people have lost all their property to these usurers. We are baffled as to why you foreigners side with the moneylenders on these issues, and make them into your protégés. People like Ted, here, do much more to help to create better understanding between our two countries, as does *Qaid* Maclean, Sir Walter Harris and the other foreigners living with us."

Coggins at that moment motioned to one of the guards, who brought forward a large package. Bowing slightly, Coggins presented this to Abdel Aziz: "Your highness, I have heard of your interest in our modern transportation. I hope you will do me the honor to accept this small token from England."

Aziz motioned to a servant to unwrap it. Kneeling on the ground, the servant removed the elaborate wrappings and uncovered, one by one, tiny but perfect replicas of a British train, complete with technically accurate engine, caboose, passenger cars, freight cars, open flat cars on which lay tiny bags of wheat. The Prince got down on his knees when the tracks were unwrapped, along with several bridges, tunnels, model trees and a city landscape. Soon, both boys were on the ground, assembling the train and accompanying small generator.

"*Choukran, Si* Coggins," said Abdel Aziz. "I hope some day we may have such a train system in my country."

While they were setting up the train, Coggins attempted to ask Abdel Aziz some other questions, mainly about the types of weapons carried by the royal army, but Ted, speaking for the prince, was easily able to deflect him.

"Those are really questions for *Qaid* Maclean. I'm sure you can meet with him later," Ted said, knowing very well that Harry Maclean would be quite unlikely to share any military information with this reporter.

Ted ventured a remark or two of his own to the reporter. "You know, foreigners aren't allowed to move around the country freely. If a British Consul were stationed here, it wouldn't be the same pleasant life he has in Tangier. Why would Britain actually want to station someone here full time?"

Coggins appeared amused by the innocence of the question. "Well, young man, many foreigners would like to get closer to the Sultan and his regent, Ba Ahmed. Your stepfather, himself, is interested in trade, is he not? If Ministers or Consuls were stationed here in Marrakesh they might get advantageous trade concessions directly from the Sultan, instead of having to deal always with the tribesmen. Of course, you know that France, England, and Germany are gradually colonizing most of Africa and Asia in order to secure their trade routes, and find new homes, in some cases, for their citizens, as France has already done in Algeria. Morocco is another piece of the world that hasn't yet found a special protector, and its strategic position is important for many reasons."

Abdel Aziz, who had managed to follow much of this exchange in English, interrupted, "We control the caravan trade routes up from Africa, as well as the entrance to the Mediterranean. And we can't forget that the French in Algeria are anxious to protect their rights there."

***

Lili met Arthur Crampton at her sixteenth birthday party while she was still in California. Some good friends of Matt held the party for this special birthday at their house in San Francisco. Their tall three-story house had a spacious entrance hall and ballroom, and they hired an orchestra so the youngsters could dance. Lili wore her first ball gown, of white satin.

Arthur was nineteen, tall and slender. He had thick blond hair and laughing blue eyes. When he smiled he had two irresistible dimples. He introduced himself at the beginning of the evening.

"Miss Lili, I'm going to try to monopolize you this evening."

"Oh, and why is that?" she said.

"I'm studying Middle Eastern affairs at Stanford and learning Arabic, and I intend to go to Tangier next year when I graduate. I'd like to work at the American Legation there. I was hoping you could tell me more about Morocco."

"It would be wonderful to have some new people there," she

replied. "We seem to get so in-bred. Of course, I love Morocco, since it's my home, but what has made you interested?"

"I'm absolutely fascinated by the tales of Sir Richard Burton and the other English adventurers who've traveled in the region. Articles by Sir Walter Harris and Budgett Meakin, Jr. have piqued my curiosity. Then, of course, I also have my career to make, and it seems to me that North Africa is a challenging part of the world with good opportunities for trade."

Although Lili and Arthur began by dancing, they soon found they were more interested in their discussion and ended up sitting together at a small table. Lili liked the way Arthur watched her as she talked, paying total attention.

"What does Tangier look like? Are there lots of tribesmen living in the city? Does everyone have to speak Arabic all the time? Are there lodgings for rent there? Do they have the same kind of food we do and is it easily available? Have you ever met the Sultan? Is it safe to live there?" The questions burst from him rapid fire.

As Lily laughed and tried to answer one at a time, she could see that new questions were already forming in his mind. When he found she had met both Walter Harris and Budgett Meakin, two of the Burton-like explorers living in Tangier, his questions multiplied.

"So what's Sir Walter like in real life?"

"We've been several times to his home for dinner and he's a fairly good friend of my father's. He's a bit larger than life, you know! He likes to dress in Arab clothing and really does speak Moroccan *derija*—oh, that's our word for dialect—quite well. His house is lovely and he has peacocks wandering around in the garden."

"And Budgett Meakin?"

"Mr. Meakin is a bit like you; he's definitely a romantic who wants to be another Lane; you know, that man who wrote about life in Egypt. He even has an Arabic name—I think they call him Tahar bel Mekki. He's done a lot of wandering around Morocco and I heard he was working on a book. My step brother, Ted, admires him tremendously. You would like Ted."

***

Ted and Tariq were walking in the *medina* of Marrakesh, looking for a book binder who had been recommended to them. Ted had a small volume of verses he wanted bound to give to Meriam. As they rounded a corner near the address they had been given, they saw a large group of men, talking and looking at something. Intrigued, Tariq went up to see what had captured their attention.

A man handed him two photographs. Tariq saw a pretty young woman, dressed in a French robe trimmed with ostrich feathers, one leg coquettishly peeking from its open skirt. He took a few more of the pictures; they were all of women wearing modish French designs. "My friends, who owns these pictures?" he asked the crowd.

A man stepped forward, "I do, *ya sidi.*"

"How much will you take for all of them?"

The man hesitated, then calculating quickly said, "Five hundred *douros.*"

"That is a lot." Tariq thought a moment. "All right, I will pay it. Here is my promise," he handed him a ring. "A servant will bring you the money this evening and you shall give him back the ring. Now let me have all the pictures of the women."

As they walked off, Ted teased him, "I didn't know you were so interested in pictures of women."

"These are from Abdel Aziz's harem. I know he was taking pictures with that new apparatus he has, but his women should not be seen by strangers on the street. Let us hope those men did not know who the women were."

***

Arthur began coming frequently to the convent on visiting day, and as the weather grew milder he was allowed to take Lili for carriage rides and walks on Mount Tamalpais with his sister Mary as chaperone. They never seemed to run out of topics of mutual interest, moving on from Morocco to discuss books they had both enjoyed, plays they had seen. Arthur was an attentive escort and his admiration for Lili was obvious.

When June arrived, Arthur came to say good-bye.

They sat together in the school's parlor, a nun sitting discretely nearby. As they sipped their tea, Lili chatted on to Arthur, telling him of her plans, describing her stateroom on the ship, and sharing news of Ted who was preparing to enter Oxford in the fall.

"With Ted leaving, I'm wondering how I'll spend my time. I'd like to do something to help the poor, but it's hard to know where to start."

Arthur leaned forward, "Lili, you know, I'm planning to come to Morocco next spring."

"Oh yes, I am so looking forward to that, Arthur."

"Lili, you've grown to be such a friend to me these past few months. I am going to miss you."

"I'll miss you, too, Arthur. You're one of the only people in California I feel I can really talk to."

"Lili, maybe it's too early, but, could I ask if you think

your feelings for me could become more than just those of a friend?"

Lili replied, "Why Arthur, you are my greatest friend. I don't know, I never really thought...."

"Lili, I admire you sincerely, and I hope you may come to feel more for me than friendship, as I do for you," Arthur was looking deeply into her eyes and she found herself feeling very flustered. "I hope you will think of me as a suitor. You don't have to say anything now, but I hope we can write to each other after you leave. Might I hope that by the time I get to Tangier next March, you will have an answer for me?"

Lili wrote Meriam that night, vowing her to secrecy until she arrived.

CHAPTER FOUR
1897

L ili inhaled the salt air as she squinted to catch her first glimpse of the Tangier waterfront. With each breath, the memories of her seven years in California grew more distant. Not that she wanted to forget it all. If nothing else, her education had convinced her that despite her Moroccan blood, she had become and would remain an American by education and preference, even though she was determined to live in her beloved Tangier.

Had it not been for Amelia, she might have continued happily scampering with the kitchen maids and being spoiled by Matt when he remembered that she was there. The life Lili had seen the Moroccan women lead, confined to their own quarters, constantly bearing children, lacking all but the most rudimentary education, had contrasted sharply with what she had been exposed to in Amelia's drawing room and then in school in California. There she had learned to question what she heard, and think about the morality of the extreme poverty she saw around her. Only as a Western woman could she address these issues.

As Lili scanned the shoreline she felt a familiar thrill at seeing the cliff rising before her, the gleaming green tiles of the mosques behind the stone walls of Tangier. To her left, the scrub forests reaching down to the sea reminded her of pig-sticking expeditions Matt had let her go on once or twice, before Amelia decreed it too dangerous. Even the fish mongers hawking their wares along the wharf made tears sting her eyes as she searched the crowds for her family.

Home again, yes, but different this time. There would be no more escapades masquerading as a Moroccan boy and poking her nose where young ladies shouldn't go. No, now she was committed to her corsets and high button shoes, tea parties and polite conversations. Her toes, encased in proper leather boots, scrunched uncomfortably, and made her remember her earlier barefoot days, sitting in Aisha's lap in the kitchen, hearing bawdy tales of the scullery maid's adventures with her boy friend. Were those days really over for good? She was sure Arthur Crampton would be shocked to know she actually enjoyed such things. She knew he thought of her as the perfect future diplomat's wife; in fact, she suspected that might be a large part of why this scholarly man liked her so much. Of course, she admitted, part of his allure was his interest in the Arab world and desire to come and live in Morocco.

She spotted Matt and Amelia. But where was Ted? Then she saw a patch of spiky red hair and waved at Ted's gawky arms gesticulating in the air. And there was Tariq next to him Ugh! That awful man. Why were he and Ted such good friends? She knew Ted almost worshiped this Berber prince, older than he and so capable. Tariq never seemed to do anything wrong. She took in his tall, rangy frame and gleaming black eyes, and hoped she wouldn't have to see much of him.

***

The family assembled in their terrace for drinks before dinner. Shaded by its Norfolk pine tree, the courtyard was one of Lili's favorite spots. Comfortable white cane furniture furnished the patio, and there were several couches with homey cretonne slipcovers, and enough wide-seated chairs with matching cushions to provide seating for the family. Tea or drinks time was a family ritual out here in the warm weather, when every breeze was welcome.

Matt puffed contentedly on a thick cigar while Ted served out tea to Amelia and Lili and small shots of whiskey for himself and Matt. Lili, settling into her customary chair, gazed fondly at her parents noting that the years were treating them kindly. Matt was still the rough and ready ex-soldier he had always been, maybe a bit more grizzled around his temples with deeper lines carved around his lips and nose. Amelia, she thought, had given in to her tendency to plumpness, indulging at too many of the parties and dinners she loved so much. But she still had a lovely gentle face, framed by her now graying brown hair that she wore in a becoming upsweep, graceful tendrils inevitably escaping the knot atop her head.

Amelia smiled at her family, "It's so wonderful to have you back for good, Lili! It's time for you to take your place in Tangier life."

Lili said, "I loved California and am so grateful to both of you for sending me to school there. But this is my home and I love it here. And I have the most exciting news! I have a suitor." She told them about Arthur's proposal.

"He sounds like a fine fellow," Matt remarked. "Of course, we want to meet him, but I can't imagine what we wouldn't like, if you think he's the one for you.

***

Lili and Meriam went into the newly developing European town to visit one of Tangier's recently established tea parlors. Although the walled city, usually referred to as the *medina*, had numerous shops, banks and cafes, they did not encourage female clients, nor were they attractive to the girls, being either stuffy, old-fashioned establishments, or only for traditional Arab and Jewish male clientele. But the new town, developing outside the walls on what they called 'the Mountain', had modern-style villas, millinery shops and pretty pastry shops where European ladies enjoyed visiting with each other and indulging in sweets. A Spanish waiter, crisp linen towel wrapped around his waist, served them their tea. As soon as they were seated, Meriam leaned forward, "*Cherie*, Ted has asked me to marry him! But do not tell anyone yet. I think Ted will tell your father tonight. I am so excited!"

"How wonderful." Lili leaned forward and hugged her friend. She hesitated, then asked, "Meriam, how did you know you were in love with Ted? Was it a special feeling? Can you describe it?"

"*Cherie*, how can I explain? I feel like Ted is a part of me. When he breathes, I breathe. We understand each other so well; why, we even finish each other's phrases! We find pleasure in the same things, have the same *amis*. I can not imagine marrying any other man."

"But have you ever considered any one else?" Lili doubted that her proper friend even knew any other men, aside from those at her school.

"*Non, mais pourquoi?* I am so happy with Ted. I feel wonderful when he is there. Why do you ask? Do you think we are not compatible?"

"Not in the slightest! It's just that…well, it's not quite so clear in my case. I respect and admire Arthur. It's just that…well, passion! You know, the way Jane Eyre feels for Mr. Rochester. I'm not sure I feel that way about Arthur. It's all so confusing to me!"

Meriam looked curiously at Lili and then took a bite of

her cake. "You mean like the way Harriet feels for Lazlo in *Middlemarch. L'amour*? But perhaps that is just for novels? Or those feelings come later? I do not know, either, and I can not ask Maman. I do not think she would approve."

Lili resolved to put it out of her mind.

***

The night of Ted and Meriam's engagement party there was a full moon, and a balmy Mediterranean breeze. The American Legation had a wide upstairs terrace leading to the salon and dining room, and a smaller one on the ground floor, where Matt had his office. For the party both its terraces were lit with brass lanterns hanging from trees and hooks and standing on the tiled patio floors. Masses of potted orange trees in bloom flooded the area with fragrance, and Amelia put vases of fuchsias, gardenias and roses on the small tables where guests could visit during the party.

Aisha, Lili's old nursemaid, had given her a shimmering piece of turquoise satin and sparkling silver gauze to go over it as a welcome home gift. The more Aisha talked about wearing Moroccan dress, the more enthusiastic Lili had become, and when the guests started arriving she was amused to see she wasn't the only woman to select such a beautiful and comfortable outfit for the evening. A good sprinkling of men was wearing white silk *djellabahs*, red fezzes, and elaborate turbans, spicing up the muted elegance of the others in their long black tails and white ties.

After two hours of non-stop waltzing, Lili pleaded with her partner, the French second secretary, to sit and cool off. He found them a place to sit on the ground-floor terrace and left her to get some champagne.

She moved to the fountain splashing nearby and perched

on its tiled edge, dipping her hands in the cool water to refresh her flushed cheeks. Then she wandered into the arcade that surrounded the court, hoping to find a cooler area. Hearing a slight noise, she turned slowly thinking her dancing companion had returned. Before she could utter a word, a man in a white silk *djellabah*, his face indistinct in the shadows, folded her in an embrace. She felt herself melting into him as his lips covered her mouth. Her body flooded with new and strange feelings. Every inch of her responded to this stranger.

Seconds later Lili came to her senses. She went rigid and pushed with all her might, forcing a distance between the man and herself. Drawing herself up, she slapped the intruder hard across the face.

"How dare you!" she said.

Then she saw the face of this unexpected suitor and recoiled as she realized it was Tariq. He looked at her and was equally taken aback.

"My sister Lili! I beg your pardon! In this dark, I thought you were someone else. *Allah isemmah*, God pardon me." He took her hand, drawing her to the fountain.

She snatched it away. "How could you?"

"Here, sit. I do not know how I made such a mistake. By Allah, I did not know it was you." He was staring at her. "You are grown up!"

Lili was shaken, her pulse racing. Her knees were wobbly, and despite herself, she welcomed Tariq's steadying arm. As soon as possible, though, she released it.

"Just go away, Tariq and we'll forget this happened."

Lili's companion returned, carrying two glasses of champagne. Lili rose quickly and introduced Tariq. Then Tariq bowed formally. "Please excuse me. Welcome home, little one, *ahlen wa sahlen*." He turned and melted back into the darkness.

***

Rumor had it that Ian Perdicaris wanted Matt's job. Articles started to appear in the Tangier Times accusing Matt of misusing the protégé system for his personal gain.

"Look at this," Matt said, rattling the paper and fumbling for a cigar, eggs congealing in a cold puddle on his plate. "Now that blasted fellow says my protégés are bleeding the country dry! Sucking the blood of the poor, he says."

"Now, Matt. Don't let him ruffle you," Amelia said. "You just need to write a few articles of your own and let everyone hear your side of the argument."

Matt snapped the page of his paper. "I'm gonna just call him out, that no-good adulterous rascal. Most of what I'm doing is just acts of charity, for Pete's sake. That scoundrel! Shoot, I can't say that in an article. It'd look like I was just blowing my own horn. You know, the British Minister has just as many protégés, or maybe more, than I."

"How many protégés do you think you have, my dear?" Amelia said.

"Who counts?" he said. "There's no legal limit. How'd we get any exporting done around here if we couldn't protect these traders from the taxes?"

"How do the Moroccans feel about this?" Amelia said, ringing the bell and indicating to Hamoud that he should take away Matt's eggs and bring some more coffee.

"They hate it, of course. Sent one of their *wazirs* (ministers) up here a while ago," Matt laughed. "Oh, I don't deny there may be some petty mischief going on here and there. But whenever I hear of any of my men trying to pull off some funny stuff, believe me, I put it down pretty fast."

"Mischief, dear? What can they do? I assume you're referring to the protégés?"

"Well, some of them aren't the most wholesome characters

in the world." Matt said. "You know, some of these landlords, and I hate to admit it, but some of the Jews, too. They take advantage. They lend money at pretty high rates, and I know they employ some unscrupulous methods to make the debtors pay up."

Amelia shuddered. "Haven't I heard some pitiful stories of whole families being thrown into prison to waste away and die because they couldn't pay back some of those loans?"

Matt shifted slightly in his seat, looking uncomfortable, "Well, dammit all, Amelia, oh excuse me, my dear. I can't be responsible for all their internal dealings. Fact is, people need money here and they fall behind. It happens everywhere, you know. Nothing particularly unusual about Morocco in that respect. Don't you have debtors' prison in England as well?"

She nodded.

Matt said, "When they come to me and try to get the American government to enforce their claims, I always refuse. Just because they're protégés don't mean I'm going to support them in that kind of monkey business. And that's what makes me so riled up. That's what Ian's accusing me of. Well, excuse me, my dear. I'm going down to talk to Budgett about this. I'll need to write some kind of a rebuttal."

***

Meriam and Lili were spending the day at her house. Settling down in the well-appointed parlor, Meriam pulled a newspaper out of her bag and handed it to Lili. "Did you see this article about Captain Dreyfus?" she asked, pointing to a headline on the first page.

The Dreyfus affair had rocked France and caused several falls of government since it began in 1894. Alfred Dreyfus, a Jewish artillery captain in the French army, was accused of spying for Germany. The proof offered was a scrap of paper with military secrets, found by a cleaning woman. In fact, the writing bore no resemblance to Dreyfus' handwriting and he vigorously denied the charge. Nevertheless, he was found to be guilty, stripped of his rank, drummed out of the army, and sentenced to prison on Devil's Island, off the coast of South America. His family, convinced of his innocence, lobbied for a new trial, and published pamphlets showing that his handwriting and that of the paper had no similarity.

Factions developed, the army massed together insisting on his guilt in an anti-Semitic stand, while the press argued that Dreyfus had been wrongly judged and that his punishment was excessively cruel. Several years later, a new Head of Intelligence, Picquard, discovered that another officer, Esterhazy, had in fact written the document, but had been protected by high ranking generals, who had gone so far as to forge other documents to strengthen the case against Dreyfus. Although Esterhazy was eventually turned out of the Army, the Court refused to review the judgment against Dreyfus, apprehensive about revealing the role the Minister of War and other leading generals had played in falsifying and submitting documents to the Court.

Emile Zola, the famous writer, wrote an open letter to the President of the Republic, *J'Accuse*, laying out all the dishonesty and fraudulence that surrounded the case and claiming that Dreyfus' treatment was blatant anti-Semitism. For this he, too, was sentenced to jail, as the army closed ranks to protect itself. Several French governments fell as France argued this case in the streets.

"No," Lili said. "I haven't looked at the paper for a few days. But Arthur was very interested in this and we discussed it a few times in San Francisco. Devil's Island sounds truly horrible. Imagine those poor souls locked up to die there!" She shuddered slightly.

"Well, according to this article," Meriam went on, "it now appears that someone has come forward in France, a Lt. Col. Picquart, Chief of Military Intelligence, saying that it was not Captain Dreyfus who wrote that memorandum at all."

"Explain to me again," Lili interrupted. "What was the significance of the memorandum?"

"I believe it was a list of military secrets, *très importants*, that were somehow given to *les Allemands*. They were confidential, *bien sûr*, but Captain Dreyfus definitely did not write them. Anyway, now this Picquart, who is investigating, says another officer, a Major Esterhazy, wrote them. So he too has been court-martialed. Isn't that *incroyable!*"

"Heavens," Lili exclaimed. "You mean poor Captain Dreyfus is really innocent? How horrible!"

"According to this article, until they have this trial with Major Esterhazy, Captain Dreyfus will stay in Devil's Island. French Jews are very upset about this and call for la justice. *C'est ça*, Lili, that bothers me. You know, he was one of a handful of Jews that had recently been allowed into the French army, and the minute this happened, *les français* start calling for death to the Jews and all these other shockingly hateful statements. *Probablement*, Captain Dreyfus did not even do it. It is terrible to see such hatred against us. And he is a very civilized, educated Jew."

Lili was skimming the article. "It says here that Picquart has been dismissed! I wonder why?"

"My father says these officers are a tight clique, and insist on the honor of all having the same story. Papa says it's like a big *famille* and they must not tell their secrets outside the group," Meriam said.

"Isn't that ridiculous," Lili declared, her own problems forgotten for the moment. "To think that poor man is languishing away in Devil's Island just because the army doesn't want people to know it made a mistake. It's outrageous."

Meriam looked depressed. "At the Alliance they are saying because he is a Jew no one really cares. Papa says *c'est une surprise* that he got as far as he did in the army. Now there are people in the streets crying 'Death to the Jews.' The army is almost completely Christian, so probably they welcomed the chance to get rid of him."

"The fact that Lt. Col. Picquart lost his job certainly makes it look that way," Lili admitted. "It will be interesting to see the result of the court-martial."

Lili was surprised that Meriam had brought up the subject. Her friend's family seemed so modern, so Western. Meriam and her brother, Gabriel, had been educated at the Alliance Israelite in Tangier, just as their father had attended a similar school in his native Tetouan. The Alliance, run by French Jews, had a mission in the Middle East and North Africa to educate and raise the standards of Sephardic Jews. It had instilled in Meriam an admiration of French culture and an enlightened secular view of religion, balanced with a respect for her Jewish values and traditions. Not that they denied their religion; no one did that in Tangier. Religion was part of one's identity and accepted as such. Most of the people, maybe all, who worked for the American Legation were Jews because they were the only minority in Morocco and, as such, were allowed, even encouraged by the Sultan, to trade on his behalf with the foreigners. But being Jewish didn't mean all that much, at least not among the Westernized ones Lili knew, like Meriam. No one gave it much thought. Of course, they had their differences; she knew they didn't eat pork, like the Muslims, and had special holidays.

Now, watching her elegant friend, though, Lili wondered

if there were some deeper feelings of resentment or fear that she had never sensed. Meriam had always seemed oblivious to ethnic differences. Lili, too, for that manner. She supposed she was Christian of some kind, not Catholic, though, despite the nuns. And not Muslim, although Matt had instilled a deep respect for that faith in her. But more than anything, Lili was a Tangerino, not very different from Meriam or Ted.

***

Lili and Meriam went up to 'the Mountain' to shop for Christmas presents. They wandered into one of the new fabric shops to examine the vivid wool challis prints, sturdy tweeds, and more luxurious silks and velvets.

Lili picked a violet taffeta for an evening dress. She thought it looked spectacular with her olive coloring and black hair. For everyday, she selected brown tweed that she would have made into a suit with a velvet collar, perfect for at-home visits and shopping. It was fun, she thought, to dress like a lady, after so many years of white pinafores and long stockings at the convent. Still, she occasionally longed for the adventure and freedom of her old *djellabah* and turban.

While Meriam lingered over her choices, Lili noticed a young man entering the shop. He eyed the clerks running back and forth bringing out bolts for Meriam to inspect, and made several attempts to get the owner's attention. After ten minutes he lit a pipe, which brought an instant response from the shopkeeper. Excusing himself from the girls, the owner hurried over to serve the restless newcomer, undoubtedly wishing to ask him to refrain from smoking in the cloth-filled shop. Lili couldn't help overhearing the exchange between the two.

"Let me see what you have in dark flannels," the man said.

"Excuse me, senor, but I must remind you that there is a bill outstanding," the tailor murmured.

"Just send those bills to the *Sherif*," she heard the young man exclaim rather loudly. "There's no problem with money. I don't carry sums like that around with me, you know."

"I'm so sorry, but I really must insist," the tailor began to apologize, nevertheless not bringing out any further material to show him. Lili could sense his tension; a *Sherif* was considered almost above the law. One of his relatives usually could have whatever he or she wanted, and in fact often was given gifts by people hoping for a blessing of some kind. They talked a few more moments, but it was obvious to Lili that without a settlement of the bill, the shopkeeper was not going to sell this client anything. Finally, the young man made a gesture of disgust.

"You Jews are all the same. All you care about is money. You'll be the ruin of Morocco." He removed the pipe from his mouth and knocked it out carelessly against the counter, scattering sparks, several of which landed on the bolts the girls had been examining. The shopkeeper rushed to brush them off the fragile taffeta and velvet, managing to rescue the fabric with no serious damage done. The young man left the shop, slamming the door behind him.

"I'm so sorry," the shopkeeper said, uneasily patting the other bolts of cloth, lifting them from the counter and inspecting them carefully to ensure that no stray strands of tobacco had marred them.

Lili said, "Is he one of your regular customers?"

The man nodded. "He's bought material from me several times. He goes to school in England, at Oxford, I believe. So he needs suits, don't you know?"

Meriam's ears perked up, "Really? My fiancé is also at Oxford. They must know each other."

The shopkeeper looked uncomfortable. "I don't know. This gentleman is an adopted son of the *Sherif* of Matar."

"Oh!" Both girls spoke simultaneously.

Lili said, "That must be the Kassim Ted studied with. I think I heard him mention that he had gone to study in England a few years ago, although I don't remember that he was at Oxford."

Before Meriam could answer, the shopkeeper confirmed, "Yes, that's his name, Kassim."

"Hmm, rather rude," Meriam murmured, obviously not wishing to pursue the subject. That was often her way, Lili thought. Just ignore the unpleasant and maybe it would go away. "Let us go now."

***

Matt had been looking forward to this first boar hunt of the season. He was one of the first to arrive at the village, where the village headman, Abdullah, was waiting for him, with twenty of his best men.

"Abdullah," said Matt, dismounting and giving his reins to Hamoud. "How've you been? How's your health and that of your family?"

Abdullah took Matt's hand and tried to kiss it. Matt snatched it back.

"My family is in good health, *ya sidi*, thanks to your help, may Allah bless you. And here is young Mohammed." A boy, about twelve years old, smiled broadly at Matt.

"The last time I saw you I wasn't so sure you were going to make it." Matt boomed, giving the boy a pat on the head and searching in his pocket for a few douros. Mohammed had had a bad infection in his leg which Abdullah had consulted Matt about. Matt had seen to it that the boy received medical treatment. "Now you need to go out there and impress all those young girls! Glad to see you're better, my boy!"

The boy seized Matt's hand and kissed it. Matt pulled it back, embarrassed. He beckoned to Hamoud. "Amelia's got a few of the ladies busy in her sewing club and they've sent you these things." Hamoud brought forth several mules laden with knitted goods and used clothes. "Now you just be sure, Abdullah, to let us know if you're in need of anything." Matt said. "Your men are wonderful beaters and I want to take care of them."

"*Naam, ya sidi.* Any service, at all," Abdullah said. "Please, *Si* Matt, come this way." He led him to a tent where kettles steamed on brass braziers and a table was laden with couscous, raisins, almonds and buttermilk.

As Matt left the tent, he spied Ian Perdicaris talking to Georges St. René Taillandier, the French Minister. "Well, of all the nerve!" Matt said, striding over to him.

Budgett Meakin, who had been breakfasting with Matt caught his arm, "Matt, be careful. You don't want a public incident."

"Oh, don't I? That fellow needs a lesson," Matt fumed, pulling himself free.

As he neared the men, Matt heard Ian saying, "…the whole village is under his protection."

"And what of it?" Matt interrupted, arms akimbo. "Do these people look corrupt? Do you think they're trying to extort money from the less fortunate?" He gestured at the villagers, dressed mostly in rags, waiting passively to beat the bushes for the foreigners.

"That's beside the point," Perdicaris said. "There's no legal basis for making these villagers into American protégés. It's an abuse of the system."

Lighting up a cigar, Matt laughed. "What an abuse! One person in the foreign community decides to help these poor beggars with a bit of medical care from time to time and some warm clothing, in return for which they will run for hours chasing filthy wild boars for us. And as payment I can shelter them from unreasonable taxes demanded by the Sultan. Why, do you know last year he demanded that this village, with no resources whatsoever except the pittance they get from selling their wool at the market, pay him over one thousand *douros* and send twenty boys to military service? That's all the boys they've got." He puffed away for a few minutes, trying to get his cigar going, "and how would we have had our hunting with all those boys off fighting for the Sultan?" he said.

Hamoud brought Matt's horse around. Matt mounted and looked down at Perdicaris. "Since you don't approve of these arrangements, you probably aren't hankering to hunt with us." Matt stuck his jaw out aggressively and stared down at the stocky bearded man.

Perdicaris drew himself up. The French Minister, Taillandier, backed off, smiling uncomfortably. Perdicaris looked up at Matt, "Oh, I wasn't planning to hunt. Not really my kind of thing, you know. I just needed a word with Taillandier and thought I would find him here. Now I will bid you good day, sir."

Matt struck his boot with his riding whip. "Damned impudence of the man," he said, turning his horse and riding off to join the others.

***

Everyone was talking about the Daudifrets' Christmas party at their home located at the top of the Kasbah next to the Royal Palace. André Daudifret was a struggling second secretary at the French Legation, but his American wife, Judith was an heiress. They had bought an old mansion and spent thousands of her dollars renovating it. Lili and Meriam, along with most of Tangier, were thrilled when they received invitations.

The night of the party they made their way slowly up the crooked streets of the *medina*, climbing higher and higher in their sedan chairs toward the Portuguese fort. As the bearers navigated the steep stairs leading upwards from the Sokko Chico, Lili put her head out the window to watch the wreath made from thousands of bobbing lights hanging from the sedan chairs. It seemed that all of Tangier was making its way towards the Daudifret residence.

The old palace was just as much of a masterpiece as Lili had hoped. Approaching the ballroom, they descended through a series of reception areas, each room connected by one or two steps down to the next. Graceful Arabesque arches framed the rooms sparkling with waist-high Moorish mosaic tiles in red, white and green. Yellow and red Berber rugs glowed on the polished, almost translucent, white tiled floors, setting off furniture inlaid in mother-of-pearl and precious woods. The rooms shone with warm candlelight and gave off the scent of roses and incense. Spacious window seats, piled high with soft yellow and green cushions and heaped with embroidered pillows, tempted Lili and Meriam to stop along the way, but the music pulled them towards the ballroom.

The ballroom opened directly onto a terrace surrounded by a low white balustrade framing the Strait of Gibraltar directly below them. The orchestra was already playing, and Lili and Meriam established themselves at one of the small tables scattered around the periphery of the dance floor. Lili turned to say something to Meriam and discovered Kassim al-

Matar taking a seat at their table. He bowed mockingly. "Miss Lili, I believe."

Lili began to panic, as she breathed in the alcohol fumes enveloping Kassim. She couldn't believe the Daudifrets had invited such a brutish man to the party. How could she get rid of this boor? She willed herself to calm down. "How do you do? I think we saw you a few weeks ago at the tailor's."

Kassim leaned close to Lili. The whiskey fumes almost made her gag.

"Really? I don't recall. How could I have overlooked two such ravishing young ladies? What a pleasure to meet Ted Hastings' step sister. And you must be his fiancée?" He nodded to Meriam.

Meriam colored. "*Oui*, I believe Ted has mentioned you. *Enchantée*. Are you also at Oxford?"

"Yes, I've been reading law there."

"*Curieux*," Meriam said. "Ted did not mention that you were there. He never said that there were any other Moroccans there."

"Other Moroccans?" Kassim questioned, eyebrows raised. "I believe I'm the only one, in fact."

"Oh yes, of course," Meriam said. "Ted is not really a Moroccan, that is true. He is British. *Bien entendu*, we all think of ourselves as Moroccans, but perhaps I should say Tangerinos." She turned away, casting a glance at Lili.

Kassim was sitting too close to Lili and he was staring straight down her new taffeta dress. She caught Judith's eye and sent her a silent appeal. Their hostess came over and sat, turning her back on Kassim.

"My dears, I'm so glad you could come. I have the most delicious news!"

The girls looked at her in question.

"It seems we have a famous, or maybe I should say infamous, unexpected visitor tonight! Someone told me this bandit who's been causing so much trouble in Tetouan has crashed our party."

"I haven't heard anything about him," Lili said. She was so relieved that Judith had changed the conversation that she would have welcomed anything. "Who is he?"

"His name is al-Raisuni and he evidently has a kind of Robin Hood reputation," Judith informed them. "They say he's the son of a *Sherif* in Tetouan, from a very good family, who has set himself up as a defender of the poor and the weak. He's attracted a group of followers and they've taken to the foothills of the Rif Mountains where they dispense rough justice to those exploiting the poor in the area."

Kassim interrupted, "I know the family. It's very respectable. Direct descendants of the Prophet, of course. Just like my family, the Mataris. *Moulay* Ahmed ben Mohammed al-Raisuni is just a bit older than I am. My father thinks he's a disgrace."

Judith interrupted. "Oh, are you actually related to the Mataris?"

Kassim flushed. "They've raised me as one of the family."

"This Al-Raisuni sounds romantique," Meriam said.

"This country could certainly use a bit of charity," Lili said. "I've been away for years, but every time I come back I'm struck by the plight of the poor here. No one cares what happens to them, and their own leaders seem to be bent on exploiting them mercilessly."

Kassim said, "It's the Jews we have to thank for all this. They loan money to these poor peasants, knowing they can't afford to pay them back, and then they throw them into prison for life when they default. They're sucking the country dry."

Meriam turned bright red.

Lili took Meriam's hand, "Not all Jewish families do this. I think we can all admit some of our countrymen are not setting such illustrious examples!" She glanced contemptuously at Kassim.

Kassim said, "Morocco would be better off without the Jews. They are at the root of our problems. Just look at all of them who have become protégés of the foreigners. They work against our country."

Lili could see that Meriam was near tears. "Sir, you are offensive, both to me and to my friend."

Kassim leaned closer, "Do you like waltzing?" He asked Lili.

Lili wasn't sure what to do.

"Kassim! *Te barak allah alek.* It has been years since I saw you! But *smahli*, excuse me, my sister, Lili, promised me this dance."

Tariq held out his arm to Lili and she took it gratefully. Lili looked back over his shoulder and caught a glimpse of Kassim's angry face. She worried briefly about Meriam and then saw someone else had invited her to dance. She also noticed that André Daudifret had sat down next to Kassim.

Tariq frowned as his arm circled her protectively. "Lili, do not dance with that man."

Lili looked up at him, "Don't you think I know that? I just couldn't think how to get rid of him. I suppose I really must thank you for that. He was making the most rude comments about the Jews. And they were directly aimed at Meriam. What a cad! Was he a friend of yours at school?"

"Hardly. You should stay away from him."

"He must have talked his way in tonight, because I'm sure Judith wouldn't invite him," Lili said. "I was surprised to see him and wasn't clever enough to get away!"

the sheltering mountain, and Tariq was able to hold the horse, having caught the bridle.

They dismounted and Tariq helped Ted up. "There is no harm, *ya* Ted. But I do not know why your horse was so unhappy." He brushed Ted off.

Ted said, "It's my fault. I should have asked for a gentler horse. I'm not that good a rider."

"Next time, *Insh'Allah*, 1 will select your horse, *ya* Ted," Tariq said, examining the saddle strap carefully. "This strap is old. That might be what caused the problem." He removed the saddle to replace it more securely and felt along the horse's back gently, as well as the underside of the saddle. "Allah, something is here." He examined the saddle more closely and extracted a few small sharp pebbles, then looked again at the horse's back. "Look, these pebbles cut him. I must speak to the groom. He was careless. It was the stones, not you, that made him rear."

***

At a formal dinner with the *Sherif* Ted said, "What do you think about copulation?"

Silence followed. The *Sherif* raised his eyebrows and stared at Ted.

Tariq came to his rescue, "Oh, he means the weather."

Ted glared across the table at Kassim.

***

"*Ya* Ted, you must be careful with Kassim," Tariq advised when the two were out hawking

Ted laughed. "Yes, I've taken note of that, *ya* Tariq. But thanks for the warning. Scorpions in my bed, rocks under my saddle. The message is fairly clear. I've decided to use this as a learning experience on how to protect myself."

Once a week the girls lined up in front of the several bathrooms and took their turn. They were each given fifteen minutes to fill the bath and wash in the lukewarm water, which soon turned a dingy grey. Sitting in this dirty water seemed to Lili a strange way to bathe, rather than perching outside the bath and rinsing herself with clean water as she had been accustomed to do in Morocco. Eventually she adjusted, but every summer when she returned to Tangier, she made a bee-line for the *hammam*.

***

The boys liked to hunt with hawks. The *Sherif* loaned Ted one of his younger birds, and Tariq had brought his own when he came from el Meneb. The stables had ample mounts for experienced and beginner riders. Kassim led out a fine-looking stallion for Ted. Ted looked nervous when he saw how spirited the horse was, but mounted it and followed the other boys and servants out onto the trail. Tariq, too, thought the horse more than normally uneasy, but he attributed this to its having an unfamiliar rider.

When they had been out about fifteen minutes, Ted's horse started shaking its head and hesitating. Ted leaned forward to stroke its neck, trying to sooth it, but that seemed to make the horse more agitated, and it started to rear. They were on a steep mountain path and Tariq could see that Ted didn't know how to calm it. Tariq moved forward, coming alongside him on the cliff side, and pushing Ted's horse closer to the mountain. "Just stay calm, *ya* Ted," he cautioned, reaching to take hold of the bridle. The horse reared again and as it rose, the saddle strap broke, catapulting Ted off the horse. Fortunately, the path was wide enough at this point so that, rather than falling into the abyss yawning to the side, Ted fell to the left toward

"Well, I will be sure he does not bother you again tonight."
Tariq looked down at her and smiled.

"How did you learn to waltz?" she asked.

"We learned in Fez. Prince Abdel Aziz insisted we learn
so we could have parties. But there were no women we could
dance with, so we did not get much practice."

Lili laughed, despite herself, imagining the big, tall, Arab
boys dancing with each other to the music of the gramophone.
Then she closed her eyes and breathed in a mélange of fragrances
both from the ladies' perfume and from the gardenias, roses
and carnations that many wore in their hair.

Tariq looked down at her, "You're not wearing a caftan
tonight."

She shook her head.

"Have you forgiven me?"

"Oh, Tariq, there's nothing to forgive. I know it was just
a mistake," Lili said. The more she had thought about it, the
more embarrassed she had become. She hoped he hadn't told
anyone.

"What is Ted's news?" Tariq asked. "Is Oxford pleasing
to him? I have had one or two letters from him, but not
enough."

"I think he likes it. He doesn't write to me often either.
Isn't it strange that he never mentioned Kassim was at Oxford,
too?"

"Ted and Kassim are not friends. There would be no
reason for Ted to mention him, *ya* Lili," Tariq replied, a slight
crease between his long straight brows.

"Tariq, would you mind if we sat down? It was kind of
you to rescue me, but you don't need to keep on dancing with
me now."

"Whatever you prefer," Tariq said. "But let us talk a little.
I would like to hear my brother, Ted's, news."

They found a small table out on the terrace, where a cool breeze was blowing in from the sea. Tariq sat opposite her, quietly, just looking at her.

"Tariq, Kassim says the Jews are responsible for the poverty in Morocco. Why would he say that?"

"Of course, Lili, that is not true. The Jews are valuable to us because they trade and sell to the foreigners for us. And they loan us money, which Muslims are forbidden to do."

"So why does he say that?"

Tariq said, "There are good points and bad points to their profession, just as there are to mine. I am a soldier. So you could accuse me of killing people or of protecting my country. It is the same with the Jews. They do not pay all their taxes to the Sultan because the foreigners protect them. And they charge high interest when they loan money. This is hard on the poor, who sometimes end up in jail because they can not pay. But this is normal. They perform a service; it is not charity. Life in our country is hard, especially for the poor."

Lili nodded. "I feel guilty sometimes. My life is so easy, so comfortable. But it's hard to know what we can do to really help."

"You can only help those you come in contact with. I, too, worry about this."

"You mentioned being a soldier. Is that what you've been doing these last few months?"

"I have been in Marrakesh with *Sidna* Abdel Aziz, working for my cousin, Mehdi. He is chief secretary to Ba Ahmed, our Regent, who is also a relative of ours."

"Oh!" Lili hadn't known Tariq was attached to the court now. "What do you think of Prince Abdel Aziz? Ted likes him enormously."

"Yes, he is a splendid fellow. We taught him to play

billiards last year, and now he wins over us every night. It is the same with tennis. Did you know Ted taught him tennis? We play so hard it is difficult to do our duties."

"Prince Abdel Aziz is more or less my age. How does he like affairs of state?" Lili asked.

"Ba Ahmed prefers to make the decisions. He has been the Regent since the Sultan died five years ago."

"What do you do, Tariq?" She had only the faintest notion what one would actually do at court.

"I do what my cousin Mehdi asks me. Sometimes I help Ba Ahmed collect taxes."

"All anyone hears about these days is money," Lili replied. "Your job must not always be so pleasant."

Tariq grimaced slightly. "This is the way things work in Morocco. But now I will have military education. My cousin will send me to France for officer training. Abdel Aziz has proposed to send twenty of us to Europe. This idea pleases me."

"That sounds like a fine opportunity, *ya* Tariq. How long would the training be?"

"A year. *Insh'allah*, I will go after your Christmas. I want to see Ted first, and then I will leave after the New Year."

"Ted will appreciate that. He wouldn't want to miss you." She was just opening her mouth to ask another question when she sensed a third party behind her.

Tariq leaped up. "Ahmed! How are you?" The two men embraced, Arab-style, kissing loudly on both cheeks. Lili estimated that Tariq's friend was perhaps a year or two younger than he was, maybe Ted's age. He was as tall as Tariq, fair-skinned with a short dark beard, moustache and straight eyebrows. Tariq turned to Lili, "Lili, this is my father's brother's son, *Moulay* Ahmed Ben Mohammed al-Raisuni."

Ahmed bowed coolly to Lili. He did not offer his hand, which confirmed to Lili her suspicions that he was devout, since religious Muslim men did not like to run the risk of impurity by touching a woman who might be menstruating.

"Tariq, I want to talk to you about something," he said.

Lili stood up. This was her opportunity to leave graciously; she had spent enough time with Tariq to repay him for his rescue.

"I should get back to the party. I've been ignoring my dance card." She put out her hand to Tariq. "Thank you for rescuing me."

"Lili, I am sorry; I do have things to discuss with Ahmed, but I was interested...Well, never mind." He took her hand. "We will meet again."

***

"Who was that handsome young man you were talking to so intently out there?" Judith Daudifret asked.

"Oh, that's Tariq ash-Sherif. He's a great friend of Ted's. They studied together for years." Judith, like most of Tangier, knew the story of Ted's education and was quite fascinated by it.

"Oh, one of the famous Moroccan-English boys. How interesting! Do you know who the other man was who joined you on the terrace?"

"Tariq said he was *Moulay* Ahmed ben Mohammed something-or-other, visiting from Tetouan."

"That's the Robin Hood we were discussing! They call him al-Raisuni," Judith informed her. "I'd love to talk to him," she said, eyeing the terrace speculatively. Just then, however, the orchestra paused. André stepped to the front of the musicians and announced, "Ladies and gentlemen. Our players are taking a break, and we have arranged some special Moroccan dancing for the pause. So why don't you find a place to sit and we'll dim the lights for the performance."

Lili and Judith settled themselves in a nearby couch and Meriam joined them. Servants extinguished most of the candles, leaving just a few lit around the performance area. Moroccan drummers entered the room and settled themselves cross-legged on the floor, beginning a slow hypnotic tattoo. Two young girls entered, their large eyes outlined with kohl, polka dots of red marking their cheeks. Gold thread laced their long unbraided hair, and semi-translucent chiffon dresses provided provocative glimpses of their lithe bodies. The girls moved as if in a trance as they began to undulate to the beat of the drums.

They seemed so oblivious to their surroundings, Lili wondered if they might have been drugged. The girls swayed and dipped to the command of the violin and then, sinking to their knees, they began the sinuous Soussi dance, designed to be performed in tents. The girls waved their arms sensuously as the drums impelled them, their hips moving in time to the throbbing beat, and their hands beckoning as they flung their loose hair from side to side, their bodies dominated by the music. Lili was enthralled by the beat of the drums and the insistence of the dancers' provocative moves. She found her eyes unexpectedly filling with tears. It had been a strange evening. After the dances, Lili searched the room for Tariq and al-Raisuni, but both were gone.

***

Tariq arrived at St. Cyr in winter, taking a boat to Spain and then embarking on his first train trip. Ted had told him about trains, but having traveled exclusively on horseback in

Morocco, it had been impossible for Tariq to imagine such a thing. A porter showed him to his first class cabin, where he stood, unsure what to do until a man already seated there pointed to the seat opposite him and said something in Spanish. Tariq's Spanish and French were limited to a few stock phrases, but he gathered he should sit there. He must have sat at least a half hour before he realized the train was moving. Allah, it was so smooth, so unlike a horse! Seeing the scenery move past him, he stared until it made him feel slightly queasy. It was remarkable to sit in comfort, legs stretched out, making no effort, and be transported. We should have one of these in Morocco, he thought. The Sultan could move from place to place so easily. No one would get wet or cold. And there would be no limit to what one could take along, without having to consider feeding extra horses or mules.

As it got dark, Tariq berated himself for forgetting to bring food. He also wondered what men used for a toilet. These were much easier to arrange on a horse, for sure. Using sign language, he got information from the porter on both these necessities. The dining room was another hurdle, though. He read the English menu, but Tariq had never ordered a meal in a restaurant. He scanned the unfamiliar items: Tomato madrilène, Beef Consumé, Salade à la russe, Chicken fricassée, Lemon sherbet. Nothing was familiar. He decided to choose the first thing on the menu, the madrilène. The waiter brought him a quivering gelatinous red substance. "No," he said in English. "I cannot eat this. Take it back. Do you have meat?"

The waiter did not speak English. He handed the menu back to Tariq, who pointed by chance to a steak. This was brought to him and he looked down at a large piece of meat sitting on a plate, with some long green things along side. Although Tariq had learned many things from Ted and Miss

Higgins, they had always eaten Moroccan food the Moroccan way. No one had thought to show him how to handle knives and forks. He looked around the compartment and watched the others. It did not look like something he wanted to do in public for the first time, making a fool of himself. Tariq signaled the waiter again, waving away the steak. "Some bread and some fruit, if you please." He pointed to an adjoining table that had these foods and made the waiter understand. He knew he could eat this easily, without drawing unwanted attention. By the time he got to St. Cyr, a four day train trip, Tariq was famished. More importantly, he realized there was a lot he still needed to know about the West.

***

When Tariq arrived at St. Cyr, he was spoken to in rapid fire French, handed a pile of uniforms and boots, and escorted to a room that he would share. He put his one small suitcase down and looked warily at the young boy standing there. "Please excuse me," Tariq said in English. "I do not speak French."

His roommate looked at him curiously for a minute, dressed as he was in a brown wool *djellabah*. Then he replied in Arabic, "But you must speak Arabic, surely."

Tariq relaxed. "By Allah, this I did not expect. What a pleasure. I have not heard my own language for the past week."

"I, too," Fuad responded. "But I do speak French. Nevertheless, it is much more pleasant to speak in my own language. I am Fuad al-Mahrous, at your service. Your Arabic is a little different from our Cairo dialect, but we can teach each other.".

"*Al hamduli'llah*," Tariq said. "It has been such a trip,

you would not believe. I traveled on a...train.. ," he used the English word, having nothing in Arabic to describe it, "from Spain to here. It was amazing."

"Oh yes, I like trains. They are so practical," Fuad replied.

"You have been on trains before?"

"Yes, we have many in Egypt. I always went up to my military school on the train. It was so much less fatiguing than taking a boat up the Nile."

"Our Sultan has talked of introducing them in Morocco, but the *ulema* and tribesmen are very against this."

"You have tribes in Morocco? How amusing," Fuad said.

"Don't you?" Tariq asked.

"Maybe a few in the desert of Upper Egypt and the Sinai, but mostly we have *fellahin*, peasants, you know, to grow our cotton and sugar."

"Why so much of those? You can't eat cotton," Tariq asked.

Fuad laughed. "Allah, you are asking a soldier these questions! But I think we export many of these crops and get money to develop our roads and military and the like."

"Please excuse me," Tariq said. "I did not mean to grill you. I am happy to meet a fellow Muslim and to speak in Arabic. But now I need some information." He had a thousand questions, but hated to look ignorant, so he confined himself to essentials. "What are all these clothes for? When do I wear them?"

Fuad smiled. "This is the world of uniforms; different clothes for different occasions. I know a little about this from my military academy in Egypt. Some are for special occasions, others for every day."

"How it is that you speak French?"

"Oh, lots of people in Egypt speak French. We used it at school because our teachers were French, and we actually speak it at home, too. In fact, my Arabic is not that good, since I speak it mainly with the servants or on the streets. So please excuse me if I make mistakes. But why do you speak English?"

Tariq explained his background briefly.

The two got along well. One long weekend they made the trip to Paris, once again taking the train.

"By Allah, I like this machine," Tariq repeated. "How it could change Morocco."

Fuad was busily scanning a newspaper. Tariq looked over at him. "What is that you are reading? Is it the Koran?"

Fuad looked up. "Oh this? My father sent it to me from Cairo. We call it a *jarida* in Arabic. This one comes out every day, although of course it is old when I get it. But I can find out what's happening in Cairo, who has made speeches, what the Assembly is up to. Actually, there are some Arabic newspapers published in Paris, and I intend to look for them while we are there."

"Allah, this is a very fine thing. Imagine if we had this in Fez."

Fuad frowned and read out loud, "There was a bomb thrown in a Paris suburb recently. I hope it is not near where we are going today."

"But how could the Cairo *jarida* know such a thing?" Tariq asked.

"I think they use the telegraph to get news from abroad." Fuad said.

Soon Tariq was reading Fuad's month-old papers avidly. He couldn't get enough and continually marveled to his friend about the editorials. "Allah, *ya* Fuad. I do not know what to think. This writer says Cairo should be more respectful to the Sultan in Istanbul. But then another paper here says the Turks have too much influence in Egypt. They contradict each other."

"Well, in my opinion, my brother, the second paper is right. But it is good to hear several points of view, just as you would do if you sat discussing this with your fellow officers in Fez. You would not agree with all that each said, is it not true?"

"If this were about Morocco, yes, I would find it easier to decide," he agreed.

Fuad's description of the Egyptian military, so large and well educated, impressed him. When he questioned his friend about this, Fuad said, "You know, the French came to Egypt in the 1790's with Bonaparte. We learned a lot from them and our rulers decided to become more like them."

"The French would like to do more in Morocco now, but we are against it." Tariq replied.

"With good reason. We have the British occupying us, and we want them out. Be careful of them," Fuad replied.

Although a high-ranking officer in Morocco, at St. Cyr, Tariq was treated like any other student. He endured long forced marches, drills, asking himself why it was necessary to keep such straight lines and all move their feet in unison. He and Fuad would laugh about this, "What difference does this make in fighting someone?" he asked. But over the next six months Tariq began to realize the importance of discipline, of men learning to move as a well-oiled machine, responding automatically to orders, moving together. He compared this to Morocco, where aside from the Royal Guard, most soldiers had no uniforms and received no training. They were expected to know how to shoot from their horses running at top speed, each acting on his own, hurling himself at an enemy tribe with no order, each inflicting whatever damage he could, or wished to, pillaging, and racing away. Now he began to learn an entirely different way of fighting, moving in squares, on foot. Tariq could see some advantages, in that all sides were covered, and someone was there to cover your back. He doubted, though, that this would work in mountain fighting.

The courses Tariq liked best were strategy, and provisioning troops. These were new concepts. His professor set up an exercise on a chart in front of them. The chart showed a large valley, and marked the place of various troops. Later Tariq would learn this was Waterloo. "Now, gentlemen, *vous êtes ici*, you are here." He pointed with a marker. "You are surrounded 'ere and 'ere, by the enemy. What do you do?" Tariq listened and learned, as he became proficient in French. Fuad introduced him to chess and after a month Tariq surprised his professor by suggesting dividing his army into four positions making a v-shape and closing the enemy in a vise. "Excellent, Lt. ash-Sherif. We will make a commander of you, yet."

Military logistics was taught by a series of guest speakers. One whom Tariq remembered was a General Hubert Lyautey, recently returned from Madagascar. "Your boys come first, never forget that," he counseled them, strutting around the room. "Before anything, be sure they have food and dry clothes. Otherwise all the weapons in the world will not serve you."

***

Tariq received a note from Ted announcing the date of his wedding and insisting that Tariq come back for the event. St Cyr had a break for the summer, so he was free to go. He remembered Meriam, most recently from the Daudifret's party, although she had usually been around the house playing with

Lili when he visited Ted. His best friend married! Well, he couldn't really think it was strange; his cousin, Mehdi, had discussed the idea with him several times, too. But Tariq found the young Arab girls uninteresting; they reminded him of his mother or his sisters; completely alien from his life. While he was happy for his friend, he was in no rush to become so involved; he had his meals provided for at the school, as well as his laundry, and as for sex, there were enough clean prostitutes around. Still, he could see that Ted was happy, and that was enough.

Tariq bid farewell to Fuad, who had finished his course and was returning to Egypt. "We will meet again, *insh'allah*." he told Fuad.

"I hope one of these days you will come and visit us. I want to show you my country," Fuad said. "Until then, let us exchange letters from time to time. I would like to hear more about Morocco, too."

"Let us try," Tariq said. "But unlike you, we do not have postal service yet in Morocco. When you find a friend who is coming to my country, you may give him my name and tell him to find me in Fez. That is the only way for me to receive a letter. It will be easier for me, *insh'allah*, because my people go on the Pilgrimage every year and pass through Egypt. So I can send you my news.

Tariq resolved that he would visit Egypt. He was curious to see this Arab country that seemed to resemble France more than Morocco.

***

Arthur arrived in Tangier by boat. Lili was at the harbor to greet him and laughed as she watched him being carried in from the row boat by two burly black men.

"Well, I must say, Lili, that is the most undignified entrance I've ever made," Arthur said, standing up in the sand and straightening his suit and trench coat. "Do I have to tip these beggars?"

"Of course. I think that is their only compensation." Lili said.

"It's quite a strange way to come ashore."

"Papa says the Tangier Commission is trying to have a pier built, like you have in San Francisco. But it seems to be difficult, maybe because of our weather. We prefer being carried to wading through the water. Anyway, the important thing is that you're here." Lili said. "Come and meet my parents. I hope you'll stay with us until you get settled."

They walked down the beach road. "What about my luggage?" Arthur said. "You don't suppose those good-for-nothing porters have stolen it, do you?"

"No, I wouldn't think so. They always put it down over there. I'm sure yours will be there. I've already arranged with them to bring it up to the Legation." Lili said.

"Sorry, Lili. It's just that everything is so unfamiliar to me." Arthur said.

"Yes, I remember feeling like that when I first arrived in New York. But you'll soon get used to it." Lili tucked her arm in Arthur's and led him up the steep street to the small gate that led to *Sharia Amerika*, where the Legation was located.

***

Coming down the steep hill from the *medina*, Tariq immediately spotted the three black and white royal tents set up in the sand, lit from behind by a bonfire. Ted was having a *meshwi*, or lamb barbecue, to celebrate his upcoming wedding.

There was a clear full moon. The sea air was full of the

aroma of the six sheep roasting over huge bonfires. A troupe of tribesmen hired to perform exhibitions of swordplay was assembled to the side, their faces orange in the flames of the nearby fire.

Ted, Matt and Brahim, Meriam's father, settled on cushions toward the center of the tent, putting Tariq next to Ted so he could catch up on all his news from France.

Arthur Crampton was seated on Ted's other side, next to Matt. Ted turned to Tariq and teased him that military discipline appeared to agree with him. He asked Tariq how he liked St. Cyr.

"It is good, *ya* Ted. The school pleases me. And France is interesting. I would like Morocco to have some of what it has, roads, trains, order. And, naturally, since it is my responsibility, a real army. We have much to do here. I am not sure that a handful of trained officers can pass on all we have learned to our rough Moroccan *askars*. But how are you, my friend?" he said, clapping Ted on the back and kissing his cheeks. "This is a happy day for you. *Mabrouk*, congratulations."

"Yes," Ted looked deeply contented. "How about you, *ya* Tariq? Any plans in that direction?"

"Oh, I am not thinking of it. But how is that little *afrit*, the naughty young boy we met at the *moussem*? What was his name again?"

Ted hesitated, "Uh, Larabi. That reminds me, Tariq. Let me introduce you to Arthur Crampton. He's a friend of Lili's from San Francisco."

Tariq's eyes narrowed slightly as he stared at Arthur. He saw a tall, pale man with curly blond hair and blue eyes. How could Lili like someone so bloodless, he wondered. He leaned across Ted smoothly and grasped Arthur's hand. "*Ahlen, ya* Arthur. Welcome to Tangier."

Arthur grinned. "It's a real pleasure to meet you. Both Ted and Lili have told me a lot about you."

A roll of drums announced that the entertainment was beginning and they all settled back against the cushions.

Thirty men in long white robes, belted and crisscrossed with bandoleers, formed a semi-circle in front of the guests. Some carried round flat drums over which skin had been stretched taut. They pounded out a rhythm to which the men dipped and swayed in unison as they sang. Women dressed in red, black, and pink long dresses, heads bound in fringed scarves, tattoos between their eyes and on their chins, filed out and stood facing the men. They started a kind of singing contest, men inventing a verse and the women answering back.

The fires from the barbecuing lamb glowed in the darkness, blotting out the stars, and the rich aroma made Tariq's mouth water. The men were now dancing with their rifles, throwing them into the air and approaching each other in mock battle. Tariq leaned over to Ted, muttering, "Look at those old flintlocks!"

Men started serving the lamb, placing whole juicy carcasses, still smoking from the flames, on small round tables directly in front of the guests. Dishes of salt and cumin were put along side and Ted and his friends drew closer eyeing the meat hungrily while they waited for servants to bring around kettles of water to wash their hands.

Matt began at their table, pulling away a crispy morsel and offering it to Ted, "In honor of the groom. May your wife cook as well as this!" The men laughed and in seconds all hands were reaching greedily for the succulent meat. Suddenly a young man broke through the singers and approached the tables, firing a gun in the air.

"Good evening gentlemen. I hope you are enjoying your dinner," Tariq looked up and tensed. He whispered to Ted, "Al-Raisuni."

Ted stared curiously at the young bandit, dressed in clothes very similar to the dancers.

"Ah yes, the famous nisrani who speaks and acts like us," said al-Raisuni. "*Mabrouk.* I hear you are to be married."

Ted answered with a monosyllable.

"Aha, and here is Tariq ash-Sherif. I should have expected you at your best friend's wedding dinner," said Raisuni. "Well, gentlemen, I must ask you to remove your jewelry and empty your pockets. My men will pass among you and we can take care of this and be gone in a few moments, before your meat gets cold."

Matt muttered and made a quick motion towards his pocket. Tariq leaned over and gently placed his hand over Matt's. "It is not worth it, *Si* Matt. They will shoot to kill."

The guests quickly stifled their protests as did Matt, when ten or fifteen of Raisuni's men materialized, armed with much more modern rifles than the flintlocks the dancers had been using. They passed silently among the party, holding long fringed leather bags before them into which the men reluctantly dropped their valuables. A few who were not speedy enough received slight nudges from their daggers.

Raisuni, who was standing in front of the dancers, bowed to the assembly, "Gentlemen, thank you for your contributions. These valuables will be put to good use among the country people who have not tasted *meshwi* for a long time." He and his followers turned and quickly made their escape, leaping into the saddles of their horses, which were tethered just beyond the dancers. Spurring their mounts, al-Raisuni and his men vanished.

Pandemonium broke out among the guests.

"Well, of all the nerve," sputtered Brahim, Meriam's father.

Budgett Meakin and Walter Harris, British journalists who were seated at another table, began to laugh. "You've got to give that man credit for courage," Harris said.

"We were rather sitting ducks," Meakin said, slapping his thigh.

"Hell, you're dead right," Matt said. "We were kind of asking for it, having such a public banquet with all these diplomats."

"Still," Ted said, "it seems too bad to challenge our hospitality like that."

"Personally," Arthur said, "I find this outrageous. Why, that watch belonged to my grandfather, and to my father. Why aren't the police here to do something about this?"

"I think," Tariq said, "Al-Raisuni would say we had much to go around and will not miss whatever we gave up to him just now."

"Well, it's a lesson to me," Ted said. "I must be sure to have plenty of guards at Ravenswood day after tomorrow, to prevent a recurrence of this. Once my guests might tolerate, but twice would definitely be too much."

They finished the evening, Matt and Brahim passing from table to table to express their embarrassment and regret at the incident. Once the initial shock had worn off, most guests seemed inclined to shrug it off, some like Meakin and Harris even laughing and making wry jokes about sharing out the wealth more equitably.

***

Ted and Miriam's wedding was held in the Ravenswood gardens with their sweeping lawns and graceful peacocks. The scarlet and orange bougainvillea covering the house provided a dramatic backdrop for the ceremony. Lili thought Meriam looked beautiful in her long white lace wedding dress and Ted was handsome in a long white silk *djellabah* and red fez. Lili thought it was very romantic when they both drank from the same glass and then Ted crushed it under his heel. She wondered if one had to be Jewish to include that in the wedding ceremony.

Passing among the guests, Lili came face to face with Tariq.

"Well, my sister, it went well today, I think."

"Yes, I'm so happy for Ted, and Meriam, too. They were meant for each other," Lili said.

"Perhaps. I have never thought of marriage as you do. You seem to see it as it is described in English novels."

Lili colored. "Not just in books. After all, Amelia and Matt have that kind of marriage, and so did my grandparents. And I think Leah and Brahim, Meriam's parents, do too, in their own way."

"Your grandparents? And who are they, Lili?" Tariq asked, with a slight smile.

"Actually, Papa's parents. You know, Tariq, I don't know my real family." Lili said.

"Yes, Lili. I know. But you are a Berber, like me."

"Am I, Tariq? I think I'm a European; I used to wonder who I was. What would I become? But it's clear to me, now. I'm even more European than Meriam. I understand Morocco, maybe better than most. But I'm all European now. All my education, my upbringing; I'm a Shields, daughter of Matt and Amelia Shields. My mother's family abandoned her. That seems like a pretty clear message to me."

"*Smahili*, pardon me, my sister. Now you are upset. You are not easy for me to understand. And your life is foreign to me." Tariq said. "Here marriage is a contract between two families. We are not involved. We do not choose our brides, or see them in most cases before we wed. Even after the ceremony, aside from the marriage bed, the husband continues his life with his men friends, and the women do the same. If we are lucky, we respect each other, but love, such as they describe in *Wuthering Heights*, or *Jane Eyre*, or some of the other books Ted and I read with Miss Higgins, I do not see that in my family. My cousin and his wife, for example, hardly speak. They do not spend time together. They are not unhappy. But their lives are separate. And I, when I marry…. Well. I thought for a short time…. I wondered…"

Lili was standing close to Tariq, hanging on his words. Just then, behind her, Arthur approached, "Lili, there you are! Hello Tariq. Wasn't it a grand wedding?"

Tariq nodded, barely acknowledging that Arthur was there. "So, you see, little one. Our ways are different. We try to understand each other, but there is a big space. And now I must go."

Smiling, he bowed slightly in Arthur's direction, then with a last glance at Lili, he made his way toward the gate, stopping to say good bye to Ted and Meriam.

Lili took a deep breath and looked up; Arthur was standing there, watching her. She reached up and touched his cheek. She was grateful for Arthur's steady arms and his obvious love and thought to herself, this is what I need.

***

At the Portuguese Fort at the top of the *medina,* Arthur and Lili spread out a straw mat close to the old stone wall and unpacked the cold chicken, hard boiled eggs, and sliced melon that Aisha had prepared for them. Lili poured them both some lemonade and leaned back against the wall, "The Mediterranean looks so peaceful from here. And look, I can see Gibraltar over there. Can you see it?"

He moved closer to Lili, taking her hand. "Lili, remember what we talked about before you left San Francisco?"

She nodded.

"Have you had enough time to think about that? To think about whether you would marry me? I don't want to rush you, but seeing Ted and Meriam has made me think more about marriage. I love you and I want you to be my wife."

Lili was silent for a while, thinking about Ted and Meriam and how happy they seemed. Her last conversation with Tariq flitted briefly through her mind, but she quickly dismissed it. She would never marry an Arab, and certainly not Tariq, even if he had actually been hinting at that. She could never live like an Arab wife, confined to the women's world, hardly ever seeing her husband, never socializing publicly with him. No, it was Arthur she wanted, a life she knew and had been brought up to live. She squeezed Arthur's hand, "Yes, my dear. You are right. We should marry."

"Lili, are you sure about this? You know, I've wanted to marry you almost since the night we met, but I sensed you weren't ready. Do you really feel now that I'm the man you want to live with?"

"Yes," Lili assured him. "I'm sorry it took so long for me to make up my mind."

"Do you love me?" Arthur said.

"Of course I do, Arthur. I think I would be happy if I married you. I can imagine living with you, making a life with you, sharing the breakfast table with you every morning. I think we are compatible."

CHAPTER FIVE
1900

Arthur and Lili agreed on a December wedding to celebrate her eighteenth birthday.

"A Christmas wedding," Amelia said. "We'll decorate the church with poinsettias. And Meriam, as your matron of honor can wear red velvet."

Lili reminded her that Meriam's golden skin and chestnut hair were not the ideal complement for red velvet.

"Oh, yes, dear. You're right, as usual! Well, could you carry red and white roses? And then Meriam could wear moss green velvet. That will still look Christmassy and match her coloring."

Meriam came back from Oxford with Ted and their newborn baby. She was able to squeeze herself into the matron's dress and Lili was radiant in creamy white satin. Arthur wore his diplomat's attire of morning coat, complete with cut-away tails and top hat. It was a sparkling sunny day, crystal clear and cool enough to invigorate everyone. To Lili's disappointment, the minister refused to allow the breaking of a glass, as Ted and Meriam had done. Lili suggested to Arthur that they do this at their reception, but he said, "That's Jewish. We're Christian."

The Legation's large salon had a huge Christmas tree and boughs of greenery covered the window sills, along with poinsettias. The fireplaces, at each end of the room, blazed with Yule logs.

Matt claimed the first dance with Lili. "My dear, your mother would have been so proud of this day," he said.

"I know so little about her," Lili said. "Sometimes it's hard to believe she really existed."

"You look a lot like her. But sometimes it's hard to see since you wear your hair so differently and go around with your nose in the air."

"Oh, I don't! Surely not, Papa."

"I'm just teasing. But don't you get too high and mighty, just because you're a diplomat's wife, now."

"It'll be hard enough, just learning to be Mrs. Crampton," Lili said. "But getting along with some of these wives will be a challenge. I don't know if they'll ever really accept me."

"Don't be silly, my girl. Of course they will. Now here's your groom, standing there looking like he can't wait another moment to get his hands on you." Matt spun her back to Arthur, who was dancing with Amelia, but casting longing looks at Lili.

Lili and he danced well together, and the orchestra switched into the Anniversary Waltz. Lili closed her eyes, and laid her head on Arthur's shoulder. "Oh Arthur, I'm so happy. Imagine me, Mrs. Arthur Crampton."

He hugged her tightly. "That's right, and don't you forget it."

Soon Ted claimed a dance. "Well, little sister. You're a grown up matron now. How do you like it?"

"It's too soon to tell. How about you, Ted? Are you glad to be married?"

"Definitely, I recommend it to all my friends. And it's wonderful that Meriam could be with me that last year at Oxford. It made life so much more bearable. And now little Arielle. Did you ever see a child as beautiful?"

"Never. But I hope to compete with you soon," Lili laughed.

Meriam and Amelia helped Lili change into her going-away outfit. They sat on her bed sipping anise-flavored tea. The baby girl, Arielle, had been carried upstairs by Aisha and slept quietly in a cradle near them.

Lili bent over and stroked her little hands. "Isn't it amazing how perfect they are? I'm always surprised that they have little fingernails, and little toe nails and eyelashes. Everything's there!"

"*Oui*," Meriam said, "and I assure you, I inspected every inch when she was born!"

"I hope I'll have one soon, too," Lili said.

Amelia came hurrying in. "Lili, you'd better move along. The ferry won't wait, even for you, you know."

Meriam ran to get her dress, and Lili stood up, undoing the intricate buttons of her wedding gown. "Oh, Mama, I can't believe this. I'm leaving this room as Mrs. Arthur Crampton. Do you think they'll believe us in Gibraltar?"

"Of course they will. Don't you worry about a thing!"

Meriam nodded in agreement. "Arthur will be a good husband and a good companion, just like Ted is for me. You will be happy together. Here now, step into this." And she held out a brown tweed skirt and creamy satin blouse. Amelia handed her the little jacket that fitted snugly at the waist.

Just then there was a knock on the door and Matt and Ted came in. Matt took Lili's hand. "My dear, I 'm right proud of you. You're a real picture, and you've chosen a good man. You're starting a new life. I'm just tickled you'll be spending it in Morocco with us, and that Arthur will be working with me. Now, you'd best get going. We don't want that boat to leave without you!"

Arthur appeared at the doorstep, looking extremely dapper. He pointed at his watch.

"Yes, I know, Arthur. I'm coming". Lili turned to Ted and gave him a big hug. "We'll see you in a month."

***

At the Rock Hotel in Gibraltar, the couple retired after an early dinner. Upstairs, Arthur poured them some champagne. "Let's toast our new life and the beginning of the twentieth century."

Lili sipped her drink.

"Do you need me to help undo any of your clothes?" Arthur said.

Lili colored. "Oh no. Well, maybe. I suppose I'll need help with my undergarments." She turned uncertainly toward the bathroom. "Aisha made my stays very tight so my waist would look small."

"It looks tiny," Arthur said, putting his two hands around it. He leaned forward and gave her a big, wet kiss.

Lili pushed him away, gently. "I'll change in the bathroom." In the privacy of the small room, she wiped the slobber from her mouth, then poured water into the basin and rinsed her hot face. Slowly she took off her clothes, hanging them carefully on a hook. She fumbled with her corset and managed to untie its knots by herself. She slipped on a long white silk gown and wrapped herself in a matching robe. She took a deep breath and went back into the bedroom.

Arthur was already in bed. Lili tiptoed up to him. His eyes were closed and he was snoring slightly. Why, he was asleep. An empty champagne glass stood next to the bed. After a few minutes, she went to her side of the bed and sat down, removing her robe and laying it carefully on the nearby chair.

She stretched out next to Arthur, snuggling up close to him and putting her arms around him. He murmured something she couldn't quite understand, then started snoring again.

Lili lay there a while. She rolled over on her side and closed her eyes. She fell asleep, listening to the fireworks marking the arrival of the twentieth century.

***

Matt found a lawyer to help him draft some articles attacking Perdicaris. "Tell them," he instructed him, "Ian Perdicaris is just trying to get my job. He wants to be the one who can have protégés so he can make some good land deals. He'll offer them protection in return for their real estate. I wouldn't trust that son of a bitch any farther than I could throw him," he told the confused young lawyer. "And make the point of how badly the Jews are being treated here. Without some of us foreign powers to exempt them from Moroccan law by making them protégés, their lives would be even more miserable than they are."

***

In Rome Lili and Arthur found a hotel near the Spanish steps. Their first night, at the suggestion of the concierge, they went to a small restaurant nearby. Arthur and Lili both inspected the menu, and laughed. "I can't understand a single word," he said. "Arabic and French don't seem to help much."

"Neither can I," Lili said. "But some of these words sound like Latin. This *pollo cacciatore* must be chicken," she said, "And *bistecca* is probably like *bifteck* in French."

Arthur laid his hand over hers. "Bravo." He ordered for them. "Now, for tomorrow, what about the Vatican and St. Peter's? We might as well start at the top."

"Oh yes, and while we're here, Arthur, could we go to Assisi?"

"Definitely, I've always wanted to see the Giotto frescos. And I was going to suggest Florence. You could do a little shopping, and we could see Santa Maria del Fiore, and of course, the Uffizi, and the Pitti Palace, and..."

Lili interrupted, "Oh, and we must go to Venice."

"Whoa," Arthur squeezed her hand. "Of course, we will see everything you want, sweetheart. Venice, for sure, and Siena, there are so many things. But we'll come back, too. After all, we only have a month."

Venice was cold. But Lili and Arthur spent the whole day in St. Mark's, marveling at the treasures pillaged from Istanbul. Afterwards, seeking refuge from the frigid sleeting rain, they went to one of the cafes that lined the square. They settled into a dark booth at the back and Arthur ordered them both sparkling *proseccos*. Lili wrinkled her nose at the bubbles, and sipped, "The perfect thing to warm me up."

A stringed quartet began playing sweet Mozart quartets. Lili closed her eyes and a tear ran down her cheek. Arthur reached over and wiped it gently away, "Tears, my dear?"

"Oh Arthur, I'm just so happy. This is a perfect moment, and everything is right," she said, moving closer.

"I feel that way, too. You know, for a while there in Tangier, I wasn't sure you'd really marry me."

"Oh Arthur, I was just so young. But you shouldn't have worried. I think we belong together."

"There seemed to be a lot of competition. And everyone else there seems so knowledgeable and confident. I'm the newcomer. Frankly, I feel so stupid sometimes. I can't speak Arabic well, and I can't function in four languages the way all of you do, switching from Spanish to French, to Arabic, then back to English."

"Don't be silly, Arthur. No one expects a newcomer to know all that right away. Darling, you are so much more handsome than all those dark-haired men I've seen all my life. And you know so much more about America. You're better educated than most, too. Don't forget those things."

"I miss all my friends in California," he said. "It's hard to be new somewhere and not know everyone. And all of you have seen so much more of Morocco, know it intimately. It makes me feel stupid sometimes, when Ted and Tariq talk about Marrakesh or Fez so knowledgeably and I'm the only one who hasn't been there."

***

Budgett Meakin, editor of the Tangier Times, called Matt on the phone that had recently been installed in the Legation. "Matt, I've heard Ian Perdicaris has gone off to Washington. A source has told me he's planning to meet with the State Department people while he's there."

"Hmmf," grunted Matt. "Good of you to tell me, Meakin. I just heard they were sending out some auditors to look at my books. That's probably Ian's doing. Thanks."

***

Al-Raisuni continued to prey on the rich around Tangier, demanding enormous fees for the use of any road he controlled. *Sheikh* Abdurrahman, the governor in Tangier, begged the Regent to put an end to it. Tariq, his training at St. Cyr behind him, accompanied Ba Ahmed to Tangier.

The Regent and his party stayed at the palace at the top of the Kasbah with *Si* Abdurrahman. Ba Ahmed assured the Governor that he would settle this once and for all, and sent a note to al-Raisuni, inviting him to come to town.

"With all respect, *ya sidi*," Abdurrahman said, "why do you think he will honor such an invitation? He knows we are his enemies."

"Never mind," Ba Ahmed assured him. "I am offering him a beautiful new Enfield rifle. I think this will be hard for him to resist. May Allah assist us in this."

A few days later servants came running into the courtyard where the Chamberlain and his party were assembled. "*Ya Sidi, Sherif* Raisuni is at the door and is asking to come in."

Ba Ahmed rose, wiping his hands, a contented smile on his face. Turning to the Governor, he said, "Be sure your men are well armed."

Tariq had agreed to his relative's plan, despite earlier reservations. He knew al-Raisuni was causing too much disruption in the region. Ba Ahmed looked at him. "*Ya* Tariq, al-Raisuni thinks of you as a friend. Go and invite him in for food and drink."

Tariq went to the outer gate. Al-Raisuni was seated on his horse, pacing to and fro, fifty of his armed bandits surrounding him. He frowned when he saw Tariq, "*Ahlen, ya* Tariq. What are you doing here?"

"I work for Ba Ahmed now. He welcomes you and invites you into the house for tea."

Al-Raisuni frowned. "He said something about an Enfield rifle."

"That is right," Tariq said. "He received several from the English and has one for you. But first, come in and eat with us."

Al-Raisuni's men began to dismount and Tariq held up a warning hand. "Just you, *Si* Ahmed."

Al-Raisuni hesitated, then said, "I would break bread with you before I enter, *ya* Tariq." Tariq nodded and sent someone in to bring a loaf out. He handed it to the *Sherif.*

Al-Raisuni broke the bread and took a bite. "We have shared bread together. Now you have an obligation to protect me."

The bandit dismounted and went up the stairs into the palace. They entered the sunny mosaic-tiled courtyard. Ba Ahmed and Governor Abdurrahman embraced him. Ba Ahmed gestured towards the cushions surrounding the small wooden table, where a freshly roasted lamb glistened. A servant seated nearby poured glasses of mint tea. "Please, let us have some tea. You must be hungry after your trip in from the mountains."

Al-Raisuni nodded and sat, uttering, *"Bis mi llah,* in the name of God," At that moment Abdurrahman's guards rushed into the room and seized al-Raisuni by his arms and legs. Simultaneously outside they heard shouts and shots, indicating that other soldiers had surrounded al-Raisuni's soldiers.

"I am betrayed," al-Raisuni shouted. "You sons of sin. How could you break the law of hospitality? A curse on you all. A curse on the religion of your mothers." He reached for the dagger he always carried in his belt, but Tariq grabbed it first.

Ba Ahmed replied, a satisfied grin on his dark face. "Such a technicality should not worry you. With all the evil you have committed, I have no doubts you would do the same if it suited you. Men, put this sinner in chains and take him away."

Al-Raisuni shouted curses as they wrapped him in chains and carried him from the room. Tariq followed the men out into the courtyard. Blood streamed over the cobblestones and men lay everywhere, wounded and dying. The horses snorted and whinnied, frightened by the scent of blood. "Get those horses rounded up and put them in our stables," he directed a nearby slave. He beckoned to another. "Bring that cage over here." He pointed to a wooden cage sitting in a corner. It was three feet high and the same width. "Put him in that cage."

Al-Raisuni struggled against his chains. "Tariq, how can you betray me?"

"What you are doing is not good for the Kingdom," Tariq replied. "May Allah show you mercy." He turned and went back into the palace, not wanting to watch his old friend be stuffed into the small cage. He knew the bandit would be kept in that cage for the 500 kilometer trip to Mogador's prison.

***

Sitting at breakfast, Matt opened a letter. As he read it, he slowly lowered his coffee cup to the table. When Amelia looked up Matt was just sitting, staring into space.

"My dear, what's the matter?"

"That's it, Amelia. That son of a bitch has won."

"Won what? What are you talking about?"

Matt handed her the letter. "They're relieving me of my duties. It's all explained there. I never thought he'd win." He shook his head. "I can't believe it."

Amelia read the letter quickly. "It says it will be at least six months before they can send a replacement. Maybe you can change their minds. Why don't you send a telegram? Maybe there's still something we can do."

Matt shook his head. "I can try, but I think this is it."

***

Ted knocked on Lili and Arthur's door. "Ba Ahmed's died of cholera. Tariq's sent me a message from Marrakesh. *Moulay Abdel Aziz* wants me to come down to Rabat, where they'll have an official inauguration, to cover the story and handle the other reporters, and help during this transition period." Ted was an official correspondent for the London Times and the story would be an exclusive for him.

"Golly, that's something," Arthur said, ushering Ted into the living room while Lili poured him a cold drink. "It'll be hard for such a young boy to take over this job. You know him pretty well, Ted. What do you think?"

"Of course, he's only eighteen," Ted said. "He hasn't shown much interest in ruling so far. He may do better than one would expect. I know he's interested in reform and better administration. The hardest part will be overruling the more conservative older men who surround him. He's got some good young people around him, like Tariq's cousin, Mehdi al Menebbhi. Undoubtedly there will be a struggle within the palace to see which faction wins. That will be his hardest test."

***

Matt and Arthur, along with the other ministers and consuls in Tangier, received invitations to present themselves in Rabat for the inauguration ceremonies.

Sitting at the office reading the invitation Matt groaned. "Damn, just six months till my replacement arrives. I was keeping my fingers crossed I'd be spared another one of those cursed diplomatic functions!"

Arthur said, "Are they that bad?"

"Well, young fellow, you judge for yourself. But one session is enough for most of us."

Arthur was excited by this opportunity. The Sultan did not encourage Christian foreigners to travel in the interior. Without a specific invitation from him or one of the 'men of power', as Tariq called them, it was foolhardy for Christians to travel outside of Tangier without a tribal protector and official invitation, as the traveler would be fair game for any tribesman.

The diplomats went in caravan down the coast, accompanied by troops sent by Abdel Aziz. Every night they camped near a tribal settlement, where the headmen joined them around the campfire, bringing cous cous, chickens, fresh buttermilk and whatever fresh vegetables were available. The leaders talked about the local news, the drought that continued to plague them, the excessive taxes, the pressure the Regent had put on them with his incessant demands for gold. Arthur was disgusted by the misery in which they lived, reluctant to eat the food they prepared with their dirty hands, sleeping with bedbugs and fleas. They're all just beggars, he thought. Why can't they help themselves more, like our pioneers did?

In Rabat Arthur and Matt stayed in the *mellah* (the Jewish quarter), the only place in the city where foreigners were welcome. Luckily, the Botbols, relatives of Brahim, had plenty of room for them. Their home was near the walls of the *medina*.

As one of the seven Jewish elders of Rabat, Isaac Botbol was obliged to participate in the ceremonies, and was looking very gloomy. "Jews are expected to bring valuable gifts, for which our whole community is heavily taxed. They demand bolts of embroidered silk and braid for the Sultan's clothes, and those of his harem, of course. But the worst is the gold; for events like this we're expected to give kilos and kilos of gold jewelry in tribute."

Isaac's wife Janna, bringing in the dinner, caught the last part of the conversation. "Oh, Señor Arthur, you don't know the half of it! It's not so hard for the elders, we have enough, thanks to God, but even though we try to tithe in proportion to people's means, the poor have had to come up with half their yearly wages to satisfy this tax. And just think," she concluded angrily, "for this privilege, my poor husband will have to stand barefoot and bareheaded in the sun before the Sultan for hours tomorrow, to offer these so-called presents!"

"Now, now, Janna," Isaac chided her. "The Sultan does look after us. Don't forget earlier this year when that young Jewish boy was lynched by a *Sherif* for touching him, Ba Ahmed got that all straightened out and saw that his family got their $1000 in blood money."

Janna rolled her eyes. "You seem to forget, Isaac, that that poor young Jew's only problem was that he dressed in European clothes which offended that crazy *Sherif*. I don't see why we have to be so grateful that Ba Ahmed saw that his family got a bit of money to compensate them. I'm sure they'd rather have their son."

This exchange reinforced Arthur's growing opinion that Morocco needed taking in hand. He knew most of the Jews in Tangier, at least the younger and better educated, like Meriam's family, wore European clothes and had adopted modern ways. He had noticed that here in Rabat all the Jews were required to wear black, even on their feet when they left the *mellah*. How unfair to decree what kind of clothes people could wear.

Isaac said, "We can never forget we are only here at the sufferance of the Sultan, who welcomed us when we were expelled from Spain. That's just our lot in life. Let our guests eat in peace." He started ladling out the appetizing *harira*, lentil and lamb soup.

Arthur knew that the Andalusian and more rural groups of Jews did not mix and had different customs, beginning with language. The Andalusian Jews, as the newcomers were often called, spoke a dialect of Spanish among themselves and in the intimacy of their homes dressed in clothes recalling Spain. The women wore brightly colored skirts and blouses, unlike Moroccan Arab women, who wore long dresses. The

Andalusians were merchants, often jewelers or tailors and continued many of their Spanish customs and way of life, using European furniture and clothing. They considered the rural Jews who spoke a dialect of Arabic, and generally worked in agriculture, although forbidden to own land, backward and uneducated. He wondered if Isaac spoke for all Moroccan Jews or just his fellow Andalusians.

The first day the diplomats gathered in the wide plaza just outside the palace walls. A large dais marked the young Sultan's throne, and his immediate staff and several slaves stood behind him with a crimson parasol and fly whisks to keep the ruler comfortable. Abdel Aziz sat cross-legged on the dais, his white silk caftan covered by a white silk and linen cloak bordered with gold thread. His turban was partially covered by the hood of his cloak. Behind him a bank of trumpeters announced each new event.

Arthur and Matt, along with the other Western diplomats, wore formal morning attire, complete with striped vests, grey cutaway jackets with tails, heavy cotton shirts and flannel trousers. They had been told to remove their top hats as a sign of respect to the Sultan; only Muslims could cover their heads in the presence of the ruler.

Arthur's expectations that diplomats would be treated as honored guests were rudely shattered as he saw the disdain of the official Muslim community for the Christians. They stood the whole day in the grueling sun, while various tribes and other officials offered allegiance and pledges to the Sultan. There were shows of force, mostly in the forms of fantasias, horse races, ending with mighty firing of rifles and horses brought up short as close as possible to the spectators. Tariq, now working full time for his cousin, Mehdi al-Menebbhi, to train the military, was much in evidence, putting his troops through their paces.

"Not much to admire there," Matt said sotto-voce to Arthur, as the soldiers struggled through elementary marches and maneuvers, rarely keeping in step, carrying themselves badly, and generally manifesting few signs of discipline.

Arthur, secretly pleased to see that even Tariq had trouble in some areas, nevertheless came to his defense. "Tariq's only been working with them a month or two. But Ted tells me he's sometimes in despair. They're evidently hard to recruit and there's virtually no money to pay them. And, of course, Tariq's the first of the handful of Moroccans to return from formal military training, and to try to establish some discipline."

"Yes," Matt said, "the fierce charge, every man for himself, and the quick withdrawal; that's the Arab way. Raiding's what they're good at, not disciplined military exercises. It'll be a miracle if the youngsters like Tariq are able to change this. After all, *Qaid* Maclean's been here twenty years and he hasn't made any headway."

Arthur said, "Is that him over there?" He pointed to a sturdy gray-haired foreigner resplendent in a Moroccan costume complete with Turkish trousers standing near Abdel Aziz.

"I believe so," Matt said, stretching to peer. "Ted would know. Where is Ted, anyway? I thought we'd see more of him. He seems to be damned busy!"

"I'm sure he's enjoying himself more than we are," Arthur said.

Matt looked at him more closely. "My God, you're beet-red! Do you feel all right?"

"I sure wish I'd brought some water with me," Arthur said. He was sweating like a pig. He just hoped he wouldn't pass out and really disgrace himself in this diplomatic crowd. "Now I see what you meant about this being an ordeal. Maybe we can get Ted to convince Abdel Aziz that this customary reception of diplomats is a bit barbaric."

When the ceremony ended, Ted joined the two men.

"What a day," he said, his eyes sparkling.

"I'm glad you enjoyed it," Arthur said. "To me it began to feel like torture after the first hour or so. What more do we have to endure before it's over?"

"Oh, I think there will be a day or two more like this one where various dignitaries, important family heads, tribal chiefs, leaders of craft guilds and so forth each come to swear their allegiance."

"The diplomats have to witness all of that?" Arthur said. He was wondering if he could invent some excuse to miss the rest.

"It's customary," Ted said. "I didn't realize they made everyone stand with their heads uncovered like that. I wonder.... Let me talk to Tariq tonight and see if they could erect some kind of an awning. I know it would be considered very impolite to cover your head, but perhaps an awning would be viewed differently."

"It's fine for the Sultan, since he has that wonderful umbrella shading him all the time, not to mention the imperial fly whisk," Arthur said.

"Isn't that parasol splendid? You know, that's probably the only real sign of the Sultan's office. To have someone walking beside one carrying that great tall sunshade, reaching all the way above the seated rider. What a luxury. I suppose that's why it's a sign of power, of course, always having shade."

"At least the Muslims all have their turbans. That's a big help. Personally, I've always had a hankering for one of those slaves to whisk away the flies," Matt said.

"Of course, any good Muslim always has his head covered, in respect to God. But Christians or Jews don't have that privilege," said Ted. The sartorial laws decreed that the minorities went bareheaded to show respect to the Muslims, just as they were required to always be lower in height, so that they went on foot when Muslims were riding, or on mules when Muslims were on horseback.

Early the next morning Ted did get an opportunity to speak to Tariq and his suggestion convinced the young Sultan to erect an awning for the foreign guests. Although there were still no chairs, the shade helped the foreign visitors get through the following days, during which they made sure they had water with them. Arthur and many of the other fair-haired Westerners had badly burned faces, which began to blister and peel as the ceremony slowly unfolded, but at least the awning prevented further damage.

After the ceremonies a messenger came to the door of the Botbol's house with a summons. Ted read out loud, "*Sidna* Abdel Aziz, Commander of the Faithful, summons you to his presence after the mid-day prayer." Arthur's spirits sank, but revived when he heard they would be meeting inside the palace and most likely would be sitting. He really didn't think he could take any more ceremonial events.

The men presented themselves at the Palace gates at noon. Many of the diplomats with whom they had shared the past few days of festivity were also there, standing patiently in the noonday heat. When the guards rose from their prayer mats, two magnificently dressed soldiers dressed all in white with short black cloaks trimmed in gold hanging from their shoulders swung open the small wooden door within the huge brass gates and an honor guard escorted them to *Moulay* Abdel Aziz's throne room. The young Sultan, dressed as he had been during the ceremonies, was seated cross-legged on his wide gilded throne with his pet lion beside him. A dozen soldiers holding spears stood near him dressed in white baggy trousers, with white knee-high stockings, yellow *belghah*, (slippers) and white jackets that looked like French uniforms, complete with epaulets. The mosaic tiled floor was covered with a red rug with a flowered medallion in its center, to which Abdel Aziz gestured. The British Minister, more familiar with palace customs, sat on the rug, and the others followed his lead.

Abdel Aziz addressed the group, and as he paused, *Moulay* Ali, Ted's former schoolmate, translated.

"My friends, representatives of the foreign powers, you are welcome here today. I trust you have enjoyed the past few days of festivities." Ali stopped for a moment, as Abdel Aziz seemed to be expecting an answer.

The British Minister stood to speak for the group. "Most esteemed Sultan, we, the members of the diplomatic community, congratulate you on your ascension to the throne of Morocco and wish you long life and a good reign. On behalf of everyone, we pray for your success. *Eish al malik* (long live the king)."

Abdel Aziz nodded. This seemed to be the kind of response he was expecting, thought Arthur, a touch bitterly, thinking of his sunburned head and the thirst they had suffered.

Ali continued, translating for the Sultan, "As you know, under Ba Ahmed, the *makhsen* (government) did not welcome foreigners, and we had very few representatives and councilors from the foreign powers. I would wish to change that tradition."

The men seated at his feet stirred in surprise.

"My kingdom is going through difficult times. I believe we need to change. I seek more of a dialogue with you, so that I may learn from you. Some of you probably know that we are wish to modernize our army. We have sent a dozen or so of our young tribal leaders to learn military ways in France and

England. I have also heard talk of different approaches to state administration. I want to set Morocco on a new path, and I invite assistance from our foreign friends.

"I also inform you that, although until now we have made our court mostly in Marrakesh, we will now move to Fez. Our religious leaders, the *ulema*, are there and have begged us to come and be closer to them. I therefore request each of your legations in Tangier to appoint a permanent representative to come to Fez and establish a consulate there."

He gestured to the servants standing on the sides of the room and they brought steaming mint tea to the seated men. As they passed the silver trays and the men helped themselves, the diplomats stirred, whispering among themselves as to what might be behind this surprising announcement.

"Maybe he's afraid of the French," whispered Matt to Arthur. "You know, the French seem to be making some kind of deal with the British, carving up the southern rim of the Mediterranean. I've heard talk about the French leaving Sudan and Egypt to the English. Wouldn't surprise me to hear they're going to play that same game in Morocco."

"It would make sense," Arthur said. "After all, the French have to protect their interests in Algeria."

"So," Ali continued as mouthpiece, "*Sidna* requests that within the next two months, each Legation send its delegate to Fez. For those of you who do not have suitable space available there, the Palace will assist you in finding it."

The British Minister got to his feet again. "Your Excellency," he began. "I believe I speak for us all when I say that we are deeply honored by your invitation and we welcome the chance to strengthen our ties with you. We shall all be returning to Tangier within the next day or so to confer with our foreign offices at home and should be able to send word to you in the near future about the arrangements we shall be able to make."

Abdel Aziz nodded his head as Ali translated this speech to him. Then the new Sultan lifted his tea glass to the foreigners, smiling. He gestured to the musicians who were seated in the back of the room and they lifted their lutes and violin-like *qannuns*, filling the room with Andalusian music.

Arthur groaned silently to himself, as his cross-legged position was becoming more and more uncomfortable. "I guess there's no way we can sneak out on this?" he whispered again to Matt.

Matt, who looked like he was suffering even more, shifted his weight and uncrossed one knee, stretching it momentarily in front of him to rid himself of a beginning cramp. He shook his head. They would have to resign themselves to another few hours of the music before it would be appropriate to take their leave. Arthur noticed that some of the more savvy around him had sought out the divans around the walls, or borrowed cushions, and appeared to be arranging them as arm rests and generally settling in for the duration. A few, like Matt's journalist friend, Walter Harris, and Ted, wore Arab dress, and seemed to Arthur to be at ease in their loose robes. He thought to himself that if he went to Fez, he might consider adopting this costume, at least for ceremonial occasions. Arthur started mulling over the idea of living in Fez. He couldn't honestly say he'd enjoy living in the interior, which he had heard was even less pleasant than Rabat. But he'd be the man on the spot, even if still junior at the Legation. He'd gain a lot of credibility. All in all he decided it would advance his career and realized that the idea appealed to him. He wondered what Lili would think of it.

***

Tariq sat with Mehdi and other male members of his family in a tent in Meneb. An Andalusian orchestra played softly in the background. Tariq wore all white and had a red fez on his head.

Mehdi leaned toward him, handing him a piece of succulent lamb from the *meshwi* they were enjoying. "Congratulations on your marriage, my cousin. My young sister will make you a fine wife."

Ted was seated on Tariq's other side. "I'm sorry you didn't give us a little more notice, *ya* Tariq. I should have liked to have a party for you in Tangier."

Tariq shook his head. "It is not necessary, my brother. This is just a family celebration, not one of your fancy Western affairs. And we would not be able to dance."

"True, but it is good to celebrate these things," Ted said.

"But we are celebrating," Mehdi said. "We will eat, drink and listen to good music. Later the bride will dance for her husband, in their own bedroom, right, *ya* Tariq?" He slapped Tariq on the back.

"If she likes," Tariq answered. "It does not matter greatly to me. I haven't seen Malika for five or six years. Does she dance?"

"I have heard that my sister is an accomplished dancer," Mehdi answered. "But you will soon see for yourself. I must say, it does my heart good to cement our alliance with this marriage. I know Malika will be in good hands, and you will now be my brother."

"I am honored by this symbol of your respect," Tariq answered. "I will try to be worthy of her."

"Now let us talk of more interesting things," Mehdi said. "I am not happy with this move to Fez that *Si* Fadoul Gharnit has insisted on. *Sidna* is already complaining that it is so cold and damp in Fez in the winter."

Tariq laughed, "He can light more fireworks to warm us all up."

"Yes, but truly, my cousin, I do not trust Gharnit. He has many friends among the *ulema* there. Why, I have already heard that *Sidna* has been given a list of readings from the Koran and told to study them daily, to seek inspiration for his reign there."

"Of course, reading from the Koran is highly commendable," Tariq said. "But somehow I cannot see *Moulay* Abdel Aziz staying on that path for long. I would not be overly worried."

Ted said, "I feel he's genuinely interested in making some changes. I hope the Fezzis don't deflect him from that."

A servant approached and whispered something in Mehdi's ear. He nodded and turned to Tariq, "It is time for you to claim your bride."

Tariq rose and Ted and Mehdi stood with him. Ted and he shook hands. "Good luck, old boy," Ted said.

Mehdi clapped him on the back, "I will go with you to the women's tent."

They walked the short distance to the other tent, accompanied by the musicians. As they approached, a trumpeter sounded a horn. In a few minutes, the young bride appeared, her chest covered in silver coins, which also hung from a braided headdress. A veil covered her face. Her mother and sisters stood beside her. One of Tariq's attendants led out a richly caparisoned horse with hennaed mane and tail. The mother stepped forward, holding her daughter's hand, which she placed in Tariq's.

"Auntie Khadija," he said. "I am honored by this precious gift to me. Please be assured that I will honor and protect Malika for as long as she desires it."

"I know, my son. We are honored by this alliance," she said.

Tariq gently guided Malika to the horse. "Can you see to mount, my sister?" he asked.

She nodded. He put his hands down for her to step in and she jumped lightly to the saddle, settling herself side saddle. Tariq's horse was waiting and he swung up, grasping the reins of Malika's horse. Slowly they made their way to the house in the village prepared for them, men walking alongside with lighted torches.

In the house, Tariq carried his bride to the bridal chamber, where a bevy of women shooed him out of the room. "Go, go," they laughed. "We will prepare your bride for you."

At their signal, Tariq came back into the room. Malika was seated naked on the bed, with women ranged around her. By tradition, they would stay in the room to witness the taking of her virginity. Tariq looked at his young bride; she was shaking and tears were streaming down her face. "Go, all of you," he instructed the women. "She is frightened. We will be better alone."

He neared the bed and Malika shrank back, eyes wide. Tariq saw a tea pot nearby and poured two glasses. "Here, my sister. Let us drink some tea." He sat beside her on the bed and handed her a glass. She sipped. He stroked her arm. Why don't you come and sit here, in my lap?" He gathered her up, like a little child and wrapped his arms around her, kissing away her tears. "Do not fear. I will not hurt you. And I will always take care of you."

Later that night a sheet was hung in front of the house, showing Malika's virginal blood.

CHAPTER SIX
1901

Lili wondered what she would do for friends in Fez, with Meriam so far away. Then Aisha, the housekeeper who had raised Lili, announced that if Lili was going into the interior into 'God knows what,' as she put it, she, Aisha, was going, too. Having the company and help of the woman who had nursed her as a child made the move much less daunting.

The men opted to go in January, ahead of the women, to find suitable lodgings and make arrangements. The wives, including Lili, felt that it would be far better to wait until after the rains, so they delayed their departure until early April. They would travel in a large caravan, accompanied by fifty soldiers sent by Abdel Aziz to ensure their safety, and make the trip in easy stages down the coast and then due east from Rabat.

They assembled at Souk al Barra, just outside the walls of Tangier. Lili and Aisha were among the first to arrive and stood by their belongings in the shade, waiting for the soldiers to get the group organized. Lili was chatting with Aisha when she heard a familiar voice. Looking up, her eyes opened wide in surprise as she saw Tariq giving orders. He caught her eye and saluted, and when he was through organizing his soldiers, he dismounted and came over to where she was standing. Tariq's black Turkish trousers, belted tunic with gold braid, and the crimson cloak thrown over his shoulders suited him, she thought.

"My sister, Lili, how are you? And Mama Aisha, it gives me pleasure to see you will go with this little one."

"Allah, you don't think I would let my baby go off to that primitive place without someone to look after her!" Aisha laughed. "But *Si* Tariq, I'm glad it's you leading this group of ruffians! They don't look as if they could find Larache, let alone Fez."

Tariq noted that his elegantly attired soldiers in their spotless royal uniforms seemed to be causing more confusion than order as they gave conflicting instructions and steered people in the wrong directions. "You speak the truth, as usual, Mama," he said. "But by Allah, these men can shoot. I hand picked them. Have no fear."

He turned to Lili, smiling, "I see that Larabi has made another appearance."

Lili had put her hair in a braid and was dressed in baggy pants, shirt and vest. Some of the diplomats' wives were obviously shocked by this attire, but Lili was more interested in comfort than correctness.

"Well, there shouldn't be any official receptions on this trip, and you men have such comfortable clothes."

Tariq seemed preoccupied. "We will talk later. But now, it is my duty to see to my men and be sure there is order here, so we can depart." He touched his hand to his heart briefly and returned to his troops.

He assembled the group—women mounted either in litters or on horseback, children either in saddle baskets, or with their mothers. Lili had decided long ago that she would ride, but Aisha demanded to be put in a litter where she crouched cross-legged muttering imprecations at the bearers as they struggled on the rough paths.

The first few days of the trip many of the women were

querulous and sick, and Lili spent her free hours after they were camped soothing and caring for them with Aisha's help. Tariq, too, was fully occupied, supervising and training his troops to handle the unpacking, setting up of tents, negotiating with the neighboring tribes and making food arrangements. It was not until the fourth evening after they had eaten, that Lili looked up to see Tariq standing near her.

He addressed himself to Aisha. "Tea, Mama, may Allah reward you," he said, folding himself down beside Lili.

Aisha busied herself with the preparations for tea.

"My sister, Lili, how are you?"

"Fine. I'm learning to run a household and be a wife."

Tariq nodded.

"Tell me about your wife, *ya* Tariq."

Tariq settled back on some cushions Aisha placed near him. "She is my cousin Mehdi's youngest sister. She is called Malika. She grew up with me."

Lili couldn't resist the image that came into her head of the docile little Arab wife. "When was the wedding?" she asked. Ted had told her something about it, but she had forgotten the details.

"Just after Abdel Aziz's inauguration."

"So," said Lili, counting on her fingers, "almost a year ago."

"Yes, and soon I will have a child, *insh'Allah*," Tariq said.

"I'm happy for you, Tariq."

"Lili, Malika is coming to Fez to keep house for me, and you two must be friends. She will not know anyone there."

"Of course, Tariq. I'll look forward to it," Lili said. She was curious to meet his wife and see his baby. She would know almost no one in Fez and this might be a good place to begin. "How do you like being in Fez? And what are you doing exactly?"

"You know, Lili, that my cousin Mehdi is Minister of War? We are all from the region of Marrakesh, so we prefer living there. But some of *Moulay* Abdel Aziz's advisors are, I think you would say, old-fashioned. They think he does not do enough work in Marrakesh. So they have insisted the court move to Fez. I do not know how it will be. We are all new there and do not have many friends. It is hard for us, as I think the elder royal advisors do not always approve of my cousin. They say he is a bad influence on *Sidna*. It is complicated, but I will do my best. *Sidna* Abdel Aziz wants a modern army and I will lead that effort."

"I'm thankful that they assigned you this task. You understand us so much better than any other Moroccan, and the fact that you speak French and English is a godsend. Having this trip go smoothly will do a great deal to start all the new diplomatic families off well in Fez."

"Yes, that is why I volunteered for the assignment," he said.

Aisha handed them both a glass of steaming mint tea, and squatted down near them herself with a third glass. "Allah," she said. "*Si* Tariq, this trip will kill me. All my bones are aching from that litter."

"May God give you patience," Tariq said. "I'm glad you're here to help Ted's sister."

"Tell me, *ya* Tariq," Lili said. "Why so much preoccupation with an army? Is it so necessary?"

"A strong army means a strong country," Tariq said. "The Sultan must show his power to control the Berber tribes. Now that many of the tribes are protégés of foreign governments, they are often better armed and stronger."

In addition to their commercial arrangements with the Jews, most foreign governments also had contracts in tribal areas so they could buy wool and wheat wholesale and ship them abroad. Other Legations had made the same arrangements Matt had made with his hunting village, sometimes giving tribal leaders the protection benefits in return for monopolies on buying their crops.

"Why can't Abdel Aziz just retire to Fez and let the Berber tribes in the mountains do as they please?"

Tariq shook his head. "The *makhsen* needs their money. The taxes of tribes provide much revenue for him. It would be different if we were like Egypt. They make much money from crops they sell to Europe. But we do not think that way. The Sultan looks only to taxes to keep his ministers, his army, and his family. If the tribes refuse to pay, he will lack sufficient money. Worse, they could overthrow him, if they sense that he is too weak."

"So, the country is constantly in a state of war, in a way," Lili said.

"May Allah protect us," Tariq said.

"Well," Aisha said tartly, "Those Berber sons of sin don't know any other way of life than banditry and pillaging. Oh, begging your pardon, *Si* Tariq." Aisha pulled herself up short and Lili could see she had remembered that Tariq and his cousin Mehdi came from those Berber tribes themselves, owing allegiance to one of the most powerful lords of the Atlas mountains, Madani al-Glaoui.

"Do not worry, *ya* Mama Aisha," Tariq laughed. "That is why we make such good soldiers. We are natural fighters. We drink it in our mother's milk. But now some of us are on the Sultan's side, so he also has the best."

Lili yawned. "I think it's time for bed. Thank you for coming with us on this trip, *ya* Tariq. It makes me feel safe. Good night."

She rose. Tariq took her hand and kissed it, "Good night to you, little one, and pleasant dreams."

***

Abdel Aziz inspected himself in a mirror admiring his new red uniform made in the English style, with tight fitting pants, high black boots, and a shiny black leather belt. He adjusted the high hat crested with feathers to a jaunty angle. "I like this," he said to *Qaid* Maclean. He strutted around the room where several British friends were seated, drinking tea.

"I say, let's go for a ride. You look splendid," Walter Harris suggested.

"By Allah, that is a good idea," said the young monarch.

Six Western friends accompanied Abdel Aziz as they raced from the palace to the outskirts of the city. On their route they passed a mosque; their laughter drifted back to a mosque interrupting the prayer. Two courtiers, late for the sermon, stopped in their tracks. "Was that our Sultan?"

"Surely he would not carry on in such a godless way," said his friend.

"It could not have been him, dressed like an infidel," the other agreed.

***

At the camp the bath and toilet area was set up behind the tents where the women were settled. This was always a busy location, as mothers wanted to bathe their children, removing at least some of the dust, and many, like Lili, tried to give themselves cursory sponge baths in the evening. There was never much water and the situation was always chaotic, with children everywhere, mothers and servants trying to keep some order.

Lili and Aisha were washing when they heard a woman scream. They rushed to see what the matter was and found a semi-hysterical young woman, half dressed, sobbing that one of the Moroccan soldiers had been watching her bathe. Lili, who had recently attended the wedding of this woman to a junior French diplomat, managed to soothe her and stayed with her while she completed her toilette, then saw her to her tent.

As Lili was returning from her own bath, she saw a group of officers standing in a semi-circle. Tariq was in the middle addressing a young officer who was on his knees before him. Lili saw Tariq lean forward and slap the man hard across his cheek.

That evening Tariq asked Lili to accompany him to the young bride's tent. "She is unhappy and I think it would be better if you were present," he said. "One bad thing like this could spoil the trip and I want to make it right, if I can."

They went together to where the woman was sitting, drinking tea with a few others, who had formed a protective shield around her. Tariq approached the group and bowed. The woman looked up.

"I wish to present my apologies for the incident this afternoon." Tariq spoke in flawless French, which obviously surprised the young bride.

She nodded.

"The man meant you no harm," he began.

Before Tariq could continue one of the older women interrupted. "Shame on you. All you Moroccans are the same. Always after the women."

Tariq's jaw clenched. "I wanted you to know that he has been disciplined and I have instructed him to ride with the baggage mules for the rest of the trip. So he will not be in a position to offend you again in any way."

The young bride bowed, looking like a stiff doll. An older lady sitting next to her spoke up, "Well, it serves him right, that's all I can say. We're respectable ladies and children on this trip and we're expecting you soldiers to look after us. If your men are too brutish to respect our privacy, well, who can we rely on, then? That's what I want to know!"

Tariq nodded his head, his face expressionless. "*Oui*, Madame, I agree. Again, I apologize for the incident and I can assure you it will not happen again."

A silence fell on the group. Tariq and Lili waited a few minutes, but it was clear there was nothing left to say, so they excused themselves. Walking back, Tariq said to Lili, "That which has been made crooked cannot easily be straightened. But I tried."

Lili said, "Tariq, I saw you strike that officer a while ago. That must have been humiliating for him, especially in front of all the others. Was that really necessary?"

"Why do you ask?"

"It just seemed so cruel. In the United States we would discipline someone privately, at least," she said.

"My sister, this is a hard country. This is what people understand. When people make mistakes they must be corrected swiftly and strongly. It is necessary that they understand that their actions could have fatal consequences. That man is a distant relative from Meneb and one I am close to. I did not want to do it, by Allah. But this could have created bad feelings among the wives of these diplomats whom *Sidna* Abdel Aziz is counting on to improve his relations with the West."

"I'm sure he didn't mean any harm," she said.

"Only Allah knows. That is not important. We can not create bad impressions and that man will not make another one."

The rest of the trip proceeded without further mishap, as Tariq had promised. In the evenings when all the children were in bed, the saddle-sore ministered to, and the soldiers chatting and laughing around their campfires, Tariq would come and have a glass of tea with Lili and Aisha. They became easy with each other. Lili learned more about Malika. "You see, my sister Lili. I have a Berber marriage," Tariq explained. "My wife is a young girl who will breed children for me and keep my house. She is unlettered. She has very few expectations from me, only that I provide for her."

Lili nodded, "Arthur and I have similar interests. We like the same books. We enjoy spending time together."

The night before the caravan reached Fez, Tariq came as usual for his tea. After sitting quietly an hour, he stirred. "I should be getting back. We will start early tomorrow." Tariq stood and turned to her, "My sister, Lili, we shall be friends. I like to talk to you. You listen to me, almost like Ted. It will be hard for us to see each other in Fez. It is much more traditional than Tangier. But I will visit you from time to time."

"I've looked forward to our evenings, *ya* Tariq. I want to remain your friend."

"Malika will be in Fez soon. I will call to bring you to our house, so you can meet each other. Until then, *ya* Lili." He strode away.

***

Al-Raisuni rattled his chains in the dank cavernous cell that held him and two other prisoners in Mogador. "Jailer, jailer, for the love of Allah. This man next to me is beginning to stink. He's been dead three days."

The jailer paused in his task. He was checking the chains that connected all the men to each other. He came over to where Raisuni lay sprawled and kicked the corpse next to him. Two rats scurried away. "What're you worried about? At least this way the rats won't eat you."

"No matter what this man did, he deserves a decent burial," Raisuni said.

"Burial, huh? All he'll get is fed to the sharks outside the prison gate."

"May Allah have mercy on his soul. He's already been through Hell here," Al Raisuni said. He closed his eyes, shaking away the matted hair that had grown down to his shoulders to mingle with his long beard. Those devils in Tangier. He had them to thank for rotting away in this pesthole.

CHAPTER SEVEN
1902

Lili set off to see Malika. As she had always done in the Tangier *medina*, she dressed conservatively, throwing a long veil across her hair and crossing it around her neck, so that much of her face was obscured, if not covered. Her brown velvet suit skirt swept the ground, regrettable in the dirt she knew she would find in old city, but unavoidable if she were to hide her ankles. At least the material was dark and didn't call undue attention to herself. The *mellah*, like the one in Tangier, had as many women as men walking in the streets and shopping, but when she stepped down through stairs in the wall leading to the open courtyard of the royal palace, she became uncomfortably aware that she was the only woman there and that people were staring at her. Then, as she entered a narrow street running alongside the palace leading into the *medina*, a crowd of children gathered behind her. She stopped to ask a shopkeeper for directions. The man averted his eyes and refused to answer her. She felt a small stab and realized a sharp pebble had struck her arm. She turned around and saw that about fifty children were following her now. "Who among you threw that stone?" she demanded in Arabic.

A few children looked down, but a bolder urchin in the front started chanting *"nisrania, nisrania,* Christian, Christian."

"Don't you have any manners?" she said to them. "You should be ashamed of yourselves. Leave me alone."

The mob of children laughed, and then someone threw another rock, which glanced off Lili's shoulder. As she sensed the ugly mood of this small mob Lili began to be afraid. She ducked back into the shelter of the shop where she had asked directions. "Please, *ya sidi*," she appealed to the shopkeeper. "I am a stranger here. My husband works with the Sultan. Please help me."

The shopkeeper paused, still not meeting her eyes. Then he opened the small gate that formed part of his counter and went out to the street. "That's enough, now," he said to the children. "You, Mohammed, your father would not want to see you out here. You, Ahmed, get back to the shop where you belong, *yallah*". He spoke to the crowd for a few minutes, and little by little it dispersed, children slinking off, trying to avoid his angry gaze.

He came back into the shop and addressed Lili, still not looking at her. "*Ya binti*, my child, you should not try to walk in the *medina* alone." Calling to a teen-aged boy who worked in his shop, he instructed him to walk Lili back to the *mellah*.

***

From a distance, a youngish man with a diseased left eye, watched. He had been leading his donkey through the streets, looking for work, and the disturbance had caught his attention.

"Look where you're going, *ya* Bou Hamara (donkey owner)," a rider shouted.

***

When Aisha saw Lili return, bruised and hurt, she scolded her, "*Ya habibti*, the rest of Morocco is nothing like Tanja (Tangier). Women never go out here unescorted. You were asking for trouble! If you want to see Fez, you must take an escort of one or two men, to be sure everyone knows you are a woman of consequence and honor, and not just some no-account foreigner!"

Lili set out again, several days later, this time accompanied by her steward and her face covered by a gauze veil. Old Fez was like a bowl, in which she was standing on the rim and gradually slipping down towards a river that ran through its center. Narrow cobblestone streets led from gates at the top of the city, steadily descending to the water and then up to the other side. Dingy mud colored houses rose on both sides, forming canyons that filtered out most of the light. In places the houses actually met overhead, or were connected by bridges, similar to what Lili had seen in Venice on her honeymoon. Scattered here and there colorful mosaic fountains built by the wealthy offered water to the population, but they were so crowded with users that Lili could barely make them out.

Smells of manure, cedarwood, spices, rotting animal carcasses, oranges, mint mingled in a nauseating miasma. As they descended towards Malika's house, the steward holding her bridle, Lili wanted to dismount, rather than cling to the mule's saddle, leaning over it at a 45-degree incline, as it slipped on the slimy cobblestones. But looking at the filth in the streets, she quickly decided the best course of action was to hang on.

The noise battered her from all sides. Mules carrying heavy wide loads of lumber, bags of wheat, furniture, skittered dangerously down the street, their owners running behind calling out to warn passersby that these pack animals would not stop and could well knock them down if they failed to remove themselves quickly. Donkeys brayed in protest at their loads; horses whinnied in fright as they tried to escape from the heavy traffic. After about ten minutes, Lili had to fight a powerful urge to escape, her head throbbing and her stomach churning from the overload of sensations.

Malika's house was a haven of quiet and peace, strange in the middle of the busy *medina*. Like the Legation in Tangier, its entrance hall took several turns until it reached an open tiled courtyard, shaded by a hibiscus tree growing in its center. Lili supposed the thick walls muffled the noises. She could actually hear birds singing in the cage hanging in the tree.

A slovenly-looking maid led her to the room where Malika was sitting spinning wool.

The room was furnished in typical Moroccan style, with wool-stuffed sofas lining the wall, pillows at their back making a couch-like seating arrangement on the tiled floor. The plumpness and newness of these cushions, richly covered in green damask shot with gold, proclaimed Malika's newly-married state. A five-month old baby was lying near her on a large red and black rug, crying. She struggled awkwardly to her feet, dropping the spindle, and revealing a crumpled and none-too-clean robe. "You must be Lili!" she exclaimed. "*Si* Tariq told me you would be coming, but I wasn't sure when. Ahlen, *ya* Lili, *ahlen!*"

This vulnerable young girl immediately appealed to Lili. She was slight; her skin was very fair, as Lili had noticed on many Arab and Berber women who rarely went outside. She had large, startled-looking eyes, with slight blue shadows under them. Her neck was covered with an ornate tattoo in a cross-stitch pattern imitating a necklace, and between her eyebrows and on her chin small matching motifs of this design were repeated in dark indigo. She wore her long black hair in braids wrapped round her head and covered by a scarf in such a way that it gave the impression of a crown, slightly higher in the center of her forehead.

Malika still dressed like the Berbers of her village, in two long pieces of white cotton attached at the shoulders by heavy silver ornaments that served to fasten the material. Under the robe, Malika wore a hand-knit long-sleeved red sweater.

The servant brought them tea. A silence followed, filled by polite smiles on both sides. Finally Malika burst out, "You're so beautiful!" and she burst into tears.

"So are you, my sister," Lili said.

"I'm so lonely here," Malika said, wiping her tears. "I miss my mother and my sisters. My maid is lazy; she won't do as I say. And *Si* Tariq complains every day that the food isn't good enough."

"I'm sure he doesn't mean it," Lili said. "It's just being in a strange town and not having friends. I, too, have the same problem."

"Really?" Malika looked up hopefully.

Lili felt drawn to the young, frightened girl, away from her family for the first time, saddled with a baby, a new household, and a husband who expected her to manage everything.

***

Abdel Aziz stood in his harem surrounded by a handful of his favorite wives and concubines. Several mirrors were set up and a eunuch was unpacking large crates, passing the contents to the Sultan.

Abdel Aziz held up a long turquoise ball gown. "Here, Aziza, try this. You have a small waist and it should fit. There's a corset there to help."

The young girl held the material to her cheek, "It is so soft, *sidna*. May Allah repay you."

"I ordered these from a tailor called Worth in Paris. Some one told me all the ladies there wear his clothes. Here, Fatima, try this velvet. I think it is for afternoon wear." He plucked out a dark red ensemble.

Fatima kissed his hand, "*Sidna*, you are so good to us." She giggled as she held up the bustle. "It is strange."

"There are one hundred dresses here. After you have had your pick, the other women will choose. Here is a nice ermine cape. Who wants to try this?"

Twelve hands reached as he threw it in the air.

***

Lili was having tea with Malika in the sunny tiled courtyard of her home, when Tariq came in. Smiling at Lili, he sank down on the cushions.

"Allah, this thing with the English missionary, David Cooper, is turning into a nightmare."

Lili said, "What's happened?"

"This young Christian missionary entered a very holy shrine, the tomb of Moulay Idriss, the founder of Fez. Always there is a chain across, to keep people out, but today they were careless. A pilgrim from the countryside saw Cooper. He felt he had, would you say, violated? Yes, violated this sacred place. So he took his rifle and shot Cooper. May Allah grant him peace. Cooper died immediately. The palace is in an uproar. The British insist that *Sidna* Abdel Aziz punish the assassin."

"Well, he should," Lili said. "Oh, I suppose some of the Moroccans consider the pilgrim a hero?"

"Yes, many think he did his duty, nothing more. The Chamberlain, *Si* Fadoul Gharnit, and the *Wazir* (Minister) of Foreign Affairs, *Si* Ben Slimane, and their friends, think the Sultan is too friendly with the Christians, especially the British. They insist that *Sidna* protect the killer."

These two men had been hand-chosen by Tariq's cousin,

Mehdi, to hold high office, because he had counted on their allegiance to him. But over the past few years, they had seen that Mehdi Al-Menebbhi, although holding a relatively junior position compared to theirs, had gained influence and power through his closeness to the Throne. When they realized that the riches they had expected their offices to bring were instead flowing to Mehdi, both men began to plot against him. Now that the Court was in Fez, where the religious and more conservative men's opinions carried weight, Gharnit and Ben were creating a strong faction opposed to the modernizing favored by Al-Menebbhi and supported by Abdel Aziz.

"But surely they can't ignore the fact that a British citizen was murdered?" Lili asked.

"What the British think is of no concern to most, you know. This will be difficult for Abdel Aziz. No matter what he does, some one will be unhappy. May Allah help him."

**

Ted and Meriam were arriving for a visit. Ted had been commissioned by his London newspaper to find out more about what was going on in Fez.

It will be wonderful to have company, Lili thought. She didn't particularly like the diplomatic families who had come to Fez with them. They were insular, tried to recreate their European living situations rather than adapting, told hurtful and sarcastic stories about Moroccans, and obviously counted the days until they could return to their homelands.

She and Aisha had worked hard to turn their small house into a comfortable home, but it was still dark and damp, as were so many of the *mellah,* residences. Her rooms were arranged Arab-style with mats or rugs on the floor and wool-stuffed cushions on wooden frames around the walls replacing beds. Every room except the kitchen could serve double duty as meeting or reception rooms during the day and sleeping quarters at night.

This furnishing had been dictated in large part by the near impossibility of finding Western articles in Fez, while transport by caravan from Tangier severely limited Lili's ability to bring cumbersome wardrobes, chairs, bed frames, and the furniture she was more used to. But she had become accustomed now to the convenience of the Moroccan way.

Aisha was coaxing the coals in a small charcoal brazier from gray to scarlet, and grumbling at the young kitchen assistant. "Allah, I miss that iron range in Tangier. Who would have thought in my old age I'd be back to cooking like my mother did, God rest her soul."

"Oh well, Aisha," Lili said, "at least you have plenty of help." She considered in amazement the number of servants needed to run this relatively small house: the kitchen girl, a cook, a doorkeeper, and a steward to do the daily shopping that couldn't be undertaken by women in this strict environment. "But I hope you're all ready for Ted and Meriam. They'll definitely be here by dinnertime, and we should have something ready in case they arrive early. And did you make a special treat for Arielle?"

"Don't worry about that, *ya binti*," Aisha reassured her. "We've got plenty of little surprises and treats for my favorite baby. I just wish we had one of our own in this house."

Lili poured some warm water into a large pitcher to take up for Arthur to wash, as he often liked to when he came home. He said he felt dirty after being out in the city or at court all day. She wanted a child desperately and was jealous every time she saw Arielle. Having a child would give her life some meaning. But it just wasn't happening.

In late afternoon, banging at the door announced the arrival of Ted, Meriam and Arielle, bedraggled, dust covered, sun burnt and exhausted from the long journey. Aisha hustled Meriam and the baby off to wash and rest, but Ted settled down to have tea with Lili.

As the porter helped him pull off his boots, Ted stretched out luxuriously wriggling his feet in the soft cushions, "Ah, what a change from that infernal saddle! I thought we should never get here."

"I hope you'll stay a long time. We don't get enough guests here to let them depart easily," Lili said.

"Are you bored?" Ted asked her, scanning her face.

"Not really. But there are so few of us here and it seems like we just exchange the same gossip round and round. There are no restaurants or tea houses for foreigners and of course, no theater. Thank God Matt and Amelia send me books whenever they can. "

Lili knew that Ted would be interested in the Cooper murder and told him what she knew. She was just getting to her concerns when the door sounded again and Arthur entered, accompanied by Tariq.

Lili called for more tea and told Aisha to bring some snacks for the men. They settled back down in the cozy room, as the rays from the setting sun gradually tinted it deep gold, then finally faded, leaving just the glow of the lanterns mounted on the walls. Aisha brought *milawi*, a flaky pastry cut into long strings and tossed with melted butter, sugar and cinnamon. Meriam came in, looking washed and fresh, and sank into a corner next to Lili, gratefully accepting the hot mint tea.

They settled down for a chat, while the men began discussing the Cooper murder. Lili listened with half an ear, wondering how the young Sultan would handle this crisis.

Finally there was a lull and she found her chance to ask the question that had been bothering her all day. "Is this incident likely to have any repercussions on the foreign community, Ted?"

Ted looked thoughtful. "It could. I think Tariq would agree with me that, although *Moulay* Abdel Aziz favors the Westerners, and of course, invited them to come to court, most of the other people at the palace see us as a bad influence."

Although *Si* Fadoul Gharnit, the Chamberlain, and Ben Slimane, the Foreign Minister, had hoped the move to Fez would remove Abdel Aziz from the frivolous habits he had indulged in in Marrakesh, instead he had brought his companions with him to Fez. Many of these were either young Moroccans, like Mehdi al Menebbhi and Tariq, or British visitors, encouraged to come by *Qaid* Maclean to amuse the Sultan. The *ulema*, the religious elders saw having Christians in Fez as an insult to Islam.

Ted said, "Wasn't Gharnit originally suggested for his position by Mehdi?"

"Yes," Tariq said. "It is complicated, as is everything in Morocco, you know, Ted."

In fact, Gharnit had failed to understand the strength of the friendship between Abdel Aziz and Mehdi al Menebbhi, who spent almost all of his waking hours with the Sultan. These young men were close in age, and loved sports. Mehdi was a genius at thinking of new amusements for the Court, fireworks, bicycle races, polo, tennis, bridge, there was something new every day. Gharnit had pushed for the move to Fez, but it had not changed Abdel Aziz's behavior, nor his preference for fun-loving youth rather than the serious religious elders. Mehdi was still the favorite, the games continued, and there were wasteful fireworks regularly. The conservative people of Fez, watching the skies turn pink, and blue and gold, thought it was the work of the Devil, and the *ulema*, urged on by Gharnit and Ben Slimane, blamed it all on the British.

Ted thought about this information. "If Abdel Aziz punishes the Muslim who murdered this English missionary, the *ulema* could accuse their Sultan of being a bad Muslim and not fit to be the head of Islam in Morocco."

"Yes, because Cooper broke the sanctity of the holy shrine," Tariq said. "And if Abdel Aziz doesn't punish him, the British and maybe the rest of the foreigners, could withdraw money they have promised to lend us, which we need."

Lili sighed, "It sounds to me like no matter what Abdel Aziz does, it's likely that we'll become even more unpopular here,"

"I would agree," Ted said. "And the Sultan won't be able to protect us." Abdel Aziz had his advisors around him, some of whom were trusted friends like Tariq and Ted, but many of whom had other, more hidden agendas. His favored companions like Mehdi and Tariq, wanted change in the country and Abdel Aziz was interested in their ideas to build roads, to improve the army, and have a railroad. Improving tax collection was key, but at every step along the way, they were thwarted by the conservatives, who liked things just as they were, muttering imprecations that these innovations were ungodly. More likely, Ted thought, there was less money in graft for them. He wondered whether Abdel Aziz would have enough time to learn how to play off these different factions. "Tomorrow, *insha'llah*," Ted said, "I'd like to go to the palace with you, Tariq, if I may."

Tariq said, "I know Ali wants to discuss this with you. Abdel Aziz depends on him for advice in dealing with the foreigners, and he would value your opinion. And you can write about it for London. I regret we will not see your words here. I miss the newspapers we had in France. You will see Kassim al-Matari, too. He has gotten close to the Sultan."

Ted raised his eyebrows. "I suppose I should have expected that. He left Oxford some time ago."

***

When Ted and Tariq arrived at the palace crowds of people were milling around, headed in the general direction of the Sultan's audience hall.

Dressed as he often was in a fine wool *djellabah* with a white skullcap covering much of his close-cropped red hair, Ted blended easily into the crowd and was able unobtrusively to make his way into the room, walking with Tariq. This would make a great story for the Times.

They found themselves a corner with a good view. Abdel Aziz was seated in the center, surrounded by his counselors and the ulema. Before him was a slight man, perhaps fifty years old, dressed in the rough brown *djellabah* of a tribesman. He was holding something in his hand.

Ted nudged Tariq. "What's that?"

Tariq squinted, and then consulted a neighbor to his right. "A relic from the shrine of *Moulay* Idriss. That should protect him, as it has great *baraka*, or magic. It gives him the same right of sanctuary he would have if he were at the shrine. That is what he is saying now to Abdel Aziz." Tariq said quietly to Ted, "Do you see Kassim? Right there next to Gharnit?"

Ted nodded. He focused on the Sultan and his prisoner. He was curious to see if this fun-loving young prince could exert enough authority to handle this case. Abdel Aziz's face was contorted with rage. He began questioning the pilgrim.

"Who told you to kill this *nisrani*, this Christian?"

"Why, it was *Moulay* Idriss who told me, *ya sidi.*"

"Did you ever think perhaps *Moulay* Idriss himself called for this *nisrani* to come to his pilgrimage?"

The pilgrim stuttered, "I entered the shrine to fulfill my pilgrimage, *ya sidi.*"

"So did the *nisrani*, for all we know. Our Saint is strong enough to protect all human beings, if he is so inclined, no matter who they are. So answer my question. Who told you to kill him?"

The man looked down and mumbled, "No one. It was myself."

"But what idea pushed you to murder?"

"He was a *nisrani*, a foreigner. He didn't have the right to desecrate the sanctuary."

"So tell me, you son of a donkey who understands nothing, don't you know Muslims, Christians and Jews are all men, brothers, even if they don't have the same religion? To kill a man you must have a reason and so far I don't see one."

"*Sidna, Moulay* Idriss himself told me to kill him."

The Sultan gestured for the keepers of the sanctuary who had accompanied the pilgrim to court to come forward. He held out 200 *douros* and said, "I doubt that you know the gravity of this man's action. If *Moulay* Idriss were in our place, he would have already executed him. Now think a little about all the problems that will result for the *makhsen* (government) with the Europeans, of all the compensation we must give them, and understand that I can not leave this act unpunished. I am tired of all the attacks against foreigners for one reason or another. We must make a dramatic example. The Christian was wrong to enter your sanctuary, but no one has the right to kill all those who make a mistake or do wrong. You may now withdraw."

As the holy men withdrew, the tribesman started to say something. Abruptly the young Sultan silenced him with a raised hand, his voice trembling with anger. "You say the Saint made you do it. Well, the Saint now orders me to have you killed." His soldiers surrounded the pilgrim and dragged him away.

A murmur went around the room. Ted could see people breaking into small groups, muttering among themselves. Abdel Aziz strode quickly from the room, Ali close behind him.

Ted turned to Tariq. "Now there'll be bloody hell to pay."

Tariq turned his palms upward. "The killer made a mistake in challenging Abdel Aziz like that. It was as if he were daring him. You know how *Sidna* is. It would be hard for him to resist such a dare. But Allah *awwen na*, God help us now. The *ulema* will not like this."

Shots from the courtyard announced that the execution had been carried out. Just as Tariq predicted, the killer's head hanging on Fez's walls gave all the religious fanatics, and anyone else who wanted one, an excuse to criticize Abdel Aziz. They had all the proof they needed that he was totally under the influence of the foreign devils and no longer a devout Muslim worthy to be the leader of the faithful in Morocco. People even said he wasn't truly the son of his father, but the son of *Qaid* Maclean.

***

Kassim slipped quietly out of Fez and rode fast towards the east, making sure he was not followed. The third day he arrived at a large campsite, where hundreds of white tents covered the dusty plain. He looked around, impressed. There had to be at least three thousand men here. He stopped a young boy leading a mule and demanded, "Where is the man you call Bou Hamara?"

The boy pointed to a large tent in the middle of the gathering. Kassim threw his reins to the startled boy and walked over to the tent. As he tried to enter, two burly tribesmen stopped him, "Who wants to see our Lord?"

"I am Kassim al-Matar and I have valuable information for your leader," Kassim said.

The two men hesitated and then a voice from within called out, "Let the visitor enter."

Inside the darkness of the tent he slowly made out a man dressed in white, about forty years old, tall and slim, with a wall-eye. The man beckoned him to come closer. "Well, my son, what is your business with me?"

"Are you the man they call Bou Hamara?"

"Some people call me that, yes."

"I think I could be helpful to you."

"I seek my rightful place as the Sultan of Morocco. My brother, Abdel Aziz, was wrongly put there by Ba Ahmed. I am the elder and deserve the throne."

Kassim bowed, "Yes, I have heard rumors that someone was claiming to be *Sidi* Mohammed. But others say he died at the time *Sidna* became Sultan."

"It is a lie. I am he. See, here you can see scars from the shackles that bound me in the prison where Ba Ahmed kept me. How I suffered there. But now I am free and claim what is due me."

Kassim had heard these stories from other sources. He had also heard that this Pretender was in fact a low-level engineer who had been imprisoned for theft during the time of Ba Ahmed, and had recently returned from Algeria where he had learned to be a magician. But for his purposes Bou Hamara's claim was good enough.

"People in Fez tire of our young lord, *ya sidi*. They say he is godless; some even say he is a Christian."

Bou Hamara said, "Yes, it grieves me to hear these stories of my young brother. He was always given to levity and is not fit to rule."

"I think I can be of use to you, your Excellency," Kassim said.

"In what way?"

"I am welcome at the Court and hear much information about military affairs. I could easily pass such information along to you, details about how well armed the *guish*, army, is, how many men they have, their plans."

"Yes, that could be useful. We will soon be mounting an attack. As you can see, I have many tribal leaders with me."

"*Ya sidi*," Kassim said, "there are powerful foreigners who are not happy with the situation at court. The British have too much influence there. I have talked to the Spanish and some Frenchmen who would willingly give you funds, if only to weaken the influence of the English devils."

Bou Hamara patted Kassim's hand. "I will need those funds. Make that your first priority. With enough money I can arm a tribal force that will easily overcome the royal *guish*."

Kassim bowed again. "It will be done, Excellency."

CHAPTER EIGHT
1903

L earning that her Aunt Rebecca was expecting her fourth child, Meriam insisted that Ted take her to Taza to help her aunt through the pregnancy. Rebecca had been a second mother to her when she had lived with them in Tangier, now Meriam felt duty bound to look after her.

Tariq objected strenuously. "Taza is not calm, *ya* Ted. Bou Hamara has made it his headquarters and every day more people gather to him. It is not a safe place for our sister, Meriam."

"I didn't really have a choice, *ya* Tariq. Meriam's aunt is not well and she insists on staying with her. I don't like it, either, but I don't think I can do much about it."

Bou Hamara continued to build his strength in the region of Taza. Lili became more concerned about Meriam and knew Ted felt the same. She was relieved when Ted and Tariq made a trip to Taza, traveling mostly at night to see if they could extricate Meriam. Ted was wild when they came back to Fez without her.

"By God," he told Lili. "I couldn't insist that she leave, with Rebecca looking like she would die any minute. But, Lili, what should I do? Things look worse and worse in the countryside; you can see the tension in Taza. I would have stayed if I could, but the Times is expecting weekly reports from me on this situation, and my sources are all here in Fez."

Lili spotted fifty new heads hanging high on the walls of

the city. Tariq told her these were some of Bou Hamara's men that Mehdi and he had overcome in a recent skirmish. This made the danger real to her in a way it hadn't been and forced her to the decision that had been forming in her mind.

"I'm going to stay with Meriam," she told Ted and Arthur at dinner. "I can't leave her on her own."

"That is totally preposterous," Arthur said. "I simply won't allow it. It's just too dangerous. I don't want you living out there with those wild men all around."

Ted protested, too, but Lili could tell that despite his arguments, he wanted her to go, hoping that she could convince Meriam to leave.

Lili sat down in front of her mirror and cut her hair to chin level. It would be safer to travel disguised as a boy. The mirror reflected back a youth, admittedly a bit delicate, but still a young man. Take away the dress and add a rough *djellabah* and turban and a bit of dirt, she thought, and I'll pass.

The night before her departure, Arthur drank a bottle of wine with dinner, barely talking to Lili.

In bed, Lili tried to make amends.

"I may not see you for several months."

He put his arms around her; his sour wine-flavored breath nauseated her. "Please don't go, Lili." He pulled her close.

Reluctantly, Lili willed herself to surrender to his lovemaking. It had been at least a month, she reminded herself, and it was her duty. But the wine had done its work and he was unable to perform.

"You don't realize how much I need you, Lili. It's hard for me living here. You're all I have."

"Arthur, you know I'm not doing this to hurt you. It's just that I can't bear to think of Meriam being in such a dilemma without a friend to support her. You have lots of people here. And Aisha can keep your house..."

"Aisha is a maid. You're my wife. Lili, you really don't understand. I love you! I want you near me all the time. Something might happen to you. I don't like living in Fez. Without you…. Oh, why bother to explain?" he shook his head, discouraged.

Lili took his hand, "Arthur, please. I do understand what you're saying, but I must do this."

***

As Ted and Lili set out, Tariq rode up, tall and proud. "I will accompany you." They protested, but Tariq held up his hand, "This is not a good idea and one I oppose. But as I can see that this little one is determined, I will show you the safest way to go. I know this route like my own house. And Ted should not come back alone. So it is settled."

When the trip was over Lili realized they could never have managed without Tariq. He knew all the back roads and also the locations of the enemy encampments and led them safely around them. They traveled at night and during the day he steered them to empty caves where they could sleep and hide their horses, avoiding detection. Despite the danger, Lili admitted to herself that she was happier on this trip than she had been for ages. Dressed as a boy, she was once again free to behave as she wanted; she was out in the open air rather than enclosed in the dark environment of her walled home in Fez. She loved the early mornings when they made a small campfire and sat drinking tea as the sun came up. In the evenings when Ted woke her, they would sit briefly and eat a little dried meat before mounting their horses. Tariq always took the lead. She rode between Ted and Tariq, moving quietly, staying in the cover of the trees, as there was a full moon and always danger that a stray scout or group camped for the night could detect them. Several times they passed close to a campfire, but Tariq steered them downwind and they slowed their horses to a walk. A feeling of true camaraderie grew up between the three of them. Tariq accepted her man's clothing as natural, and he referred to her as Larabi half the time.

They spent two days and nights on the road, and in some ways Lili was almost disappointed when they arrived at Taza the morning of the third, just as the city gate was being opened.

They hurried through the just-awakening city, avoiding the clusters of ragged men who Lili assumed were Bou Hamara's scouts. Tariq kept his face down and moved quickly by them, tugging Lili's horse. Momentarily she thought how dangerous this was for Tariq. If he were caught, he would undoubtedly be shot on the spot. But if Tariq thought of this, he didn't show it.

***

Sitting at a small café drinking coffee, Kassim looked up curiously when the three riders went by. He was always interested when he saw newcomers. The patch of red hair caught his attention and he whistled to himself as he recognized Ted. He grabbed the sleeve of a passing coffee boy and threw him a coin, "There'll be more of this if you follow those three riders and tell me where they go."

The boy grinned and ran off. "Don't worry. I'll find them, *ya sidi.*"

***

Lili and the two men rode quickly to the squalid Jewish *mellah.* Lili held her breath to avoid the stench of rotting garbage; she watched dogs and goats competing with scrawny chickens for any edible items left along the sides of the road. Ragged urchins squatted, defecating near piles of debris. They looked ill, undernourished, but she thought that wasn't surprising. With all the rebel movement in the countryside, regular markets were meeting less often and provisions were scarce. Even at this early hour Lili could see lines of barefoot children forming near the few shops not yet open. She suspected that whatever supplies there were probably went straight to Bou Hamara and his troops. She noticed that many of the houses, even in this quarter, looked abandoned. Many must have fled when the Pretender moved in, figuring that things would just get worse.

Ted led them straight to Rebecca and Israel's house which, although unprepossessing from the outside, was spacious and comfortable inside. One of the children admitted them and led them to the large first floor room, where they found Meriam sitting around a table with the family, having breakfast. Meriam's face showed disbelief, quickly followed by a relief, so pure and transparent, then replaced by sheer joy, as she took in all members of the party.

"Ted and Tariq and...oh *mon dieu*, is that you, Lili? *Ce n'est pas possible*! I can not believe it! What are you all doing here?" she said, laughing and crying as she hugged them all.

Lili gave her friend a big kiss. "You need my help more than anyone else right now," she said. "So I made them bring me."

Rebecca's boys, Michel and Gerard, were sixteen and fourteen. Michel was a thin, tall boy with the beginnings of a moustache. He wore scholarly round-framed glasses to strengthen his weak eyes and was shy and unsure of himself. His family had encouraged him to become a rabbi, and he spent most of his time pouring over the Torah and studying Hebrew with local scholars.

Gerard was a lively, sturdier boy who assisted his father in his money lending activities, often accompanying him as he visited debtors to collect payments or assess the value of property offered as collateral. Hannah, eight years younger, was the long-awaited only daughter of the household.

Lili unloaded the supplies they had brought; dried apricots, pickled lemons, olives, dates filled the kitchen with their fragrance. Sacks of flour, cinnamon, chickpeas, lentils, almonds added to the profusion. Lili had carried twenty loaves of sugar in her own saddlebags. She produced cooked lamb and beef, packed in oil by Sarah Benoliel, Leah and Rebecca's mother, who lived near them in the Fez *mellah*.

"*Quel luxe*," Meriam said. "What treasures! It has been *très difficile*, trying to keep this family fed. I can hardly remember when we have had meat, or fruit. And I finished our last olives weeks ago. *Merci*."

"Well, we'll find ways to use it sparingly," Lili said. "Ted will bring us more." Lili was dismayed that her friend, usually so well groomed, was bedraggled; her hair barely combed; her skin sallow making her freckles appear prominent on her much-thinner face. Her eyes were dull, and she had a strained and tired look. Meriam was no longer dressed in her modish French clothes, but was wearing the full silk skirts and black velvet vests worn by traditional Jews. She later explained to Lili that without her maid she couldn't maintain her lovely ruffled and pleated outfits. These were much more practical.

"Oh, *cherie*," Meriam said, "It has been so hard! Rebecca is really *malade*, and I do not know what to do for her. I have been trying to keep the house and feed the children, but *ce n'est pas facile*."

"Well, we'll manage better together," Lili comforted her, hoping it was true. "I can cook and look after Hannah, and keep you company, at least!"

Later that day, Tariq took Lili aside. "It does not please me to leave you here. This is dangerous."

"Tariq, I understand. But Meriam shouldn't be here by herself. She needs help and it's just as dangerous for her."

"All right." A small frown of annoyance creased his forehead. "I see I can not change your mind. So, it is necessary for you to take these." From a knapsack he pulled out a long, sharp dagger, as well as a shorter, even more lethal one.

"This small one, *ya* Lili, wear it always. You can attach the scabbard to your leg where it will be hidden. No," he held up his hand, as she started to remonstrate, "you must promise me never to be without it. And the longer *jenbiya*, my sister, hide this somewhere where you could get to it in a hurry. Think like a soldier. If someone broke in here, where could you find it before them? Put it there, maybe under the cushions in one of the main rooms. Somewhere you could reach it if you need it."

As Lili started to refuse, he stopped her, gently putting his hand on her arm, "By Allah, things may get very bad here. No matter which side wins, if Taza is taken, soldiers will overrun this town. And they will break into these houses, looking for loot. If that should happen, Allah forbid, you must be prepared to use these. Do you understand what I say, *ya* Lili?" He took her hands, and looked intently into her eyes, studying her face and then releasing her with a sigh. "Be careful. I will come when I can, or send someone who can bring me messages from you, if you need me. If it is not me who comes, the messenger will use the code word 'Larabi'. You can trust him."

***

Although visibly pregnant, the rest of Rebecca's body was emaciated. Her skin was waxy and yellow and her hair, once her finest feature, was thin and dry. Her eyes appeared huge in her sunken face, in which every bone stood out. She clutched at Lili. "I know I look awful. I hope I don't frighten you."

Lili leaned over her reassuringly, covering her hand with her own. "Nonsense, I'm just so glad to be here to help you and Meriam." Nevertheless Lili fled the sickroom as soon as she could, feeling powerless to help and ashamed of her revulsion at the stale odors of the sick bed.

***

Abdel Aziz stood in the front courtyard of his palace, running his hands over the sleek exterior of a Hispano-Suiza motor car. "Look, *ya* Mehdi, is it not beautiful? I have even had a man trained to drive it."

Mehdi smiled, "But I would like to drive it, myself, *sidna*. Will you allow me?"

Abdel Aziz called for a servant to crank up the car. "Yes, take us for a ride."

They settled themselves on the soft leather cushions and soon the car's engine turned over. Mehdi put his foot on the gas the car lurched forward, stopping with a loud backfire. A curious slave who had been watching shrieked and ran into the palace, crying, "It is the Devil!"

Mehdi tried again, with no better success. He got out and signaled to the chauffeur, standing nearby. "Take us for a drive."

"Yes, my lord."

The two young men got into the back and the driver started the engine with little trouble. He drove several times around the cobbled courtyard.

"Take us outside," Abdel Aziz commanded.

The courtyard doors opened and the car bumped out, both

men gripping the seats as the tires met rocks and holes in the unpaved surface, while unwary passersby scattered in terror. The ride got rougher and rougher; the car slid into a deep mud hole and came to a stop. The driver got out to inspect. "My Lord, there is nothing I can do. I think the axle is broken."

Abdel Aziz and Mehdi descended, sinking up to their knees in the mud. The young Sultan slapped Mehdi on the back, "It was fun while it lasted, was it not?"

***

Lili went down to breakfast to be greeted by three hungry men and the child, Hannah. "What can we eat, sister Lili?" Hannah asked, too young to be embarrassed.

Lili found bread and eggs and started water boiling for tea. Meriam had forgotten to bank the fire the night before and it took a half hour to get the brazier hot enough. "Tomorrow," she said to Michel, "if you come down before me, get these embers hot and put on the kettle. Then it'll be easier and faster for us to eat."

"I can wash the floor." Hannah told her after Israel and the boys left. "Do you want to see how I do it?"

Lili rose just as Meriam came down the stairs with a huge bundle of dirty linen. "Here," Lili said. "I'll do those. You sit and have some tea." Meriam sat for a minute, then started making fresh tea for Rebecca.

Hannah ran around the room, showing off her washing skills. Then she went into the salon and came back with the rugs and mats that covered the floor. "Shall I put these out in the sun, sister Lili?" Lili nodded. She had forgotten that was a daily chore. And what to do about this linen? She remembered seeing Aisha boiling big cauldrons of water and asked Meriam if they had such a thing. Meriam pointed to the courtyard where a huge copper pot rested. "Lili, it shames me to admit how long it has been since I washed clothes. Or myself."

"Well, that's why I came. No one could do all this herself." Lili was grateful to discover that the Rabines had their own well in the court and for the next half hour she drew buckets of water from it and filled the cauldron, which she had set boiling on another brazier. When the water was warm enough, she called Hannah, who was playing in the room with Rebecca. "You and Meriam take some of this warm water and wash yourselves. Then Meriam can use some to wash Mama."

"Tante Meriam washes Mama every day," the child said.

Of course, that was so like Meriam. Lili plunged her arms into the remaining soapy water and rubbed the sheets and clothes up and down on a scrub board. After ten minutes her knuckles were bleeding.

Meriam, clean and fresh from her sponge bath, came out and found her sitting on her knees, holding her hands in pain. "Oh, *cherie*, I had the same experience! *Finalement* one's hands toughen. Here, I will finish this. Maybe you could clean the lamps."

The lamps. Lili had never given them a moment's thought. They were always sparkling in her house. Hannah began bringing them out into the courtyard. All were black with soot. Lili and the little girl took soft white rags and washed them, trimming the wicks and refilling them with kerosene. "Is it hard to get kerosene?" she asked Meriam, scrubbing away beside her.

"Not for the moment," she said. "The shops still sell that, probably because even the soldiers have need of them." A weak call came from upstairs and Meriam dropped her washing.

"I'll finish," Lili said. Most of the laundry was clean and just needed to be wrung out and hung to dry. Lili looked at the little pocket watch she carried. It was two o'clock. "Hannah, you must be hungry." The child nodded, shyly. Lili stood up stiffly and went to the kitchen where she scrambled some eggs and mixed them with tomatoes and cumin. Meriam joined them and they ate hungrily, using their fingers and pieces of bread. Thank God, Lili thought, the men don't come home for lunch. But she probably needed to start thinking about dinner soon. She took some lentils from the provisions they had brought and put them in a bowl to soak. And bread, oh God, she had totally forgotten. "What time does the *ferran* (public oven) open?" she asked Meriam.

"At the afternoon prayer."

Quickly Lili assembled flour, yeast, salt and found Rebecca's kneading bowl. Aisha had shown her once or twice when she was young, but she wasn't sure she remembered how to make bread. Meriam had gone back to Rebecca, and Hannah watched her critically, as Lili's hesitation made her inexperience obvious. As Lili poured the flour into the bowl and made a hole in the middle, Hannah handed her a small bowl of yeast starter. "Mama always uses this, and then when she's done kneading, she puts a little back in here."

Oh yes, Lili remembered. Aisha did that, too. It was like the fire. You never let it all go out. She mixed and kneaded, and kneaded until she thought she couldn't move another inch. But Hannah looked critically at the dough and said, "Mama's doesn't look like that. Hers has just little bubbles and is smooth."

So she kneaded some more and then pronounced, "That's it. Even if it's not great bread, we should be able to eat it." Lili patted the dough into four rounds and put them on a board. "Here, Hannah, can you take these to the *ferran*?"

Hannah nodded. "They want one or two *fils*" and she held out her hand.

Lili stood up and handed her a few pennies. Her back was breaking. She looked outside and saw the rugs and blankets, still hanging on the wall. Moving slowly she gathered them up. Meriam came back down, apologizing again for not being able to help. Together they put everything back in the salon and shared a moment of satisfaction at the freshness and neatness they had created.

They finished preparations for a simple dinner of lentils, bread and some dried figs. The family sat together and ate, almost silently, no one complaining about Lili's lumpy dry bread. Lili was almost in tears, but Israel patted her hand and said, "Bless you, my sister. Do not fret. You will learn. And bread is sacred, no matter how it is made."

At least, Lili thought, I'm glad we eat Arab style. Just one plate and no utensils. The washing up was easy and only took a few minutes. As soon as she could, she crawled up the stairs and collapsed into bed. Lili promised herself in the future never to underestimate the efforts of Aisha and the rest of her staff in Fez.

***

In Mogador, one of Al-Raisuni's supporters came to see him. The *Sherif* had been moved to a better cell with a window. He was still draped in chains, which had rubbed festering sores into his arms and legs.

"*Ya Sherif,*" the visitor said. "This is a very special loaf of bread for you. *Insh'allah* it will raise your spirits."

"May Allah recompense you for your generosity," Al-Raisuni replied.

The man kissed the filthy rags covering the *Sherif*'s shoulder and left.

Al-Raisuni moved to a corner of the room and broke open

the loaf. "My friends," he said to the two other prisoners in the room. "Allah has blessed us." He lifted a heavy metal file from the bread. "At night we will start working on these bars. I will send out a message to have a boat waiting for us when we are ready."

***

In Taza there were little reminders of the preparations for war going on outside their door. Often in the night bands of men marching by the house woke Lili. More than once, she heard them banging on the doors of nearby houses. When no one answered, the sounds of doors breaking, and curses told her they were rummaging inside, looking for gold, calling back and forth to each other, "Look harder. These Jews always have gold hidden somewhere." Lili and Meriam, who shared a bed, would clutch each other and sob soundlessly, paralyzed with fear that their house would be next. One night Lili looked out into their courtyard, thinking she had heard an intruder and saw Israel sitting there in a half crouch, an axe in his hand. After that, she slept better, but still always listening.

Ted came twice, smuggling in meat, flour, sugar, lentils and beans. The news Ted reported was discouraging. The situation in Fez was no better; people were losing confidence in the young Sultan, who they felt had betrayed his country to the foreigners. Ted told Lili that many were talking against Mehdi, Tariq's cousin, and even against Ben Slimane, the Minister of Foreign Affairs, saying Mehdi and he were taking bribes from the West.

"Don't all these rumors make it hard for Tariq and his cousin to lead the army?" Lili asked.

"Well, that's exactly the problem," Ted said. "The troops are losing confidence in their leaders. They think Mehdi is too pro-British, and Tariq, too. Many are questioning their authority, calling them 'non-believers'. These rumors are undoubtedly being spread by Gharnit and his followers. They count anyone in that category who's friends with the Westerners. It's definitely undermined their credibility.

"Sweetheart, I've just heard from London," Ted said to Meriam. "They've asked me to go to Algeria for a month or so to look at the situation from that side. They're particularly interested in a General Lyautey who's just been posted there. Tariq met him in France."

Lili knew this was a great chance for Ted. It was what he had been hoping for for a long time.

Lili thought Meriam did a great job of summoning up enthusiasm, *"Cheri*, how wonderful. You must do it."

"Yes, it's just what I've been waiting for. But, will you be all right?"

"Non, non. Do not worry yourself about that. Tariq is also around, do not forget. We will be all right. This is your big chance," Meriam assured him.

"You know, this Lyautey is an interesting chap. He's been leading attacks on Morocco from the Algerian side. I should like to know more about him. And it could be helpful later to know him personally."

"Vas-y cheri, do it, Ted. We would both be sorry all our lives if you did not take this opportunity. It will be fine," Meriam said.

When Ted mounted his horse that night to leave, Meriam turned away, clinging to Lili, unable to bear watching her husband depart.

***

The prison bars had all been filed through. *Sherif*

Raisuni and his two fellow prisoners were just attacking their chains when they heard two guards talking. "The Governor will be visiting us tomorrow. You'd better look sharp, *ya* Mohammed."

"Allah," Al-Raisuni said to his mates, "This ruins our plans. The boat will not be here for four more days."

"*Ya Sherif*, we cannot wait. They will see that we have broken the bars," one of the prisoners said.

"You are right. We will have to go tonight and trust in Allah to make good our escape."

When it was dark, Raisuni went first, crawling through the opening, dragging his chains behind him. He had lost so much weight that he easily slid through the narrow aperture. The two other men followed him. They landed on the rocky shore and started making their way towards a distant cottage, their manacled feet impeding their progress. When they neared the house, Raisuni paused. "You two, go with Allah. I will go another way. They are more interested in me, and if you are alone they will let you be."

Al-Raisuni crept to a road running by the camp. It was getting light by the time he reached it. He crouched by a tree and slept a little, praying for inspiration. When he woke he saw two soldiers coming toward him, still unaware of his presence. He pulled back into the shadows until one was close, then leapt out and fell on top of him, strangling him with his chains. He grabbed the soldier's gun and shot the second one before he could recover from his surprise. He looked up and saw the Governor approaching with fifty men. Raisuni took aim and picked off three men. Then he called to the Governor, "I will keep shooting unless you agree to free me."

The Governor paused, looking uncertain. Raisuni shot two more men.

"Enough," the Governor shouted. "Let us talk. You are outnumbered and we will eventually overpower you, *ya Sherif.*"

"By Allah, I will go back to the prison if you swear on the Holy Koran to go to *Sidna* Abdel Aziz and have him pardon me. I have been rotting in this prison for four years. It is enough."

A month later *Sherif* al-Raisuni was greeted with cheers as he walked out of the Mogador prison a free man. Mehdi al-Menebbhi and other friends in Fez had obtained his pardon.

***

Ted found a caravan departing for Ain Sefra the following week. He and his manservant Amin traveled due east, crossing the Moulouya River, heading first for Ras el Ain, and then across the no-man's land that formed a border between Morocco and Algeria in the minds of the foreigners.

Ted hadn't heard much about General Lyautey and wondered what to expect. Normally, military men were a bit out of his field of his interest, but the Times had hinted that Lyautey was different, more interested in native customs and beliefs than most military men. They had sent him a brief biographical sketch, so he knew Lyautey was 49 years old and that he had served with distinction in Indochina and Madagascar before being assigned to Algeria. Ted had also heard rumors that the General was a homosexual and he was intrigued to see how a military man could handle such a predilection and still rise to the top ranks. Ted, raised in North Africa, was used to homosexual behavior but he knew Europeans did not have the same tolerance. In the Arab world where boys and girls were kept strictly segregated, many were attracted to their own sex. This had never particularly appealed to Ted, but he found it normal in others. The Times had also enclosed a controversial article Lyautey had written early in his career castigating the service for its lack of attention to its recruits and its neglect of the opportunity it had to form its enlisted men into motivated soldiers. It should be an interesting trip, he thought.

The Times had notified Lyautey that Ted would be coming to interview him, so when Ted arrived in the desert town, he found what he took to be one of the general's native soldiers on the lookout for him. The man was dressed in a spotless white turban, a long flowing red cape, polished knee high boots, white baggy trousers, and a wide red cummerbund. Ted had heard that Lyautey was somewhat of a dandy and believed in the value of appearances, and he had to admit to himself that this uniform would command respect among the nomads.

The *spahi*, as Ted later found out these troops were called, found a mule for their baggage and led them to the military camp, located not too far from the market. There a smartly clad French officer showed Ted to his quarters.

The officer bowed slightly and said, "M. le Général is having his siesta, but was expecting you to arrive today. He invites you to dine with him at 7 p.m. Dinner dress is formal." He saluted and left the room. Ted sat down on the cot in exhaustion. "Dinner dress, indeed!" He had heard the general was meticulous but hadn't really expected it to go this far. He searched his luggage: nothing but the Arab clothes he usually wore and one tweed jacket. But those gave him an idea. He headed for the Arab quarter of town, where Ted was sure he could find a *hammam* and scrape off the dust of the week's trip.

That evening, bathed and rested, he presented himself at Lyautey's tent. The guard raised his eyebrows when he first saw Ted, but then bowed and showed him in. Once inside, Ted drew a breath of surprise. The tent was enormous. It must have been a thousand feet square, he estimated, as he passed through various sections that had been divided off with embroidered Berber hangings. He passed into a reception room furnished in the Arab style, with luxurious couches upholstered in silk brocade, Persian and North African carpets under his feet, woven hangings covering the walls and shimmering in the light cast by the brass lanterns that hung throughout the room. Hubert Lyautey was seated on one of the couches, with several French officers grouped around him. He noticed Ted and laughed slightly, beckoning him to come closer.

"So you are the famous English reporter, Ted Hastings. Somehow I had expected an English gentleman, but instead I see a Moroccan *Sherif*. How do you do?"

Ted smiled and shook his hand. "I regret my unconventional attire, but I had not thought to pack a dinner jacket when I set off from Fez by camel caravan. Still, in Morocco this would be acceptable in just about any circumstances." Ted wore Turkish trousers with a wide green suede cummerbund trimmed in gold braid. A white collarless shirt was tucked into his pants and covered by a black embroidered vest. To complete his outfit, he had purchased a red fez and traditional yellow *belghah*.

"Oh, quite, quite, my dear chap." Lyautey said. "Many of us prefer to wear Arab dress. It suits the climate so much better, one finds. Will you have some champagne with us?"

Ted nodded his thanks.

Lyautey introduced him to the other officers. They chatted politely, asking Ted questions about his trip, what conditions were like in Morocco, discussing Bou Hamara and the unrest he was causing in the countryside. Then a *spahi*, dressed like the one Ted had encountered on his arrival, announced that dinner was served. The dining room was elegantly appointed, and as large as the one in the Legation. The table was set with silver,

Limoges china, and candles in heavy gilded candlesticks. He was not disappointed to find that the meal, like the trimmings, was superb; this general traveled with his own cook.

During the dinner Ted had the chance to observe Lyautey. He was slight, his gray hair cut straight across the top, *en brosse*, as the French called crew cuts and the yellowed edges of his bristling mustache revealed his well-known addiction to cigarettes. The mustache, Ted decided, must be waxed nightly, as it ended in elegant points. Lyautey carried his head regally, had piercing blue eyes that changed quickly from cool disdain to genuine amusement as he listened to his fellow officers discuss art, politics, literature throughout the evening. His manner could be imperious and impatient, Ted thought, watching him direct the servants, yet underneath that, Ted detected a genuine fondness and an almost paternal affection for his men. Ted found he was looking forward to the coming days when he would have the chance to interview him one-on-one. Momentarily Meriam crossed his mind, but he quickly dismissed her situation; if worst came to worst, Tariq was always there. At the end of the evening they made an appointment to meet the following day, when Lyautey promised him several hours.

The next morning, Ted found the general exercising his horse. Today the Frenchman was wearing a vivid purple Arab-style *burnous* (cloak) bordered in gold with the silver stars of his rank scattered over its breadth. Lyautey rode up quite close to him and pulled his horse to a quick stop, forcing it to rear. Used to these maneuvers from his Arab friends, Ted did not flinch. Lyautey looked at him approvingly. "Ah, M. Hastings. *Bonjour.* I trust you slept well? Shall we ride a little? My horse needs the exercise, and so do I."

Ted agreed happily, and a horse was found for him. They

rode, not speaking. Ted had the impression the general was testing him, putting his horse through various paces, trotting, cantering, galloping, and even jumping over occasional small obstacles. After about an hour, they came to a small oasis with a well and a few palm trees casting some shade. Lyautey suggested that they dismount to rest their horses. They could start the interview here.

The equerry jumped down and spread a rug, setting up two campstools. He busied himself lighting a small camp stove; Ted realized he was going to make them tea.

"So, M. Hastings, you ride like an Arab as well as dressing like one," Lyautey said.

Ted explained his background to him.

"Excellent, excellent," Lyautey said. "You have the kind of experience I wish my officers to have. If we are to pacify these noble tribes and lure them to the French side, we must first understand and respect them. Speak their language fluently. I have a few men who can do that. Laperrine.... He's a first-rate man. Has his troops eating out of his hand. They call him *Sheikh* because he understands the nomads so well. He's forming his own tribe out of his camel corps, the *Sahariens*; they'll do whatever he wants, because they respect him. This is what I'm trying to do here."

"Yes," Ted said, accepting a cup of thick sweet tea, brewed nomad style with a generous dollop of milk, from the equerry. "I've read a bit about your years with Gallieni in Tonkin and then in Madagascar. Would you consider yourself his disciple?" Ted was referring to the charismatic officer whom Lyautey had served as chief of staff. Apparently many now thought of Lyautey as his successor in forging a new kind of military behavior and philosophy for the French.

"Yes, I suppose you could call it that," Lyautey said. "It

just seems like common sense to me, but that's often in short supply in the military." He searched through his pockets for a cigarette which the equerry quickly sprang to light for him. "The thing is, you know, we can't bring thousands of French boys to these far-flung outposts. If we're going to make the natives part of our empire, we have to do it through the locals themselves. That shouldn't be such a hard task. After all, we have so much to offer them."

Ted raised his eyebrows slightly. "For instance?"

"Oh, I'm not suggesting they become French. Far from it. But we can teach them to keep peace; to stop their endless feuding and raiding, such as you now see in Morocco. Let's face it, this constant fighting prevents them from developing, from producing, from trade. And trade, now, that's what's important in the long run. Commerce, my boy. Buying and selling. It's the secret to prosperity, to the growth of culture, of art. But without peace, which we can teach them to maintain, none of that is possible."

"Just look at your home," he said. "Morocco is a shambles. That young sultan, Abdel Aziz, he claims this Eastern Desert as part of his kingdom, but he can't keep order here. His army, if you can call it that, is pathetic! Why, they can't even tame this Bou Hamara fellow who's running around the country. What kind of government is that?" He puffed away at his cigarette for a few minutes and then tossed it carelessly aside. The aide quietly found it and ensured that it was extinguished.

"Now, we French, you see, we can offer good government. Look what we've done here in Algeria. That tells the story. It's basically the same country as Morocco. But fifty, sixty years here and look at this place. It's peaceful; there are productive farms. People are employed. The Arabs have their own space.

"Oh, I think we've made a few mistakes, don't

misunderstand me. If I had it my way, I would never have made Algeria a French *départment.* That was unnecessary and an insult to the Algerians. We should have established a protectorate, as we did in Madagascar. Let the natives rule their own country, but help them keep the peace, build roads, establish systems for governing. They rule and we tutor them. In the process, we establish links of trade, cooperation, and friendship. They keep their culture and traditions, we keep ours; there is mutual respect. Now that's what I believe and you're right, my friend. Much of this I learned from Gallieni."

Lyautey's philosophy seemed enlightened to Ted. It was certainly not what he had expected from a military man. He opened his mouth to ask some other questions, but Lyautey rose, brushing off his trousers and gesturing to the equerry to take up the carpet.

"We can talk more tonight. But now, I need to get back to my troops. These legionnaires are more trouble than they're worth. But I mean to make my mark here, no matter what kind of material I've inherited." He stalked off, gathering the reins of his waiting horse and mounting it, leaving Ted to follow as quickly as possible. The equerry was left in their dust.

***

In Taza, the Friday prayer was said in the name of Bou Hamara, alias *Sidi* Mohammed. He now dressed in royal garb and was accompanied everywhere by a slave carrying the crimson parasol.

Kassim went back and forth regularly between Fez and Taza bringing agreements from the Germans and Spanish to provide arms and ammunition in return for promises of mineral rights in the Rif Mountains.

***

Ted got an hour, sometimes two if he was lucky, with Lyautey during the day. At other times he observed and chatted with the other French officers drilling the troops, particularly Laperrine, whom Lyautey had mentioned to him. There was such a variety of soldiers. Those under the control of Laperrine, the *Sahariens*, were the roughest, reminding Ted of the Berber tribesmen controlled by Madani al Glaoui, Tariq's powerful relative.

They were simple tribesmen, who, Ted learned, had been recruited in the desert. Riding their camels, they were able to race through the sand. Laperrine assured Ted that they could actually find their way in the dark. "They can detect ancient water sources and make their way by their scent. By God, it works. And their food, *mon dieu*, they can exist for days on a few dried dates, lamb fat and salt. No need for cumbersome caravans to ensure supplies. These men are worth twenty French soldiers each." Ted could also see that they worshipped the French officer, who had been working with them for years, and who spoke their guttural desert dialect fluently.

The French legionnaires were predominantly German. Lyautey despised this group, which was a rough undisciplined lot, forever getting into brawls, drinking too much, and more than occasionally selling their rifles to pay off gambling debts. Lyautey suspected them of selling military secrets to the Germans as well, and he refused to use them for any but the most routine tasks, allocating them to the rear and forcing them to oversee supply wagons.

Lyautey had brought with him some handpicked French officers to supplement the regular troops he had inherited. Those who had been there before him, he complained to Ted, were almost useless.

"They're too disciplined," Lyautey said. "They've been

trained in the old ways. They move in squares, marching straight forward into the desert, where the Bedouin raiders demolish them. They haven't been trained to think for themselves, to dodge, to fade into the territory, to feint. In the desert, they become sitting ducks."

During the interviews Lyautey shared his vision of military procedures with Ted. "We're hopelessly old-fashioned in France," he said. "Those of us who've been overseas, we *coloniaux*, have learned a different kind of warfare. Maybe the so-called German system works in European theaters, but it's useless in this part of the world. We learned that in Tonkin, we learned it again in Madagascar, and I mean to apply it here.

"What we need is small bands of men, desert men, my *goumiers* and *spahis*, led by good French officers that I have trained. These men are fighting Bedouin, after all. They need to learn to operate like them. The tactics of the desert raid, in and out fast, attack and run, retaliation. Give these tribesmen a taste of their own medicine, but with discipline and perseverance behind it. Then, when they see we're serious and surrender, we go right in with medicine and markets, help them dig new wells, improve the roads. That convinces them they've made the right decision. That's the way to go."

Lyautey was proud of his handpicked officers and as they sat at dinner every night, reviewing the day's exercises Ted got to know them. Lyautey took a keen interest in his officers, quizzing them in minute detail about their activities with their soldiers, progress they were making, even asking about the quality of food the men were given, their health. Lyautey insisted that all his officers speak Arabic fluently, so that their interaction could be direct and immediate with the men.

Although his men sometimes joked about Lyautey's homosexuality among themselves, they appeared to accept this as part of him in a manner-of-fact way. Ted had heard that there had been serious opposition to Lyautey's appointment because of this predilection, most particularly from General Fernand O'Connor, supreme commandant in Algeria. But Lyautey's sterling reputation and strong recommendations from his mentor, Gallieni, plus support from the colonial bloc in France, had won the day.

***

Mehdi Al-Menebbhi began the campaign, or *mahalla*, that must definitively capture Bou Hamara. Since they were not far from Taza, Tariq managed another visit. Lili found him moody and taciturn.

"There is little food in the countryside, and the people do not want to fight for the Sultan." Tariq told her. "He tries to collect taxes, which makes him even less liked. We have had reports that they have sold the guns we gave them, probably to Bou Hamara. I am worried, *ya* Lili. The French could easily take us over."

"Would that be so bad? From what I've heard, France has done a lot of good for Algeria."

Tariq stared at her, his face flushing with anger. Algeria had been colonized by the French in the 1830s, and since then it had been made an official part of France. French settlers had streamed to the warm Mediterranean country with its fertile soil and long growing seasons. They now supplied early vegetables and fruits to metropolitan France. They had built roads, established a railroad service, had regular post, most of the services France had.

"What Algeria has, what Egypt has, these things I want for my country. We are backward; we need roads, easy ways to communicate, education. It would be good if we could raise money from agriculture. But colonization means giving up our fertile lands to the Christians. Letting them reap the rewards of our soil, our mountains, and our people. Sending our profits so that those people can drink champagne and eat caviar. How would we benefit from that?"

"Papa says when a country gets colonized, the colonizer builds roads, improves agriculture, brings markets for produce. They bring jobs and prosperity."

"Prosperity for whom? The French own Algeria, just as the British benefit the most from Egypt. The Algerians work for the French. In Egypt, decisions are made by their Lord Cromer. There is no profit for the Arabs. Their country is not theirs. All good things are for the European powers. It is like Tangier, only larger. Nothing good is left for the natives.

"*Ya* Lili, what Algeria has, the roads, postal delivery, schools, I want this for my country. Very much, Allah willing. But we Moroccans must profit from it. Not the French, or the British, or any *nisara*, foreigners. This is wrong."

These arguments were new to Lili whose family and friends had always stressed the benefits of colonization. She and Tariq spent a long time discussing nation building, a topic she had not really thought about critically before then. It was true, Moroccans needed these services. But the Europeans who came with them seemed to take over the best land and also to benefit most. Even in Tangier, this was true. She was impressed that Tariq had been doing so much thinking about these things. And what he said made sense. It left her thoughtful.

***

Ted needed to get back to Morocco.

Before dinner on his last night he and Lyautey were sitting among the cushions, relaxing after a long day in the sun. It was still hot inside the tent, but flaps had been raised at both ends, creating a cross draft. Lyautey was dressed in a long blue Saharan robe, its V-neck trimmed in white braid, and Ted wore his Turkish trousers and white collarless shirt without the vest. Lyautey puffed away contentedly at the water pipe. "So, Ted, my friend," he said, "I trust this visit has been profitable for you."

"Oh, yes, M. le General. I have lots of good material. There's just one final topic, though, that I was hoping we could discuss this evening. I'd like your perspective on the French attitude towards Morocco."

"Ha!" Lyautey said. "I wondered when you'd get around to that! Well, of course, it's complex, as you know. There are a growing number of us now in France that people are beginning to refer to as les *coloniaux*. Those who lead this faction have an Algerian slant, like Charles Jonnart, governor general of Algeria and Eugène Etienne, the Oran deputy to Parliament. Gallieni and many of us who have served in foreign posts belong to this group. We believe France will be greater if it can expand its markets overseas, become powerful through trade, recapture, if you will, the glory that we lost after the war with Germany in the 70s. And to do that, we need strong colonies in our camp. Like Algeria is. Like Morocco, perhaps, could be. At a minimum, we need peaceful borders, which is my responsibility."

"But maybe more than that, too?" Ted said. "Doesn't France have more ambitious plans for Morocco as well?"

"Of course, I'm just a soldier, and politics are a bit out of my realm," Lyautey said. "But I would say that others in France, led by our lily-livered Foreign Minister, Delcassé, probably want Morocco. Everyone wants it one way or the other. What we disagree on is method. Delcassé thinks he knows everything, since he was Minister in Tangier. He insists on working through this Abdel Aziz. Now I actually agree with him about that, in principle. You know my theory; tutor, lead from behind. But I must say that this youngster doesn't strike me as very impressive so far. I'm not sure how much there is to really work with. What do you think? I believe you know him rather well."

Ted laughed. "Well, I don't know him that well. But I shouldn't underestimate him. He needs time to become accustomed to ruling. He has some good men around him as advisors. Unfortunately, he also has quite a few who are corrupt and self-interested. What will matter, ultimately, is which faction around him gains the upper hand."

Lyautey nodded. "That's pretty typical of these backward countries. The backbiting and scheming at court. Of course, we have quite a bit of that in France, too. But Delcassé has been in power for much too long, and many of us would like to see some new blood. At any rate, Delcassé and his followers, among them the present Minister to Tangier, St. René Taillandier, are insisting that we work through Abdel Aziz. They're also so damned afraid of the Germans that every time I make any move at all to secure the borders here between Morocco and Algeria, they almost piss their pants."

This last bit of information was of special interest to Ted. Despite his years at Oxford, he still had trouble sometimes capturing the European perspective. The European powers had been lining up alliances and dividing the world below the Mediterranean for the past twenty years, but Germany didn't have what it considered its fair share. France, having been trounced in the Franco-Prussian war, was still gun shy and reluctant to take Germany on again, at least not until its position was stronger.

"Come, my boy. I know tonight is your last night." Lyautey clapped him affectionately on the back. "I've prepared a special surprise for you. Here, let's go outside." Lyautey rose and led Ted toward the open flap of the tent. Outside, a group of twenty legionnaires were gathered. When Ted and Lyautey approached, at a hidden signal one stepped forward and began to sing. Strains of German lieder filled the night. They quickly found places among the rest of the staff where they sat for the next hour, enjoying the cool breeze that had risen off the desert and the surprisingly beautiful music issuing from these hardened soldiers.

***

Lili and Meriam sat in the salon with Rebecca's new baby, Rachel. A midwife was nursing the puny child, since Rebecca had no milk.

Lili stroked the infant's tiny hands. "Meriam, I don't think Rebecca is recovering very well, do you?"

Meriam sighed. "Is it not stupid of us? We thought our troubles would be over when *Tante* Rebecca gave birth. *Mon Dieu*, what were we thinking? She is very weak."

Lili said, "I hate to say this, Meriam, but there may be something more wrong with her. You know, she didn't look very healthy even at the start of the pregnancy."

Meriam nodded. "I do not see how we can leave as we had planned."

***

At the Palace in Fez Kassim ran into Arthur, who was sitting alone in an antechamber, looking bored.

"Hullo, old chap," Kassim said. "What are you up to?"

"Waiting to see *Si* Gharnit," Arthur replied. "I've been

here all morning. You're Kassim al Matari, right? The one who studied with Ted?"

"Yes. I say, what are you doing for lunch today?"

"Nothing special."

"Well, why don't you come to my place? I have a good cook."

"I'd love to," Arthur said. He was tired of eating alone and it was nice to speak English with this young chap. He accompanied Kassim deep into the *medina* where the Matari palace was located. Kassim had a suite there, along with whatever other family members were in town. They made themselves comfortable in a small chamber facing an open courtyard. As they dipped their bread into a cinnamon spiced lamb tajine Kassim said, "I heard your wife's in Taza?"

"Yes, she's helping her sister-in-law look after a relative," Arthur said. "She's been there a damned long time."

"Is Ted there, too? I haven't seen him for a while."

"Oh no, he's in Algeria. Some kind of interview."

Kassim leaned back more comfortably on the silk cushions, signaling a servant to bring water so they could wash their hands. "Well, you shouldn't be all on your own. Come and visit me whenever you want. We can find some things to do." A servant brought a small brazier of incense and passed it over the men's clothes. Then he handed Kassim a small pipe and helped him light it. Kassim puffed. "Umm. Have you tried this?"

"What is it?" Arthur asked.

"We call it *kif*. It's a kind of tobacco mixed with herbs from the Rif mountains. Very relaxing. Here, take a puff of mine."

Arthur puffed and coughed. The second puff was easier. His head started to spin very slightly, as though he had had a few whiskeys. "Very pleasant."

***

Lili opened the door to a grimy Moroccan peasant. She was about to close it in the man's face when he smiled at her and said 'Larabi'. Lili pulled him quickly through the door. He held out a small piece of paper that she snatched; then, remembering her manners, she ushered him into a sitting room and called for Gerard to bring him water and soap, while she prepared something for him to eat.

The paper had just a brief message, "My sister, you and the family must depart as soon as possible, preferably tonight. We will be in Taza soon. It will be too dangerous then. This man will guide you to safety. Destroy this note. May Allah keep you safe."

***

Meriam and Lili sat up late with Israel and the boys discussing what to do. Meriam brought in a small brazier and boiled water for tea. They ranged themselves on the plump divans in the salon, Gerard sitting on a cushion on the floor with his head against Meriam. Hannah cuddled herself against Lili, sucking her thumb. They all watched in silence while Meriam completed the tea, pouring it back and forth into the glasses and back to the pot several times before it was pronounced good by Israel.

Meriam smoothed down her red silk skirt and fiddled with her long auburn braids as she said, "You must leave tomorrow. The soldier won't wait any longer than that. You can break yourselves into small groups, perhaps Lili and the baby with Michel; Gerard and Israel with Hannah. It will be necessary for you to leave at different times."

Israel, dressed in his long rusty black caftan, removed his black skull cap and rubbed his balding head. He said, "I did not hear you mention yourself and Rebecca."

"That is correct. The rest of you should go now. It is too *dangereux* for everyone to stay."

Lili said, "I have absolutely no intention of leaving you here."

"*Cherie*," Meriam said. "I speak the truth. Why expose the whole family to such danger? It is not logical."

"I understand that," Lili said. She shifted her legs, able to sit cross-legged on the divan because of the baggy pants and loose shirt she had continued to wear in Taza. "But can't we think of a plan to get Rebecca out too?"

Meriam said, "I do not think so. Rebecca has *la diarrhée*. It reminds me of that cholera epidemic we had in Tangier."

They sat quietly together, sipping their tea, each trying to think of an alternative plan.

Lili said, "We could construct a stretcher of some kind and carry Rebecca out with us. The men are strong enough to carry her."

"That would not work," Israel said. "There are several problems. We would be instantly noticed and challenged by Bou Hamara's troops. And Lili, we are Jews, they would harass us. You know they would."

Lili paused. She was ashamed of the treatment she knew was meted out to the Jews in these interior cities, but it couldn't be denied. If they went out as a big group, the men would immediately be seized for military service, at best. At worst...she shuddered. She had seen the kind of baiting of Jews that could go on, especially among idle soldiers. And she could imagine the fate that might await the young women. No, that clearly wouldn't do.

"Well," she said, "we just have to wait and do everything we can to get Rebecca better quickly, so we can all leave together."

"No, *cherie*, it is not possible," Meriam said. "There are Hannah and baby Rachel to consider."

Israel said. "This is craziness. What are you thinking about? I will stay, and you will all leave, separating as planned, into two groups. When Rebecca is better, I will bring her out."

"But *Si* Israel," Meriam said, "you need someone to care for Tante Rebecca, and someone to cook. You can not do this yourself."

Israel considered a few minutes, and then nodded, "Yes, you should stay with me, Meriam. You are part of Rebecca's family. And I can look after you, when we are able to leave. That makes sense."

Lili protested, but Israel cut her off. "That is final. You are not one of us and I can not accept responsibility for your well being. My family owes you a great debt, but this would be more than we could accept. You must leave with the children. But the baby will stay here and can come out with Meriam. That is the most sensible solution, and that is the way it will be." The paternal declaration had the ring of authority that both the women recognized as final. "You will make preparations and go tonight, just before the city gates close," he said, standing up and ending the discussion.

When it seemed the last word had been said, the two boys spoke up, Michel leading, "We are not going either. We are not sissies to run away with the girls."

Gerard agreed with his brother.

Michel added, "Hannah should definitely leave. It is too dangerous for girls. And our sister, Lili, should not stay longer and endanger her own life for us."

Israel put in the final word, "I only wish our beloved Meriam could go with you, Lili. You two have rendered this family an invaluable service. Please do not think for a moment that we are not grateful. But now, my daughter, you must leave, and take Hannah with you. God willing, we will follow very soon with Meriam and Rebecca and the baby."

Reluctantly, Lili made preparations to leave with Hannah that night. She couldn't believe she had agreed to the plan, but couldn't see any way out of it. Someone had to take Hannah out. She comforted herself for what she felt was abandoning Meriam by promising that she would deliver Hannah safely to her grandparents in Fez, and then would come straight back with Ted. She told Meriam about the weapons Tariq had left with her, transferring to her the dagger she had faithfully kept strapped to her ankle, and showing her the other, hidden under the cushions in their sitting room.

She smuggled out a note out to Tariq's man, who had settled down several doors away, squatting in the street and playing cards with some young boys. The note said they would leave in the late afternoon just at prayer time and meet him at the city gate.

Lili cut off Hannah's curls, to howls of anger, and added little rips and tears to her robes, then she rubbed both her and Hannah's hair in mud, tousling it to give them as unattractive and dejected an air as she could. The stains from Hannah's tears as she began to realize what was happening contributed to her general state of dishevelment. Lili covered both of them in huge *djellabahs*, effectively hiding their bodies and much of their faces. Lili kept their farewells as brief as possible. She pulled Meriam aside for a final few words:

"Meriam, you know I'm not doing this willingly."

"I understand. Please, do not worry," Meriam said. "With luck we will be out of here ourselves in a few days, with Rebecca walking beside us." She managed a brave smile.

Lili thought to herself, much more likely Rebecca will die, and found herself disloyally wishing she would. She guessed Meriam felt the same, at least some times, but was not going to admit it. She squeezed her hand, speechless with unshed tears.

They embraced, and then Lili turned away quickly.

Lili and Hannah stepped out the door. Once she was out in the street, Lili was terrified. Although she was used to posing as a boy, she had never been completely on her own before. And this time the consequences could be so much more serious. She told herself, I must set a good example for Hannah, whom she tugged along by the hand. Walking the back alleys, she left the Jewish quarter as quickly as she could. The presence of a young Arab boy there could have been suspicious. Once into the main town, Lili forced herself to walk slowly and more confidently, looking as though she was running some errands for her household. There was a group of Bou Hamara's soldiers near the market and she steeled herself not to flinch as she neared them. She could see the men were looking at her speculatively and gripped Hannah's hand tighter. One of them started walking toward her and she froze, unsure what to do. Just at that moment a hand clapped her back and she jumped, then relaxed as she turned and saw Tariq's man, Mohammed, standing next to her. He made some passing comment, as though recognizing a friend. Lili noticed out of the corner of her eye that the soldier who had been closing in on her turned away, and she breathed a sigh of relief. She could hardly move, and commanded her body to loosen up.

Mohammed walked by them briskly murmuring, "I will meet you at the city gate. Follow me, but at a distance. People should not connect us, in case I am recognized."

Lili was grateful for the suggestion that she follow, as

she had no idea how to find the city gate, having rarely left Rebecca's house. Hannah was crying softly, and Lili offered her words of consolation describing how happy her grandmother, Sarah, would be to see her and the special treats she would have waiting for her when she arrived. All the while her heart was pounding, afraid of discovery, of challenge, of failure. They reached the gate, where Mohammed joined them. There he cautioned Lili, "Say nothing. I will do the talking here. Keep your eyes on the ground and keep the child quiet."

Both did as he directed. They squatted down on their haunches near the wall, where groups of beggars and women were clustered, some selling bread, some staring listlessly into space. Lili hugged Hannah close, telling her all kinds of nonsense to distract her. Mohammed strode off to talk to the guards watching the gates, and Lili, stealing a timid peek when she could, saw that he had obviously made a deal with the men long ago which probably involved a handsome bribe, as the guards appeared very deferential. After a few minutes, Mohammed beckoned to them. Lili, clutching Hannah's hand, approached them, trying to walk casually, with her hood drawn almost completely across her face to shadow it.

Almost before she could believe it, they were out the city gates. Before her stretched the Atlas mountain range that lay between Taza and Fez, and the open plains, scorched dusty brown in the summer heat. They must hurry, take Hannah to safety, and then come back, hopefully with Ted and get the rest of the family out before the attack. How much time did they really have?

***

In Fez Lili was as nervous as a cat. "When exactly do you think Ted'll be back, Arthur? We shouldn't delay very long. I could see the troops massing as I left!"

Arthur went to his study and rummaged around, coming back with a one-page letter from Ted. "He says 'I should be leaving here at the end of the week. Plan to stop briefly in Tangier to see Matt and mother and will then proceed directly to Fez. So you should see me around mid-July'."

"Mid-July!" Lili said. "That's two weeks from now. I can't wait that long."

Lili put her glass down decisively. "Time is critical now. Send a messenger. He may prevent Ted from overstaying in Tangier and also convince him to come here as fast as possible."

***

A police officer came to Tariq's home early in the morning. "*Smahli, ya sidi*, excuse me, my lord," he began. He held his head bowed, seeming unwilling to meet Tariq's eyes. "There is something, something most unfortunate, most terrible, that we have discovered. I am not sure, uh, what to do. I do not want to cause trouble, but…uh, well, could you come down to the river with me? It is unpleasant, but someone of your rank should see this, I believe. Then you can tell me what is best to do."

Thoroughly mystified, Tariq threw on a long black cashmere cloak and called for his horse. Following the officer, he wove through the back alleys of Fez until they came to its outskirts, where much of the sewage of Fez had accumulated as it flowed into the river dividing the city. The officer dismounted.

Tariq got down from his horse, trying not to breathe in the noxious fumes. It was misty and damp; the ground sank under his feet as he approached what seemed to be a pile of twigs and debris near where the officer was standing. When he got near he saw a little brown hand sticking out. He recoiled. "What is this, my uncle?"

The officer reached down with his stick and pushed aside more of the debris. Gradually the form of a young African girl emerged. Her belly had been slit open and a small fetus protruded with its neck cut. The girl's breasts were slashed. Tariq reluctantly brought his eyes to her face. The eyes were wide with terror and her mouth was frozen in a scream. He turned away, "*Ya haram*, what a sin. May Allah punish the perpetrator of such an abomination." Tariq ran his hands over his face, which he realized was wet with tears. He stayed with his back to the officer for a few moments, trying to collect himself. How could anyone do this to a defenseless young girl?

He turned back to the police officer, who was standing quietly, gazing at the girl.

"*Ya sidi*, in all my years I have never seen anything to equal this. What should we do?"

Tariq thought quickly. It would have to be hushed up. Abdel Aziz's reputation couldn't withstand another scandal. "My uncle, a terrible offense has been rendered to this young slave. But now the best thing we can do is bury her quickly. We will never know where she came from, or what slave dealer she belonged to. I will send some trustworthy men from my house to bury her. You did right to come to me. Please accept this small token of my gratitude for keeping this a private matter between ourselves. Let us pray to Allah that she has found peace in Paradise." He handed the officer a purse of coins. As he rode off, he saw the girl's terror-stricken eyes. His jaw clenched. He knew that face. It belonged to the slave girl Kassim had bought in the market.

***

Tariq reviewed his troops. They were not a pretty sight. He felt frustrated and depressed. With material like this, how could they ever pull their country out of its misery and put its citizens on the path to a better life. Everywhere he looked he saw ignorance, disease, injustice. How long would it take his people to rise up from their poverty and injustice? Would it be possible to create a better world for them?

The *guish* had uniforms of some kind and boots. He had trained and drilled his regulars so that they could shoot more or less correctly, kneeling and aiming before firing, at least most of the time. But the others, the men levied from the tribes, they were a sorry lot. All barefoot and wearing ragged *djellabahs*, they were the dregs of the countryside, sent by tribal chiefs who wanted to get rid of them. He guessed their ages ranged from seventy to ten, with the oldest and youngest in the majority. Many of the oldest were blind or lame and, while there was more hope for the boys, most were very slow to learn. Tariq was particularly frustrated by his complete failure to teach any of these recruits to shoot; they insisted on holding their antiquated firearms at the hip and firing blindly, sometimes injuring a fellow soldier, one of the horses, or just wasting the precious bullets uselessly.

The royal army was gathered at Meknassa Tehtaniya, a valley less than a day's march from Taza. Mehdi was in charge, and Tariq was there with his other powerful cousin, Madani al-Glaoui, from the High Atlas mountains south of Marrakesh. With them was another Berber chief, al-Goundafi. With the tribal recruits and the *guish* they had over 30,000 men and this time they were determined to flush Bou Hamara out of his stronghold. Mehdi's enemies in Fez, led by *Si* Fedoul al-Gharnit had been quick to criticize him for his failure to eliminate this threat to the Sultan and there was talk of replacing him; this time they had to trap Bou Hamara. Tariq had waged a strong campaign for two months earlier in the year, as attested to by the fifty heads Lili had seen on the wall in Fez. But every time they thought they had finished him off, the Pretender would show up somewhere else, stronger than before, and he was deeply entrenched in Taza.

Allah be praised, Tariq thought. At least Lili is not there. He refused to think about Meriam; he understood why Ted's wife had stayed, but it would be a miracle if she survived this siege. Her fate was with Allah now.

Tariq, Mehdi and the two *sheikhs*, Glaoui and Gandoufi, had staff to pitch their tents and get them organized, so the four men each took a different section of the camp and wandered among the soldiers, seeing that their tents were securely set up, ditches dug around them for drainage, animals safely tethered. The prisoners and camp followers settled nearby, and on another side the merchants and vendors who followed the *mehalla*, or campaign, set up shop.

Tariq found himself in an area of recruits, rather than among his own *askar* or soldiers. Two young boys, named Hassan and Hussein, quickly attached themselves to him, kissing the hem of his *djellabah*. They spoke only Berber and liked this officer whom they could talk to.

"*Ya sidi*, what will the battle be like? Do they really have European guns? We heard they have more cannons than we do, and bigger. What if they shoot the cannons? What's it like? Will we explode if it hits us?" The boys were shivering, despite the intense summer heat and their eyes were huge with fear.

"Whatever happens is the will of Allah," Tariq said. "But where are your tents? Have you eaten?"

The boys shook their heads. "We just have these soldiers' crackers." They pulled some dried pieces of bread, made of millet and sorghum that looked like rocks, from their pockets.

Tariq tousled the matted hair of one of them. "Come by my tent later and there will be some couscous and lamb for you. And get my man to shave your heads. You are covered with lice." The boys grabbed at his hand to kiss it, but Tariq pulled it away. He hated these gestures of servility, so common in Morocco.

Tariq strolled off to see how the other recruits were doing. Smoke was beginning to rise from thousands of campfires and he could see the men's wives squatting over small braziers fanning them into crimson glows. The smell of *bessara*, a stew made of mashed chickpeas, was everywhere. Small children ran around, darting between the fires, searching for firewood, taking hay to the animals, happy to be camped and off the march.

He came upon a cluster of soldiers with their backs to him, listening to a bearded man in their midst. As he got closer, Tariq heard him say, "...why they are almost Christians. They associate all day with foreigners, with English. They are not real Muslims like Bou Hamara..." he was interrupted as Tariq seized his arm.

"Who are not real Muslims?" he demanded.

"*Ya sidi*, some of our leaders in Fez," the man stuttered, not recognizing Tariq.

"He is from Bou Hamara's camp," one of the recruits shouted. Others confirmed this, all wanting to clear themselves of any suspicion.

"Is this true?" Tariq demanded.

The bearded man looked at the ground, refusing to answer.

Tariq drew his pistol and held it to the man's head. "We are true Muslims and have no room here for followers of the Pretender, Bou Hamara." He pulled the trigger. Brains, blood and bone scattered everywhere. The men moved away in haste. "Allah is great." Tariq shouted.

He passed into the area where his *askars* were assembled, sickened as he brushed what he could off his *djellabah*. Mustn't show it, though, he cautioned himself. He would not hesitate to blow the head off a snake and spies were just a different kind of snake. He could not falter now.

***

Lili was about to start out on her own when Ted arrived. Lili almost knocked him down as she threw herself at him. "Thank God, you're here at last! Did you get our message in Tangier?"

"No," Ted said. "What's wrong?"

She dragged him into the salon and explained the entire situation. As she went through her recital Ted became more and more alarmed. "We can leave tonight," he said when she finished.

Lili eyed her brother's sunburned and peeling face, the fatigue lines drawn around his eyes. His whole body was clearly drooping with exhaustion. But they had little choice.

***

It was getting dark as Tariq made his way to Mehdi's quarters, easy to find because of the pennant topping his principal tent, signaling the authority of the absent Sultan. He entered the audience chamber, glowing with lantern light, and furnished with wool-stuffed cushions spread over rugs. Mehdi, Madani al-Glaoui and Tayyib al-Goundafi were already there, lounging on pillows, sipping tea; to the side several musicians were playing softly.

Mehdi waved at Tariq and beckoned him to sit beside him. "Is everything all right in your section?"

Tariq nodded. "Yes, but I am uneasy. I did not like those shots at us this morning when we were on our way here. We are deep into Hayaina country and they are Bou Hamara's men, one hundred for one hundred."

Madani al-Glaoui moved closer, grimacing at one of the wounds he had received earlier in the *mahalla*. "It will be as Allah has written. I do not trust some of our recruits. Some are Hayaina, and those sons of sin are known to be treacherous. If they can, some will sneak out tonight and report our position to the Pretender."

Mehdi agreed with his companions. "It is true. We subdue one area, they give us tribute, fine Negresses, horses, and recruits. One week later their men have disappeared with our rifles and are shooting at us. Well, Allah will decide, but we will be ready and protect *Sidna* Abdel Aziz. Let us not forget that Bou Hamara cannot win. He is a nobody and a trickster; his family cannot trace its roots to the Prophet; Allah will not support him. If he wins today, he will lose tomorrow. Allah is on our side because we are in the right."

***

Just as they had finished eating the sharp retort of a cannon interrupted them. Then another, and another.

Mehdi jumped up, overturning the platter. "Quick, back to your troops. It is starting."

Tariq and the other *sheikhs* roused their men with all the speed possible in the total darkness. In the inky night they made their way to the edge of the camp, stumbling over pots and pans abandoned by frightened women, now huddled in tents quieting the children. Bullets continued to harass them, but less frequently with the lights out. Still, an occasional shriek indicated that another bullet had found its mark. When they reached the limits of the encampment, Tariq stationed the machine gunners at strategic points. At least they could shoot well, he thought, thanks to his hours of working with them. He circulated among his men. "I know you can't see, so wait until they fire. Then fire at their light. We must work as five fingers on one hand." He thought to himself, *insh'Allah*, God willing. He saw an old man who he knew was functionally blind. "You, my father, sit here next to young Khalid. He has one of our machine guns. You can pass him ammunition and help reload his gun. Let him shoot." Hassan and Hussein turned up again near him, and he grabbed Hassan's arm. "My son, go carefully around the camp from the left, while you, Hussein, go from the right. Go until you meet. Then come back here as fast as you can and tell me if our men are in place all around. If you see holes where there is no coverage, mark them and report that to me. Now go."

Tariq's eyes searched the black void surrounding them. How to fight in the dark? As light from a shot opened the void, he commanded, "There, get that man." Volleys rang out. Some of the spots did not light up again.

It seemed to Tariq like forever until Hassan came back without Hussein. The young boy's eyes were wet; he rubbed them on the back of his filthy *djellabah*. "*Ya sidi*, there are men all around my part. But Hussein.....he did not make it all the way."

Tariq hugged him. "Well done my boy. Your brother is now in Paradise; be happy for him." He felt sick.

A scout ran up from Mehdi. "*Ya sidi*, the whole circle is closed with our men. My master asks that you send some ammunition. We are taking more fire on our side."

Tariq sent Hassan. The busier the boy was, the less time he would have to think about his brother. He asked the scout, "How many casualties, do you know?"

"No, *ya sidi*. But not too many, I think. It is hard to tell in the dark."

"All right. How are the Hayaina recruits behaving?"

"Our soldiers are shooting them if they attempt to run off," the scout informed him.

Tariq began to make out his men's haggard faces in the early dawn. Mohammed came up to him. "My lord, the firing has stopped."

Tariq listened. All he could hear was moans from the wounded. He hadn't noticed, he was so caught up in the battle. Slowly the men put down their arms. Many had wounds, but thanks to Allah, they had not had too many casualties. While he had cursed the night fighting, Tariq now thought in some ways it had been a blessing from Allah, because it had made it hard to hit his men. Now, as his dazed men looked around and realized they had made it through the night, smiles began to appear. One man shouted, "*Allah al Akbar*, God is Great," and the others took up the praise. Whoops and hollers filled the morning as they celebrated their survival and praised Mehdi al-Menebbhi and the others for guiding them in a good defense.

***

The encampment was a shambles. Many tents had been ripped into shreds by bullets, pots and pans lay where they had been abandoned, dogs licked at food lying where it had been spilt in panic.

They rested a day and then advanced on Taza.

By afternoon the *mehalla* reached the banks of the river below Taza. Shots were falling all around them. Tariq could see tribesmen stationed on the city's ramparts and even in olive trees. Briefly he noticed that they did not look like Bou Hamara's regular army, which had a semblance of a uniform, but he was too busy with security preparations to reflect on what this might mean. On Mehdi's orders, Ben Sedira positioned the cannon, facing straight at the main gate to Taza.

"Now, *Si* Sedira, you may show them the gates of Hell," Mehdi said.

Sedira, an Algerian who had been loaned to the Sultan to help train the army, grinned. He had been waiting for this moment all through the last night's fighting.

***

"We must occupy the town now," Mehdi said.

"Maybe we should wait until tomorrow," Tariq suggested. "It is late and the men are tired."

"No, if we leave it until tomorrow, those cowardly Ghiata tribesmen will slink back and make it harder for us. We must take it, now that we have opened the gate."

Tariq agreed, despite his misgivings. "Let us take the best men from our regular *guish* and all the machine gunners. The others can stay behind and begin establishing a camp here. I will put Mohammed in charge of that."

They assembled five thousand of their best mounted horsemen. With Mehdi at their head, Tariq, Madani al-Glaoui and al-Goundafi, waved their rifles toward the city gate. "*Yallah*, my brothers. Taza is ours," Mehdi shouted, racing up the steep mud road leading to the gate.

They crowded into the main street which opened into a square near the gate. Mehdi held up a hand. Kneeling in a line, ready to meet him, were what appeared to be a group of city elders, holding milk and dates.

At a gesture from Mehdi, Tariq dismounted and approached the group. He wondered briefly where they had found the delicacies they were offering, knowing how scarce supplies were in Taza. He made eye contact with the man who appeared to be the spokesman. The man seized the hem of his *djellabah* and kissed it. "*Ya Sidi,*" he said in a quavering voice, "the *makhsen,* the government, is welcome in our city. Please accept our hospitality."

Tariq signaled to Mehdi, who dismounted and approached, grasping a riding crop in his hand.

The spokesman abased himself even further, almost prostrating himself on the ground. Mehdi went up to him and nudged him with his foot. "You dog, how dare you challenge the authority of the Sultan Abdel Aziz, the rightful heir of *Sidna* Hassan?"

"*Ya sidi,*" the man babbled, "the Ghiata made us do it. They took over the town for Bou Hamara and we had no choice. They became our masters. And now those sons of sin have deserted us, leaving us and our families unprotected. *Allah isemmah* (may God pardon us). We meant no harm to the Sultan, whom we respect and honor."

Mehdi and Tariq conferred with the two *sheikhs,* al-Glaoui and al-Goundafi, who were standing in the shade of their horses.

"What do you think we should do?" Mehdi asked them.

"Chain them and throw them in prison," the angular al-Goundafi advised, his dark face twisted with anger.

But the wily Madani al-Glaoui urged mercy. "These people are not our enemies. They are victims of the Pretender, just as we all are. I say we be lenient. Let them lead us to the Pasha's palace and we will establish ourselves there. They can go in front of us, should there still be sharpshooters in the town. They may have good information for us about Bou Hamara's whereabouts."

Mehdi assented. They tasted the milk and dates, to the

visible relief of the men still kneeling in the dust of the square. Then the elders led them to the governor's house where Mehdi and the others established a headquarters.

Tariq turned his horse in the square to go back to see how Mohammed was doing in setting up the camp, but his way was blocked by the *guish* troops behind him. They had been standing at attention while Mehdi and the others were talking to the elders, but as Mehdi moved off to the palace, they broke ranks. The soldiers streamed by him, preventing Tariq from making any progress in the other direction. Their battalion leaders did not try to stop them, but were also pushing forward. They raced in all directions, heading for the town's shops, driving their horses through the doors, breaking windows, seizing whatever pitiful supplies remained in the town. The few citizens, who had been cowering in their doors watching Mehdi and his troops enter the cities, fled as it became clear that the soldiers were about to take their revenge.

Tariq and Mehdi, who had heard the commotion, tried to insert themselves among the men, screaming, "Stop in the name of Allah. This is not permitted!" They waved their pistols and threatened to shoot, but quickly saw that it was too late to take control of the angry men, many mourning comrades who had fallen last night or during the *mahalla*. This was their chance to punish, and to seize what they could, the bounty of war.

***

As Lili, and Ted approached the city, Lili saw huge clouds of dust in the air. Searching the sky, his hand shading his burnt face, Ted was silent and then said, "The army must be camped around Taza. Nothing else could cause such dust."

In another half-hour they saw an enormous army settlement

encircling the city and stretching for miles. Squinting in the dust, Ted called a halt, and examined the camp from his horse. After careful scrutiny, his face relaxed slightly and he told the others, "This is the *makhsen* army. I can see Mehdi's pennant. Tariq must be here, too. Wait while I look for him."

Thankfully, Lili slid down from her horse.

***

Meriam heard the soldiers as they broke down the doors to the *mellah*. Her first thought was for Rebecca, but Israel anticipated her. "I will go up to Rebecca and the child," he announced.

Then as Meriam ran to find the two boys, she remembered the daggers. She shoved her arm under the cushions in the salon. Where was that *jambiya*? Ah, there it was. And the other. She patted her leg, yes, it was still there. She and the boys huddled in a corner of the room. "What can we do?" she asked them.

Gerard hugged her. "I will protect you, *Tante* Meriam. Here, let me have that *jambiya*."

Michel started to pray. Meriam looked at him, angrily. "Is there nothing more useful you can do?"

The door to their courtyard splintered. Ten ragged soldiers burst into the empty space. They swore as they discovered nothing of value. One man broke into the salon. "In here. I've found one kind of treasure, anyway."

Meriam and the two boys flattened themselves even farther against the wall. Michel began to cry. Gerard moved forward, clutching his dagger. "Leave us alone. Can't you see we're just two children and a defenseless woman?"

The soldier smiled, showing a mouth with two teeth. "Oh yes, I see that." He moved his rifle almost casually, and shot Gerard in the leg. Gerard doubled over at the pain, and dropped the knife. "You bastard," he shouted. Two soldiers grabbed Meriam, who was standing paralyzed with fear. As they focused on her, Michel raced from the room.

Meriam looked around desperately. There was no one to help. She reached down to her ankle for her dagger.

A voice called to the others, "Here's a pretty piece of Jewish cunt for you."

Meriam gasped. That was a familiar voice, but whose? Before she could think a soldier threw her on the floor and slapped her hard. She lifted the knife and stuck it in his neck.

The soldier screamed, and grabbed at his neck, where blood was bubbling out. Three of his companions, seeing this, attacked Meriam. She felt her nose break, as another soldier, his face covered by a scarf, hit her, hard. He laughed. "A little spitfire, but we know how to take care of these Jews, all right."

Meriam passed out.

***

Tariq galloped to Israel's house. Men were swarming in the streets, carrying off screaming women and any portable goods. Jewish men trying to protect their families were stabbed or shot, and others were running for their lives, children in their arms.

At the house, he found the door already broken in. Tariq dismounted. Those pigs, it hadn't taken them long to find the homes. Pistol in hand, he went in cautiously. It was deathly quiet inside, in contrast to the violent street. The courtyard was in shambles; the plants Lili and Meriam had carefully nurtured overturned; the orange tree in the middle broken and burning. Inside the main hall he saw a baby's body lying beside the wall, its brains bashed in. Tariq began praying to himself. "Allah the almighty and all merciful, have mercy on us all. Please let this not be so."

He entered the salon. One of the boys was there, he thought it was Gerard. He was on his stomach; pants down at his ankles. Tariq turned him over. His battered face was still wet with tears.

Where was Meriam? Tariq stumbled over a dead soldier. Looking closely he found the dagger he had given Lili so long ago, plunged into his neck. But no Meriam. Cautiously he made his way up the steps to the sleeping areas. Rebecca was lying on her bed, her arms crossed, eyes closed. He thought, she died before this started, praise to Allah. But Meriam was nowhere to be found. He opened the small door that led into the dark water closet—nothing. Heartsick, he made his way back to the main floor. I should have come here faster, he told himself. He wandered around the house a few more minutes, hoping to find a clue, any kind of sign. At least, he told himself, it is good that her body is not here. Pray Allah she is still alive.

Tariq walked back out into the street. His horse was gone, of course. Well, that was the least of his problems. He pushed his way through the marauding men, so involved in their pillaging and rape they failed to notice one of their commanders. Ahead of him, Tariq saw several soldiers attempting to auction off a terrified young girl. He ran. The men, noticing his interest, called to him, "*Ya sidi*, here's a nice one, almost a virgin," they laughed. "Come, you can have her for free."

Enraged, Tariq pulled out his pistol and aimed it at the men. "This is not how the Sultan's army conducts itself. Release that girl at once."

The men let go of the girl, looking abashed. She looked dazed, hardly noticing her new freedom. Then she pulled her tattered clothes around her and crept away. Tariq thought to himself, someone else will get her in a few minutes. There's nothing I can do to stop this. He made a disgusted gesture to the men and turned on his heel. There was nothing more he could do here.

***

The sun was only a faint crimson when two figures appeared in the distance. Looking up, Lili realized that Ted was approaching with Tariq.

Tariq shook hands gravely with Lili. They sat.

Ted said, "Tariq's told me that basically, the fight is over. They overwhelmed Bou Hamara's men, but unfortunately, he has gone to ground."

Lili said, "So now you have Taza."

"Yes, Lili, but I do not take much pleasure from it," Tariq said.

"Why?"

"How can I tell you this? I am shamed for my people." Tariq was hesitating, Lili noticed, searching for the right words. "After those gates were opened, our soldiers rushed in. I should have been prepared." His brow wrinkled in anguish. "My soldiers went wild. The others said it was normal. 'Those are the spoils of war, the reason men fight,' they explained."

Lili and Ted looked at Tariq with expressions of horror, as it began to dawn on them what he was trying to tell them.

***

Inside the gates a very different scene existed from what Lili remembered of the day she left. The streets were now full of men, mostly soldiers. Many appeared drunk. Doors to houses stood ajar, some off their hinges. Windows were broken, and furniture and debris littered the streets. Here and there a frightened woman could be seen, her clothes often in tatters, eyes wide in shock, hair bedraggled, wandering down the streets in search of water, or perhaps simply looking for lost family members, absent children. When the women saw them, they shrank back into the shadows or a doorway. Lili's heart went out to them but she couldn't help searching every face for Meriam.

They came into the center of town, near the main mosque. Hassan, who was leading them, paused. He had heard rumors of a red-headed girl being held by a slave dealer who lived in this area. He went to ask a group of men standing on a corner.

Ted sat rigidly on his horse. Lili's eyes turned briefly toward Tariq, sitting straight and imperious on his stallion. He masked his thoughts well, Lili thought. Tariq felt her glance on him and looked at her briefly, but his mind was clearly elsewhere.

Hassan returned. "They say the man who organized the auction lives in that house." He pointed towards a blank white wall about a block away.

"Good," Tariq said. "Ted, just you and I will go first to talk to this man."

Lili waited with Hassan. Tariq beckoned to them.

Lili saw that Ted was crying. "Lili, she's here. She's...she's not very good.... But she's alive. She wants you."

Lili pushed quickly past Ted, and went straight up to the house. In its courtyard she heard the groans of many women being held here. She glared at the fat merchant, "How much for my sister? Take me to Meriam." She shoved money into his hands. The merchant gaped at her, not knowing what to make of this young woman in man's clothing. He pointed towards a corner of the house. Lili turned and ran for the room. Entering its gloom, she was blinded for a moment, then, as her eyes became accustomed to the darkness, she saw a small figure, huddled in a corner, coiled in a fetal position,. At first she thought it was a child, Meriam was so tiny. Lili went up to her and knelt down.

"Meriam, we've found you! We're here, all of us. Ted is here." Meriam huddled farther into the corner when she heard Ted's name and began to sob. Lili leaned closer to Meriam, putting her arms around her and stroking her hair. "There, there," she soothed her. "It's all right now. We're going to get you home and take care of you. Everything will be fine," she said.

Meriam continued to sob uncontrollably. Lili kept talking. "We'll go back to Fez now. Maybe you and Ted will want to go right back to Tangier. Arielle is waiting there for you." She sat with Meriam at least a half an hour, cuddling her, rocking her. Gradually Meriam's sobs diminished and she lay against Lili, exhausted.

Lili looked up. Ted was at the door of the room. She spoke again to Meriam, "Now Meriam, we're going to leave. We're going to walk out of here, and we're going to put you on a horse, and we're going to ride out of Taza. Can you do that?"

Meriam nodded.

"Good. Now, Ted is standing right outside the door. Shall he come in and help?"

Meriam shook her head vigorously. *"Non."*

Ted looked stricken, but Lili held her hand up in warning to him and shook her head. She motioned him to stand back.

"All right. Now it's just me, and I'm going to help you. And when we get outside, you and I are going to get on a horse together. I'll sit in front, and you'll be behind me, hanging on. Can you do that?"

Once again, Meriam nodded in assent.

"All right. So we'll take this one step at a time. Now, let's get up." Lili released Meriam and rose to her feet. "Now, take my arms. That's good. You're doing fine. Good. Now, stand up. Can you stand up? That's all right. It doesn't have to be perfect. We don't have far to go. Just try to get on to your feet. Good, good." Meriam was slowly rising. For the first time, Lili saw that Meriam's face had several bad gashes on it. One eye was closed. She seemed to be all black and blue, and her face was terribly swollen.

As she rose and heard Lili's involuntary intake of breath, Meriam paused. She touched her face and shrank back again.

"Here, *habibti*," Lili said. She pulled off her *djellabah*. "Let's put this over you." She arranged the long voluminous garment over Meriam and pulled the hood over her head, hiding most of her face. "That's my good girl. Don't worry. All those bruises will go away. You'll be fine. It's all right."

Lili half carried, half led Meriam out of the darkness into the bright courtyard. Ted came quickly toward them as they emerged, but Lili caught his eye and shook her head at him. "Not now," she mouthed. Meriam did not see him, keeping her gaze fixed on the ground. They moved slowly towards the front door, Ted following behind. The merchant hovered in the background, murmuring meaningless phrases.

Tariq was standing at the door. When he saw them, he also moved automatically to help Meriam, but Lili waved him off, too. Meriam did not want these men to see her or help her. At the open door Meriam moaned and held on to the door frame. She sank to the ground, and clung to Lili's knees. Tariq, seeing what was happening, went out into the street. Quickly he brought their horses right up to the door. He scooped Meriam up in his arms and deposited her on Lili's horse. Quickly, he picked Lili up, too, and put her in front. Patting Meriam gently on the back, he spoke to her in soft Arabic, "It is all right now, my sister. Here, put your hands around Lili. That is good. Now, Lili, start riding slowly behind my *askar*. I will follow you and so will Ted. Do not fear anything. Everything will be fine." He patted Lili's horse on the rump and it began to walk sedately, following the *askar*, who was riding beside him.

They made their way out of the city. Tariq led them to a campsite shadowed by tall eucalyptus trees; it was quiet, cooler, and best of all, completely private. They spread the blanket under a tree, and he and Lili assisted Meriam to dismount and lie down. Meriam gathered herself again into a tight knot, hands clasping her knees, and lay on her side facing the tree.

***

Lili wandered around her house in Fez's *mellah*. Ted had taken Meriam back to Tangier and suddenly Lili felt useless. She entered the kitchen where Aisha and the other maid were cutting vegetables, preparing lunch. She picked up a knife, "Here, I'll chop that parsley for you."

Aisha clucked her tongue, "Better give that to me, *ya binti*, I don't want you cutting off your finger."

"But I've been doing this for months, Aisha," Lili said. "Now it's all being done for me."

"We have our duties here that we are used to doing," Aisha said. "You've forgotten, my girl, with all that time in that cursed Taza, may Allah damn them and all their families to hell."

"What did I used to do with my time?" Lili said. "It seems like another life."

Aisha clicked her tongue. "Well, there are plenty of people in Fez needing help. Lots of families came in with all that fighting that's been going on. Allah knows, they're a miserable lot; children sick, not enough food, people not used to being in a city."

***

Wearing the Moroccan clothes she was used to now with a shawl, or *haik*, wound around her head and covering her mouth and nose, Lili mounted a mule. Their porter, Ahmed, accompanied Lili to carry her provisions, as well as for the general protection she always found prudent in this city. They arrived at a refugee area outside Bab Mahrouq. She sat uncertainly on her mount, taking it all in and wondering how to make contact with someone, how to figure out what might be done to help these people. The camp reminded her of the military encampment in Taza, although less well-organized. People had erected flimsy tents, some using the woven black wool of nomads, others settling for old rags or whatever they could find. The ground was a foul mass of mud, mixed with straw, ashes from cooking fires, excrement, dead rats. Donkeys and chickens wandered undisturbed and flies sat in the corners of children's eyes. Lili could not detect any natural source of water aside from some small donkey carts with metal containers full of water being sold by the cup or bucket full. Noticing this, she understood why everyone looked so dirty; this water was much too dear to be used for washing.

A group of scruffy boys approached her, ready to taunt, but cautious when they saw a respectable Arab woman accompanied by her porter. Lili noticed an angry look in their eyes that she knew could quickly change to vicious if she didn't handle the situation well. She decided to take the lead. "Where are you boys from?"

One of the older boys, maybe twelve years old, dressed in

a short *djellabah*, his hair wild and unkempt, answered, "We're Hayaina."

Lili recognized the name of the tribe that had been so treacherous during the Taza *mahalla*. "Who's in charge here?" she asked.

The boys looked uncertain, consulted each other. Finally the same boy said, "People go to *Sheikh* Omar when they need something."

"Take me to his tent," Lili said.

Plunging into the depths of the camp, they took her to a wider enclosure where a black tent was pitched. An effort had been made to provide privacy by erecting a cane fence around the area and in this sheltered space two women were squatting cleaning chickens. They gestured for her to go inside. Entering, Lili blinked in the gloom, then began to make out six or seven women sitting drinking tea, most with children tied in slings on their backs or sitting in their laps. They invited her to sit and poured her a glass of tea, politely incurious about who she was or what she was doing there.

A young woman, who looked about the same age as Malika, Tariq's wife, continued her pleading with an older woman sitting near her, who Lili judged was one of *Sheikh* Omar's wives. "*Ya Lalla* Fatima, no matter how often I feed my baby, he cries. And he has diarrhea."

The older woman looked sympathetic and took the child in her lap. "*Meskine*, may Allah have mercy on him."

Lili leaned forward to see the infant. Its yellowish skin hung from its body in folds. "Excuse me, my sister, but your baby needs more liquids to help him get better. If someone can bring me some clean water, God willing I can help you."

The older lady looked at her in surprise. Soon Lili was explaining her background to them and the little she knew about dehydration. She mixed the water with a little sugar and salt and made sure the mother washed her hands. Then she instructed her to dip her finger in the liquid and drip it gently into the baby's mouth and to continue doing this until he had absorbed the whole bowl. Lili sat there all afternoon with the women, watching the mother carefully administer the fluids to her baby.

As they talked, Lili discovered many of these women were widows. Their husbands or fathers had died in the last six months, or gone to fight with Bou Hamara. They were surviving by begging at the mosques in Fez, or getting handouts from relatives in the city who had no room to keep them. Lalla Fatima began to talk, "Since Ramadan ended (in January) we have not had a life. Fighting, fighting. We moved all the time to escape the soldiers. There was no time to plant crops. Our animals are all gone, killed by the *makhsen*, the government troops. Now we must depend on Allah."

"Where do you get your food?" Lili asked.

"Allah provides," Lalla Fatima told her. "Sometimes the elders of Fez send us bread and soup, or some *tajir*, merchant, slaughters a bull for us. And the mosques give us food. But it is not much. That is why our children are suffering."

***

Lili sat at the dinner table staring at her plate. "Do you think the Legation would be interested in helping these refugees?"

"I doubt it," Arthur said, pouring himself a whiskey and sipping it. "We're short on funds ourselves, as you know. And I'm not sure it's such a good idea for you to be down there, Lili. It's probably dangerous and full of disease. Who knows what you could catch?"

"But they need help. And no one else seems to be doing anything for them. I feel it's my duty," Lili insisted.

"Your duty, your duty. That's all you seem to think about. But what about your duty to me?" Arthur was slurring his words slightly.

"There's not enough to keep me busy here," Lili said. "I need something to occupy my days, since I don't have children." As soon as she said it, she regretted this.

"Well, whose fault is that? There's only one way to get children that I know of. But that doesn't seem to interest you much, either." He threw his napkin down and pushed away from his uneaten food. "I'll be upstairs reading."

Lili sat there thinking. She hadn't slept with Arthur in a long time. She detested it when he breathed strong fumes of alcohol in her face, making her feel he didn't even know it was she. But when he was sober it was even worse, pawing around, hurting. She gave a small laugh thinking about all the romantic literature she had read. What was that passion they described? Poetic exaggeration. She made an effort to put Arthur out of her mind, since it was so depressing. What could she do to help these people? They needed so much. Maybe the British would be willing to help. She would call at their consulate tomorrow and see.

***

"The tribes are saying we do not have a Sultan," Mehdi told Tariq at the Governor's palace in Taza. "They have been so influenced by Bou Hamara, they do not believe *Sidna* really exists. If he does not show his face here soon, they will turn against us again. We will be trapped in this city with enemy tribes surrounding us."

"My cousin, you must go to Fez and remind *Moulay* Abdel

Aziz of his promise to come. Even though we did not succeed in seizing Bou Hamara, we do have this town, which is important for trade. Perhaps you can remind him of that."

Mehdi nodded. "I will go today. He must understand how important this is."

***

Mehdi joined the Sultan in his garden, where he was dining with *Qaid* Maclean. The Scotsman greeted him affectionately, "Well, laddie, good to see you. How are our boys holding up out there?"

"Our regular troops are performing well, but we continue to have trouble with the recruits. I do not know how long I can convince al-Glaoui and al-Goundafi to stay. They are restless now that we have taken the city," Mehdi told him. "It would give everyone new courage to see our Sultan's face. Then he could appoint a new Governor and leave a garrison there, to keep the peace. And we could continue to hunt that rascal Bou Hamara."

Abdel Aziz said, "That is our big problem, *ya* Mehdi. My *wazirs* complain that you have not yet caught this Pretender. They tell me I should wait until the tribes have submitted."

"Excellency, the tribes say they will submit only to you. If we are to retain Taza, you must show them your face," Mehdi told him.

Abdel Aziz stretched. "So many problems and so much advice. It is hard to know what is best. But I need a change from this palace. So I have given orders to prepare. We will leave with you tomorrow."

Mehdi kissed his hand. "My lord, you have made a good decision."

***

Al-Raisuni had been gathering his forces together in his mountain fortress of Zinat, near Tangier. Without warning he attacked a *mehalla* led by *Si* Abdurrahman to assist the Sultan in fighting Bou Hamara. Raisuni slaughtered the army and seized not only the Governor, but also an uncle of the Sultan's, Abdel Malek.

When appeals by Abdel Aziz had failed to gain their release, Mohammed al-Matari, Ted's mentor from his school days who was now the *Sherif*, was called in to mediate. The *Sherif* arrived and took up residence in his villa in the city, where he took advantage of his recently installed telephone to call Ted, who was in Tangier with Meriam, to see how they could collaborate on this task.

Ted spent several days when he first arrived, closeted with Mohammed discussing the best way to deal with Raisuni. Then, with a retinue of Matari supporters, the *Sherif* and Ted rode out to al-Raisuni's fortress, a half-day's ride from Tangier. It was a beautiful early fall day and the sun was still hot on their backs. They ascended the winding mountain paths, passing golden tangles of shrubs baked by the summer heat. A hawk circled over head, reminding Ted of some glorious and not so glorious days at Matar. They camped within eyesight of the fort and *Sherif* Mohammed summoned one of his men.

"You, my son, go to al-Zinat and tell *Sherif* al-Raisuni the *Sherif* of Matar desires an audience with him. Here, take this flag so they can see who we are. Allah go with you."

The man rode off and was back within the hour, bearing the news that the *Sherif* was welcome, but was not to bring his escort.

The *Sherif* and Ted entered the large stone fortress. Ted thought how unprotected they were inside this seemingly impregnable palace, but he reminded himself that no one would dare to harm the *Sherif*, whose sanctity as a direct descendant of the Prophet was almost as strong (or maybe stronger in the present circumstances) than Sultan Abdel Aziz. As they passed through the gate and crossed the stone paved courtyard, Ted noted heavily armed men everywhere, carrying the latest European weapons. He even glimpsed a cannon or two. All those years of raiding caravans and robbing rich men at their weddings must have paid off, he thought.

They entered a large guestroom, covered in red and gold Berber rugs, with low couches lining the walls. Ted guessed there were about twenty-five men seated there, with al-Raisuni seated in their center. Al-Raisuni came to the *Sherif*, bowing and kissing his hand and his shoulder. He led him to the space where he had been sitting and sat down next to him, Ted crowding in next to *Sherif* Mohammed on the far side. Ted thought he would never have recognized the once handsome young man, no more than three or four years his senior. The years in prison had turned his hair grey; his face was lined, his features gaunt.

"*Ahlen, ya sidi*, I am honored by your presence," Al-Raisuni said.

"I, too, my son, am honored to be here. How is your health after your unfortunate stay in Mogador?"

"I am recovering, thanks be to Allah."

The *Sherif* nodded. "You know it was *Sidna* Abdel Aziz, and Sidi Mehdi al-Menebbhi who intervened to have you released from that hell-hole."

"Allah will recognize the just. But it was not he who sent me to that torture."S

"Allah rewards the compassionate, my son. But you have in your keeping Abdel Aziz's uncle, Abdel Malek. And Abdurahhman is the Sultan's representative in Tangier. This is not a good way to show your gratitude to our Sultan."

"That son of sin, Abdurrahaman, welcomed me into his palace and betrayed me, along with my own relative, Tariq ash-Sherif. And now, with *Sidna's* permission, he has seized my land. I cannot forget that. But let us talk of better things. Tell me, *ya sidi*, how is your family, your children? How goes it in al-Matar?" Smoothly, al-Raisuni led the subject to more general topics. He called for tea, whispering something into the ear of a henchman.

They sat for an hour. Ted thought, he has good reason to want revenge.

Suddenly Ted heard loud banging and cries; the doors burst open and the two men were thrown into the middle of the room.

Ted sprang up and went down to help the two elderly prisoners. He gasped as he approached Abdel Malek. "My God, you've blinded him!"

Sherif Mohammed rose. "*Al Hamdui'llah*, at least they are alive. But you, my son, could have shown more mercy."

"*Ya sidi*," al-Raisuni said, "these sons of sin do not deserve the mercy I have given them. They tricked me. Abdurrahman does not deserve to govern Tangier. I would be a better ruler. Let this be a lesson to them. And now, my men will escort you back to your guards. Go with Allah." He turned and strode from the room, leaving Ted to deal with the wounded men.

***

A huge entourage set out from Fez for Taza. At the head of the party the Sultan's royal guard announced his passage with trumpets. Two slaves followed throwing coins to the populace. Behind them stretched a line of horsemen, including Mehdi, *Qaid* Maclean, and five or six British friends who had been visiting the Palace. After them came Abdel Aziz, seated on a dancing white horse, and surrounded on both sides by slaves holding his stirrups. Behind him a servant held the crimson parasol. Bringing up the rear was the royal harem, carried on covered sedan chairs, and escorted by eunuchs. An army of servants followed them.

In the areas near Fez that were loyal to the Sultan, the tribes lined the road. Women held out bowls of milk and Abdel Aziz stopped from time to time to dip his finger in the milk. Such blessed milk would give the children extra strength.

Mehdi suggested they set up camp outside the city since Tariq had sent word that their hold on Taza was precarious. *Qaid* Maclean confirmed this decision, speaking later to Mehdi, "This way we can spread out, and eat off the land. That ought to make the tribes a little quicker to submit, so we will leave them alone."

Abdel Aziz and his friends lounged in the main tent, and the young sovereign called for his female orchestra. He told Mehdi, "These Circassian musicians are a gift from my friend Omar al Tazi. He has been very kind in your absence."

Mehdi thought to himself that it had been dangerous to stay away so long. But he had had no choice.

Mehdi organized his troops to spread out in the tribal areas, where they commenced to burn fields, kill animals and seize slaves. Soon a Hayaina *sheikh* appeared in the camp, demanding to see the Sultan. He was escorted to the royal enclosure, passing through the honor guard that flanked its entrance. Trumpeters announced the arrival of the *sheikh*, who came on foot, leading a bull. When the *sheikh* was close to the Sultan, he knelt and kissed the hem of his caftan. "The Beni Hassan of the Hayaina wish our sovereign, Abdel Aziz ben Hassan, a long life and good health," he proclaimed. He seized the bull by its horns and slashed its neck, letting the blood run in front of his sovereign.

Abdel Aziz, with Madani al-Glaoui seated on one side and al-Goundofi on the other, inclined his head toward the *sheikh*. "It is good that you have come, my uncle. Come and sit with us."

The *sheikh* bowed his head, then signaled towards his men. One came forward leading ten armed men with fully fitted out horses. "I beg you to accept these slaves, my Lord, as a symbol of my loyalty."

The tribes continued to trickle in to submit for a month. Then, exhausted and suffering from the raids of Abdel Aziz's troops, they began to rebel.

***

Two slaves stopped Kassim on *Sherif* Raisuni's doorstep in Tangier. "Who are you and what business do you have with our Lord, *Sherif* Raisuni?" they demanded.

"I come as a friend," Kassim said. He held out a bag of gold coins, "I wish to present these to the *Sherif*, to compensate him for the losses he has suffered at the hands of his enemies."

He was admitted to Al-Raisuni's presence. He hardly recognized the young *Sherif*, who looked as if he had aged fifteen years. His skin hung loosely from his bones, and wrinkles lined the once-handsome face. "*Ya sidi*, I am sorry to see you so affected by your unfortunate imprisonment," he said.

The *Sherif* gave a faint smile. "Such is the fate Allah gave me. But thanks to the Prophet, you see me now a free man, although much reduced in circumstances. That son of sin, Abdurrahman, has stolen most of my property and goods."

"Please accept this small gift in recognition of your suffering," Kassim said, tendering his bag of coins.

"Allah will compensate you," Raisuni said, weighing the bag in his hand. "Let us have some tea. I think of all the things

I missed in Mogador, the sweet taste of fresh mint caused me the most pain. But what brings you to my door?"

"I have some thoughts on how you might take revenge on *Si* Abdurrahman and perhaps on the *makhsen*, as well," Kassim said.

Al-Raisuni's eyes brightened. They spent the afternoon closeted together.

***

Abdel Aziz and his *mehalla* returned to Fez. He was tired of fighting the tribes and in the last month he had lost many of his men to tribal conflict. They still had not captured Bou Hamara, who had moved farther north.

***

Tariq shook his head wishing he could lighten the weight of his country's problems; nothing they had done had helped. In fact, all this fighting had increased the wretchedness of the ordinary people. He was preparing himself for a meeting at the palace. Mehdi had only told him tersely to be there after the noon day prayer and he wasn't sure why they were going. Surely at this moment they had little to say to Abdel Aziz. He adjusted the hang of his black felted cloak trimmed with gold braid and slipped his feet into new yellow *belghah* as he left his house. Five of his men were waiting at the door holding his white stallion, richly caparisoned with a red saddle and bridle trimmed in gold. They passed through the narrow streets of Fez, out the gate and entered Fez Jdid, arriving in the broad courtyard outside the palace just as the call to prayer sounded. Tariq dismounted, throwing his reins to his equerry and the large brass doors to the palace swung open to meet him. Two black slaves, dressed in the palace regalia of red Turkish pants and military style top with gilt braid crossing their chests, escorted Tariq to a small red and green tiled chamber in Abdel Aziz's personal quarters, where he found Mehdi. Abdel Aziz was the only other person, which Tariq found strange, as usually he would have a small orchestra playing in a side room and at least a few other foreigners, like *Qaid* Maclean and Ted, or Walter Harris. He wondered why this solitude.

The young Sultan gestured for him to enter and rose to kiss him on both cheeks. They then settled down on the plump brocaded cushions. Aziz did not keep them long in suspense. Looking unhappy he began, "My friends, these past few months have been bad. Bou Hamara is still in the countryside, threatening the peace of this land. The poor Jews of Taza persecuted by our own troops. The *ulema* are making it very difficult for me. They are constantly complaining that I spend too much time with foreigners. While we were in the field, the *ulema* dismissed all the Westerners who were not with us on the *mahalla*. Perhaps you have noticed this. Only *Qaid* Maclean was spared, because he was with us."

He took a long breath. "Many here are accusing me of being a *nisrani*. Can you imagine? Me, the commander of the faithful, a Christian! It is so stupid." He slammed his clenched fist into a nearby cushion. "I am ashamed for my people. They are backward and ignorant. They do not understand that their Sultan is interested in new ways and that only I can bring them out of this state of backwardness. But with Bou Hamara still at large, many are angry at me and are pointing their fingers, saying I have ruined the country by my godless ways." He sighed, his large dark eyes staring off into the distance.

Mehdi leaned forward. "*Sidna*, I, too, have heard this gossip. I know most of the *ulema* are blaming me, saying I have encouraged you to listen to foreigners. They say we cannot defeat Bou Hamara because Allah is on his side. But you know they hate me because I am your friend."

Abdel Aziz sighed again and twisted the prayer beads he had taken to carrying in his hand. "It is not so easy to be Sultan. I do not understand my people and they do not understand me."

Mehdi moved forward and kissed Abdel Aziz's hand. "My Lord, with your permission, Tariq and I will go on the pilgrimage to Mecca. Perhaps if we remove ourselves this will ease the problems."

Abdel Aziz nodded his head, reluctantly. "Yes, I think that is best. Go for a few months and maybe things will calm down here." He motioned for a slave to bring some tea, which Tariq and Mehdi drank, but Tariq knew Mehdi's mind was churning with plans and impatience to be gone quickly before his enemies could hurt them. As soon as was possible, the two took their leave.

Once they were outside the palace walls, Mehdi, who had been silent as they walked through the corridors, turned to Tariq, "The *ulema* and that son of sin, *Si* Fadoul al-Gharnit, will try to seize our belongings. As for me, I propose to send my valuable horses and other animals, as well as the gold I have accumulated, to Abdel Aziz. I would prefer him to have my property rather than those jackals."

Tariq nodded. He would do the same. At least this would buy some good will, he thought bitterly. He was disappointed with his Sultan, but also beginning to understand that, although friendly and amusing to be with, Abdel Aziz was not a strong man, maybe not a man to be trusted. He wondered what hope there was for his country with such a weak-willed ruler.

Mehdi continued, "I propose that we leave at daybreak tomorrow, even though I have accepted a dinner invitation from

Si Ben Slimane for tomorrow evening. My people tell me there are plots in Fez to kill us, such is the displeasure and hatred of the *ulema*. I do not trust Ben Slimane's sudden friendliness. Be ready at the dawn prayer and bring very little. The sooner we leave, the safer we will be."

This last news stunned Tariq. After all the good they had done, all the months they had spent trying to capture Bou Hamara, suffering hardships to save their country. He smiled bitterly to himself; this was another lesson he must learn well. Where there is no success, there will be no gratitude, no matter the effort you have made. He shook hands with Mehdi. "My cousin, I will await you at the city gates at the dawn prayer. Now I must go quickly to make plans. May Allah protect us both."

***

Lili went up to Tangier to help Amelia settle into their new home. She found little pleasure in Arthur's company these days and welcomed the change. Matt and Amelia had moved to the villa they had been refurbishing. The house, called Mt. Jefferson, was on the mountain outside of Tangier's city walls.

Lili was happy to see that Matt appeared content with his new life. If anything, she thought he was more popular than before. The Sanitary Commission, the powerful body of foreigners that ran Tangier, had asked him to take part in its administration, and he was engrossed in the town's affairs.

As Lili grew up, she had come to realize that Tangier's status was unusual; in many ways it was not exactly a part of Morocco. It was the diplomats and foreign businessmen who kept the streets more or less clean, and saw that electricity was installed, and it was the only city in Morocco with such a luxury. The Tangerinos were even lucky enough to have telephones, although they only worked within the city itself. But thanks to Matt and other members of the Commission, they also had a means of communicating with Gibraltar by flashing lights in Morse code.

Matt and Amelia had invited their friends to say goodbye to Tariq and Mehdi. Lili found herself looking forward to seeing Tariq and regretting the fact that he would be leaving. She realized, with some surprise, that aside from Ted and Meriam, he had become her closest friend.

Lili was dreadfully worried about Meriam who had failed so far to recover from the incidents in Taza. Meriam had been staying with her parents, the Ben Simons, since August so that her mother, Leah, could try to nurse her back to health. But she had remained despondent, barely speaking, spending hours staring into space. Meriam spent almost all her time now with Arielle, sharing her bed, playing quiet games in the garden, reading to her, or just sitting silently and rocking her.

***

When Ted arrived at the Ben Simon's house, located near the Legation in the *medina*. Brahim showed him in, and took Ted aside immediately, "Ted, my son, I'm so glad to see you. Our girl is so low. I hope you can do something to cheer her up a little, don't you know?"

Arielle was there, and climbed on her father's lap as they sat in the stiff salon, decorated with gilded French furniture and Aubusson rugs, sipping the coffee that Leah poured. Ted amused the child, but kept looking anxiously toward the door. The lunch hour neared, still no Meriam. Leah said, "Please stay for lunch. Meriam will feel better in the afternoon."

They ate quietly, Arielle sitting next to her father. A servant brought in lentil soup with lemons. The only sound in the room was that of their spoons clinking politely against the soup bowls. A boiled brisket of beef with mashed potatoes and peas followed. Each person helped himself silently as the maid passed the dishes. Ted leaned over to cut Arielle's meat into small pieces. "Papa, will you stay here this time?" she asked, breaking the silence. Ted cleared his throat, "Actually, sweetheart, I have to go back to Fez. But I will be here for Christmas. We'll have a good time then." Leah and Brahim exchanged glances but said nothing. When the meal was over, Leah put down her napkin and announced, "I'll go see how Meriam is." She went upstairs to Meriam's room. She found her lying in bed, face turned to the wall. "Meriam, dear, Ted is here to see you. Won't you come down for a while?"

Meriam shuddered and Leah saw that she was crying.

"Don't you think it would be a good idea to talk to him, Meriam? I know he wants to see you."

"No, I cannot." Meriam mumbled. "I just can not, *Maman.* Maybe some other time. *Peut-etre...*" she hesitated so long Leah almost thought she had gone to sleep. "Perhaps, *oui*, tell him to come day after tomorrow, in the afternoon. You are right, Maman. In fact, I must talk to him, but I am not strong today. Tell him, after tomorrow I will see him."

***

Two days later Ted came back. As before, the Ben Simons made much of him, forcing delicacies on him, offering juices and coffee. But no Meriam. After several hours passed, Ted decided he had to do something. "Excuse me, Mama Leah, but if she can't come down I am going upstairs to see Meriam."

Leah wrung her hands, "Oh, I do not know, Teddy. She might not....she might...."

Ted smiled. "What can happen, Mama? She's my wife. I need to see her and I think she needs me."

Leah threw up her hands. "Yes, it is for the best. You know the way."

Upstairs, Ted found Meriam in almost the same position Leah had found her, face to the wall, shoulders shaking. He sat down on the bed and pulled her to him, "Sweetheart, why can't you talk to me? I know this has all been horrible, but I'm here and I want to help you."

Meriam continued to sob, and Ted cradled her, rocking her and attempting to comfort her.

After fifteen minutes her weeping subsided and Meriam pulled herself away, pushing back her hair and sitting up. "Ted, we must be strong. Life has not been fair. This was a terrible thing that arrived in Taza. But now it is worse."

Ted looked at Meriam, "What could be worse, my dearest?"

"*Cheri*, I am pregnant." Her eyes welled with tears again.

Ted drew back. His face reddened and he clenched his fists. He was silent, holding Meriam. Then he said, "Well, there are ways to solve this. There are doctors."

Meriam stiffened and pulled herself away. "*Oh non, mais non*! This I will not do. Never!"

It was Ted's turn to sit up straight. "How can you say that, Meriam? Why on earth would you want to keep such a child?"

"I know it is difficult to comprehend. But Ted, this is my child, too. And think, this is a Jewish child, it is part of me."

"Yes, but the other part, sweetheart. The other part is those brutes. Why would you want to have a child by them?"

Meriam's eyes burned. "I have thought and thought, *cheri*. To me, the best thing I can do is have this child and raise it to be a good Jew. Those men who attacked me, they hated Jews.

They said it, over and over, 'dirty Jew, dirty Jew'." Her eyes flashed. "Now I will have this child and I will raise it to hate those men."

Ted was shocked. His sweet gentle wife, who would have suspected such a streak of vengeance. "No, no, Meriam. I can't allow this. I want nothing to do with such a child, who would always remind me of that terrible crime against you."

"*Cheri*, this is my decision. You cannot change my mind." Meriam sat up very straight now. "I think, Ted, the best thing for me to do is to go to Paris, to my brother. Gabriel. If I can leave soon, no one here need know. You must allow me to go."

Ted was speechless. "No, Meriam. Please. There must be another way. You must have an abortion."

"Absolutely not!" she snapped. "This I insist on. If you will not help me, then my father will, if for no other reason than to spare the family this shame. I should tell you, Ted, that I do not envision returning to Tangier. I do not want to live here any longer. Now that I see how they hate us here, I refuse to live with this hate. I can not."

Ted's shoulders sagged. Never had he envisioned an outcome like this. "But Meriam, what about me?"

She hesitated. "You can come to Paris with me. I would love that."

"I can't do that. You know that. My whole career, everything I've worked for, is here in Morocco."

Meriam sat up straighter, "Ted, everything is about your career. But I am your wife. I always come second. Now I have need of this time in Paris. I must go. I am desolated that we do not agree, but I must go. Will you help me or not?"

"Of course, if that is your wish," he said.

***

Mt. Jefferson was at its best; this would be Amelia's first big party and she had spared nothing for these friends of Ted. All the rooms were lit with candles, fresh flowers were banked in the receptions rooms, fires crackled in the salon and dining room to warm the chill fall air. Other guests included Walter Harris, Budgett Meakin, and Sir Arthur Nicholson from the British Embassy. Amelia had also invited Alice Watson, Kassim's step mother and wife of the late *Sherif* of Matar, who had died some years ago, leaving her a widow who many believed to have *baraka* of her own. There were about twenty people, Lili counted, going over the guest list mentally, as she performed her hostess duties during the cocktail hour.

Having made sure she had not neglected any of the guests, she finally approached the group where Ted was talking to Tariq and Mehdi about General Lyautey. "You know, especially now that you and Mehdi are gone, *ya* Tariq, there'll be no stopping Lyautey. He's organized, has disciplined troops. These slow incursions along the border are going to grow. I predict that eventually he will take at least the eastern section of Morocco."

Mehdi looked depressed. "We never had the troops we needed, or the equipment, to fight Bou Hamara. We should have accepted British help instead of relying on the French. At least *Qaid* Maclean understands us. It will be hard to stop the French, if that is their goal."

"Lyautey's approach is not so bad," Ted said. "He would improve conditions here, and with his emphasis on trade, he could bring prosperity to Morocco."

Tariq could not hold his tongue at such a pro-colonial remark, "*Ya* Ted, I disagree. You are not reading into what he says. But I do not want to argue about what I have not experienced for myself. After the *Haj*, the Pilgrimage, I will stay in Egypt. I want to study colonization for myself and see how it has worked. You know that I want the best for my country, but I do not think French rule will bring it. *Insh'allah*, I will find out."

"As for myself," Mehdi said, "I will return to Tangier. Did you know I have now become a British protected person? What do you think of that? Ah, here is your sister, *ya* Ted."

Lili joined them saying, "Haven't you three seen enough of each other recently? I'd have thought you'd be tired of each other's company after that long trip up from Fez."

Mehdi greeted Lili. "Why, Mrs. Crampton! It is always such a pleasure to see you. And what a lovely party your parents have given us. You must forgive us. We were talking politics once again. Such a fascinating subject, we never tire of it. Your brother was just telling us more about this General Lyautey, the Commandant who seems to have his eye on us. He is causing quite a bit of trouble along our Eastern borders."

"Somehow," Ted said, "I suspect this is not the end of your involvement. It's probably best for you to think of this simply as a well-deserved vacation. It wouldn't surprise me to hear that when you both return from the Pilgrimage to Mecca, there will be plans afoot to reinstate you or find something equally useful for your talents."

"Only Allah knows," Tariq said. "But for me, I will not come back to Morocco soon."

"Oh?" Ted and Lili spoke together. Lili blushed furiously and bit her lip, hoping no one had noticed her unsuitable interest in this news.

"I will visit Egypt and stay some time there," Tariq said. "I have heard many stories from my friend, Fuad, about what both the Turks and the British have done there. I am curious and this is the perfect opportunity."

Ted nodded. "I must say it sounds quite a good idea. There's really no reason to come rushing back to Morocco. Things are so unstable here at present. How long do you think you'll stay?"

"Perhaps a year or two, maybe longer, whatever is the will of Allah."

"I've encouraged Tariq to take the opportunity," Mehdi added. "We need to know more about our Muslim brothers. I think it will be very valuable for him, *insh'Allah*."

Dinner was announced. Lili hadn't realized Tariq was leaving for so long; why, it might be years before she saw him again. And yet, Ted was right, there was no reason for him to stay here. Oh, she supposed his wife Malika might miss him, but probably not that much. She would stay with her family in al-Meneb and probably be quite content with her children, her sisters and her mother. Why shouldn't he go? She had absolutely no reason to expect that Tariq would stay; in fact, she had no right. And that was that, she kept telling herself. She felt desolate; she could hardly concentrate on what people were saying around her at the table. And straight across, facing her, sat Tariq, not meeting her eyes. She fought for self-control.

During the dinner she made a pretense of talking to her neighbors at the table, but she had no idea what they were discussing. It was agony for her, trying to avoid Tariq's gaze. She choked down a few bites of food and prayed that she would not lose her composure before the party was over. She was embarrassed, too, hoping Tariq wouldn't notice, since she was sure he would be surprised at her reaction. After all, they were just friends.

After dinner when the men rejoined the ladies, Lili continued determinedly to talk to the ladies refusing to even look in Tariq's direction. She was listening abstractedly to Alice Watson talk about a health dispensary she had established when Tariq came up to their group. He stood chatting politely with the women for a few minutes, until Alice excused herself. Tariq looked down at Lili, "My sister, Lili, I wanted to say *b'slaama*, goodbye, to you. I will be leaving tomorrow, *insh'Allah.*"

Unable to move her tongue, Lili nodded speechlessly.

"Allah willing, things will go well for you and Arthur. And *insh'allah*, our sister, Meriam, will be better. I have told Ted to send me your news. And I will let him know about my travels." Tariq looked down at Lili, his face a mask of politeness.

Lili struggled to maintain her composure. "You've been a very good friend to us all. Without you, Meriam might not be here right now. Maybe I, too, wouldn't be here. I want you to know that I'm grateful, that I consider you a friend, and that I value that. I'll miss you, but I'm glad that you have this opportunity and that you're free to go." She spoke carefully, formally, willing herself to be unemotional, wanting her words to convey friendship but no more than that. Furiously she struggled against the tears she could feel brimming her eyes, praying he would not notice the one rolling down her cheek.

Tariq stood looking at her for a few minutes; he seemed to be evaluating her comments. Then he shifted. "Yes, it is best, I think, *ya* Lili. God willing, our paths will meet again in the future." He bowed slightly, turned abruptly and left.

Lili watched him as he made his way through the room. Despite her best efforts, a few more tears trickled down her face. Tariq had always been there. What would life be like without him? Would she ever see him again?

***

After Tariq's departure Ted spent most of his time with Meriam and Arielle. He came back to the house in Tangier every evening looking haggard, not inviting conversation, closing himself up in his room and asking for a tray for dinner. Amelia and Lili consulted with each other about whether to intervene and on the third day were about to deputize one of themselves to approach him. Just at that point he came to the small sitting room where the two of them were having tea and asked if he might join them.

"Oh, yes, please," Amelia said. "Here, come and sit by me on the couch, and I'll give you a nice cup of Earl Gray." She patted the space beside her invitingly.

Ted sank gratefully onto the couch, "Whiskey would be better, Mama, if you don't mind." He sat, sipping it moodily and staring out into the darkening night. Finally he said, "Well, you might as well know. Meriam wants to leave. She's asked me if I will help her go up to Paris to stay with Gabriel. I don't know for how long. She'll take Arielle. She doesn't know if she'll ever want to come back to Morocco." He rubbed his hand wearily across his face and looked down at his hands. "In other words, she's leaving me."

"Oh Ted," Lili said.

"Oh, my dear," Amelia said simultaneously.

Ted smiled grimly. "Yes, it's rotten. I suppose one can't really blame her. Perhaps I'd feel the same. In fact, I do feel that way about what happened to her. But I'm not ready to give up on Morocco. Among other things, it's my entire career; it's where I have all my contacts, all my education and knowledge. I can't just leave and start somewhere else. But I do understand how she feels."

"Yes, and of course, there's also the anti-Semitism," Lili said slowly. "That's part of what she's feeling, and something we can't fully understand."

"She talked about that with me, too. Of course, it's true. Jews have a bad situation here and now Meriam understands that in a way she never did before. And," Ted hesitated for a moment, searching for words, "you might as well know it all. She's pregnant."

There was a stunned silence in the room as they absorbed this final piece of information.

"My God," Amelia said, "what are you going to do?"

"I don't have much choice. I respect Meriam's sentiments and understand them perfectly. I think she has to go, at least for now. It's too late to get rid of the baby. Excuse me, Mother, for being so frank. Of course, I don't want her to keep the child, once she's had it. But she wants to. Can you understand that? I cannot. Maybe after she's been in Paris for a while, she'll feel differently. But I'm afraid I'm going to lose her. Our lives are going in different directions. And I can't see what to do about it." He stood up and began to pace in the small room. "If only things had been different. If only I'd gotten back earlier from Algeria. I wish.... But, it's useless. What happened, happened and we just have to live with the consequences."

"Will you help her to go?" Lili said.

"Of course. Gabriel already has a place there, and I know he would welcome having his sister for company. I always thought he was a trifle lonely. It won't be that hard for me to give her some kind of an allowance to live on. After all," he laughed bitterly, "she's my wife. And there's Arielle, too. They're my responsibility, no matter where they are. It's just that, well, I certainly never envisioned it being like this. And now, this new child. What to do about it." He groaned and sank back down next to his mother on the couch.

"Oh Ted," Amelia said, putting her arm around him. "Who can tell how Meriam will feel in a few months? You'll go up and stay with her when you can, and maybe in a while she'll see things differently. It's quite possible."

***

Ted handed Lili a sealed envelope showing signs of wear. "Sorry, Lili, I meant to give this to you earlier. Tariq gave me this for you the morning he left."

She took it eagerly and hugged it to herself until she was able to find time to be alone. In her room she looked at the sealed envelope, wondering what Tariq could have written her, half-dreading to read it, yet finding it hard to control her longing. Finally she tore it open. It read:

> Lili, my sister. I wanted more time to say good bye to you, but it was not possible and maybe it was for the best. I think now that I made a mistake a few years ago, and sometimes I think you also feel that. But now that time has passed for us. I do not like being reminded of what I can not have. I will miss you, little one. Please tell Ted to send me news of you from time to time. God keep you, Tariq

Lili sat back on her bed holding the note. Despite her sadness, she felt exhilarated. The thought kept running through her mind, he does care. It's not just me. Deep despair immediately followed as the full implications of her situation began to sink in. She knew he was right; there was nothing to be done. Then she got angry. Why hadn't Tariq discussed this with her instead of simply making a decision on his own, assuming he knew best for both of them? But she was stymied and she knew it. She had married Arthur and now knew it had not been a good decision. But her promise had been given. She wasn't some light woman, about to run off from her husband to join her lover. Her lover didn't even want her to do that, she reflected. Maybe, she thought to herself again, Tariq is right. This is the best thing. But the logic did not stop the yearning and emptiness she felt knowing that Tariq was gone and wondering when, if ever, she would see him again.

***

The entire family was at the port to see Meriam and Arielle off. Meriam had made a special effort to dress and looked almost her old self, although still pale. Arielle danced around her parents, unaware of their inner anguish. Lili noted with approval that Ted tried to act normal for her sake, but he was very withdrawn, finding it hard to talk to Meriam. Lili knew that he wanted to be supportive, but it was obvious that he couldn't suppress his resentment that, in his mind, Meriam was fleeing him, as well as Morocco. His frustration at his inability to reach his wife was obvious to Lili, if not to the others. She couldn't help noticing that, although he hugged Arielle and told her she was Papa's girl and he would see her soon, he and Meriam barely spoke to each other.

Lili watched as Meriam stepped into the small boat that would take her out to the steamer. Ted and she embraced briefly and formally, touching cheeks, barely looking at each other. Meriam turned as if to leave and Ted, holding her by the arm, said, "Meriam, please. Let me know when you need me. You know I'll come." She looked up then, almost as if she had forgotten that Ted was her husband, nodded and said, "Certainly, Ted. We shall be in touch. God keep you."

L ili started a clinic to expand the work she was doing with the refuges. She met with the French Court Physician, who gave her material and moral support. In fact, he told her that the present French administration was talking of setting up medical clinics in all the principal Moroccan cities within the next few years. "So this can serve as a pilot project for us, my dear," he informed her.

Abdel Aziz donated an abandoned guardhouse near the camp, and Lili and Aisha scrubbed and cleaned it, covering its walls with fresh whitewash. Lili furnished a waiting room with Moroccan couches, using cheap cotton to stuff the mattresses and pillows and cheerful calico with pink flowers to cover them.

When they opened their doors, no one came. Depressed, Lili looked at Aisha. "Maybe they don't want this kind of health care. Do you think I was wrong, *ya* Aisha?"

"*Ya Allah*, my girl. Don't be silly. They are just stupid. We will have to go out and talk to them, to make them realize the value of your clinic. These women are too ignorant to understand."

Lili and Aisha spent each morning going to a different neighborhood, knocking on doors, and talking to the women. Their reception was mixed, but most women were at least curious to hear that a doctor would be available to see them and their children. Deep in the *medina* they spent the morning in an old palace talking to the women of a large extended family. The eldest woman spoke first, "We like our own medicine, *ya lalla*," she told Lili. "These Christian ways do not work for us. You see, here and here," she pointed to round burned spots on her arms. "When I was young I had many pains in my bones. The holy man put hot coins there and the pain went away."

Another woman said, "When my son was sick last Ramadan, a *siyyid*, holy man, wrote me a verse from the Holy Koran. I dipped it in water and my son drank it. It cured him."

Lili said, "Many of your cures are very powerful. But I suspect all of you have lost young children, despite these treatments."

The women nodded. "It is so. In this house two of our babies died in the last year, despite all the blood we drained from them. It is Allah's will."

"You are right, my sister. Whatever Allah wills, we cannot change. But we do not know his will in advance. And there are other things we can do, especially to treat sores, the running stomach and the fevers. Let us add to what the *siyyed* does and see if we can save more of your babies."

Finally, the women started to come in, probably as much from curiosity, Lili thought, as anything else. But also, she found, they came if they had tried everything else and the children were still sick. The first child brought was about five years old. Its mother was weeping as she handed it to Lili. Lili placed the young boy, shivering with fever, on the examining table. He was filthy, his skin caked with henna and dirt. His clothes smelt of vomit, feces. She started to strip off his clothes. "No," the mother took her arm. "He is too sick. The cold will hurt him. Leave his clothes."

"Yes, my sister, he is very sick. But we should put him in clean garments and wash him a little. The dirty clothes do not help him get well. Let me try," Lili coaxed her. "I will do it quickly, with warm water, and we will dry him completely, so the cold cannot strike his skin." As she spoke, she sponged the boy with warm water, and rubbed him dry with a soft cloth. Aisha brought a clean *djellabah* that they pulled over his head.

"Now, my sister," Lili told his mother. "You must try to make your son drink, although I know with the fever he does not want to. But he must have some nourishment. Take these sheets and put them on his bed; wash what is on there now with hot water. Boil a chicken and let him drink the hot water from it. Let him sleep, well covered, and be sure there are no drafts in his room. If he awakes and the sheets are wet with his sweat, change his clothes and change the sheets to dry ones." She showed the mother how to drip soup from her finger into the child's mouth. "Be sure to do this at each call to prayer and once in between, my sister, until he has drunk a whole soup bowl. *Insh'allah*, Allah will spare his life. If you will allow me, I will come to your house tomorrow to see how he is."

As she visited with the mother the next day Lili asked her, "Have you washed your boy again?"

"No, *ya lalla*," the mother said. "We do not have enough fuel to heat water."

"But you have enough to make this tea I am drinking," Lili said.

"You are our guest," the woman replied.

"My sister, heat water for your sick boy and go without tea," Lili said. "Your son is a greater treasure than a guest."

Lili was very lucky. The boy recovered and word spread around the *medina* that she could help sick children.

***

Although Ted had promised Meriam he would come to Paris soon, he convinced himself his duties in Fez were more urgent. Every time he thought about her decision to keep this baby, he got more angry. He knew that under those conditions it would be pointless to go to Paris. And then, the Times was hungry for news on Abdel Aziz. Thanks to Ted they were aware of the threat Bou Hamara was making to the throne and wanted weekly reports on the state of the *makhsen*. All this made it easy for Ted to linger in Fez, although he knew he should be with his wife.

In Fez, he and Lili heard the boom of the cannon that announced the first day of the holy month of Ramadan. This month was one of the holiest obligations of Islam. During this time, Muslims would refrain from eating, drinking, or smoking from sunup to sundown. Menstruating women, the sick and the old, as well as children were technically exempt, but with the exception of menstruating women, the others often kept the fast as well since dying during the holy month ensured direct entry into Paradise.

Since Islamic months followed the moon, the holy month and other Islamic holidays rotated, occurring each year approximately eleven days earlier than the year before. Ted was grateful that Ramadan fell in the winter this year, when the days were relatively short and the weather cool. In the summer, it could be agony to go all day in the blazing sun with no water.

Lili, Ted and Arthur had been arguing all day about when Ramadan would start, since no one ever could pinpoint the exact day in advance. It all depended on whether one of the *ulema* sighted the new moon, so even a cloudy night could delay its announcement.

"Jolly good," Ted said, when he heard the boom of the cannon. "This will liven things up at least."

Arthur looked puzzled. "I've never understood why people look forward to Ramadan. Isn't this a time of fasting and prayer?"

"It's not like Catholic Lent. After Muslims get used to the fasting, which takes a week or so, they use the evenings when they break their fast to socialize and invite in friends. It should give me some good entrée to people in the court."

Day break and sundown were announced every day by men walking through the *medina*, blowing long trumpets. The last meal of the fast would be eaten just before dawn, when trumpets were accompanied by vigorous thumping on the doors to rouse the sleepers. After this last meal, many slept away the day, doing business or meeting with their friends in the evening. The evening meal, called breakfast since it was the first of the day, became a joyous occasion.

On the tenth day of Ramadan, Ted received an invitation to come and break the fast with his former schoolmate, Prince Ali. Ted wandered over to the Palace early, as there were several comfortable nooks where he knew he could relax and take a nap and it would be easier to get to Ali's on time from there. One didn't arrive late when the host had been fasting all day long.

Ted found a little alcove off one of the courtyards, its three sides well supplied with wool-stuffed cushions and pillows and painted doors, which he shut to keep out the winter drafts. He settled down with some late editions of the Times that he had brought along, intending to give them as a small gift to Ali.

He was deep into an article about Germany's Kaiser Wilhelm when he recognized a familiar voice just outside. Kassim, he was sure of it, and, yes, that was *Si* Feddoul Gharnit, the grand *wazir*. Ted put down his paper and started listening.

First Kassim. "Now that Mehdi is out of the way, *ya sidi*, I know a few foreign interests that might want to do business with you, *insh'Allah*."

"Hush," Ted heard the other man say, "It is not good to talk of such things in the palace."

"No one is here. All are resting at this hour," Kassim assured him. "You know, Bou Hamara is gaining strength since he retook Taza. He would welcome more supporters in the *makhsen*. *Moulay* Abdel Aziz has shown himself to be godless. Even though so many of the *nisranis* are now gone, thanks to you, he still prefers to spend time with *Qaid* Maclean and Walter Harris. You could help put a stop to this. I know Bou Hamara would show his gratitude."

"You may be right," the other man said. "The fact that Mehdi and his army could not capture Bou Hamara shows they did not have Allah on their side. A curse on all these Christians. They are stealing our kingdom!"

Kassim laughed, and Ted heard his name mentioned, but couldn't make out what Kassim said as the men were moving away from his door.

Damn that Kassim for a traitor and a scoundrel, he thought. Well, now I have proof that he's a spy for Bou Hamara. I wonder how he dared to talk so openly to Gharnit. The *wazir* must need money enough that he doesn't care where he gets it. How long would he, himself, be welcome at court, with this poison being spread? Ted fell asleep thinking about all these ramifications and dreamed about Meriam.

He was awakened by the palace trumpeter, walking through the courtyards summoning people to break their fasts, as he could no longer make out a white thread in the growing darkness, a sign that the sun had truly set.

Ted rushed through the palace labyrinth, wishing he had

one of Aziz's bicycles, but he arrived in Ali's apartments just as the men were sitting down to glasses of milk and dates. "*Ramadan karim,* generous Ramadan," he muttered as he sipped the milk sweetened with almonds. "Sorry, Ali, I fell asleep."

Ali smiled and nodded. Everyone was hungry so they devoted all their attention to eating. Then they sat back and some of Ali's friends lit small pipes, closing their eyes in contentment as the nicotine revived them after a whole day's abstinence.

Ali said, "*Marhaba*, welcome, my brother. You've been away too long."

"I had family affairs in Tangier," Ted said.

"Yes, my brother. I am so sorry to hear that our sister, Meriam, has gone to Paris. The attack against our Jews in Taza was unforgivable. You know, Abdel Aziz was furious when he heard about it. Did you know he deducted a month's salary from all his soldiers?"

A rich aroma of fresh coriander, cumin and lamb filled the room as servants brought in the *harira* that was the centerpiece soup of every Ramadan breakfast. Once again all fell silent as they drank the nourishing mixture of chickpeas, lentils and lamb. Ted was always surprised to find that, although he'd been fasting all day, he never could eat more than one bowl.

They sat back, sated. Then Ali said, "Ted, Aziz is so bored now that all his *nisrani* friends have gone. Can you come and spend some time with him this evening?"

"Of course." Ted knew they would probably stay up all night, playing bridge, or maybe even charades. And eating, of course. Then just before dawn they would have a final meal and he could go home to Lili's to sleep, just as the city gates were opening. This became a nightly routine for him.

***

Kassim sat in the tent that *Sherif* Raisuni used to receive his guests. Steaming glasses of mint tea sat near them.

"That son of a dog, Abdurrahman, continues to enjoy himself on the fruits of my property," Raisuni complained. "But thanks to your advice, I did profit from that attack on his *mehalla*." He leaned back on the cushions.

Kassim noticed that the *sherif* was no longer gaunt; in fact he looked quite portly. "Your freedom has improved your health," he said.

"Thanks be to Allah. There is nothing as good for the digestion as a home filled with women and children. But I still need my revenge on that cursed traitor."

Kassim twisted on his cushions, leaning forward, "Some of these foreign countries would be willing to pay large sums to protect their citizens. Have you ever thought of seizing some Christians and holding them for ransom?"

"That would be a good way to embarrass the Governor," Al-Raisuni said, looking thoughtful. "Maybe there would be a way to use such an action to my advantage."

***

"Can you believe it?" Abdel Aziz exclaimed. He stretched himself when the bridge hand was over. "That annoying Frenchman, the Count de St. Aulaire, has announced he's on his way here to discuss the terms of that loan with me." He pouted, signaling a nearby slave to pour him a large glass of lemonade.

Walter Harris, the British journalist and one of the few foreigners who had not been banned because he, like Ted, was a trusted friend, looked up from the score sheet. "There's no need for Your Majesty to see him, just because he comes here. Certainly not right away."

Abdel Aziz looked interested. "Yes, that's right. But," he said, "I do need money. I can't forget that."

Ted backed Walter up. "Sir Walter is right, my lord. You can keep him cooling his heels for a while. Show him who's in charge. He won't go away. Make him wait until the end of Ramadan, at least. The French are very keen on that loan."

"Right," Walter said, "let him wait. And then bargain hard."

Abdel Aziz said, "He will stay at the Tazi palace."

The Tazi palace was known in Fez as an elegant but crumbling ruin, famous for the size of its nasty rats with large pink feet. These rats were fearless and had been found swarming over the couches and beds of the palace, waking guests from their sleep by nibbling on their toes.

***

Ali appeared at Lili's house after lunch seeking Ted. She and Ted and Arthur were all sitting on the roof, enjoying the warmth of a early spring day. Ali settled down comfortably on the cushions strewn around the straw mats and leaned back, casting an appreciative eye at the flat white rooftops and green tiled mosques of Fez.

"It's such a beautiful city. I should look at it more often," he said. "We're so involved in politics and debt, it's my whole life these days. It's nice to be out of the palace for a while and among friends." He smiled at Lili and Arthur. "My sister, Lili," Ali said, "I hear good things about your clinic. One of my wives was telling me a story the other day about how her maid took a very sick child there, and she claims you accomplished miracles!"

"Well, hardly miracles, *Sidi* Ali," Lili said,"but it's amazing what a little hot water and salt can accomplish sometimes.

Especially with infections. I wish I could teach everyone that one simple idea of soaking septic wounds in hot water. It's so easy and sometimes it does look like a miracle."

"We're all grateful you're doing this, Lili. Our children suffer so much here," Ali said.

"I wish I could do more," Lili said. "I'm thinking of going up to Paris, maybe next year, and taking some training in nursing. There's so much I don't know."

Ali nodded politely at Lili's comments and turned to Ted. "Ted, my brother, Aziz asked me to come to you and tell you that he has agreed to meet tomorrow with the French count, St. Aulaire, to discuss the loan. He wants you to be there."

Ted said, "I wouldn't dream of missing it. How is St. Aulaire feeling, do you think?"

"I cannot imagine," Ali answered. "We just sent a messenger over to the Tazi Palace today officially summoning him to the meeting tomorrow. I have not seen him personally, and no one else has either."

Arthur, who was well briefed by Ted as to the state of play, said, "He must be pretty miserable after three weeks in that dungeon. I hear he's been complaining all over town and in fact, sentiments are running pretty high in the French community over his reception."

"Pity," Ted said, "he did ask for the meeting."

"But the French are offering to bail Morocco out of a bad debt situation, when all is said and done," Arthur said.

"But you could also say they are just sitting around like crocodiles, waiting for us to fall into their open jaws," Ali said. "And after all, they are responsible at least to some extent for the fact that we owe so much. And it is to their advantage to have us in their debt, because they are then in a position to dictate to us."

Arthur said, "But we can't forget that the Sultan made some rather rash expenditures."

Ted saw that Ali was looking very polite, which meant he was getting annoyed, and intervened, "You Americans have your own history of being a country dominated by another power. It's not a pleasant situation to be in. At any rate I shall be delighted to participate. I just hope Aziz will hold his own."

"Do not worry about that," Ali said. "He has learned in the past year how to handle situations like this. It is not easy, but he knows how."

***

Ted was shown into the vast Andalusian garden in the palace interior. With its small pools, flowering orange trees, and birds in cages suspended from the branches, it was a fragrant oasis in the middle of the dusty old city. Chairs had been set up near the area where Aziz kept his lions, and Ted watched them as they strutted around their pens, stretching lazily in the afternoon sun. Ali joined him in a moment.

"My brother is in a temper," Ali said. "I do not know how this will go today. We must pay close attention. Under no conditions should he accept what St. Aulaire offers."

They settled down under a large orange tree shading a paved area where comfortable rattan chairs and divans stood. "It is easy," Ali said, "for these diplomats to threaten us. And Aziz is so used to being obeyed that he simply does not know how to react when these Westerner powers give orders."

Ted caught sight of a slight young man, dressed in grey striped pants, a cutaway jacket, white vest and bow tie, carrying a high silk hat in his hands. In his polished black shoes with white spats, St. Aulaire, the French representative, picked his way down the garden path, obviously trying to avoid the muddy spots. The Count approached Ali and Ted, obviously not recognizing them from a distance. As he got closer Ted saw a look of surprise cross his face. He offered his hand, with raised eyebrows, *"Mais, dis-donc,* I thought this would be a private meeting?" he said, looking at Ali.

Ali smoothly introduced himself, "Good day, M. le Comte. I am *Moulay* Ali ben Hassan, the Sultan's brother. And I believe you know Ted?"

"Oui, bien sûr." St. Aulaire shook Ted's hand. *"Mais,* I do hope these proceedings will be kept confidential, Ted? We are *certainement pas* ready to report anything to the press at this stage, *n'est-ce pas?"*

"No, of course not," Ted said. "His Excellency, the Sultan, invited me to be present at this meeting. Perhaps he felt it would be good to have another foreigner present."

The Frenchman permitted himself a skeptical smile, *"Peut- tre.* In all cases, it is nice to see you, to be sure. How is your charming mother? And your lovely wife?"

Ted assumed St. Aulaire knew what had happened to Meriam, as did most of Tangier, so he bowed coolly, refusing to rise to the bait. "My wife, as perhaps you know, is visiting her brother in Paris for a few months. Thank you for asking."

A servant appeared, offering refreshments. They made their choices and sat for some time exchanging banalities about the weather, the garden, until Abdel Aziz made his appearance. Watching him draw near Ted had to admire his sense of drama. The young Sultan was dressed in sparkling white, white stockings and *belghah,* white baggy Turkish trousers, a white silk collarless shirt trimmed with white silk braid, and a white wool and silk cloak attached to his shoulders with a golden chain. On his head he had a white and gold skull cap. Two trumpeters heralded his approach and one of his favorite slaves proceeded him, leading a pet lion on a golden chain. The cub, probably about 8 months old, had a diamond collar encircling its neck, and frisked about as if it were ready to play.

Abdel Aziz seated himself cross-legged on the divan and signaled to the slave to stand to his left, coaxing the lion to settle under the couch. This last turned out to be harder to achieve, as the young pet was curious about his surroundings, and wanted to go to each guest, sniff his feet, explore his clothing, and familiarize himself with everyone.

The large cat showed particular interest in St. Aulaire. It circled the French diplomat, sniffing him suspiciously, licking his hands, and poking his nose into his crotch. The poor man squirmed in agony and fright while trying to pretend it was perfectly all right. Ted thought he detected a gleam of amusement in Abdel Aziz's eyes.

After the formalities had been exchanged, Abdel Aziz addressed St. Aulaire directly, "I hope you find my pet amusing? It was a gift from the Sultan of Mauritania, Bou Einaiya."

"Quite charming, quite entertaining," St. Aulaire said, wiping his perspiring forehead with a large white handkerchief. "It's just that I have a slight allergy to large cats. They make me, how do you say, sneeze," he said, coughing to illustrate his point.

"How interesting," Aziz said. "We do not have problems like that here in Morocco. Perhaps we are more used to savage things. We are a wild country, you know." He laughed.

"Yes, well, I want to thank you, Your Majesty, for seeing me at this time," St. Aulaire began.

Aziz nodded regally.

"You know, Sire, that *la France* wishes to help Morocco and is aware of its present financial difficulties," St. Aulaire said.

"To help us, or to buy us?" Aziz said. "I know that France signed this Entente Cordiale with Britain, our close friend. Am I right in assuming that this agreement means Britain, my friend Ted's country, has *given* Morocco to France?"

"Your Majesty, that was surely not the intent," St. Aulaire said. "The Entente covered many areas. It tried to define spheres of interest where one European country would be the main patron."

"And why do the Europeans divide up the world this way?" Abdel Aziz said.

"Your Majesty, it is for commerce in *Afrique*, that is all. France wanted to prevent further conflicts with Germany, France and Britain, and to clarify which country would have predominant rights in which countries of Africa."

Abdel Aziz said. "I do not remember discussing this with your Ambassador, M. Taillandier."

"Your Majesty," St. Aulaire said, "No insult was intended. Perhaps that was an oversight on the part of the European powers. I believe we thought the African countries were already aware of the trading arrangements in their domains. At any rate, I assure you that I will convey your sentiments to Paris. At this moment, I have, unfortunately, not been instructed regarding this point. My appointment today was to discuss with you the terms of this new loan which is being offered to the Kingdom of Morocco by the Banks of Paris and the Netherlands."

"Yes, yes," Abdel Aziz waved to him to continue. "But this Entente does not please me."

"*Certainement*, your Majesty," St. Aulaire said. "I will send for instructions tonight. In the meantime, I am instructed to advise you of the terms required for this new loan. The Banks wish Morocco to set up a Debt Commission in Tangier to administer it. They also desire to have a State Bank established to oversee Moroccan revenues, and to ensure that loan repayments can be made promptly."

The Sultan shifted restlessly in his chair. He fiddled with his lion's leash. "Who would be controlling this bank?" Aziz said.

"I believe the suggestion is to have the major foreign powers, that is, France and Spain, and perhaps Britain as well, set up a board to administer it. The Bank requests that the new institution collect all Moroccan revenues, make the periodic disbursements, and negotiate all new loans."

"Is that all?" Abdel Aziz said, his voice shaking and his fists clenched. Ali translated this, keeping his voice even.

"Your Majesty," St. Aulaire said, looking like a guilty schoolboy as he perceived the Sultan's anger, "the other request is for a port or customs police force to be established, with officers provided from Spain and France. This would ensure that customs are collected regularly and that the proceeds are correctly deposited in the bank, as they are the most important source for the debt repayment."

Ali, seeing that his brother's face was turning scarlet, cut into the conversation himself. "How would Morocco benefit from this loan, M. le Comte?"

"It would be able to pay off its debts. Is that not enough?" St. Aulaire said.

"I can see how France would think that," Ali said, "but we do not. We need money, but what you are suggesting will not give us funds. You will be taking most of our income. How are we to explain this to our people? Is France prepared to do anything to help Morocco? Something concrete?" He stopped to translate as Abdel Aziz glared at him, being unable to follow the English.

"I was not instructed in that respect," St. Aulaire said.

"Well," Abdel Aziz said, unfolding himself from his cross-legged position on the divan and rising to his feet, "Go back to your superiors in Paris and ask them for further directions. I will not agree to this loan unless my country benefits. And you can tell Paris that I have received another offer that is suggesting more favorable terms. Many Moroccans do not like this second French loan that gives France power over us. Just as your Entente would seem to suggest. Good day, M. le Comte!"

Aziz turned and quickly strode away, followed by the slave tugging on the leash of the young cub who reluctantly left off his examination of St. Aulaire and followed his master.

***

Lili ran out to meet Ted waving a telegram. "Ted, it's from Paris. I've been burning to open it all afternoon. I'm sure it's from Meriam. Please, tell me what it says. I've been so worried about her."

He tore open the envelope, quickly scanned the contents and then read out, tonelessly,

"Meriam gave birth to a healthy girl yesterday in Paris. Mother and daughter doing well. Regards, Gabriel."

Ted balled up the paper and tossed it away from him. "Well, that's done it, then. I have to admit I was hoping the child would die. Then, maybe, we could start again. But now... I don't know, Lili. I feel only revulsion when I think of that child, that *creation* from such an act of violence!"

Lili sank down near him. "I understand how you feel. But

the child is innocent. And Meriam is still its mother. Don't you think you should at least go up to Paris and see it and talk to Meriam?"

"Of course I will, Lili. But I don't want to see the child, or have anything to do with it. If Meriam would agree to give it up...but we've already discussed that and she seemed dead set against it before she left."

"That's a hard thing to ask. She's the one who has to decide. "

Ted said, "Maybe, but I know how I feel, too."

***

A slave pounded on the door one afternoon, just as they were finishing lunch. Ted answered.

"The Sultan desires your presence, immediately, my lord. He said I was to wait and accompany you back to the Palace."

***

Tariq arrived in Alexandria on a sunny morning, having opted to return from Mecca by way of Jerusalem, then taking a boat to Egypt's famous port. Fuad was at the harbor to meet him. They spent the day visiting the historic city, since Fuad wanted to show it off to him, before continuing to Cairo.

"We could be in Marseilles or Paris," Tariq said, as they traveled by streetcar through the center of the city. "The architecture is the same. I do not hear much Arabic spoken here, either. Are you sure we are in Egypt?"

Fuad explained that Alexandria had large Greek, Coptic and Jewish populations who used French as their lingua franca. They passed a large building with a grassy park surrounding it. "Is that the Palace?" Tariq asked.

"No, that is the site of Victoria College," Fuad explained.

"It will open next year and will be very exclusive. Most of their courses will be taught in English. You know, until now we have been taught mostly in French."

"No Arabic?" Tariq asked. "By Allah, can Egyptians read the Koran?"

"That is a problem, I admit. The schools are beginning to add Arabic as a course. But some of our newspapers are in Arabic, as you know."

"A strange kind of Arabic, though."

"Well, they write the way we speak. It is easier for us to understand." Fuad shrugged his shoulders. "Let us go and have a coffee and then we will catch the train to Cairo."

On the main square of Alexandria, Tariq saw the Cecil Hotel. To its left was a grand marble building with large plate glass windows. Fuad led him into the place, which he called a coffee shop, but looked to Tariq like a sumptuous restaurant, with crisp white tablecloths and sparkling cutlery. "Shall we have a sweet, as well?"

"No, my brother, and I prefer tea, if that is possible. But I cannot rid myself of the feeling I am in France. Is Cairo like this, too?"

"You will see." Fuad laughed.

The train ride took them through the Delta, with its cotton and sugar fields all along the track. "So these are the famous export crops you spoke of," Tariq said. He noticed big bundles of cotton stacked along the rails. Fuad explained that the train would pick these up and deliver them to Alexandria's port to be sent overseas.

From the station in Cairo they hailed a carriage to go to Fuad's home. They traveled down a broad boulevard, where Tariq saw more Italian and French-inspired four and five story stone buildings. "Who lives here?" he asked.

"Some foreigners, and some Egyptians. The Egyptians are probably *muwaddafin*, bureaucrats."

Tariq raised his eyebrows in question.

Fuad explained, "We have a large class of people who work in the Administration. Of course, the top positions are held by the British, but under them are many Egyptians who have studied here and abroad. They receive a monthly salary. This is part of the British program for us. Lord Cromer talks continually about our being better organized."

They passed a large garden where Europeans strolled, men and women together. "That is Ezbekiyya Park," Fuad informed him. "It is nice, is it not, to have a public garden in the middle of our dirty, dusty city? And there, just across the street is Shepheard's Hotel, where that large terrace is? Just beyond is our Opera House."

To Tariq's relief, the terrain they were passing through began to change as they entered the eastern part of Cairo, which Fuad explained was the oldest part of the city. While there were still European style shops and apartment houses lining the road, he caught glimpses behind them that looked more like the *medina* in Fez or Marrakesh. He spotted many minarets. Fuad told him, "We are known as the city of a thousand mosques, and most of them are near my house. It is because we are such an old city and every merchant or ruler who wanted to ensure his way to Paradise would build a mosque."

The carriage turned off the main boulevard, and Fuad pointed out a white marble building with red horizontal stripes. "That is Al Azhar, site of our Islamic university."

The road here, while flat, reminded Tariq in many ways of Fez. It, too, was crowded with shops, people, mules, donkey carts, and their way was slower. He began to feel more comfortable. "Thanks to Allah, now I feel I am in a Muslim city."

Soon they were in Fuad's family home, only a few blocks

from the bazaar, but like the palaces Tariq was used to in Fez and Marrakesh, peaceful and quiet inside its solid stone walls. To Tariq's eyes, the huge home was familiar, but different. It had several stories, which was common in Fez, although not in Marrakesh. But Cairene houses, he would find, were built in black and white marble and lacked the colorful red, green and black mosaic decorations always found in Morocco. Their court yards did not always have fountains, but their main salons often had marble depressions in their center, which could hold a fountain or a charcoal burning brazier in the winter. A feature he much admired in Fuad's house was carved wooden lattices covering the windows, often with small apertures that could be propped open. As he looked at the one in Fuad's reception room he exclaimed, "It has something written in the lattice, 'May this home be blessed.' By Allah, that is beautiful. I must tell them about this in Marrakesh."

***

Ted found Abdel Aziz in the same garden where they had all met St. Aulaire. The soft air of April and the scent of orange blossoms caressed him as he made his way to where Walter Harris and Ali were puffing on water pipes while Abdel Aziz paced back and forth.

The Sultan greeted Ted, without slowing his steps, "Ted, at last! You will not believe what that son of sin Raisuni has done now!"

Ted was totally baffled. What did this have to do with St. Aulaire? "*Sidi*? I don't understand? Raisuni?"

"May God curse his mother and his father! Allah cast a shadow on his soul. That ingrate! Woe the day I allowed Mehdi to convince me to release him from prison. What a mistake. I should have known, especially after the way he insulted my poor uncle." Ted watched in alarm as Abdel Aziz strode back and forth with a small whip in his hand, striking the table, the teapot, the trees, anything in his path in his fury.

"Your Excellency," Walter spoke from his chair, "I'm sure we can find a solution to this. It's just a question of money."

"Money, money! My eternal problem! But money will not rid me of al-Raisuni," said Abdel Aziz.

Ali motioned Ted over. "Al-Raisuni has kidnapped Ian Perdicaris and his stepson, Cromwell Varley. Not only is he asking for a large ransom, but he is making impossible demands, such as that he be made Governor of Tangier."

Ted couldn't help exulting silently. Perdicaris deserved it after what he had done to Matt. But he tried to look impassive.

Abdel Aziz heard Ali explaining and said, "Bah, someone should rid me of this man. This could turn into an international scandal or worse!" He waved a piece of paper in his hand. "Look at this! I have a telegram from President Theodore Roosevelt insisting on the immediate release of these men, who are American citizens."

Now Ted saw the full enormity of the situation. He sank down into a chair and gratefully accepted the glass of mint tea a slave was offering. "My God! Where has he taken them?"

"Same bloody hole he had me in last year," said Harris.

"Oh, right. I had forgotten your own experience with Raisuni," Ted said, now recalling that Harris had been imprisoned by Raisuni for almost a month.

Harris said, "But perhaps this isn't quite the time..."

"You two shut up and pay attention," Abdel Aziz said. "I need suggestions. How am I to handle this situation?"

"What's he asking for?" Ted said, turning to Ali for details.

Ali leaned closer to Ted, speaking softly, while the young Sultan continued to pace restlessly around the garden, slashing out at the flowers and any servant unwise enough to approach too closely. "Raisuni wants to have *Si* Abdurrahman recalled. He is also demanding that all the Governor's property be turned over to him. He wants all his men released from prison. There are some other things, including a large sum of money, which of course, we do not have."

Abdel Aziz said, "That son of a donkey has the gall to require that the British and the American ministers guarantee that the conditions be met. May Allah curse the day I ever took pity on him."

"Outrageous," Ted said, despite himself admiring the bandit's cleverness in seizing such prominent Western hostages.

Walter said, "This is going to be hard to negotiate."

Abdel Aziz said, "Walter, you and Ted must go to Matar, talk to *Sherif* Mohammed and get him to settle this. We cannot make enemies of the United States."

Ted's heart sank. Despite his assertions to Lili, he had just about made up his mind to go to Paris within the next few weeks. He needed to see Meriam and talk to her. But this was an irresistible opportunity. He could get a first hand account of what was sure to be an international incident. This would have to take precedence.

Within a few days Ted and Walter were on the road to Matar accompanied by a troop of soldiers. They stopped there a few days while they conferred with *Sherif* Mohammed, who agreed to join them as soon as he could in Tangier.

***

Ali and Abdel Aziz met for a second time with St. Aulaire. This time the Sultan received the French diplomat in the same reception room where he and Ted had met with the British journalist, Fred Coggins.

St. Aulaire looked relieved when he saw that the lion did not accompany Abdel Aziz in this meeting. He bowed deeply and Ali indicated that he should sit on one of the red-flocked mahogany chairs. Abdel Aziz sat cross-legged in a similar chair with an extra-wide seat, made to accommodate his preferred mode of sitting.

"Excellency, I hope you have had time to consider our loan agreement?" St. Aulaire said.

"Yes, we have studied them and discussed your terms with our *wazirs*. I accept your loan, and I will sign the papers."

St. Aulaire relaxed. "That is great news, my lord. I have the papers right here."

The Sultan signed, and St. Aulaire handed him a check. "If I may say so, this is a good thing for Maroc."

Abdel Aziz held up his hand, "Yes, I accept the loan, but I do not agree on your other conditions, setting up a police force, starting a customs bank, and so forth."

St. Aulaire sat straight up, his body rigid. "Pardon? Perhaps I did not understand correctly?" He looked at Ali perplexed.

Ali inclined his head. "We will take the money but do not accept your conditions," he repeated.

A frown wrinkled St. Aulaire's brow. "*Mais*, it is all part of a package."

Abdel Aziz leaned back and clapped his hands for a servant. "Bring us something to drink." He drummed his hands on the arms of his chair. "There are other things we need more than what you are suggesting. We need roads, health clinics, training for our army, military supplies. If France could provide some of these things, perhaps I might be able to convince my advisors to accept your terms. Otherwise your loan is of no use to us."

St. Aulaire mopped his forehead with his handkerchief. "*Alors*, I will report this to my *superieures* in France, Highness, and come back when I have a response." He accepted a glass of chilled almond water from a slave and sipped. "There is one more thing my President has asked me to mention. We are most deranged by this terrible incident in Tangier, the taking of M. Perdicaris and his son by this ruffian Raisuni. My government requests that you do everything in your power to have them released as soon as possible."

Abdel Aziz smiled slightly. "Unfortunately, as you know, he is asking for a large sum of money. I may have to use some of this loan to pay what he asks."

"Your Highness, I must warn you that it is unlikely my president will agree to drop those conditions," St. Aulaire said.

"I could never accept the conditions without taking this news to all my people and making sure they agree," Abdel Aziz told the diplomat. "As you can see from this kidnapping, we are a wild people and would not easily accept a foreign group to police us." He stood up, ending the interview.

***

The first thing Ted and Walter Harris saw in Tangier was a harbor filled with ships. "Those look like warships to me," Harris remarked.

"I suppose this shows President Roosevelt is serious about his threat," Ted replied.

Ted and Walter separated after arriving in Tangier, Ted going to stay with Matt and Amelia, while Walter went to his own nearby villa near the beach.

"Personally, I don't have a shred of sympathy for Ian," Matt told his stepson. "It's time he got his comeuppance. But I was down today talking to Sam Grummere at the Legation, and it looks like it's getting politically complicated."

Ted knew that Samuel Grummere, Matt's replacement at the Legation, had become fast friends with Perdicaris, enjoying the parties and entertainment always available at his villa.

"What's Grummere doing about this?" he said.

"From what I can tell, he's the one that's upped the ante," Matt said, lighting up a big cigar. "Sam contacted Nicholson, the British representative here, and the two of them think this could mean the beginning of a take over of Tangier by those ruffians. That'd be the end of the only spot of civilization in this country. So Sam telegraphed the State Department and asked them to send a battleship or two down here, just in case."

"He's probably right to be cautious," Ted said.

"Then this fellow you know from Matar, Kassim, I believe his name is. He came up and went to talk to Raisuni, according to Sam," Matt said. "That was the first we heard about the money."

"I wonder if Kassim might have suggested that part to Raisuni?" Ted said.

"Dunno, Raisuni's a pretty greedy fellow. Always seems to need money, and he's learned that kidnapping is the easiest way to get it."

"It has worked well for him, hasn't it?"

"This Kassim fellow has some kind of meeting tomorrow with Sam. Mebbe you should join them. See if you can make any sense out of it."

***

Kassim was already there, deep in conversation with Sam Grummere when Ted entered the office. Samuel stood up, shaking hands with Ted and offering him a chair. "I believe you two know each other?"

Ted nodded at Kassim, who extended his hand lazily, "Yes, we were school mates many years ago. How are you, Ted? How's that lovely wife of yours? Did I hear she'd been in some kind of accident? She was staying with her aunt in Taza, wasn't she?" He smiled. "It doesn't do to leave women unattended these days, you know."

Asking about a man's wife in the Arab world was a deep insult. Whatever, Ted promised himself, he would not give Kassim the satisfaction of reacting. Instead remembering what Tariq had told him, he replied, "Speaking of our women, how is that little slave girl you bought?"

Kassim's face darkened. "A woman of no honor. She is no longer with me."

That was one way of putting it, Ted thought. There was nothing to be gained in pursuing this. Not now, not in public. "I understand you've seen Raisuni. What did he have to say? How were the hostages, by the way?"

"We were just talking about this when you came, Ted," Sam Grummere said. "Kassim said Ian and his stepson, Cromwell, were being kept in a wooden hut, very primitive and uncomfortable. I want to send up some things with Kassim, see if we can at least make them more comfortable. It may take a while to work this affair out."

"Sounds a good idea," Ted said, keeping his eyes fixed steadily on Kassim, as if he were a snake. "The money is going to be hard to arrange. I thought he was more interested in getting his fifty-six men released from prison and ousting the governor. Would he settle for that?"

"A little money never hurts," Kassim said. "Helps to sweeten the pot, I always say."

"President Roosevelt's pulling out all the stops," Grummere said. "He's sent a telegram to the Sultan saying 'Perdicaris alive or Raisuni dead'. It made the headlines of this evening's edition of the Tangier Times, plus quite a few international papers, too, I believe. All hell seems to have broken out in Fez. I just got a telegram from your brother-in-law, Arthur. He said all the foreigners there are panicking because of these warships anchored here. The Moroccans are worried the Americans may fire on them and there's a lot of anti-foreign sentiment."

Ted realized that he and Sir Walter were going to have to do some tough bargaining to dispel these tensions. Fortunately, they would have the *Sherif* to do the main negotiating. Kassim's involvement was a wild card he hadn't expected. He was sure one way or the other it would complicate things. He wondered how long it would be before he could get to Paris.

***

Ted and Walter rode out to Raisuni's fortress to see how Ian and Cromwell were doing. To his surprise, Ted thought that they actually seemed fairly content.

"He's actually quite a good fellow," Ian Perdicaris told Ted. "Just as Walter found. He's smart and I think he wants the best for his country."

Ted raised an eyebrow. "I'm sure he wants what's best for himself, at any rate. After all, the $70,000 he's demanding will just about beggar Abdel Aziz. I wouldn't let Raisuni fool you that he wants what's best for Morocco." If the ransom had partly been a suggestion from Kassim, it had been a brilliant maneuver on his part to weaken Abdel Aziz's power, perhaps fatally.

Ted and Walter visited Raisuni again with the two Ministers to see if any room for bargaining existed, but they had to admit finally that the bandit seemed ready to hold the two men forever. Meanwhile pressure was mounting. Murmurs in the European community were quickly becoming public statements about the weakness of the government and its inability to control its own countryside. At the same time, Roosevelt was shrewdly using the affair at the Republican convention to remind his constituents that he was a man of action and the heroic leader of the Rough Riders who had led his troops to victory in Cuba.

In late June *Sherif* Mohammed of Matar arrived. Ted and Walter met with him in his house in the *medina* to bring him up to date on the status of their discussions with Raisuni. "My friends, I am happy to see you. Please excuse me for not rising, but the long trip has exhausted me." He waved them to the velvet divans lining the room. "Please, be comfortable and I will have some chilled juices brought." He clapped his hands and another slave appeared to take his order. "Now, what are we going to do about our friend, al-Raisuni?"

"Excellency," Ted said, "you may not be aware that your step-brother, Kassim, is here and has visited Raisuni several times to see to the comfort of the hostages."

"Ah, so that explains why he is here. Some in our house mentioned his presence, but I have not seen him," the *Sherif* said. His brow furrowed. "*Insh'Allah*, he can be helpful, and not just make more trouble. I will discuss this with him, and meet with the American Minister. Then you must allow me a week to recover from my journey. After that, we will go to al-Zinat. Let us hope we will have better luck than the last time, *ya* Ted."

***

Raisuni, as always, was hospitable to the *Sherif.* As a fellow *Sherif,* although without the special mediating and healing powers of *Sherif* Mohammed, he honored his position. After they were once again settled in his reception room, he said, "You are always welcome in my home. I am thinking of keeping a special room for you, since I am so often favored by your presence."

Sherif Mohammed smiled, settling himself into the cushions. "Without insulting your hospitality, I would prefer to stay in my mountains during this summer heat."

Raisuni nodded.

"Now, my son, let us come straight to the point. Your capture of these two Americans is causing grave damage to our Sultan. Our country is already in a bad state. Your actions weaken it further. The Western powers speak ill of us, saying there is *fuda,* anarchy, here. The warships in our harbor threaten to invade us."

Raisuni shifted in his chair, looking as a child might when scolded by his father. "*Sidi,* the Sultan makes excessive demands on us. He has seized much of my property and given it to *Si* Abdurrahman. He asks for taxes that will beggar us. We cannot continue like this."

"Nevertheless, as a *Sherif* of this country, you must improve your actions, my son. We should behave as five fingers on one hand, each helping the other. Now, for the sake of peace in our kingdom, and to protect Islam, *Sidna* has acceded to your demands. Let this be the last time."

"And what of *Si* Abdurrahman?" Raisuni asked.

"It will be as you asked. He is packing his bags today. My son, you have won this round. *Sidna* awards you the Governorship of this land. Mind that you bear this responsibility seriously, and remember who is your Commander, and Commander of the Faithful."

Raisuni looked down. There was a silence. "*Ya sidi*, it will be as you say." He hesitated, then almost defiantly added, "When my men and the money are brought here, I will release the two Americans."

Sherif Mohammed nodded. "*Si* Abdurrahman is assembling the money as we speak. He should arrive soon. We will wait and accompany the Americans back to Tangier."

By late afternoon, a caravan of thirty mules wound their way slowly up the mountain, carrying the load of $70,000 dollars in Spanish silver coins. Ted and Walter stood waiting for the funds to arrive. Al-Raisuni counted the money to assure that it was all there, while Walter Harris watched, making snide asides to Ted. When Raisuni was satisfied, he gestured to his men to release Perdicaris and his stepson, who had been standing by, talking to Kassim, who had appeared with the mule train. *Sherif* Mohammed waved two horses in the direction of the hostages, and all took their leave of al-Raisuni. Kassim, however, remained behind, bidding Perdicaris and his stepson farewell.

As he rode off, Ted commented to Walter, "I wonder how much of that $70,000 is his finder's fee? Two thieves working together. God knows, I wouldn't trust either of them farther than I could throw him."

The trip back was quiet. Perdicaris rode alongside Ted, not speaking. Then he looked up, "I'm through with this country. It's just getting too damn dangerous. Why, we could have lost our lives there. As it was, al-Raisuni wasn't that bad, but if there were a next time, who knows?"

Ted answered neutrally, trying to disguise his anger. The thought of all that money going to such a scoundrel, while Abdel Aziz was fighting off bankruptcy disgusted him. Truly, there was no notion of the common good in this country, despite

Sherif Mohammed's words. A little discipline and education from the French could only be good for Morocco, in the long run.

Ted remained in Tangier a few more weeks to tie up loose ends. He was reluctant to begin the trip to France, dreading what he would find there.

***

Ted accompanied his mother to the market in Souk al Barra, as always dressed in Moroccan baggy trousers and shirt. Probably some thought he was her servant as he was holding the basket while Amelia looked over an array of fresh tomatoes, bargaining with the vendor as she pinched them to see how ripe they were.

"Two *douros* is definitely my last price," she insisted.

"For you, my aunt, I will do it. You are my valued customer," the vendor said, piling the vegetables into the open basket Ted held out.

Just then five burly men in brown wool *djellabahs* pushed through the crowd, shoving Amelia rudely aside. Ted caught her before she fell, and swore at the men, "Watch it, you shameless men. Don't you have respect for women?"

Four of the men ignored him, but the last one turned back and stood, arms akimbo, staring at Ted. "She is only a *nisraniya*. Why do you care?"

"Since when do good Muslims act this way toward any woman?" Ted demanded.

The man grinned. "We do as our lord, *Sherif* Raisuni, bids us. If you have a quarrel, you may take it up there." He pointed to the middle of the marketplace where Ted now saw a circle had gathered.

The man walked away and Amelia begged Ted to forget

it. "There's no point in making a fuss," she insisted. "No real harm was done."

But now Ted was curious. "Don't worry, Mother, I won't start a fight. But stay here a moment. I'm curious to see what's going on over there."

Ted approached the circle. As he got nearer he could see that al-Raisuni was seated in the center, with a table in front of him. On each side sat a white bearded man in a long white robe and a turban wrapped around a fez, indicating his status as a Haj, someone who had made the pilgrimage to Mecca. Ted pushed to the front and saw that a tribesman, judging from his short *djellabah* and dirty turban, was kneeling in the dust before the *Sherif.* When he stopped talking, Raisuni and the two men, who Ted decided were probably *qadis*, or religious judges, appeared to be conferring. Ted heard al-Raisuni say, "You are guilty of a heinous crime. For this you shall be beaten!" And as Ted watched, two of the thugs he had just seen with Amelia came forward and pulled off the peasant's *djellabah* leaving him in just his baggy pants and shirt. Another came forward with a whip and began counting the strokes.

Ted backed off, shocked that his beloved Tangier could revert to such a primitive level. He hurried back to Amelia. "Are you through here, Mama? I think we should be getting home." He didn't want to tell her what he had just seen. As they passed through the main gates to the Souk, Ted looked up and saw, for the first time in his memory of Tangier, that heads were hanging on the wall, just as they did in Fez. He hurried Amelia along, keeping up a patter of conversation to divert her attention, hoping she would not see the grisly sight.

"Raisuni seems to have rather a lot of ruffians in the *medina*," Amelia remarked later at lunch.

"Sounds like we're reverting to barbarous traditions even

here in Tangier," Matt said. "The next thing you know, we'll see heads on top of the city walls again. Who knows, maybe we would be better with the French running this country."

. "Well, I wouldn't say that very loudly these days," Ted said. "Abdel Aziz is quite sensitive on that subject, and I can't blame him. But it's too bad he can't keep people like Raisuni in line. It doesn't pay right now to look so weak, with the French and British circling like vultures. But this latest change of events, with Raisuni as Governor, won't do much for Morocco's image either."

***

It was a hot summer afternoon in Paris when Ted descended from the wagons-lits car. He stretched and looked around the Gare de Lyons for a porter. He had traveled with Georges St. Réné Taillandier, resident French Minister in Tangier, who had been called to Paris for the negotiations of the French loan. Ted also had instructions from the Times to cover this event, so he planned to stay three or four weeks, through early September, when it took place.

He had accepted the Taillandiers' invitation to stay with them, at least for the first few days until he could see how things lay with Meriam.

A carriage took them from the station on the hour-long ride to the suburban neighborhood of Neuilly, just beyond the Arc de Triomphe. It was late in the afternoon, and Ted drank in the sights of this wonderful city as they made their way. He didn't know Paris well, but he had always enjoyed his short visits there.

Ted watched mothers and nannies walking slowly with their children or charges in the Luxembourg Gardens, looking tired from an afternoon of frolic. From the open windows of the coach he could hear them calling to each other desultorily, in low voices, hushing the children, urging them towards home and teatime. He couldn't help thinking of the last time he had been here with Meriam, returning from Oxford, and the fun they, too, had had in the park. Could his life really have changed so much in a few short years? They approached the Quai d'Orsay, where their meetings would be held in a few days.

He looked across the river, spotting Notre Dame, sitting there in all its majesty and saw small clusters of tourists gathered in its Grande Place, guidebooks in hand, listening to a guide extol the mysteries of the ancient cathedral. He wondered if they were as carefree and happy as they looked, or if they, too, hid unhappy secrets. He shook his head. He must rid himself of this gloom; after all, he would see Meriam soon and maybe they could somehow put all the sadness behind them. Yes, she had suffered tragedy, but he still hoped it wouldn't ruin their lives forever.

As always, returning to Europe from Morocco, Ted marveled at the vast differences. Even in the dust and heat of late summer, France seemed so organized, so neat. There was a sense of logic, of systems, that to Ted's Arab soul seemed vaguely disquieting, so sterile, so antiseptic. He missed the hustle and bustle of Tangier, the beggars darting through the crowds, vendors hawking their wares, the press of people, mules, carriages, litters that were so familiar to him. Europe was an alien place for him. Even the smells were wrong. Here in Paris the main odors were river water, urine, coffee, cigarettes and linden trees. Not his smells. Paris somehow lacked the appeal of Tangier, the whiff of cumin, the acrid trace of henna, the smell of kebabs cooking in small braziers along the curbs, the pungent scent of fresh mint being sold on street corners, the ever pervasive odor of cedar shavings. Ted smiled to himself and turned to address Taillandier, "Well, how do you feel, being home?"

The elder diplomat unexpectedly echoed his thoughts. "I do not really think of Paris as home any longer. Of course, my wife prefers it. She misses the shops, the theatre, you know, *la vie*, she would call it. But for myself, well, I have lived in Tangier for the past five years. Naturally, I like Paris, seeing my family. I enjoy the restaurants. But," he gave a Gallic shrug, "Tangier is my home, really. I have adapted. I have become a Tangerino. We have a nice life there, don't you think, *mon ami*? And Paris seems a bit, how should I put it, boring, predictable. *N'est ce pas?*"

Ted laughed. "I think, *monsieur*, we are lovers of adventure, of the unexpected. Yes, I must admit, I share your sentiments." He leaned back and lit a cheroot, enjoying the luxury of being transported in a carriage. They had crossed the Pont St Michel and turned left, traversing the Rue Rivoli, and were now entering the broad Champs Elysées. The cafes lining the boulevard were crowded with well-dressed men and women sipping aperitifs and whiling away the early evening. Ted watched in fascination as their horses trotted sedately up the boulevard.

"You know, *monsieur*," he said, "our life is wonderful there, you are right. But I tend to forget about this life. Look at these ladies and gentlemen, sitting happily together at these cafes, in full public view, drinking their *pastis* or sherry, with never a care in the world. If someone told them it was unseemly for men and women to sit together like this in public and to sip alcoholic beverages, they would simply laugh. And yet, for us, it's a way of life we take for granted, even though these people here are really our people, not the Moroccans. Don't you find this strange?"

"*Ah oui,*" the Frenchman said. "I think some part of us likes that. Maybe we enjoy perversity a bit, do you think? Perhaps we are destined by our own natures to always be strangers in countries not our own."

The carriage passed under the Arc de Triomphe and drew away from Paris. Taillandier busied himself directing the coachman and fifteen minutes later they pulled up in front of a large ivy-covered villa set back from the road by a curving driveway.

***

Ted went by carriage to Rue d'Auteuil where the Ecole Normale Israelite Orientale was located. He wanted to find Gabriel at the school first and discuss the best means of approaching Meriam. He was nervous. He was determined not to accept the baby and apprehensive about even discussing this with Meriam. Now that the baby was born her maternal instincts would be even stronger.

He entered the building, sniffing the familiar scents of ink, chalk, old books, so reminiscent of all the schools he had known. Boys of all ages crowded the corridor, but he saw with relief that they were quiet and disciplined. They were rigorously dressed in European suits, hair cut close to the head, boots polished to a high gloss. No caftans and slippers in sight. At first glance it was hard to believe that these were young oriental Jews, most, he knew, from Lebanon, Syria, North Africa. But then he remembered that the Alliance Israelite in Tangier required this dress of all its students and in fact was militant in its pursuit of modernism and westernization.

An older boy showed him into a guest parlor and said he would fetch Professor Ben Simon. Standing in front of the empty fireplace, Ted thought back. It had been, what, five years at least since he had seen Gabriel? The last time must have been at his wedding.

Gabriel had been in Paris eight or nine years, first studying, then later teaching at the Institute. The Alliance Israelite had sent him to complete his education and to be trained as a teacher. He was supposed to go back to Tangier and play some prominent role in the school there. If Gabriel still planned to do that, Ted thought, he must be almost ready to return. He did some quick calculations; he himself was now twenty-six, so Gabriel must be twenty-seven.

The door opened and a tall slim man entered the room. Like the students Ted had seen in the hall, Gabriel had his curly black hair cropped very short, probably not more than half an inch long. He wore round wire-rimmed glasses and was dressed in a dark suit with a gold watch chain stretched across the waistcoat.

Gabriel strode quickly across the room and embraced Ted. "Ted, *mon frère,* why didn't you let us know you were coming?"

"St. René Taillandier suggested I travel with him, so I was a bit unclear when we would actually depart. I thought it would be best to simply contact you when I got here. You look wonderful, my friend. Very grown up and dignified."

"And you look more like a Westerner than I'm used to," Gabriel said. "I'm not sure I knew you owned a full three-piece suit."

Ted laughed. "It's true. I've really grown to prefer Moroccan dress. These trousers seem so confining, and the boots are hot! But I did wear these clothes when I was at Oxford, you know."

They drank the small cups of coffee that a servant had brought to the room. At length a pause developed and grew.

The two men looked at each other. Ted was the first to speak, "How is Meriam, Gabriel?"

"*Ya* Ted, she is much better now than when she first arrived. And of course, now she has Laure as well as Arielle," Gabriel said.

"Laure?" Ted said.

"You know, the baby," Gabriel said.

Ted's face hardened. "And she's in good health? Meriam, I mean?"

"Excellent," Gabriel said. "She's gained some weight and has begun to take much more interest in the world here. She's even made a few friends. Coming here was the best thing she could have done. It was good to get away from Morocco, to put that all behind her...." He colored, letting his words trail off in confusion. "She and Mama are staying with me, as you know. You will come and dine with us this evening, won't you?"

"I'm looking forward to it," Ted said.

***

Gabriel lived in the Sixth Arrondissement, near the Rue du Bac. A concierge let Ted into a large cobbled courtyard and gestured to the far side where he found a stairway.

Meriam opened the door with Arielle at her side. They smiled, almost shyly at each other.

Ted thought Meriam looked very well, slightly older and less full of her old air of openness and joy. A serenity and peacefulness had replaced this. She was very slim but not gaunt. Her face seemed paler; her freckles had faded away, probably, he thought, because she had not been out in the sun much in the past few months. She wore a full black skirt, a silk blouse of rich crimson, and an embroidered black velvet vest. Her hair was very simple, hanging down behind her back, caught with

TANGIER, A NOVEL

a ribbon. With a shock, Ted realized she was still dressed like the Jews of the *mellah* in Taza.

Meriam reached out her hands to him. "Welcome, Ted," she said softly. Before he could do more than grasp her hands, Arielle clamored for attention and he swept her up into his arms, breaking the awkwardness of the moment, as he fussed over her and offered his presents.

In the sitting room, Leah, Meriam's mother, was sitting with Gabriel. Ted realized gratefully that they had deliberately chosen to let Meriam and himself have a few moments alone. Carrying Arielle, he greeted Leah, kissing her on both cheeks, and shook Gabriel's hand.

Ted stood awkwardly, wanting to sit next to Meriam, but seeing that she had chosen a chair that stood by itself. Leah patted the seat next to her on the brocaded couch. "Ted, my son, come and sit next to me."

He sat, taking in the room as he did so. They were in a spacious, well-appointed salon, which opened directly from the front hall. There was a small fireplace, glowing quietly, despite the summer weather. Ted recognized the work of Meriam and Leah in the needlepoint cushions that covered many of the chairs.

"The flat is lovely," he said to Leah, assuming she must have been most responsible for its décor.

"Thank you," she said. "When Gabriel came up here to study and we knew it would be for such a long time, we decided to buy this apartment. That way we knew our boy would be comfortable, and we would all have a place to stay when we came to visit him." Leah was eager for news from Tangier. "I just can't believe that ruffian Raisuni has actually become our new Governor! How could such a thing happen?"

Gabriel turned from where he was directing a servant

to pour champagne. "Ted, we also heard that Raisuni's thugs are regularly roughing people up in the town. This is terrible behavior for someone who's supposed to be in charge of law and order in Tangier. As far as I'm concerned, the sooner the French end this polite dialogue they're having and simply take over, the better for all of us.

"But I forget my duties as a host. Let's all have some champagne and drink to your presence here tonight and the reassembling of your family in Paris."

They all raised their glasses. Ted appreciated the effort the Ben Simons were making to ease a difficult situation. He glanced in Meriam's direction. She sat slightly apart, in a chair with its back to the fireplace, between Gabriel and her mother. So far, although she raised her glass in the general toast, she had taken no part in the conversation.

Ted said, "You know, among other things, I'm here because Abdel Aziz asked me to participate in the French discussions about the reform package accompanying this new loan. And, Gabriel, you may get your wish. But frankly, I can't help feeling Abdel Aziz hasn't been given that much of a chance to prove himself."

Gabriel looked doubtful. "Nice thoughts, Ted, but what you're suggesting could take decades. Meanwhile Morocco itself is suffering. People like Bou Hamara and Raisuni are running wild. For the good of the country as a whole, we need law and order."

Meriam spoke then, for the first time, "Ted, how can you support *Moulay* Abdel Aziz? The situation there is cruel especially for the poorer Jews, and he does nothing to make it better."

Ted was taken aback by this outburst. Although Meriam had always been mildly interested in Jewish affairs and had followed the Dreyfus case avidly, he had never heard her make direct remarks about the situation of the Jews in Morocco.

"You know, Meriam, one could say the same about most Moroccans as well. It's a hard country; conditions are tough there, and the poor always suffer disproportionately."

Meriam looked as if she were going to say more, but just at that moment dinner was announced and Leah rose swiftly, "Oh, let's not keep the cook waiting. She gets into a fret when we don't come promptly. And she's so good, it's best to humor her."

Arielle's nurse looked in at the door to take Arielle upstairs. She murmured in Meriam's ear. Meriam rose and excused herself.

"*Viens*, Arielle. We will pay a *petite* visit to Laure to say *bonne nuit*." She turned to the others. "Please start without me. I will not delay, but I do not want your dinner to be cold."

They sipped at their soup. It was a delicious cream of mushrooms with morels floating on the top.

Gabriel said, "Ted, we've invited a few of my friends in for coffee and dessert. I hope you'll find them interesting. Some of them are working with Theodore Herzl. Have you heard of him?"

Ted nodded. "I've heard the name, not too much else. Wasn't he one of the reporters who covered the Dreyfus story at the beginning?"

Gabriel nodded. "That's the one. You might be able to get some new material here for an article or two."

At that moment Meriam glided in and took her place quietly.

"Is everything all right with Laure?" Leah said.

Meriam nodded. "*Oui,* she's just a little fussy. I held her for a few moments, and she quieted herself and now she is fast asleep again." She looked directly at Ted, somewhat defiantly, "She is a *belle petite fille*. You do not wish to see her?"

Ted could feel the blood rising straight to his red hair. "I have no desire to ever see that ill-conceived child, Meriam. I think you are aware of my feelings in that regard. I simply cannot understand how you can tolerate having her here." He put down his spoon, having lost his appetite.

"To me she is just an innocent child, Ted," Meriam said quietly. "She can not help the facts of her conception. If anything, she reminds me every day of Morocco and the problems we Jews have there. She is a victim, just as we all were."

"You're reading a lot more into her than needs be," Ted said. "And who knows what she'll be like? Her paternity…." he couldn't go on and took a large gulp of his wine.

"She will be what I teach her to be," Meriam said. "After all, she is one half me, too. And one cannot abandon a defenseless child who is my flesh and blood, to be brought up in the streets of Paris."

Leah changed the subject. "Ted, I hope you'll have a chance to talk to Françoise Cohen this evening. She and Gabriel are quite good friends. She studied at the Alliance and is originally from Algeria. She's also planning to be a teacher."

Ted appreciated Leah's effort and tried to regain his equilibrium. "Do I detect more than a casual interest, Gabriel?" he said.

"Yes, I hope so," Gabriel said. "We have been friends for several years now and I recently asked Mlle. Cohen to be my wife. She is very keen to go to Tangier with me, and we will both teach there."

Ted raised his glass in a toast. He and Meriam had been as happy as Gabriel, but it didn't seem to have lasted. He hoped his friend would have better luck. He knew this evening was not going well and regretted the strain he was putting on Gabriel and Leah. Perhaps it had been a mistake to have come at all.

Gabriel's friends arrived just as the servant was clearing the dishes from the main course. Mlle. Cohen was an earnest young woman who was dressed in a rather severe suit and wore spectacles, a bit like Gabriel's. In fact, Ted thought, she looked more like Gabriel than Meriam. He supposed she was what the British called a blue stocking, or maybe even a suffragette although he didn't know whether that concept existed in France. She shook his hand rather briskly, staring him straight in the eye. The others were an international mixture. There was Ytzak, a blonde, blue-eyed Jew from Germany, Natan and Chaim from Algeria, and Yusef from Egypt. They settled into the parlor and the servant brought in a beautiful Ile Flottante, which was served *flambée*.

Ted and the Ben Simons switched to French, in deference to their guests. "I understand from Gabriel that some of you were working with the late Theodore Herzl?" Ted said.

Ytzak, the German snorted. "That dreamer! I don't like to speak ill of the dead, but the man was such an idealist."

Ted raised his eyebrows in question.

Ytzak continued, "Well, you know his general theme, I suppose. He believed that the Jews should form their own nation. That we should have a state. So impractical. We are well on our way to becoming totally assimilated into European society. So why discourage this trend? A state would just encourage all the downtrodden Jewry to cluster together and promulgate their anachronistic beliefs and practices, instead of slowly having these simply fade away, as have many of the more traditional practices of the Catholic Church."

Natan, one of the Algerians, interrupted, rattling his coffee cup slightly, "Creating a new ghetto of all the poor Eastern European Jews might be a problem, but in fact, what Herzl wanted wasn't even that, my friend. He was not a very religious man. I believe he may have been a Protestant formally. The state he wanted to form would have been secular. That is one of the tragedies of Herzl, in my opinion. He never could mobilize all that much support from the Jews, because so many of the rabbis opposed what they saw as a secular idea."

Ted finished his sweet and carefully placed the plate on a table near the chair. "I'm not that well informed about Herzl really, although I have heard, of course, that he was trying to create interest in some kind of a separate Jewish nation. Zion, isn't it? Didn't I hear that he had made several trips to Turkey to discuss this with the Ottoman Sultan?"

Yusef smiled, putting his plate aside as well. "Yes, it was amazing. He had this idea that maybe the Sultan would grant or sell the Jews some part of Palestine. He even talked to Kaiser Wilhelm to see if he would plead his case before the Sublime Porte. Just before Hertzl died it was looking hopeful. Now, who knows?" Yusef was a striking man. About six feet in height, he had light brown hair and unusual pale gray eyes. Like some powerfully built men, this Egyptian Jew emitted an overall sense of gentleness, as if he recognized that his strength was something to be kept in bounds, used only to protect. Ted couldn't help noticing that Meriam appeared to hang on his words.

Françoise gave a short laugh, stirring her coffee vigorously. "It was all such nonsense. Why would all the Jews of the world want to congregate together anyway? Most of us do not believe in that superstition. Old men going around in rusty black caftans and slippers mumbling Hebrew and practicing black magic, saying spells over food. And the very idea of everyone moving to Palestine! I cannot imagine such a thing."

Meriam spoke up hotly, "Well, I do not think it is such a crazy idea. Do not deceive yourself that just because Jews convert to Christianity and adopt Christian ways people are ready to accept us as one of them. How can we all forget the Dreyfus Affair so easily? That poor man is still in prison out there on Devil's Island, even though the evidence points overwhelmingly now to the fact that he was innocent all along. And there are so many other examples. Look at that case in Italy where that young Jewish boy was baptized secretly by his family maid when she thought he was dying. And then later the Church ruled that it had the right to remove him, actually remove him from his family and raise him as a Catholic, just because of that secret act of the maid. I think you are wrong, Françoise, if you think that Jews can assimilate into the West. The Ashkenazim have trouble, but we Safardim would find assimilation even more difficult. We do not look like Europeans; we have different customs. Herzl was right. We need a home of our own, our own nation, where we can be accepted as ourselves and not live in fear and hatred."

Chaim, the other Algerian, said, "I think Mme. Meriam is right. I went to several of the congresses Herzl held in Basle and the man was inspired. As you said, M. Ted, he covered the Dreyfus case as a reporter, and I think he saw clearly then that things had not changed much for the Jews and were not likely to. He said that that was the beginning of his dream for a Jewish state and I have never seen a man who worked so hard to gather support for this dream. You know, he literally worked himself to death. But he was right; we do need a nation of our own. We are really not welcome in other countries, either in the East where I come from, as do most of us in this room, or in the West either, despite what some of my colleagues appear to believe."

Meriam spoke up again, "Ted, you should read his book, *Der Judenstaat* where he lays out his whole dream for a Jewish state. It is thrilling, it is so beautiful. He has everything planned. He even describes the new opera house, what it will be like. People will farm; imagine Jews will farm! And they will run everything and have their own Parliament. There will be schools everywhere. Just think of such a place!"

"There are some settlements like that now in Palestine, aren't there?" Ted asked. "It seems to me I've read somewhere about some agricultural colonies founded by Baron de Hirsch."

Yusef answered him, "Yes, there are some small settlements. But they are there at the discretion of the Turks. And, although I think the Baron funds them generously, they are very small, and I believe settled primarily by rather backward Eastern European Jews. You know, that was de Hirsch's main interest. He wanted to save those poor Jews from the pogroms in Poland and Russia and to offer them a better life. That is one of the differences between Herzl and the big philanthropists. They wanted to save the most unfortunate Jews, to remove them from the ghettos. I think Herzl, while interested in that, had a more global dream."

Ted found himself liking this man and could understand why Meriam seemed attracted to him. He was intelligent, sensitive and dedicated to the dream of Zionism. Ted could hardly imagine a better advocate, or one more likely to catch Meriam's attention. He asked, "Now that Herzl's dead, what will happen?"

"It is hard to know," replied Natan. "I do not think the dream will die. One thing Herzl did was to create a lot of interest and support for Zionism—that is how we call it now. It has been hard to find a place for the new nation. It seems that all the negotiations for Palestine fell apart, which was a great disappointment, because there we could be near our Temple. But there has been talk. The British seem to be much more supportive than the Germans were. And places in both Egypt and East Africa have been mentioned."

Chaim said, "The Uganda option is definitely out. The Russians were against it, and they are big supporters of the movement. And Egypt does not look promising. I think they decided there was not enough water in the Sinai, which is where they were proposing. Fitting, but also referred to in the Old Testament as the 'wilderness' for good reason. So we are still wandering Jews, to answer your question."

"But," Ted said, "were there leaders to take over from Herzl? Do you think the Zionist movement will continue?"

"Yes," Gabriel answered him directly, "I think so. You know, there were quite a few congresses, and we now have a permanent steering committee. Have had for several years, which is fortunate. So it was not all left in Herzl's hands. He was a visionary, but not the best manager of people and plans. So, thanks to the fact that other people were involved, there are several men to carry on: Max Nordau, Professor Warburg, Jacobus Kann. The new president is a fellow named David Wolffsohn, a German, who was very close to Herzl during his life. Actually, Wolffsohn seems to be making some progress. He is more of a diplomat that Herzl, who managed to alienate many of the people he needed the most. Perhaps he can gain the support of the Rothschilds. They did not see eye to eye with Herzl, which was a shame, since we need their financing."

"Well," Meriam spoke again, "we are collecting dues from tens of thousands of Jews who belong to the Zionist movement. It would be nice to get Rothschild money, but I do not like to think it is essential. After all, if we want something enough, we should be willing to pay for it ourselves. And a Zionist state could be self-supporting. What we really need now is to find a location. Until we can either convince the Ottomans to give us some land, or find another spot, nothing can be put into action." Her face was flushed. Ted realized as he watched her that clearly this had become her dream.

Ted took his leave, making the long trip back to Neuilly. He had decided to continue staying with the Taillandiers, who had offered him a comfortable bedroom and seemed content to let him come and go, refraining from asking intrusive questions. Ted assumed that Georges had brought Marie up to date, as she had avoided making further comments about Meriam.

***

Not daunted by the disastrous dinner with the Ben Simons and Meriam, Ted invited Meriam out to a restaurant. He hoped they could do better in a more intimate setting, where perhaps they could recapture some of the romance of their earlier years.

Meriam wore a similar outfit to that she had on the night he had come to the apartment. In the carriage he asked her about it.

"It is necessary for me to admit my heritage, *cheri*," she said. "We Jews in Tangier, and many here, too, make such an effort to be French, or European. But we are not, and no one is deceived. I prefer to be honest and show the world that I am a Jew."

This confirmed what Ted had suspected that night at the Ben Simon's. Meriam had seemed very enthusiastic about Zionism, and now Ted realized she was even more committed than he had thought.

It was relatively early by Parisian dining standards, and the downstairs was quiet as the waiter greeted them and led them past tin trays where glistening oysters were on display, banked in ice.

"Those look good," Ted said.

Meriam shuddered slightly. Although her family prided itself on being Western, their eating habits still retained enough of the Jewish tradition that shellfish was something she avoided. This had always been a joke between them, as Ted loved shellfish of all kinds, a taste that had been nurtured in Amelia and Matt's household.

A cold bucket of champagne was sitting next to the table in their private room and Ted poured two glasses, thinking it might relax them both a bit.

Ted ordered for both of them. He knew Meriam was content to leave this task to him, since he knew her preferences and he recognized that she was too tense to concentrate on such an extraneous chore. After the waiter left, Ted said, "Meriam, what do you think is going to become of us? Do you think of coming back to Morocco?"

"*Cheri*, how much I have been dreading that question. *Honnêtement,* I do not think I can," she said. Her words came out in a gush. "I cannot go back there. After Taza, I see things so differently, Ted. There is no place in Morocco for us Jews. They hate us. I know that now."

Ted's heart sank at the implications of her statement.

"Well, what are you thinking of doing? How will this affect our lives together? When you came here, I thought it was just for a short time. To...well, to give you a pause to get over, to get over Taza...."

Meriam said, "To give me time, and to allow me a private *accouchement*, to spare us the shame of having our friends know what happened to me." She paused. "You know, *cheri*, I remember so little about the attack. But there is something I feel I should remember, something about it that I think was important."

Ted still found the whole Taza incident painful to refer to; he was surprised that Meriam could. "Best to just put it behind you, my dear. It's too painful." He patted her hand.

The waiter came in with their food, so they changed the subject until he left, exclaiming over the delicious veal medallions with mushrooms he had ordered for Meriam, while he eyed his steak au *poivre vert* appreciatively. As soon as the door closed, he took up the subject again.

"So, where does that leave us now?"

Meriam was matter of fact. "Me, with a new *enfante* whom I love and you cannot accept. Me, happy in Paris, where I must start to live again."

"Without me," Ted said.

"Ted," Meriam said gently, laying her hand on his arm. "I am so sorry. You speak truly. I did not intend this, God knows! What happened was beyond our control. But we are left with the consequences. You and I have different reactions. Maybe that leaves us with different futures."

Ted stared at her blankly. The dreaded words were out in the open. His worst fears seemed to be coming true. "But Meriam, I still love you. Isn't there any way?"

"I do not know, *cheri*. Believe me, I have thought and thought. It is not just Laure. I know how you feel about her. It is more than just that. Your future lies in Morocco, where you are valuable to your paper. Mine lies elsewhere, *peut-être*. I have heard about a Zionist state. It is becoming my dream. If I can do anything to make it come true, I want to. We Jews will never be at home without a nation of our own, where we are not a hated minority."

Ted nodded, not trusting himself to speak. He noticed that Meriam, too, had barely touched her food. He pushed his scarcely-eaten steak away from him.

Meriam was staring earnestly at him, her eyes sparkling with tears. *"Cheri,* I still love you. We grew up together. We have shared so much. You will always be my *cher ami* and my hero. But I do not see a future for us. Our lives have grown apart. Perhaps we married too young, before we were completely formed. I know so much more now than I did then. You were the center of my universe. I defined myself in connection to you, as your wife, mother of your child, keeper of your house. And I was content that way.

"Maybe I would have continued like that if Taza had not happened. Who knows? But Taza made me see things so differently. Those soldiers made me see myself as a detested person, a person not welcome in many of the places you were. And there is nothing you can do to change that. It is a fact I ignored before. I was too protected, too sheltered, in Tangier. I do not want you to change for me. I would never ask it, *jamais.* You would no longer be the Ted I love and admire. But we must accept reality." Tears were rolling down her face as she struggled to finish her sentence.

Ted sighed. He fiddled with the silverware, lining the knives and forks up straight on either side of his plate. He brushed away a few breadcrumbs near his hand.

"I guess what we're discussing is living apart. You pursue your interests here, and I'll go back to Morocco and continue doing what I do. And we'll see each other from time to time, whenever I can get up here. And we'll just see where we go from here."

"Oui, Ted, I believe that is what we are agreeing to," Meriam said softly. "And I do love you. Please believe that, *je te prie,* I beg you."

Ted squeezed her hand gently. He handed her a fresh handkerchief. "It's all right, sweetheart. Don't cry. I understand. And I'll wait; I'll wait forever if I have to. Don't worry." He brought her hand to his lips and kissed it softly. "Everything's going to be fine. I just want you to be happy. We'll survive. You wait and see.

" Now," he said briskly, "I think we should be going. Tomorrow I have meetings at the Ministry of Foreign Affairs, which will be quite intense. I need to be ready for them. And then in a week I'll be heading back down to Fez to discuss whatever happens with Abdel Aziz. I'll be leaving early next week." Ted wanted to end this discussion as quickly as he could, before he became emotional. He had so much to think over. He settled the bill with the waiter and they rose, Meriam gathering her shawl around her.

They were quiet in the hansom cab on their return to the Ben Simon's apartment. Ted and Meriam sat not touching and spoke very little. When the carriage reached her apartment, Ted got down and helped Meriam to the ground, escorting her to her front door. He bowed and kissed her hand. "Sweetheart, I want you to be well and happy. I may not see you again on this trip. Perhaps it's for the best. Give all my love to Arielle and tell her I'll write her soon. So, *b'slama, habibti*, good bye, my beloved. God keep you until we meet again."

He spoke in Arabic, suddenly feeling more comfortable in that language that evoked so many early memories.

Tears came to Meriam's eyes again. "Oh, Ted!" she said, and turned to kiss him, but he was already hurrying down the stairs, struggling with his own emotions and wishing to end this painful meeting.

Ted spent the next few days at the Quai d'Orsay with Taillandier, Théophile Delcassé, Minister of Foreign Affairs,

General Lyautey, and Eugène Etienne, the French deputy who was Lyautey's major supporter, and various other bankers and diplomats. The meetings were a welcome diversion, allowing him to put aside the painful memories of his last meeting with Meriam. Perhaps, he thought to himself, some conclusion might become more obvious to him if he just left it alone for a while. So he immersed himself in the tense meetings, enjoying the give and take of the various French factions, amused as each side subtly bargained for its preferred position.

Emotions were running high, because the diplomats, led by Delcassé, former French Minister in Tangier, and St. René Taillandier, wanted a peaceful penetration of Morocco, led by debt reform with a gradual take-over of the economy by France, when Morocco proved unable to pay its debts. This group was angry with Lyautey, who had occupied Moroccan territory in the East in June, deliberately ignoring orders from the Foreign Minister. This takeover had seriously undermined Abdel Aziz's already weak confidence in the French and caused many misgivings about the recently signed loan. Unfortunately for the peace mongers, the Premier, Emile Combes, under pressure from the many French families settled in Algeria who wanted to safeguard their property, sided with Lyautey's aggressive approach.

Ted watched and took notes as the two sides argued their points of view. As he knew, Lyautey did not see himself as a military bully and was upset at the way his actions had been interpreted. Nevertheless, the general did admit that he preferred a slow military take-over to the more insidious endebtment campaign, which the French seemed to have copied from the British powers in Egypt. And Lyautey pointed out to the group that the debt strategy was not working, in any case. The Sultan was balking, not wanting to agree to the reform program, understanding full well what the French were up to.

It was an exhausting meeting and Ted was glad when it was finally over. He knew Abdel Aziz was unlikely to accept the reforms willingly. Too bad, Ted thought, the Moroccans could use some fiscal management, since no one could control Abdel Aziz's extravagant spending. Ted trusted that Lyautey's approach would keep a Sultan on the throne but train him to be a better ruler. But the incidents of violence and anarchy manifested by Bou Hamara and Raisuni did not bode well for the country's fragile stability; a faster military approach might in the long run be more merciful for Morocco and its citizens.

Ted drafted a short report to telegraph to London. In his heart he realized he had accepted the fact of French take-over; it was just a question of how they would do it.

> Discussions finished. Delcassé's peaceful penetration has won, but many support Lyautey's military approach. Reform program to be discussed with Sultan on Minister St. René Taillandier's return will include establishment of a Debt Commission to control customs receipts. A mixed group of Europeans, led by the French will manage this. Delcassé also suggesting medical missionaries and other humanitarian assistance. I plan return Morocco immediately. Will attend Taillandier-Abdel Aziz meeting and then send full report. Predict reforms will not be easily accepted. Request leave of absence after Fez meeting.

***

Tariq loved Cairo. It was a real city, more like Tangier than any other city in Morocco, but flat and hot like Marrakesh. But they had services he had never dreamed of in his native city. Of course, just as Fez had its Qairouine, Cairo had an even more famous Islamic university, Al Azhar, where Muslim scholars studied the Koran and debated religious policy issues with the intelligentsia of the Muslim world. It was the heart of Muslim culture, closer to Mecca, with famous shrines and antiquities. Its newspapers were read all over the Arab world, even by a few in Morocco. And, as he had discovered in Paris, there were many points of view.

There was such a contrast to the traditional Moroccan world he had left behind, where there was no education available to children, aside from Islamic schools offering only the most limited subjects, he sometimes had to remind himself he was still in the Orient. Of course, he admitted, there was good education for the elite Jews in Moroccan cities, but this was not available to Muslims. After seeing these marvels in Egypt, Tariq began to dream; if this Arab country could do it, why not Morocco?

***

Abdel Aziz was eager to hear a full report on the Paris meetings and sent a steamer to bring Ted down to Rabat where the court had been spending the summer. Ted enjoyed the fresh sea breezes and the trip, so much easier than horseback. It had not yet started to rain, and the sailors aboard grumbled to him, worried about the late rains and the delay in their planting season. They told him people were saying Abdel Aziz's lack of piety was the cause of their misfortunes.

They anchored at Sale, the former pirate colony nestled in a curve of the Bou Regreg River facing Rabat. From the boat the walled city of Rabat lay directly in front of them. On its left lay the Tour Hassan, now in ruins, the tower still tall and square, the mosque itself long-fallen with just remnants of its pillars left in even rows to mark the size and splendor of a bygone era. To their extreme right was the walled *Kasbah* of the Oudaia, traditional home of the Sultan's African troops, scaling the cliffs facing out into the Atlantic Ocean. And beyond the cemetery of the *medina* was the fortress-like Koubeiba palace of the Sultan built on the cliffs facing out into the Atlantic Ocean.

Being a Tangerino, Ted always regretted that the Sultan used Koubeiba less than his palaces in Fez and Marrakech. Ted preferred the coast, with its waves washing the beaches, the seagulls perpetually whirling and whistling in the air. He found the air fresher and cooler here; even in full summer he could suddenly get flashes of cold sea mist.

Luckily the steamer was able to land, as the tide was high enough to cover the sand bar at the junction of the Bou Regreg river and the sea. Ted and his escort made the easy ascent to the *medina*, and followed the coast to the palace.

Ted entered a large, elegantly tiled room with ornate designs carved into plaster ceilings. On either side of the large hall, lacy white arcades led the way, either to the harem where the Sultan's wives and children were housed, or in the opposite direction, to the Sultan's public quarters.

Through the arches Ted caught glimpses of a lush garden, planted in the traditional Arab style, roses, stock, delphinium, cosmos, zinnias all allowed to bloom in profusion, colors clashing regally, but somehow achieving a harmony amidst tiled pools and splashing fountains. It was quiet, but Ted could hear in the far distance the sounds of harem children playing.

A slave showed Ted to a tiled guestroom with silken

banquettes flanking its walls. In a nearby *hammam*, he gratefully sluiced off the salt residue of the past five days and changed into baggy cotton pants and a long cotton caftan, pushing his feet gratefully into soft yellow leather *belghah*. Returning to his room, he found a platter of chilled Persian melons and a pot of steaming mint tea.

Ted happily settled himself comfortably on the couch, adjusting the cushions behind his back, while he helped himself to the cold fruit. He leaned back contentedly, allowing his mind to flash back to Paris for the first time since he left. He couldn't help comparing it unfavorably with this, his preferred way of living. Why people chose to wear those uncomfortable tight-fitting clothes and boots, and sit on hard chairs, he could not understand. Even Meriam had abandoned European clothing in favor of Oriental garb, although for different reasons. The plump cushions lulled him into a deep sleep from which it seemed only minutes later he was aroused by a servant, gently shaking his shoulder.

"*Ya sidi, Sidna* will see you now," a servant murmured bending over him.

Ted rose, a bit groggy, and splashed his face with the cool rose-scented water that had been provided in a silver dish earlier.

The servant ushered him into the salon where Abdel Aziz was smoking a water pipe and playing with his two young sons. Ali was there, too, also smoking and counting his prayer beads, as usual. Servants moved noiselessly around the chamber on bare feet, placing jewel-colored glass lanterns along the red, green and black tiled walls as the evening prayer rang out. The glowing colors of the lanterns threw brilliant reflections on the white plaster above the tile, complementing the rich red and green silk brocade on the couches where the Sultan and his brother were reclining.

"Ah, Ted," Abdel Aziz greeted him affectionately, reaching out an arm to draw him down near him. "It seems such a long time since all that business with that son-of-sin al-Raisuni, may his soul rot in Hell. How are you? How is your family? *Insh'Allah,* all are well in Paris?"

Ted knew Abdel Aziz spoke partly in polite formulas, since Moroccan rituals of politeness demanded that no direct questions be asked before one's health and the situation of one's family had been investigated. He answered in kind, "All are well, thanks be to God. And I hope I find you and all the people of your household in good health?"

"Praise God, all are well." Abdel Aziz returned the formulaic greeting. "But please, sit. You've come a long way. I hope you rested? Is your room to your liking?"

These familiar phrases put Ted at ease; slowly he re-adapted to the rhythm of Arab life, with its predictability, its formal questions and answers that assured the guest that the host cared about him as a person, as a family man. He relaxed back on the cushions, putting one knee up and folding his other leg akimbo. Ali offered him the water pipe and he inhaled deeply, realizing he had missed the apple-flavored tobacco, the fragrant tea, the iced melon, the rose-scented water, the orange blossoms, the wool-stuffed cushions, the peace and the comfort of Morocco.

They sat for a long time sipping tea, puffing at the pipe, desultorily exchanging polite comments: It was hotter than usual, the rains were late this year, Abdel Aziz's favorite son had a new pony, but his mother was afraid to let him ride it. Ted told a few stories he had picked up in Tangier about Raisuni, bringing grunts from the twenty-five year old Sultan and worried looks from Ali.

The hours passed; the young children curled up near their

father and gradually fell asleep. Shadows lengthened in the room as they talked, finally, about Paris and the conditions the French were likely to impose on the Moroccans. Other men drifted into the room, silently dropping onto the couches near the Sultan where they listened, clicking their prayer beads, and occasionally muttering a phrase or two in agreement with Abdel Aziz or Ted. Among them was the new Minister of War, Mohammed Guebbas, who had been brought back from Algeria to replace Mehdi. He asked for Ted's assessment of the positions held by Lyautey and Delcassé. Fedoul al-Gharnit, secure in his power as the grand *wazir* since Mehdi had left, sat near Ted. From a corner of his eye, Ted noted that Kassim had also slipped in.

Gharnit did not favor the French loan. Ironically, now that Mehdi was deposed, *Si* Fedoul had in fact allied himself with Mehdi to seek German funding as an alternative to get them out of debt. This was so Arab, Ted thought. Once you have defeated a threat, keep him sweet by co-opting him in some other way. You never knew who could be useful to you someday, and Mehdi was still a good friend of Abdel Aziz. And there was money to be made from the Germans, who, while not exactly interested in Morocco, wanted some of Morocco's mineral rights. The Germans were looking at Morocco from a more global perspective, more desirous of blocking their enemies, the French, from plucking this ripe fruit. Ted had even heard rumors that they were supporting *Sherif* al-Raisuni. The other courtiers were split; some favored the French. Some, like Mehdi, still preferred the British, but at this point England had ceded its interests. Many, including Tariq, wanted no outside intervention, preferring to develop their country themselves. And, of course, the *ulema* and most of the tribes, just wanted things to stay as they were. Kassim, Ted was sure, was playing both sides, looking for the advantage. Ted suspected, however, that he was increasingly inclined towards the French and against Abdel Aziz.

Finally a silence developed. The Grand *Wazir* spoke, "*Ya sidi,* we must take these issues to the people of Morocco. They are too serious to be decided in this room. Let us call together the *ulema* in Fez to discuss the French proposals and see what the people think."

Guebbas, the Minister of War, frowned and looked as if he would speak. Ted wondered what inducements the French might have offered him to support their point of view. But before he could say anything, Ali supported the elderly Grand *Wazir.* "Yes, Aziz, *Si* Gharnit has a good idea. We should discuss this more widely, see how others feel about accepting the French proposal."

Another official spoke up, "There are too many foreigners making decisions about our country. *Si* Gharnit and *Moulay* Ali are right. We should see how much support there would be for these reforms. If the people are opposed, then they will back our decision to refuse."

Kassim spoke then, for the first time. "Excellency, my name will give me great access in the countryside and I would be honored to approach the rural *sheikhs* for you."

Yes, Ted thought to himself, taking the case to the people was an excellent way for Morocco to procrastinate, stall on a decision. And Kassim could easily develop factions and play them off against each other for his own advantage, fomenting disruption and violence in the countryside. He wondered how he could warn Ali of such a danger.

Abdel Aziz stretched. "This is a good idea. We shall consider it. Thank you, my brother Ted, for bringing us this information. We shall return to Fez next week. You will come with us. I believe Minister St. René Taillandier intends to come to Fez to present these demands to me, and I want you to be there."

Ted had been hoping the decision could be reached here in Rabat. He wondered how soon he would be able to extricate himself from Morocco. He needed to get away and get some perspective on his own life. But he acquiesced. He supposed his personal affairs would keep a little longer. The meeting would be interesting and he knew the Times would want to know how things were progressing.

The rains still did not come. There were stories of increased banditry along the routes as hungry tribesmen took the law into their own hands. The people at court were uneasy. They talked about the skyrocketing price of wheat, which was now at over five times its price of last year. People speculated worriedly about a possible drought.

***

Lili's clinic was busy. She had overcome the fear of the Fezzi women as their children's health improved. The mothers would already be lined up when she arrived and while Aisha scrubbed and readied the room, Lili would talk to the mothers and look at the children, trying to sort out the most serious cases. She had made an arrangement for the royal physician to come for an hour or two each day and she saved the cases she knew she could not handle for him to deal with.

Lili was proud of her successes. One day a mother had come with her son who had a festering wound in his leg. Lili took one look at it and called for hot water and salt. She removed the filthy piece of cotton wrapped around it, working as gently as she could, soaking it first in water to loosen it. Then she sat the child down next to his mother and coaxed him slowly to lower his leg into the hot water, little by little as he accustomed himself to the heat. She had him sit there until the water was cold. The sore still looked raw and full of pus, but Lili said to the mother, "Now, my sister, bring your son back every day at the same time. We will continue this. Let him rest at home and not run around. He will be better." She wrapped the wound in a piece of clean white cotton, cautioning the mother not to touch it until the next day. After a week, the boy's wound was healed. Mothers started bringing all their children with festering sores and Lili's biggest problem became keeping enough hot water on hand. Sometimes, of course, she could not heal the sore if it turned out to be yaws or something more serious. This made her yearn for more training. Surely, with proper medicine and more knowledge she could be more effective.

Eye infections were another very common complaint. Over time Lili had seen the flies that clustered around children's eyes causing trachoma, a scarring of the cornea that affected sight. Once again, she found simple soap and water to be effective, and counseled the mothers to wash their babies' eyes and faces and not let the flies sit there. "The sticky stuff in their eyes when they wake up attracts these flies," she explained. "And the flies will harm your child."

"Yes, my sister," they would answer. "But there is little time. And the water is cold for the child. He could catch a chill." The mothers were skeptical, she could see. How could simple soap and water make such a difference? But over time, when they saw the results, they became convinced that Lili was a miracle worker.

***

Ted and Ali took horses early in the morning and galloped out to race along the beach in Rabat, enjoying the salty breeze. As they sauntered back to the palace, Ted said to Ali, "What do you think is going to happen now?"

"It's hard to tell, *ya* Ted. You know anti-foreign feelings are increasing in the countryside. People are blaming the French for all their problems, for the drought, the banditry, everything. They don't want these reforms, even with the improvements being offered."

"That was pretty clear last night," Ted said. "Frankly, Ali, I think it's inevitable that France will come in. Morocco is badly in debt; the countryside is constantly in revolt; the general impression in France is that a firm hand is needed."

"Best for France and for their Algerian farmers, I think," Ali said. "But we have managed for centuries without foreign help. I do not see why we need them now."

Ted shrugged. For him it was just a question of when the French would gain power and how much bloodshed there would be along the way. And some of what the French offered would help the country. The health situation alone, in Ted's mind, would justify an intervention. But he didn't see how to convince his friends. He decided to bring up Kassim's involvement. "Ali, what is Kassim's role in all this? He seems to be more active at the court these days."

Ali said, "He is looking for something to do. You know, he never got along well with his stepbrother, Mohammed. I couldn't tell why."

Ted thought to himself that this was typical of Ali. He was so trusting of people, something like his brother. He had always been oblivious to most of what was going on with Kassim when they were young. Several times he and Tariq had tried to warn him, but Ali seemed incapable of understanding such perversity, and finally they'd stopped trying. Now, though, he worried. Kassim was definitely dangerous, and Ali should be made aware of this.

He tried again. "You know, Ali, the fact that Kassim doesn't have Mohammed's respect is due to bad behavior on his part over the years, starting with the unexplained murder of that young slave girl in Fez."

Ali raised his eyebrows. "Nothing was ever proved."

Ted sighed. How could he ever convince Ali that Kassim was a potential threat? "Since he doesn't have the position he wanted in Matar, as you say, he's looking for something else. You know there were rumors at one time that he was associated with Bou Hamara."

"There were rumors that almost everyone was associated with the Pretender at one point or another," Ali laughed. "But lately, Kassim spends most of his time at court. And wasn't he useful in solving that Perdicaris thing? Didn't I hear he and you worked together on that?"

"Not exactly. Frankly, I think he's the one that suggested Raisuni ask for the money. He knew it would put Abdel Aziz in a tough position and weaken him. Honestly, Ali, I wouldn't trust him too far. He may be working against you."

Ali turned to Ted, "*Barak llahu fik*, may Allah bless you for this, my brother. I find it hard to believe, but we will watch him more carefully."

***

The many cases Lili could not help saddened her. A child was brought to the clinic, shivering with a high fever. "Please, my sister," the mother begged. "He is burning up."

Lili tried the few things she knew. She bathed the boy in cool water. He lay peaceful for a while, and then started shivering. She covered him with blankets. Soon he was drenched in sweat. She told the mother, "He has malaria, my sister. The mosquitos bring this."

The mother made a futile gesture. "Mosquitos are everywhere. What can we do?"

Lili shrugged. She had heard that there was some bark which, boiled in water, produced a bitter liquid that seemed to reduce the fevers. "I am sorry, my sister. There is nothing I can do. You must pray to Allah. Try to let him rest, give him broth, and keep him sheltered from insects. That is all I can suggest. May Allah be generous to you."

She came home just before the gates were closed. Ted was sitting in the salon when she entered and threw herself down on the divan. "We've been working all day on a child with a very high fever. I think it must be malaria, but we don't have anything to give him. I hated to leave, but there was nothing more to be done."

"What will happen?" Ted asked.

"I told his mother to take him home and let him rest. You know, they just don't do that. I know he'll be running around, or at least trying to. I think he may die. These children, some of them at least, just aren't that strong. They don't have inner resources to fight off these diseases. I guess it's in God's hands, now." The maid came in with hot water and Lili thankfully put her tired feet into the basin. "Ah, that feels good. I wish I knew more. I'm sure I could do more for them, if I just had some training."

"Nevertheless, Lili, this work seems to agree with you." Ted said.

"I do love my clinic," Lili said. "I feel so needed, and in our own small way I think we're making a difference with the children. We try to get them now to come every few months, just to see they're eating right and growing properly. The ones we see often have fewer eye problems; their skin is clearer; they have less ringworm. There's definitely a difference, and that means everything to me!"

"France is quite keen to send medical missionaries to Morocco. It's part of their campaign for peaceful penetration, and not a bad idea. I hate to see children suffering and dying just from ignorance," Ted said.

"That would be wonderful. I hope they'll also provide some medicines and materials. You wouldn't believe how expensive these things are."

"You're becoming more Moroccan every day, Lili," Ted said, observing her long dress and overskirt.

"I guess I'm reverting to my heritage," she said, laughing. "But working all day in that clinic, these clothes are comfortable and modest and easy to move around in. It seems so much more practical. Any seamstress can run them up for me. Anyway, you should be the last one to talk, since you never wear Western clothes yourself. I do sometimes feel I should do more about my hair," she admitted, touching her head. "I know braids are simply not in vogue. But, on the other hand, who would notice? And they're easy," she said.

Ted thought to himself, yes, who would notice? Arthur seemed not to be around all that much, and when he was there, he was very withdrawn.

They sat together companionably, eating melons to finish their meal. Ted had told Lili a little about Meriam, but he was reluctant to discuss the details or what the implications might mean for him. He was grateful that Lili decided to follow his lead, for the moment, and treat the subject cautiously.

After a while, Lili said, "Have you any news from Tariq?"

Ted looked at her curiously. "I've had two letters, Lili. Actually, he's a better correspondent than I would have expected."

"What does he say?" she said. "What are his plans?"

Ted stretched out more comfortably on the cushions, pushing aside the melon rinds, "It sounds like he's planning to stay in Egypt for a while. He's quite good chums with this fellow, Fuad, who invited him to stay with him." He watched Lili as he said this. He had been curious for some time about her relationship with Tariq, sometimes even wondering if they were lovers. But he knew Tariq would never seduce his best friend's sister. It just didn't fit his code of honor. And he was pretty sure Lili wouldn't do such a thing either. Still, there was something between them, he was sure of it.

"Surely he can't mean to stay there forever?"

"I don't know, Lili. There's not much reason for him to come back here, really. Malika is fine, maybe even better off back in her village. And Mehdi is more or less exiled in Tangier since he's become a British protégé."

"To be honest with you, Ted," she hesitated, "I miss Tariq dreadfully." She colored slightly. "I would hate to think I would never see him again."

"I miss him a lot, too. In fact, as soon as I can get Abdel Aziz to agree, I'm going to go to Egypt for a while. I need a break and I'd like to see my old friend."

Lili brightened. "Maybe you can talk him into coming back. It would be truly awful if he abandons Morocco altogether. This country means so much to him."

***

Kassim produced a pack of cards. "What do you say, Arthur? Our usual game of casino, or do you want to play blackjack?"

"Black jack," Arthur said, watching as Kassim refilled both their glasses. "Maybe I'll have more luck."

"I want to smoke," Kassim said, clapping his hands for a servant to bring him the water pipe. "Would you like to try this?"

"Sure, why not?" Arthur said.

Kassim turned his back to Arthur and prepared the pipe, mixing the apple flavored tobacco with some hashish he took from his pocket.

Kassim handed him the pipe. "Here, have a puff."

Arthur took a long puff on the water pipe, hearing the gurgling sound as his inhalation stirred the water in the bottle at the far end of the long hose. He coughed. "That tobacco is rough! Like everything in this God-forsaken country."

"Rough, but effective. A few more puffs and you'll feel better. Take another pull, and then a sip or two of the whiskey. You'll like the way you feel," Kassim said.

Arthur followed his advice. "Hum, you're right. I feel kinda strange, but good. Now I think I'll be lucky at this blackjack." He turned to one of Kassim's friends, who was also smoking. "Are you dealing?"

"Gladly. How much do we play for? One hundred dollars?"

"All right," Arthur said. "It's just a game. But I don't have that much with me."

"Never mind," the man said, "you are a friend of Kassim, and we know where to find you." He dealt out the cards.

Arthur had a king and a four. Kassim had a king and a ten.

"All right, hit me," Arthur said. The dealer turned up a nine. "Damn," said Arthur, "well, let me give you my pledge. I'll give the money to Kassim tomorrow, when I see him at Court."

Kassim said, "Here, have some more *kif.* Why don't you try again? Maybe you can win back what you lost."

Arthur took another puff and another good swig of whiskey. He was feeling very strange. "Better luck this time."

The man dealt him a four and a five. Kassim had a nine and a ten.

"I'll take another card," Arthur said. The man dealt him an ace. Arthur brightened.

Kassim asked for another card. The man dealt him a two.

"Blackjack!" Kassim said, "tough luck, Arthur."

"That's enough for me for tonight." Arthur rose to his feet unsteadily. "I should be gettin' back. Gonna close the gates soon." The room swam in front of his eyes. He grasped at the door jamb to steady himself.

"Can you find your way?" Kassim asked.

"Tha's all right. My man, Ahmad, is outside. He'll get me back. Thanks, old man. Let's do this again soon. Nice to have a lil fun here." He clapped Kassim on the back. "Good to have a frien' in this grubby town."

***

Georges Saint René Taillandier came down to Fez and presented the French reform package to Abdel Aziz. The Sultan informed the French that he would have to consult with his people before making such a momentous decision. Sentiment against foreigners grew, and Ted couldn't help seeing the fine hand of Kassim in the mumbling he heard. Ali informed Ted that the Sultan had issued a letter to all foreign missions demanding that they withdraw their foreign advisors. Ted knew this was directed particularly at the French, who were instructed to remove all members of their military mission that had gradually been increasing in number, since Ben Sedira had proved so effective with the cannon.

Ted refrained from taking part in the increasingly delicate situation. He decided it was time to approach the Sultan and take his leave. He didn't see any role for himself or any other foreigner in Morocco in the near future. He raised the subject one late afternoon when he and Ali were sitting with the Sultan playing bridge.

"*Sidi*, I think it's time for me to retire for a while, with your permission."

"Certainly, *ya* Ted. You can't take losing at bridge all the time, right?" Aziz said, slapping down a trump on his king.

"I'm getting used to that," Ted said. "But I don't mean just for the evening. I'd like to withdraw from court life for a while. I need a rest, and I don't think you need foreigners at court right now, with feelings continuing to rise against us."

"But I must have a tennis partner," Aziz said. "Ali's getting too fat to be any good."

Ali said, "My brother, what Ted is suggesting might not be a bad idea. We ourselves have just asked the foreigners to withdraw. Symbolically, Ted's leaving for a few months at least would show you take this command seriously."

Aziz considered this. "Where would you go?"

"To Egypt to visit Tariq, if your Excellency has no objection."

"Ah! So that's where he is. That's an interesting idea."

"You know, Aziz, Ted could be of service to us," Ali said. "Tariq too, for that matter. Maybe Ted and Tariq could find some Egyptians who'd come here and work for us, to replace the Christian advisors."

Abdel Aziz liked this idea the more he thought of it.

***

Ted, Arthur and Lili traveled to Tangier together, to spend the Christmas holidays with Amelia and Matt and celebrate Lili's twenty-second birthday. Ted planned to book passage for Alexandria as soon as he could after that.

They made good time going to Tangier. It still had not rained which made the going smooth, as the ground was hard-packed and easy for the horses to traverse, but Ted noticed many signs of hardship and famine. The livestock looked weak, and they passed many carcasses rotting on the way, frightening their horses.

The trip gave Ted a good opportunity to observe Arthur in greater detail; he looked gaunt and less well groomed than usual. He was high-strung and nervous, often irritable for no apparent reason. In the evenings when they camped, he was withdrawn and anxious to get to the whiskey. After four or five shots he was noticeably relaxed, and would then launch long, boring monologues on topics of little interest to Ted and Lili but to which they were expected to pay attention, at risk of provoking his bad temper. It was not a pleasant trip.

CHAPTER TEN
1905

Tariq booked a room for Ted at Shepheard's Hotel and encouraged him to find permanent accommodations in the growing European quarter of the city. "My brother, I know your preference would be to live in Old Cairo with me," he said. "But I believe you would benefit from living closer to the British. You would help me, too, by doing this, as I want to know their thoughts on Arabs. This is something I cannot learn here."

Ted didn't completely understand why his friend would suggest such a thing. "*Ya* Tariq," he said, "does this mean I have to dress and act like a European? You know I don't particularly like that."

Tariq laughed. "Look at me, *ya* Ted. Only *fellahin* (peasants) wear traditional clothes here." Tariq was, indeed, transformed, and had adopted the Egyptian upper class style of dress, wearing European suits with a red fez, symbol of the Egyptian gentleman. Tariq had never worn European clothes in Morocco, but the uniform at St. Cyr had familiarized him with such styles. He laughed at the fez when Fuad first showed it to him. "Only our Sultan wears this," he protested. But he got used to it. As a good Muslim, he needed to wear something on his head, and this was the most refined choice.

Seeing that even Tariq and Fuad dressed this way, Ted accepted it as the custom of Cairo. But he was less enthusiastic about living among the English. After a few weeks at Shepheard's, he found a *dahabiyeh*, or houseboat, moored along the western bank of the Nile. This seemed to him a good compromise, since it was neither European nor Arab, but marginal, the boats being used for brothels and Europeans who wished to travel to Upper Egypt.

***

Tariq took Ted to see the construction going on for the new Fuad al Awal university. The land had been cleared and construction was just beginning, but as they wandered around, it was clear it would have at least five buildings, and Tariq informed him they would teach agriculture, law, the liberal arts and maybe even medicine.

Ted was impressed. "These changes are due to the British."

Tariq said, "Yes, my brother. It is a gift from the British. Most of the professors will be British. With these foreign teachers, the university will colonize the population; it will draw the educated away from Islam, and make the Egyptian elite into second class British."

"Still, to train Egyptian doctors and engineers, surely that's what we all want. We, that is, the Arabs, need to take what's best from the West and adapt it to Arab ways. Some things the West has are worth copying, especially medical advances, education." Ted was standing in front of a large hole destined to become the main administration building of the new school.

Tariq took his arm and led him away as a work crew approached. "We are sending our military officers for training to France. We have begun that process. But we are just at the beginning of this path. Egypt started long before us. But we can do this in Fez, in Rabat. We do not need Christians to do it for us."

Ted said, "Of course you can. But it's a European model. No matter who does it, it's not an Arab concept. And I don't see what's so wrong about that. This school would never have happened if three generations of Egyptians hadn't studied in the West and been inspired to bring those ideas to this country."

"Yes, Egyptians brought back the ideas, but they are not teaching here, or holding first class positions in government, *ya* Ted. That is my point. Do you know that the British hold many ministerial positions here? The Army itself is commanded by Lord Kitchener, not by an Egyptian.

"We Arabs can learn those things at European schools and then run our own schools at home. Just look around you here in Cairo. There are thousands of foreigners in Egypt, and they are profiting from the country, instead of the Egyptian *fellah*. Egyptians are earning this money for foreigners who own Egyptian factories and cotton plantations. And just as in Morocco, these foreigners do not pay taxes and are exempted from the law of the land. I do not agree with that. Allah forbid that Morocco will be colonized. I know *Sidna* Abdel Aziz does not want this, but he may not be able to withstand the French."

"Abdel Aziz's idea about recruiting Muslim experts is at least a step in the right direction. With Turks or Egyptian professionals, at least Morocco wouldn't run the risk of undermining its Muslim values," Ted said.

"Yes, my brother. And I am happy to assist you in this." That wasn't the only thing Tariq was recruiting, but he kept these thoughts to himself.

***

Tariq, Fuad and Ted met on the large inviting terrace of the Semiramis Hotel facing out over the Nile. They found a table and settled in the chairs, enjoying the warmth of the early spring sun. A waiter appeared and they ordered the tiny cups of sweet Turkish coffee that took the place in this country of the mint tea Ted and Tariq had been accustomed to.

Fuad lit a cheroot and offered some to the other two, who refused. While Tariq had adopted some European customs since he had been in Egypt, he did not like tobacco or alcohol.

Tariq stretched out his long legs and crossed his ankles. "Allah, these shoes are not nearly as comfortable as our *belghah*. And they are hot."

Fuad, who had dressed like this all his life, answered, "Well, gentlemen can not go around barefoot, unless you want to be taken for a *fellah*."

Tariq stiffened. "Our Sultan himself does not wear shoes."

Fuad just smiled, opening up his Al Ahram paper. "Different countries, different customs. I say," he said, scanning the front page, "it looks like the French are nearing victory in Morocco."

"Victory?" Tariq said, "that is not the word I would use. Domination describes it better."

"The Moroccans have rejected the French demands for fiscal reforms and the French are calling for an international conference to settle the matter," Ted said. "It's too bad. Aziz did everything he could to resist those reforms."

Tariq groaned. "We will never accept all that foreign control. I pray Abdel Aziz will be strong enough to resist."

"Aziz needs more friends around him," Ted said. "He's playing with sharks, and not all of them are French. Trying to steer a course and make good decisions in that environment is more than a man should have to do. I'm not optimistic about any big meeting like that, where all those diplomats will overwhelm him."

Ted had been providing articles to the Times on a fairly regular basis, about Egypt and also the other countries of the Ottoman Empire. He was due to leave the next morning for visits to Palestine and Istanbul, as the paper had asked for more information about some of the discussions on-going between Kaiser Wilhelm and the Ottoman Sultan Abdul Hamid. Ted wanted to see more of Palestine, intrigued by what he had heard from Meriam, so he was looking forward to the trip.

***

Mimi Abduh's parties on her houseboat were convenient places to meet the influential men of the city, make contacts, and gather news. The food was good, liquor flowed freely, and the company was merry and compliant. There was a little dancer there, Fatima, whom Ted occasionally spent time with, and Tariq had a few favorites, too.

The boat had a room big enough to hold Mimi's *'oud* (lute), violin and flute ensemble. Couches lining the walls were scattered with embroidered velvet cushions, and low tables with brass trays ensured that all the guests had access to plentiful refreshments. The windows were heavily curtained with ornate tasseled draperies. There were several smaller rooms behind the main salon, containing just beds, for the more private entertainment that some of the men might seek from the women.

When Tariq arrived, Ted was already settled on one of the couches drinking a whiskey soda, with Fatima snuggled near him. Tariq waved but went to talk to a group of young officers he saw standing in another corner. Some, like Tariq, were drinking fruit juices.

Mimi circulated among her guests, kissing some, rubbing up against others with her voluptuous breasts. Even after almost a year in Cairo, Tariq had still not accustomed himself to the lewdness of these entertainers, but he enjoyed their rough give-and-take and their complete lack of pretense about their trade. Not for the first time, Tariq considered the different standards of beauty between his country and Egypt. Mimi was quite fat and not a day under fifty, whereas the Moroccan dancers were generally petite and young. To him the older dancers like Mimi were just overweight and beyond their prime. But they attired themselves in tight fitting or diaphanous draperies and both expected and received admiration for their fat bellies, drooping breasts and plump legs.

Other men milled around, many drinking whiskey. Several women appeared from the back room to mix with them. The musicians started to play and Mimi settled herself on the head divan and began to sing of disappointed love, romance and frustration. Fuad arrived while she was singing, and he and Tariq came over to where Ted was sitting, nursing his drink.

Mimi stopped singing and began a provocative belly dance to the music while a young male in her entourage sang out, commenting on her generous hips, teasing her to shake them harder, making references to the sexual act, parts of her body. Tariq watched and was reminded of an evening, so long ago, in Tangier, when he and Ted and Lili, disguised as a boy, had gone to see a belly dancer. Ted must have read his thoughts, because he turned to him half way through the performance and laughed. "It's not the same as Tangier, is it, *ya* Tariq?"

No, it's not like Morocco, Tariq thought. "I miss that young friend of yours, Larabi."

***

Lili had taken on several young widows who had more freedom of movement than unmarried girls, and was training them to help her. Nadia, probably about forty, Lili guessed, had lost her husband in the struggle with Bou Hamara, and, in fact, Lili had met her when she was working in the refugee camp. She had shown up at the clinic one day, dressed in immaculate white. "My sister, Lili, I have no children and now my husband is gone. Can I be of help here?"

Lili threw her arms around Nadia. "You are welcome, indeed. Here, you can start by boiling these bandages. They must be very clean before we can use them." She gestured to the back of the clinic, where a fire was burning and a large cauldron stood ready to receive the cloth. Lili took an hourglass and set it upside down near the steaming pot. "When they have boiled for the time it takes the sand to run through this glass, take them out with this stick and hang them to dry over there. Be sure the stick stays on this table, so it is clean."

Nadia shook her head. "Maybe we should have two pots. And we could put a little lemon juice, to make them whiter."

"May God bless you, *ya* Nadia. That is a good idea."

Lili later discovered Nadia had been a mid-wife in her village. She settled into the clinic and eventually brought another friend, who was equally effective. Lili found they were sharing the work and realized it would be possible to leave the clinic in their care, if necessary.

***

Arthur was coming home later and later. "God damn it, Lili. You're always harping at me. Can't you see I'm tired and just want my bed?"

Coming to the threshhold, Lili looked at her husband, once so fair and handsome. He had become soft, fat around his face blurring its shape. His hair was unkempt, as were his clothes.

"Arthur, I know you're tired. But we need to talk. Come and sit down by me. I won't keep you long."

He came in reluctantly, reeking of alcohol, cheap tobacco and *kif.*

"Actually, I do have some news, m'dear. Got a note today via the diplomatic pouch. Seems my dad is not doing too well. I was thinkin' mebbe we'd go back there to San Francisco for a little while. See how the ole boy is. Who knows, it may be my las' chance. I'm due for some leave, anyway."

"I'm sorry about your father, Arthur. Yes, you must go. Maybe it would do you good to leave Morocco for a while, at any rate."

"Wouldn't you come, too?"

"No, Arthur. You know, for some time I've wanted to study nursing. I could be so much more useful at the clinic if I had more training. This would be a perfect opportunity, now that Nadia and Fatima are so familiar with our routines. I could go and stay with Meriam in Paris."

"You won't go with me? Oh no, of course, your clinic is more important. It's always about that damned clinic."

"The clinic is important to me, Arthur. Sometimes I feel it's my whole life now. I can be helpful and can make a difference," Lili said.

"So it's the same thing again. There's always something more important than me, over and over again."

"Arthur, I hardly ever see you. I could say the same. It seems that drinking and gambling are more important to you than I am."

"Well, I need something to do in this God-forsaken place," Arthur said.

"To me it's home. I don't find it God-forsaken," Lili said. "Maybe we need to have a little time away from each other. You go to San Francisco, and I will go to Paris. When I finish my course, I'll come back to Fez, and we can start again."

Arthur looked at her, his eyes not quite in focus. "All right. If tha's what you want. I'm leaving at the end of the week. We can travel down to Tangier together."

***

Tariq began to formulate a plan that he had been thinking about and discussing with Fuad for months. He was convinced Abdel Aziz would ultimately concede to the French. He knew many friends in Morocco shared his concerns.

Tariq came to two conclusions. The first was that, with his military training, he would lead some kind of resistance to the French. He knew the weaknesses of the Moroccan *guish* and decided that, even if they had a leader stronger than Guebbas, they would not be sufficient to hold off the French. They would need reinforcement from a better trained commando force, which he could provide. The second was that Abdel Aziz was not the leader Morocco needed; he lacked the will to resist.

***

"Ted, it's so wonderful that you've actually been in Palestine," Meriam said to him one Saturday afternoon when he was visiting, after his trip. They were both at Luxembourg Gardens watching Arielle ride on the gaily-painted carousel. "Tell me about it."

"Well," he said, unsure just where to start and not wanting to be overly negative, "you did read my article, didn't you?"

"*Oui, cheri*, but it was so political. What is interesting to me is to know about Palestine, physically. What does it look like, the part where there are settlers? What are their houses like? What are the settlers themselves like?"

"Well," he waved briefly at Arielle as she came around again, "of course, it's an Arab country, or, strictly speaking it's Ottoman or Turkish-run, but most of the people who live there are Arabs, Meriam. Many are Christian, I believe. But it's not unoccupied. You must remember that."

She nodded. "*Oui*, you speak the truth, Ted. We think of it as just empty space, but it is not really, is it?"

"Not in the least. Jerusalem, which is the only real settlement in the region, is a small Oriental city with the normal *souks*, earthen houses, unpaved streets, a nice medieval bazaar, parts of which are also thought by the Christians to be the Via Dolorosa. The Jewish settlements are quite a way from the city, though, maybe several hours by horseback. So they're fairly isolated. What I saw, Meriam, wasn't too pleasant. There were dusty little settlements, with mean little huts. Very few amenities; I don't remember noticing electricity, and I would imagine the sanitary facilities are quite limited, not nearly as good even as small towns in Morocco like Taza. Not a place you're used to living in, Meriam. The Jewish settlers seem to have high rates of mortality; I think there's quite a bit of cholera and dysentery."

"Well, do not forget that most of them are from Eastern Europe," Meriam remarked. "They are not accustomed to that climate like those of us from the Arab world. They do not know how to manage."

"But what I want you to think about, Meriam, is that the life seemed very hard. And not so friendly Arabs, often Bedouins, surrounded them. The general climate was tough. I really can't imagine your living in that sort of atmosphere. It would be rather like being a frontiersman in America, hard backbreaking work, a brutish life, no comforts, general hostility from tribesmen. Is that what you want?"

"I know it would be hard. But if we can get any kind of accord from the Ottoman Sultan, so that we had some protection, it would be worth it. We could valorize it, you know. It does not need to stay like that. They must need teachers, there will be *enfants* there. I could be useful without actually doing the work of a *paysan*. Gabriel and Françoise are also thinking seriously about this."

Ted's heart sank. If Gabriel and Françoise, due to be married soon, were considering moving to Palestine, it would be very logical for Meriam to take the children and go with them.

"You have to consider Arielle, too," he reminded her. He steadfastly refused to discuss or even refer to Laure. "Are you willing to expose her to such a hard life? There will be many health risks for a child."

"Of course, Ted, we will need to consider this together. You would have to be willing. But she is healthy and young. It would be better to move before she is older. Then she and Laure can grow up in a new country, in a Jewish nation, away from discrimination and prejudice. Yes, there are risks, but I prefer those risks to some of the ones she would be confronted with in France or Morocco."

"Don't forget that at present Palestine is another Arab country. She wouldn't be free from discrimination. It would be like Morocco in many ways," Ted reminded her.

"But it is not *entierement* Muslim. I believe that it will change," Meriam responded, a bit illogically. "We are all working so hard. If enough people come there, and we take land that no one really wants, and we can make something of it…. and *we* can, because we will bring educated people,

Westerners, with culture...then they will *have* to give us some of the land. And that will be the difference, Ted."

Ted couldn't help but be struck by the similarity of this conversation with some of those he had had with Tariq and Fuad. At least, he thought, he and Meriam seemed to agree about the benefits of Western influence.

***

Lili shared a room with Meriam in Gabriel's apartment. She enrolled in a nursing course and loved the classes. After so much practical work in Fez it was wonderful to find answers to some of the medical questions that had plagued her there.

Meriam and Lili spent many evenings just talking, and Meriam began to talk a little about Taza. "It is so strange, Lili. Most of what happened to me there is just a blank. But I feel there is something important I have forgotten. Sometimes I wake thinking I have just remembered it, and then it is gone."

Lili shuddered. "Probably it's better to just forget. In my classes they talk about shock and how loss of memory can be a protective cushion for the brain, almost like a bandage. I wouldn't worry about it."

"Probably you are right, *cherie*. And I am content with my life now. I miss Ted, though. I don't know if it will ever be the same between us."

"At least you still love each other," Lili said. "I wish I had that."

CHAPTER ELEVEN
1906

The city was heating up and putrid smells and swarms of flies from piles of rotting garbage assailed Ted as he made his way past vendors and fruit stands into the crowded alleys of the area near al-Azhar where Fuad lived.

A servant greeted him in the open courtyard and Ted appreciatively inhaled the sweet fragrance of the fruit trees that were already in blossom in this spacious paved area, erasing the memory of the garbage in the streets just outside. He mounted the wide marble stairs at the far end, going to the loggia on the second floor that overlooked the courtyard through its fine wooden lattice of *meshrabiya* work. The floors were finished in intricate black and white marble designs that to Ted's eyes seemed cold after the red and green tiles of Morocco. He supposed they were more elegant but his taste had been formed by the color of North Africa.

Tariq and Fuad were deep in conversation with several young men, but ceased their discussion abruptly when they saw Ted. The guests stood up, shook hands and left the room almost immediately. Fuad, too, excused himself, explaining that he had a few errands to run before lunch and would see them in a little while.

Ted crossed his legs and settled into the cushions, accepting a water pipe that stood near by. "I feel I interrupted something."

"No, no. Those friends of Fuad's were ready to leave." Tariq smiled reassuringly at his friend and poured him some tea.

They sat contentedly, catching up with each other's news. A pause developed. Tariq leaned back and asked, "*Ya* Ted, you do not speak of Meriam. Have you seen her? How is she? How is it between you?"

"There's not much to discuss, *ya* Tariq. I did see her when I was in Paris. We do talk now, so I guess that's an improvement. But I don't know if there's any way we can go on. It's, well, it's complicated."

Tariq raised his eyebrows. "Women are hard to understand. I agree." His smile and inquiring look encouraged Ted to continue if he wanted.

After a long silence, Ted said, "Tariq, you know, she's had this, this child. I hate it! I can't accept that it's there and that Meriam wants to keep it. I simply can't understand how a child conceived under such circumstances could be welcome. To me it's an abomination! And now Meriam has become very militant. She feels she and all Jews are not welcome in Morocco, that they are despised there. I, well, frankly, I just don't know how to react to all this."

Tariq listened as Ted poured out his problems. Mostly Tariq just asked questions, making Ted talk and think about his own feelings and examine them more carefully, offering very few opinions of his own. After about an hour, Ted talked himself out. They sat companionably for a while sipping coffee.

Finally, Ted said, "I guess I've just been having trouble accepting the truth. Basically, Meriam and I have changed because of what's happened. The circumstances have made us different people. I want to turn back the clock, to pretend that everything's the same. But the truth is, we no longer have the same goals. Meriam wants to be safe, to be where she can be accepted. She feels passionately about a Jewish state, and I'd be a fool to say I didn't understand why. But there may not be a place for me in that new world of hers, and that's just something I'm going to have to accept." He stared morosely into the courtyard.

Tariq nodded. "That may be the truth, *ya* Ted. I, too, have had a problem with a woman. I had to accept what Allah had written. I understand, my brother." A shadow crossed his face as he spoke.

"*Ya* Tariq, please tell me if I'm intruding, but are you, by any chance, referring to Lili?"

Tariq's expression became guarded. "An outrageous idea, is it not? How could a Berber from the High Atlas Mountains who never wore shoes until he went to school with the *Sherif* think of such a thing? I agree. It is not meant to be. I fought with fate, *ya* Ted, and I saw that this was *mektub*, written. I was tempted when we were young. But Allah did not permit this. And then our sister, Lili, married Arthur. Still, *ya* Ted, I love your sister. I mean no disrespect."

Ted frowned. "She said something similar to me before I left Fez. I'm not an expert on these things, as you can see. In fact, I'd say I've made a complete balls up of my own life. But you and Lili. Of course, I'm not offended. There was some kind of a spark between the two of you, from the beginning. Well, who knows? I don't think Lili is all that happy with Arthur. But they *are* married. That's rather final. So, I reckon we're in the same boat, in some ways."

"We cannot let these things ruin our lives, my brother," Tariq said, "but it is hard. We must find other interests. Love is a gift from Allah. If he chooses not to give it, well, that is our fate. We must still fulfill our destinies. Do as we Arabs do. Devote your time and energy to politics and war."

He rose to greet Fuad, who was just coming up the stairs, and the servants brought in lunch, ending the conversation and leaving both men with much to think about.

Fuad was interested in Ted's visit to Istanbul and asked him about the situation there. "I've heard they've formed a group that's pushing for reforms; they call themselves the Young Turks. Did you hear much of them?"

"Not too much," Ted said. "I was mostly interested in Sultan Abdul Hamid himself and the state of the Sublime Porte. It didn't look too good, I must say. The Sultan is old and he's not too stable mentally, from what I could tell. The Germans are really courting him, you know. I think they feel they can make their alliances to the East, through the Balkans and the Ottomans. But it's an unholy alliance. And you're right. I got the impression that the army has a significant faction that doesn't support Sultan Abdul Hamid."

"Quite right," Fuad said. "I know many of those officers here in Egypt. They're ready for reform. They want to do away with all that Ottoman bureaucracy. We, too, need to make a clean sweep, rid ourselves of the British and other Europeans who are running Egypt. We need to institute more democratic practices, and have equal treatment under the law. Right now foreigners aren't even subject to our laws. If the Ottomans could change, they'd be a good ally for Egypt, much better than the British. We Muslims need to stick together and stop being so dependent on the Westerners."

"That's more or less what Mustafa Kamil is promoting here in Egypt, isn't it?" Ted said.

"Lots of people feel that way these days," Fuad said. "Kamil would go further, though, I think, and even break our ties with the Ottomans. Personally, I see no need for this. They are our brothers, after all. My grandmother was Turkish. But the British have no good reason for staying on now. They got us out of debt, and that was good, although you could say the foreigners played some role in getting us into debt in the first place. But there's really no excuse for them to linger on here. They are taking advantage of our cheap cotton to furnish their industries, but we are not benefiting."

Tariq glanced significantly at Ted. "This is what I fear for Morocco. It is the same story. Now that the Algeciras meeting is over, we know the French will come in and set up a Debt Commission. They will control all our revenues and our expenditures, just as Lord Cromer does here. And they will not leave."

Ted nodded. "Yes, the French prevailed on all their points. So we'll see many more French there controlling the banks and collecting customs intake. They want to be sure they get their money back. They're even going to set up a French dominated police force. Just as you have British police here in Egypt."

"Even though many of us, like my family, have over three generations of men trained in Europe, who are ready and able to run this country without their help," Fuad said bitterly.

Ted shook his head. "At this moment, if you'll excuse me saying so, Tariq, I think Morocco could benefit from some French intervention. I agree that the problem will be getting them to leave. But look at the state Morocco is in, whatever the reasons. Sultan Abdel Aziz has brought the country to bankruptcy. Corruption is widespread. People are suffering there from injustice, bad management, and disease. The powerful have all the advantages, and the poor are helpless victims. These things should change. You know this, yourself, *ya* Tariq. You and Mehdi tried to bring about reforms, but you couldn't overcome the people working against you, who stood to lose from reforms. Those same people are now the ones most opposed to the French. It's complex. This fellow, Lyautey, has some interesting ideas. He certainly seems to respect the culture, to want to empower local leaders rather than replace them."

Fuad said, "They all say that. But mark my words, when it comes right down to it, they choose leaders who are willing to follow advice, basically to do what the foreigners want. And I do not believe the colonizers always want what's best for the country. They have the interests of their own country at heart. It's just logical."

They finished their lunch, moving on to topics of more general interest. Ted confided to Tariq that Abdel Aziz had pleaded with him to return, missing his old tennis partner, as he put it. Privately, Ted thought he liked having a Western ear to listen and give him advice. But Ted wasn't quite ready. The Times liked the series he had done for them on Egypt and the Ottomans and had asked for more. There was nothing really drawing him back urgently. He wanted to expand his expertise to cover a larger region, hoping he and Meriam could find a neutral place in which to live.

Tariq, too, was not ready to leave. He knew he was not welcome in the present court of Morocco.

Ted was just preparing to leave when Fuad stopped him. "Ted, Tariq and I have one more thing to discuss with you. Do you have a few more moments?" He nodded and settled back down among the cushions.

Fuad said, "No doubt you've noticed that Tariq and I have been meeting numerous times with groups of men." Ted inclined his head in agreement.

"We wish to tell you about our plans, as Tariq assures me you are to be trusted as a brother. I think you know, Ted, that I am a nationalist. I don't want the British to stay here.

We should rule ourselves. This sentiment was what originally brought Tariq and me to be friends. When I came back from France I started enlisting men, mostly military colleagues, but also others, who shared this feeling. Since Tariq has joined me, we've begun training these men, as well as Moroccans whom Tariq encouraged to come here, to learn para-military techniques. We're teaching them how to disrupt things, activities that will encourage the British to leave."

"Insurgency," Ted said.

"I prefer to call it nationalism. I think it's justified. The British are putting down roots here, as we were saying earlier. They have to be convinced that it's not going to continue to be that comfortable for them," Fuad said.

Tariq said, "My brother, we propose to take you to see our camp. Someday you can write about this, but for now it must be a secret. I know we can trust you."

"I'd like to see it," Ted said.

***

Arthur was enjoying his stay in San Francisco even more than he had anticipated. His parents' home, high on Nob Hill, was spacious and comfortable. He had forgotten the wonderful cool weather and clear days of his home town. His father was not that well, and he was glad he had come. The doctors talked gravely of his heart and how important it was that he rest. Nevertheless, Arthur's mother had a series of small parties for her son, to show him off to all her friends. At Arthur's request they got tickets for the opera. The famous Enrico Caruso was singing. This was the kind of thing he never got to do in Morocco, not even in Tangier, although they occasionally had some kind of cultural event.

In his white tie and tails, Arthur escorted his mother to the event, where they sat in the family box.

At the intermission, Arthur left and came back with two glasses of champagne. "To you, Mother, and to San Francisco. I wish I had never left it."

"Can't you get another post, dear? Maybe in Paris or London?"

"I mean to talk to them in Washington, before I go back. I'm certainly ready to leave Morocco."

That night they talked a little in the stuffy Victorian parlor, as they sipped a night cap. Mrs. Crampton brought up the subject of Lili again. Arthur fidgeted and then said, "Mother, to be honest, Lili and I aren't getting along too well. If I leave, which I want to, I doubt she would come with me. I'm afraid our marriage was a serious mistake."

Mrs. Crampton leaned over and patted his hand. "Now don't you worry. You just go back to her in Paris and spend some time with her there, outside of Morocco. Maybe it's the country itself that's pulling you two apart."

Arthur sat up late after his mother went to sleep, staring into the fireplace and thinking about his life. He doubted he could win Lili back. Lili was a Moroccan, more so now than when he had met her. And he didn't like Morocco and doubted he would like any other part of the Arab world. He wanted to live in the West, with his own kind. It was as simple as that. Downing the remains of his brandy, he went to bed.

Sometime in the early morning he was awakened by a loud explosion. He leapt from the bed; the floor was shaking, everything was shaking. Arthur rushed for the door, but before he could get to it, the ceiling fell in, knocking him off his feet. As he scrambled to right himself, the floor collapsed. Arthur fell as blackness surrounded him.

***

The new train took Ted, Fuad and Tariq as far as Alexandria. After Alexandria, however, Tariq told Ted, "Now, my brother, you will feel you are back in Morocco."

They went to the camel market, located on the outskirts of Alexandria. The animals packed the huge enclosure tended by their Sudanese vendors, who had herded them up from the south. Tariq had a cousin who had died as a result of a camel bite and both disliked and distrusted these animals, so he had only reluctantly accepted the necessity of acquiring them. But for a desert journey he knew they were the only real option. He picked out three young males for himself, Fuad and Ted, since he was the only one with any experience with these kings of the desert. He also bought enough camels to provide them with transportation and portage of the equipment and training materials Fuad had brought along.

"It's best to buy these animals and sell them later," Fuad explained to Ted. "That way, no one has a record of where we have gone."

"Why not horses?" Ted asked.

Tariq laughed. "Yes, you and I always prefer horses. But Ted, this country is not like the High Atlas that we know. It is real desert. Camels are more practical in the sand."

A day of traveling proved Tariq's point. The sand was fine and soft and horses would have been as miserable as the men were, having no protection from the furnace-like heat. The men dressed as Bedouin, a welcome change for Ted and Tariq, putting on black baggy pants, black shirts and capes and voluminous turbans to shelter their heads from the sun. Not only was this practical, but it ensured that should they pass a casual traveler, they would excite no questions. Debonair Fuad looked uncomfortable in the voluminous wraps, and the two Moroccans struggled not to laugh as he fought to keep the turban in place, and the cloak on his shoulders instead of dragging behind him in the sand.

The young Hassan, whom Tariq had befriended on his last disastrous *mehalla* in Morocco, met them at the market along with a Bedouin from the camp to guide them to the water spots. Hassan had had no place to go when the campaign ended and Tariq had asked if he would like to go to Egypt with him and maybe do something to help his country. The boy had accepted immediately and had joined Tariq soon after he arrived. Now he was working at the camp, running errands and learning at the same time. Tariq looked at him with some satisfaction. At least the youngster looked clean and well-fed.

They traveled for three days through desert very different from that Ted and Tariq had known in Morocco. There the terrain they knew was rough and dry with scrub bushes and areas of gravel. Here vast stretches of sand extended as far as the eye could see, broken only occasionally by an oasis marked by a small cluster of palm trees. Luckily, their guide knew the area by heart and led them easily from one water spot to another. Occasionally they encountered small groups of Bedouin with their flocks, but their guide hailed the groups from a distance, giving the impression his companions were all part of his tribe. They passed without further notice as they plunged further and further into the southwest.

Tariq enjoyed the nights under the stars. They set up simple tents and ate dried foods, dates, and nuts. The guide had brought bread and clarified butter and they made tea. The men sat up each night in front of the campfire and Tariq regaled them with descriptions of the *mahallas* he had been on.

On the afternoon of the fourth day Tariq said to Ted, "Come, my brother. Tell me when you see our camp. Since the desert is so barren, maybe you can find it easily."

Ted kept alert, his eyes probing the distance, but as the day wore on, he said, "I don't see a thing, *ya* Tariq. Just a small oasis, like the others, with a few huts. That can't be it, can it?"

Tariq laughed. *"Mezyan*, good, my brother. That is our camp. I think it fooled you a little, did it not?"

Ted nodded. "It's a good job of camouflage, not that you have much to worry about, you're so far from civilization out here."

"Yes, but even so, it is good to be careful," Tariq said.

As they neared the settlement, several men, appearing to be simple tribesmen examining strangers coming too close to their homes, approached them. When they were close enough to identify them, they broke into cheers of welcome.

The party rode into the settlement and dismounted. To the casual eye there were maybe three dozen mud houses connected by high adobe-brick walls enclosing courtyards that were much larger than they seemed. They had planted prickly pear fences on the outside of the walls, as well as palm trees that effectively masked any activities taking place inside. The mud huts were connected, and concealed barracks filled with bunk beds so they could accommodate the several thousand men housed there. Similarly, some outlying sheds that looked like enclosures for camels or sheep, sheltered cannons and other armored equipment.

After they had rested and eaten, Tariq said, "Ted, I will drill the men for you. You shall see what they have learned."

They sat in the shade of a tent and the men marched by in blocks of one hundred. Ted said, "What a contrast from Morocco, *ya* Tariq. They look so fit, for one thing." He was commenting not only on their cleanliness and clean khaki shirts and trousers, but the marching. "I've never seen men lift their legs up so high when they parade."

"We learned that in France," Fuad said. "It looks good, but more importantly, it makes very strong legs."

"Now, let us move on to a few exercises," Tariq suggested. They walked to a small hut standing alone in the middle of one of the enclosed courtyards. Several men moved efficiently around the outside of the house, quickly assembling a small device. One darted inside and connected some wires to a post. He ran outside and another man pushed down on a lever, speeding away as fast as he could. In seconds the hut blew up, bits of clay and mortar falling in all directions. A few shards hit them, and Tariq was knocked down by a large piece. He sprang up quickly and dusted himself off; there was a scratch bleeding on his face. "It is nothing serious," he said, wiping off the blood, "but it is a good way to know how far damage can spread. We can learn from that, *insh'Allah.*"

"How are you planning to put these men and their training to use?" Ted wondered aloud.

Fuad said, "You'll see a few signs of this before long. Among other things, the men need to practice. They must gain confidence and a sense of power. They need to believe that they can have an effect on the British. That is essential for our success."

***

Screaming headlines announced an attack on the railroad between Alexandria and Cairo. The train had been carrying British replacement troops to Cairo. According to the paper, fifty men had been wounded when the rail blew up, and at least ten were dead.

***

At a dinner party given by the British Ambassador Ted found himself buttonholed by senior British military officials.

"Could we have a word?" they asked.

Ted recognized Sandy Miller, head of military intelligence and Terence Robinson, a friend from Oxford who was now in a senior position in the police. The third man was a stranger to him. They indicated the Ambassador's library, where they would be sure to have privacy. Making himself comfortable there in a well-cushioned leather chair and provisioning himself with a generous whiskey soda, Ted raised his eyebrows in question.

The unidentified man said, "Thank you for meeting with us."

Ted smiled. "I usually like to know with whom I'm speaking."

"Why don't you think of me as 'John Smith'?" the man said. "Let's just say it's a rather sensitive matter."

"Quite," Ted said, trying to hide his apprehension.

"We'd like to ask you a few questions about this Fuad al-Mahrous, as well as your friend, Tariq ash-Sherif. We have reason to believe that they are involved in establishing some kind of insurgency operation here. We'd appreciate your telling us anything you might know about this."

Ted's instincts as a reporter competed heavily with his strongest inclination to protect his friend. He decided on cautious honesty, resolving to follow their line of inquiry carefully and see where it would go.

"I should tell you, before we go any farther, that Tariq ash-Sherif is my closest friend, closer than a blood relative. You need to understand my allegiance before we continue this conversation."

The officers nodded. "We appreciate that. In fact, we're

more interested in al-Mahrous, although from what we understand, Mr. Ash-Sherif is quite closely associated with him."

"The second thing I should clarify," Ted said, "is that as a reporter, I'm bound to professional confidentiality. So in fact, if I did happen to know anything in particular, which I'm not saying I do, I really couldn't tell you a thing. This is extremely important to my reputation. You know, I spent some time with General Lyautey a few years ago. The same thing was true then. I was only invited on the firm assumption of privacy. But to the extent I can, I'll cooperate, of course."

'Smith' smiled. "Most of our information is classified, I'm afraid. But I suppose it wouldn't be too much to tell you that we understand al-Mahrous has organized a group of like-minded young officers here in Egypt who are against the British rule. There's nothing particularly surprising about that. But now we've heard that they've set up a camp of some kind over near the Libyan border, somewhere near Marsa Matrouh and it seems that they're doing military or para-military training. We've heard there are as many as 1000 men there, and we're curious about the purpose of this."

Ted was relieved that they hadn't mentioned the train bombing and wondered if they hadn't made the link or just weren't saying. "I've been gone much of these past three months," he said. "I'm afraid I wouldn't know anything much about that. I can certainly confirm for you that Fuad is a nationalist. But probably you're aware of that."

His friend, Terence, said, "We think this camp has intensified its activities since January."

Ted smiled, shrugging slightly to indicate he had nothing further to say.

'John Smith' seemed to realize Ted was not going to be

forthcoming. "Sorry to have troubled you. We shall be pursuing our inquiries and, of course, anyone found to be involved in these activities would be considered guilty of treason, with the usual consequences. If you do hear anything we'd appreciate your keeping in touch. And please do keep this confidential. Thanks for your time."

During the next few days Ted pondered what would be the best thing to do. He suspected they intended him to warn Tariq, since their close friendship was well-known in Cairo. Why? Perhaps because they'd be just as happy if Tariq left the country, which he might do if warned.

***

Ted's manservant brought him a telegram. He thought it was a routine message from his editor and started to put it aside to read later; then he noticed that it was from Tangier and quickly tore it open.

Arthur dead in SF earthquake. Can you meet us Paris? Fondly, Mother.

He stared at the paper for several minutes. He had read about the earthquake, but had completely forgotten that Arthur was out there.

***

Tariq came quickly. "Ted, my brother. How terrible. May Allah be merciful to Arthur." Tariq embraced him and took a seat near him on the deck. Tariq was in a silk caftan. He had obviously been relaxing at home and had not paused to change into more formal street wear when he received Ted's note, but had simply had his horse saddled and had ridden over to be with his friend quickly. "What do you know?"

Ted shook his head. "I read about the earthquake yesterday in the paper. One can only hope it was a quick death. I can't imagine what it must be like to have the very foundation under one's feet betray one like that, something so fundamental, so seemingly permanent. Just like that, the whole city destroyed, from what one reads in the paper."

"Lili is in Paris, is she not?" Tariq said.

Ted nodded. "Yes, Mother and Matt are going there straight away. I'm trying now to find passage to join them."

"Lili must have her family around her now. This will be a terrible shock. May Allah give her patience," Tariq said.

Ted scrutinized his friend's face wondering if he had detected a slight sign of something other than grief. "Tariq, I need to tell you something before you go."

Ted went into the salon of his houseboat. Tariq followed him.

"My brother, I want to warn you," Ted said. "The British police approached me last week with questions about Fuad's and your activities. They know about the camp near Marsa Matrouh. Fortunately, however, they don't seem to have made the link between your people and the train incident."

"Thank you for the warning, my brother. I know this puts you in a difficult situation," Tariq said.

"I don't want you to get arrested and spend the next twenty years rotting in a British jail," Ted said.

"Have no fear," Tariq said. "I will take immediate steps to protect us all. Now, go with Allah."

***

Ted followed Lili to Gabriel's familiar parlor, carrying Arielle who was thrilled to see her father although not completely sure of the circumstances that had brought him to her this time.

"Honestly, Ted. I know so little. Their neighborhood was hard hit; I think it must lie right on the fault line. Arthur's mother escaped miraculously, and it was she who notified me. She said the house just collapsed, and both Arthur and his father were killed. The roof fell in on them, I believe...." Tears came into Lili's eyes.

Ted hugged her until Arielle pushed for attention.

"Where is *Maman*?" Ted said to Arielle. "I thought she would be here."

"Oh no, *Maman's* at the office."

Ted said, "Really? She's working?"

"She works for the Zionstate," Arielle said, running the foreign words together.

Ted looked inquiringly at Lili.

"I thought you knew, Ted. Meriam should be here in a few minutes and she can explain it best, I think. But, as I understand it, she works for a fellow named Marmorek. It's all volunteer duties. Something to do with this Zionist movement."

"I see."

"There's quite a nice young man who works with her," Amelia said. "From Egypt, I believe. His name is Yusef. Did you meet him last time you were here, Ted?"

"Yes," he said. Yusef had stopped by after dinner, but Ted only recalled him vaguely. A bear of a man, who had had the very gentle manners big men often have. Ted had thought at the time that Meriam seemed to admire him. Now he felt uneasy that they were in daily contact.

Lili watched Ted. She realized there was more to this than met the eye. She resolved to pay more attention to Yusef, whom she had liked, but Meriam had mentioned nothing to her of any special feelings.

Lili had been staying with Meriam and Gabriel in

Paris for several months when the San Francisco earthquake occurred. She and Meriam had talked for hours about Ted, Laure, her future. She knew that Meriam was still far from healed, psychologically, from her trauma in Taza, and doubted she was ready to resume any kind of life with Ted. And there was always Laure, now over a year old, and an active infant, demanding attention from everyone and usually getting it.

***

Lili vowed that nursing and working at the clinic would now become her life's work. As for love, she would put it behind her, as a failed experiment, or maybe just not for her. She knew that she was partially to blame for Arthur's dissipation; if she had paid more attention to him probably he wouldn't have succumbed to the temptations of drinking and gambling. But, she had to be honest; they really hadn't had enough in common. After all, she thought, it didn't turn out too well for Meriam, either. Maybe marriage just isn't for everyone. Some of us are missing something in our personal makeup that allows us to form lasting relationships. These were the kinds of thoughts she and Meriam had spent most of their time discussing since she arrived, sitting up late at night in Meriam's bedroom after the children had gone off to bed.

***

After the memorial service Lili resumed her classes at the medical faculty. Ted met her there one afternoon as she was finishing for the day. "I thought I might take you for a drink. We haven't had that much time to ourselves, and I'll be leaving tomorrow."

"Wonderful! There's a little cafe near here. Unless you had some place specific in mind?"

"No, that sounds fine." They walked down the Boulevard St. Michel and along its side streets until they found Lili's café. Settling themselves outside in the warm evening they sat companionably for a while.

"Ted, you haven't told me much about Egypt. How do you like it?" Lili said.

Ted told her about the country, how different it was in many ways from Morocco, how much larger and more developed Cairo was than Tangier, about his houseboat, his British friends.

"And Tariq?" she said.

"Oh, he's fine. I think he's been quite happy there, although he may not stay that much longer. He and I have been interviewing many young professionals and recruiting them to go to Morocco to work for the Sultan. But the way things look now I wonder how much more we should do. It looks as though the French are gaining a foothold in Morocco and sending more of their own people under Foreign Minister Delcassé's program. They're probably going to object to these Egyptian advisors before long."

"Is he still friends with that military officer...Fuad, wasn't it?" Lili said.

"Yes. They're quite good friends, sharing the same military interests, I suppose. They have a very active circle of acquaintances. Just between you and me, they're forming some kind of anti-British network. In Tariq's case, it's more freedom fighters for Morocco. I wouldn't be surprised if many of the 'advisers' he sent back to Morocco were really his troops. I was told to warn Tariq off, just before I left last week. In fact, I would wager he leaves quite soon, now that he's under surveillance."

Lili looked worried. "Will they arrest him?"

"I got the impression they would much prefer that he just leave. They may arrest Fuad, though. Tariq told me not to fret. Still, one does. He sent you his condolences, by the way. I sent a note over to him straight away I had the news, and he came right over. He seemed genuinely sorry to hear about Arthur."

Lili nodded. "What do you think he'll do?"

Ted considered. "It's hard to say. We didn't have much time to talk before I left, after I told him about the British. But I wouldn't be surprised if he goes back to Morocco quietly."

Lili stirred her coffee thoughtfully.

"How will Arthur's death affect your life, Lili?" Ted asked. "It seems like it's a bit bleak right now. Just like me, both of us alone again. Would you like to come out and keep house for me in Egypt?"

Lili laughed. "I don't think so, Ted. But thanks for the offer. I'll have to leave Fez now. I can't stay there on my own. I've been thinking about that. There was some talk about a French doctor being assigned to my clinic, even before I left, so I've been planning to talk to the French here and see if that can be arranged definitely.

"I'll go back to Tangier and work in Miss Watson's clinic. She's getting on, and since she was really my inspiration for starting the clinic in Fez, it would be fitting for me to contribute my services to her in Tangier. I'm enjoying this nursing course, you know." She looked up at Ted. "It's so satisfying to get the skills and knowledge about healing, understanding more about the causes of the diseases we see so frequently among the children, and know that there are steps we can take to cure them. And I'm eager to put them to use."

She concluded, wiping her mouth with her napkin and folding it neatly next to her coffee cup. "I'll be here at least a year and probably return to Tangier next June. So it may be some time before we see each other again. Unless you think you'll get back here before I leave?"

Ted glanced at his watch. "Hard to tell, Lili, I'd like to, to see Meriam and Arielle. I'm going to London tomorrow you know, and I'll have to find out what the Bureau has in mind for me. I shall certainly try. But if I don't, I'll come to Tangier next summer to visit you and Mother and Papa."

***

Ted and Meriam dined together before he left. They went to a little restaurant on the Quai Voltaire that they both liked. Ted ordered bouillabaisse and Meriam selected veal in wine sauce. Halfway through the meal, Meriam put down her fork and wiped her mouth carefully with her napkin. *"Cheri*, I have something rather strange to tell you."

Ted looked up.

"You know, I said I thought I had forgotten something important about Taza?" she said.

"Yes."

"Well, I think I have remembered. It is so strange, I cannot be sure that it is true." She hesitated, tears coming into her eyes. "But I thought you should know."

"What is it, sweetheart?"

"I remembered that, when it was just the two boys and I in the salon, and we heard the soldiers in the other room, I heard someone cry out, 'there's a Jewish girl in the other room' and, this seems very odd, but I knew that voice."

Ted stopped eating and stared at Meriam. "Who was it?"

"Well, it sounded like that awful man you went to school with, that Kassim. I know it is very unlikely, but I could swear it was his voice."

"Did you see him?"

"No, *cheri*. I think when the soldiers came into the room, well, I just don't remember that part." She stopped, and put her handkerchief to her eyes.

"Kassim al-Matari. That's the voice you think you heard."

Meriam nodded. "I think so, Ted. I do not know why he was there, but it was his voice."

CHAPTER TWELVE
1907

Ted arrived first in Tangier, fresh from Syria, where he had spent several months for the Times and Lili came a day or two after him, triumphant with her nursing certificate and full of ideas for Alice Watson's clinic.

Morocco was baking, the land barren brown, leaves covered with dust, but the Mt. Jefferson house on the mountain with its high ceilings, French doors and deep porches had been built to catch the breezes. The family tended to congregate on its wide back porch, where Amelia had massed window boxes of bright pink geraniums and spicy trailing petunias that perfumed the air. This shaded area, overlooking the Mediterranean, with the Kasbah of the city in the foreground to the left and the new Customs House the French were building in the center of the beach, was the coolest part of the house.

Ted settled himself comfortably in the biggest wicker rocking chair, and poured himself a generous Pernod with a splash of water, a drink he'd become fond of in the Lebanon. Lili found him sitting there, gazing contentedly out at the bay. "Where's that chic Parisienne who stepped off the boat just a day or two ago?" Ted teased her.

"It's much too hot for all those stays and belted waists and lady's undertrimmings," she said, arranging the loose folds of her caftan to sit on the swing. "Isn't it glorious to be home? Why do we ever go away? How could we leave such beauty and comfort behind us and go into those murky cities with coal dust and traffic and noise?" She leaned back, her one foot that was resting on the ground pushing the swing languorously back and forth, creating a modicum of breeze. "Ah, this is heaven, really."

The twilight lengthened. Amelia and Matt joined them and they sat peacefully watching the gas lights of the city flicker in the hot summer evening.

"I'll have what Ted's having. It looks good." Lili said in response to Matt's unspoken question. She sipped and wrinkled her nose slightly. "It's licorice! I wasn't expecting that. But it's refreshing. It is hot. Not that it was all that cool in Paris by the time I left. But it's different here. A drier heat, I think."

"How were the Ben Simons?" Amelia said.

"Just fine, Gabriel's wedding was lovely, very quiet, partly in respect to me. But it was a nice ceremony. I think Leah and Brahim were thrilled to see him settled. Françoise will be a good wife for Gabriel."

"Are they still talking about going to Palestine?" Ted said.

"I think so. But they haven't made any definite plans yet. Neither of them seems to be in much of a hurry. They're so comfortable in Paris, and Meriam enjoys her work, as you know, Ted. I wonder if they'll really bring themselves to do it."

"But what about Arielle?" Amelia said. "Ted, surely you don't want her to go so far away and be raised in such a primitive environment?"

"Not particularly, Mother," he said, "but I can't really offer her a home, the way I live."

Matt stretched out his legs. "Who can, these days? I wonder how much longer we're going to have that privilege here."

"What?" Both Ted and Lili spoke at the same time.

"Nothing to fret about right at this moment," Matt quickly assured them. "It's just that things are looking mighty shaky here. I reckon you two are a little behind the times."

"I've been rather occupied over in the Levant," Ted said. "What in particular makes you feel this way, Papa?"

"There've been at least five attacks on foreigners, most of 'em French."

"It no longer feels as if we're welcome, not even here in Tangier now that Raisuni is in charge," Amelia said.

"The murders, though, they haven't been here in Tangier?" Ted said.

"No, with that one exception of the young military officer killed on the beach by Raisuni's thugs. The rest have been in the interior."

"There was one particularly horrible incident a few months ago," Amelia said. "Didn't you hear about the man in Marrakech?"

Lili said, "The one accused of being a spy?"

"Yes, that was quite awful," Amelia said. "They stoned him to death. Some reports say they dragged his body all over the city. Maybe the time is coming when we'll have to leave."

"I've read that General Lyautey continues to push the Algerian border onto Moroccan soil," Ted said.

Matt said, "It's a darn sight worse since Delcassé was replaced by this Clemenceau. He's a lot hungrier for action, a real warmonger and is urging Lyautey on. And, of course, Taillandier's out now, too. I reckon you knew that? Replaced by a fellow named Regnault. So it's all different. The French seem set on taking over."

"Probably for the best," Ted said.

They sat on the porch talking as the sky gradually

darkened. It was a beautiful clear night, and the lighthouse at the top of the Kasbah cast a golden light out over the bay.

Lili said, "It's so lovely, so peaceful here. I can't believe anything bad is going to happen. This is our home. We're Tangerinos. Those attacks that you talk about, Mama, those Frenchmen must have done something to provoke the people. They were probably offensive in some serious way. Surely that kind of thing isn't going to affect us."

***

Lili went down to the *medina* to find suitable material for some more caftans. She spent an agreeable hour at her favorite cloth shop, chatting with the vendor, Uncle Ali, a long-time favorite of hers, catching up on the news of his many children, wives, and in-laws. When the evening prayer was called she realized she would be late for tea. She hurried through the small open area full of tea shops known as the Sokko Chicco. Still musing on some of the stories Ali had told her, she wasn't paying too much attention, when she heard a familiar voice. To her surprise, she spotted Tariq. Dressed in a *djellabah*, with the hood pulled over his head shadowing his face, he was hard to distinguish but she knew him immediately. Tariq had just bid three men good-bye and now he was walking straight toward her, his thoughts obviously elsewhere. Without thinking, Lili walked forward and touched him on the arm, "Tariq!"

Tariq's eyes widened as he saw Lili. Gesturing to her to be silent, he quickly took her arm and drew her into a nearby dark entrance hall to a house. "I thought you were in Paris." Without warning, he pulled her close and kissed her, a long, hungry kiss. Despite her surprise, almost shock, at seeing him, being pulled so quickly into the dark, not having a chance to speak, Lili melted against him, responding to his body warmth, the comfort of his embrace, the sheer joy of finally being where she had thought she would never be. They stayed wrapped together, hidden from the outside world behind the fly-speckled glass of the door for what seemed to her an eternity.

Finally, they separated. "Tariq!" she said, "what on earth?"

"Lili," he spoke at the same time. He looked into her eyes. "*Marhababik*, welcome, little one."

"But Tariq, I thought you were in Cairo?"

"I will tell you. But not here, *ya* Lili. People should not see me. But I must see you. Are you free now? Can you come with me?"

Lili thought quickly. Mama and Papa would be worried, but she couldn't bear to be parted from Tariq. She said, "Yes, Tariq. I'd like that more than anything. Let me just send a message to the house, so they won't worry."

Tariq said, "One of the boys from the cafe will take a note up for you. He can take your packages, too. That way they can know you have not been kidnapped."

Lili laughed, confused. She was having a difficult time adjusting so quickly to the surprise of seeing Tariq, to the wonderful kiss, which had made her feel a bit lightheaded, to her incredible feeling of happiness. She wrote quickly, just a few lines telling Amelia not to wait dinner for her. The boy, summoned by Tariq, trotted off with a handsome tip in his pocket and promise of more to come when Tariq had been assured that his mission had been successfully completed.

Tariq paused to think a minute. "Lili, we will go to my villa. It is the best place. There are too many people everywhere. I do not want my presence known. And I do not want people to talk about you, either."

She smiled. "Such secrecy!"

"There is a good reason." He said. "So I will go first. If you lose sight of me, I will find you in Souk al Barra. There we can take a carriage."

***

Tariq drew her through the house and pulled her gently into a small sitting room. He closed the door firmly, looking straight at her. "Now we can talk, *habibti*. Here, let me take your wrap." He reached around her shoulders to release it, and almost without thinking, Lili turned and was in his arms. Lili's body pressed against his willingly this time, her mouth open to receive his kiss, her mind empty of any emotion except what she was feeling and sensing.

Gradually, as the embrace continued, Lili could feel Tariq running his hands down her body. She shrugged off her wrap and reached her hands higher, circling his shoulders to intensify their closeness. He seemed to relax and cupped his hands around her buttocks, pulling her body tightly into contact with his sex. Lili's body contracted into a series of orgasms. She clung to him, overcome. Tariq picked Lili up and carried her over to one of the couches where he laid her gently down.

Sitting down beside her and looking down into her eyes, he smoothed back her hair and said, "Lili, *habibti*, I want you. I've always wanted you."

Lili had never dreamed such feelings were possible. Her entire body demanded that they continue. Without even thinking, she held up her arms to Tariq. "Please," she said, "please, don't stop. Not now."

Tariq laughed. "*Habibti*, I was not planning to stop."

Gently then, as an overhead fan revolved lazily in the heat, Tariq proceeded to disrobe Lili, stroking and kissing each part of her body as he divested her of her Moroccan clothes. Finally she lay totally exposed in the semi-darkened room, lit by now only by the light of the setting sun. She watched as he shed his rough *djellabah*, Turkish pants, cotton vest, and shirt. She gasped as he turned back to her, fully aroused.

"Lili, my heart. I love you."

"Yes, yes, Tariq."

He came to her then, first lying beside her, his sex gently grazing her body as he stroked her, kissed her breasts, warmed her body, slowly, bringing her back almost to the state of orgasm again. She sighed with pleasure, thinking how amazing that she had never realized this was how it was between a man and a woman.

He was above her, looking into her eyes searchingly.

"Yes," she replied simply, her entire body craving his, shuddering already in anticipation of receiving him. And then they were together. Lili could not believe her body was capable of such sensation. Almost from the moment of contact, waves of orgasm swept over her; she felt herself going in and out of consciousness with each of Tariq's motions. She opened her eyes to find him watching her. She moved slightly and was overcome again.

Tariq said, "Lili, we were meant to be together."

"Tariq," she began, but couldn't continue, as his rhythm increased and she was swept away again. Soon she began to moan. Her emotions were primordial, there was no thought left as he continued to insist with his body, more and more, faster and faster. Finally they reached a climax; Lili heard herself cry out, as if from a distance. She must have dozed then, for she woke up later to find Tariq beside her, propped on one arm, watching her. She said with a start, "Oh, Mama and Papa will be worried about me! It must be late."

Tariq took her into his arms and kissed her. "Lili,

my dearest, I sent a note to them saying you would not be home tonight and they should not worry. Was that all right, *habibti*?"

She relaxed. "What will they think, do you suppose? But it's too late now to worry about that, I guess. Thank you. Thank you, Tariq, for everything," she said. "I've never, you know, I've never experienced anything like that before," she said, blushing slightly. "I really didn't know love could be like that."

"It isn't very often, my heart," Tariq said, stroking her breasts lightly. "This is something very special, between just the two of us, Lili."

She shuddered, and noticed that he was aroused again. Her breasts felt so tender, his fingers gently probing. Her whole body was tingling, burning. She relaxed as his hands continued to explore, moving down her body till they reached her swollen lips. They were so moist, so ready, his hands slid between them searching for the hidden interior. She let her legs fall open and abandoned herself again to the wonderful new sensations of love.

Hours passed in their lovemaking. Lili reveled in these new feelings, becoming aware for the first time of her own body and of Tariq's, too.

In the middle of the night Tariq threw on a silk *djellabah*, and went out to bring them some food from the kitchen. Lili stirred, offering to help.

"No, my dearest. You stay here. I do not want the servants to see you and start talking. I will serve you."

He came back with a plate of warm chicken that must have been prepared and left for them earlier. Lili sat up and smelled the aroma of cumin, garlic and tomato sauce appreciatively. "I'm starving! How did you guess?"

Tariq laughed. "I, too. We have been working too hard, my sweet."

***

There was a little round table near the couch and they drew up some cushions and settled themselves around the table, eating ravenously with their fingers, mopping up the sauce with bread Arab style. Tariq made them some tea and they sat contentedly, satiated in all ways, sipping it.

Finally Lili broke the silence. "Tariq, you must think I'm completely shameless." She blushed, overcome at the thought of her own abandon.

Tariq tilted up her head and stared fiercely into her eyes. "Lili, never be ashamed. I love you. We have always loved each other. This is right. Do not let shame ruin it. Be proud of yourself, of your emotions." He smiled at her and kissed her softly on the lips. "I am proud of you. You are an honest woman. You are passionate." He brushed her breasts gently with his fingertips and groaned. "Allah, you are an enchantress!"

Tariq held her close, his hands once again exploring her body. She moved in delight.

She said, "Tariq, I was wrong. I shouldn't have married Arthur. It was a mistake. I realized that. The more we were together, the more I knew I had married the wrong man. I was so miserable."

"Yes, *habibti*, I know. I felt the same. I wanted you so much. I hated to watch you with him. But I thought he was what you wanted. So I went away. I felt bitter. I am not sorry he is dead, may Allah have mercy on his soul."

"It was sad, wasn't it?" she said. "To die so young. And I felt in some way I had contributed, because he knew I didn't love him really. I tried so hard not to let it show; not to let it be true."

Morning came. They had spent the night making love and talking. Both were exhausted, but Lili did not want this to end. Just as she was about to suggest something to Tariq, he spoke, "Lili, must you leave now? Can you stay longer? I have a few days before I must travel. Can you stay with me?"

Taking a deep breath, she said, "Papa and Mama are probably already scandalized, so I have nothing more to fear. I can't bear the thought of leaving you, either. I don't know how I'll explain this when I get back and they want details, but I'll worry about that later."

Tariq nodded. "Please Lili. I wish you could tell them the truth, but no one must know I am in Morocco. After these few days, I must leave for a while, but we can share this time at least. We will close out the world until I go. I will dismiss my staff, and we will be private. No one need know you're here."

"Can you explain to me why it's such a secret that you're here?" she said.

"You should not know too much. It is dangerous for you. Just believe I am working for the good of Morocco."

"Ted told me that you were involved training resistance forces in Egypt. Was that for Morocco?"

"I had to leave or face jail. Fuad is now in prison. But his friends will get him out very soon. It was time for me to come back to Morocco, in any case. But I do not want to discuss this with you. It is dangerous for you to know too much. You must not be involved." He pulled her close.

"Are you working on something like that here?" Lili said, her eyes anxious. She didn't think she could bear to lose him now that she'd finally found him.

"Hush, my dear, we will not discuss any more of this. We

have to keep my presence a secret for the moment. And you and I have better things to do."

Lili was curious but understood from Tariq's tone that he was not going to say more. She nodded and wrote a short note to Amelia, "I've run into some old friends and have decided to go with them to Gibraltar for a few days. Please don't worry. See you soon. Love, Lili."

The days passed all too quickly. They had the house to themselves. Tariq's staff prepared delicious meals and left them in the kitchen, then retreated to their own quarters leaving them in perfect peace. Their lovemaking became more leisurely as their initial urgency abated. Lili relaxed completely; she was amazed at how at ease and comfortable she felt with Tariq. Even more surprising, she thought, was that he was the same with her. She thought to herself, we're having a honeymoon. Night turned into day. They wandered through the house in simple robes, not bothering to dress fully, so that each was available to the other at any moment. Everything faded into the background.

Their last night came. They were sitting on the terrace, enjoying the breeze and picking at some salads left by Tariq's cook. Lili was trying not to cry as the desolation of being parted from Tariq began to descend upon her. Tariq was quiet, too. He sat there watching her as she poked half-heartedly at the food. Finally, he moved the plate away from her. "Lili, my beloved, I can not bear to see your tears."

"Tariq, it's hard to have just found you and now to have to separate."

"I know, my heart. I feel this, too. But I must go, for a while. I have responsibilities. But I will come back soon. I can not stay away from you. You know that." He kissed her. "Now we will marry."

"But what about Malika?" Lili said, guiltily remembering the sweet young girl she had befriended in Fez.

"*Habibti*, we both made our mistakes and have to accept the consequences. Malika is my responsibility and so are our two children. She knows I don't love her. We have not shared a bed for many years now. She does not even know I am in Morocco. But unless she wishes to leave me and marry again, I must care for her. This is our way, you know, *ya* Lili. We are allowed more than one wife for this reason, I believe. It is the humane way. Women must be looked after. I trust you will not object to my continuing to support her. You will be my true wife, my love. We will have children together, *insha'llah*. Malika and I will not have other children. She will remain in El Meneb with my family. You and I will live here or elsewhere, together."

Lili considered all this. "Yes, Tariq, what you suggest is right. I hope my heart can accept what my head tells me makes sense."

Tariq took her hand and kissed it.

They woke just as the sun was rising. Tariq had his man saddle two horses and assisted Lili to mount on one while he mounted the other. "*Habibti*, I will escort you to Mt. Jefferson, just to the gate. It is early and no one will see us. Then I will continue from there, taking this horse to another who is waiting for it."

They rode quickly through the city, passing the Souk al Barra as the farmers were just arriving from the countryside bringing produce to sell in the market. It was still cool and fresh. A few roosters crowed in the background and a dog or two barked at the horses as they passed. Lili smiled at Tariq in delight; it was so wonderful to look at him, riding beside her and to realize that finally they were united. "Tariq, I will miss you."

"I, too, little one. But the time will pass quickly." His dark eyes flashed in a smile.

"*Insha'llah*," she said. They arrived at the gate to Amelia and Matt's house. The guard, who had been asleep, rose groggily to his feet. "Oh, Miss Lili. Good morning! I wasn't expecting anyone so early." He glanced curiously at the two men accompanying her, but Tariq quickly turned his horse around, not wanting to be seen, and galloped away, leading the spare horse by its reins.

***

Lili had been working at Alice Watson's health clinic two weeks when Alice invited her to dinner. "Just a few family friends, dear, I think you'll enjoy it."

When Lili showed up at Alice's house she was dismayed to find Kassim there. It had completely slipped her mind that Kassim was Alice's step son.

Alice introduced them. "Lili, my dear, Kassim said he had met you once or twice, many years ago, so you two know each other?"

Forcing a smile as she recovered from her surprise, Lili acknowledged that they had met before. Kassim was assiduous in his attentions during the entire evening and, as he was seated next to her at dinner, it was hard for Lili to avoid him. "Surely someone as young and attractive as you will remarry," he said.

Lili tried to look noncommittal. "I haven't really given it any thought. You know, Arthur only died a year ago."

"We wouldn't want you to languish in our midst," he said. "There are so many amusing things to do in Tangier."

Lili thought about all the amusing things Kassim had

introduced to Arthur with an inward shudder. She said, "I often go about with my brother, you know. He's separated from his wife at the moment."

"My word, I haven't seen Ted for ages. I think the last time was actually during the Perdicaris kidnapping. He was most helpful then."

Alice leaned over. "Oh, you're being too modest, Kassim. Surely, you were the leader in solving that problem."

"I did what I could to help the poor man, Auntie," he said. He turned back to Lili. "Now that Ted's back in Tangier does he plan to stay here? He was in Cairo for over a year with Tariq, wasn't he?"

Lili became wary. "Ted's just visiting our parents. His job takes him far and wide, all over the Mediterranean, really. Maybe he'll keep his place in Cairo and also spend some time here. He hasn't said."

"So, he'll be here for the next month or two, you think?"

"He hasn't discussed his plans with me."

"And what do you hear from Tariq?"

Lili could feel herself reddening. "I've heard he's quite content in Egypt."

"Didn't I hear about some trouble there with the police?"

"Not that I know of." Lili turned the conversation to more general topics, directing questions to Alice about the clinic, affairs around Tangier.

She went home as soon as she could politely excuse herself, but not without a final interlude with Kassim in which he invited her to go to the pig sticking with him the following weekend.

"Unfortunately, my family has already made plans," she replied. He bowed, then, and promised they would see each other soon. She fled, vowing to warn all their servants to refuse him entrance to the house, should he make good on his promise.

As Lili's carriage drew up to Mt. Jefferson, she noticed a horseman standing near the entrance. She motioned to the carriage man to stop. She peered out. It was Tariq.

***

At the villa, once again conveniently free of servants, Tariq and Lili fell hungrily into each other's arms. Then they settled down to talk. Lili told him she wanted to let Ted in on their secret.

"Yes, of course," Tariq said. "Tell him I will see him soon. What have you done since I left? Where were you tonight?"

Startled, she remembered. "I had the most unpleasant evening. Alice Watson invited me for dinner and when I got there, I discovered Kassim was one of the party. He pestered me all night and before I left he actually asked me out."

Tariq went very still. "Lili, you must have nothing to do with that man."

"Well, of course I wouldn't." She was indignant at the thought.

Tariq told her about the death of the young slave girl whom Kassim had bought when he was sixteen, about suspicions they had of his role in getting Mehdi and himself dismissed from the court. When he had finished, they sat for a while in silence, Lili leaning against Tariq's knees, he stroking her shoulders.

She said, "I knew he was horrible, but I didn't realize he could be lethal. Now I'm frightened. You know, he asked me lots of questions about you and Ted. He even started to talk at the dinner table about your problem with the police in Egypt. He was quite well-informed."

"Lili, do not have fear for us. But I am afraid for you. It

would be easy for him to hurt you. I cannot take a chance. I will leave a guard with you. Do you remember the man who came for you in Taza? Mohammed?"

She nodded.

"He is here with me now. He will stay with you. Maybe *Si* Matt can find some place for him in your coach house. Do not move without him. Will you promise me that?"

"Yes, if you think it will help, but who will protect you?"

Tariq laughed. "I am my own best protection, with Allah's help. You should not fear for me, *habibti*. I have plans for Kassim, but they need a little longer to come to ripen. In the meantime, though, you must not be in danger."

"Tariq," Lili said. "Ted's planning to go to Casablanca soon. He said he's heard about civil unrest there and the Times wants him to do an article on it."

Tariq paused. "Where will Ted be staying? Do you know?"

"No."

"Well, as soon as you do, tell Mohammed. He can get word to me. I will contact Ted. We need to talk, about you, among other things." He pulled her close and kissed her gently. "I wish we could marry now." He paused, thinking. "Lili, for the moment, shall we sign a contract, the two of us? I will give you this ring." He drew a heavy silver signet ring from his finger, embossed with the star and crescent of Islam. "Abdel Aziz gave me this a long time ago. Wear it around your neck as a good luck piece. Then, as soon as I finish this project I am working on, in August or September, we will have a proper ceremony."

Solemnly he wrote out a marriage contract in Arabic and then translated it into English. It was very simple.

I, Tariq Ash-Sherif, do this day of 30th June, 1907, take Lili Shields Crampton as my lawful wife and promise to protect her and be responsible for her and any offspring produced by this marriage from this day on.

They both signed it. "There," he said. "I want to do so much more, but at least you have this. Please, little one, hide this carefully, as well as the ring. This would prove to anyone looking for me that I am in Morocco. I can not afford to have people know that, at least not for a few months."

Tariq left later that night. Lili was in a daze. Too many things had happened. Tariq assured her as he left that Mohammed would show up at the house in the morning.

"Tell Ted to take care of him," he said. "He can think of a way to explain it to Matt without mentioning my name. But I am serious about this, *habibti*. Be careful." He gave her a final kiss and rode off.

***

Lili was certain she was pregnant. She was struggling with her thoughts at breakfast, elation that she and Tariq would produce a child, nausea and fear, how could she explain her pregnancy without revealing that Tariq was here? Her worries were interrupted when Ted announced that he would leave the next morning for Casablanca.

Amelia said, "Why on earth would you want to go down there now? It's hot and unpleasant and there's no decent place to stay. Perhaps you could stay with the Clarks? They like having company, don't they Matt? Isn't he something in the wool trade?"

"Yes, my dear, something of the kind. You want us to

contact him for you, Ted? Why in blazes do you want to go there now, anyway? Your mother's right. It's right unsettled there, from what I hear."

"I think I should go and take a look. There might be a good article in it."

Matt said, "I heard something about Casablanca from Regnault the other night. Remember, Amelia?"

"Not really," she said. "I believe I was talking to young Miss Price at that time. She was telling me a fascinating story about a new play she saw recently, and I was simply riveted. What did he say, dear?"

"Something about some new customs police. It looks like the French have sent their own people down there to start collecting the taxes, to pay back the debt, just like they've been threatening to do, and the people are protesting. The same old thing," he said, motioning Hamoud to pour more coffee.

"You know that whole area around Casablanca is a tinderbox," Ted said. "Most of it's owned by foreigners now, either straight out or by farmers who are protégés of some foreign power. So they're already a rather mutinous lot. And there are complications. The Compagnie Marocaine is building a jetty at the harbor and they've brought in French and Algerian labor, which has caused a stir. It sounds as though it has the ingredients for a good story."

Amelia said, signaling Hamoud to clear away the dishes, "it sounds hot and uncomfortable, but I suppose that never did bother you, dear."

Ted nodded. "I've ordered the horses for tomorrow morning. I'll join a French party that's headed in that direction. I'm not sure how long I'll be gone, but I'll try to get a message back if it looks like I'll be there long."

Ted checked in with the Clarks in Casablanca, who

were happy to have him and to hear news about Tangier. They confirmed that things were very tense in the young city, occupied mainly by foreigners representing various trade interests.

George was an old friend of Matt's and represented a large American company that bought wheat and wool from Moroccan farmers. He and his wife, Marie, had been living in Casablanca for the past ten years. He put it succinctly, "We're trying to build a modern town, get a jetty built at the port so larger boats can land here to pick up produce. We finally have good international police to ensure that taxes are collected properly. But these people are so damned backward. You know, we've installed a little train track, just a work train that goes out to the quarry where they're getting rocks for the jetty. It makes it a lot easier to get those heavy stones to the beach. But now the natives are raising holy hell. Seems they don't like the whistle."

Ted said, "Don't forget these people have never seen a train before. It's a scary thing. And whistles are considered very unseemly here, very improper. Haven't I heard that the train passes through a cemetery? That would really compound the problem; they'd think it was disturbing the sleep of their dead. Also, bringing in Algerian workers probably didn't contribute much to its popularity."

"Well, the Moroccans are too lazy to work themselves, so I don't know what they expected," was George's only comment.

At the quarry Ted found two dozen or so Algerians loading a small train with the stones destined for the jetty. The French engineer seemed to be finding special delight in blowing its shrill whistle. A crowd of tribesmen was gathering, getting more and more angry each time they heard a toot. He wandered over to the Moroccans and started chatting with them. Someone plucked his sleeve discreetly. "Please, *ya sidi*," a young boy said, "come with me. A man wishes to speak with you."

Ted hesitated for a minute. He knew it was foolhardy, but he was curious. So he followed the scruffy looking boy about 200 meters to a small hut, where some men were gathered, drinking tea. The lad motioned him to join them and he squatted down with the men.

"*Marhaba, ya* Ted."

He looked up to see Tariq next to him, offering him a glass of tea.

"I wasn't expecting you here, of all people!"

"Ted, this is not a good time to talk. And do not look at me. Later I will explain, but now, my brother, I want you to leave immediately. Some bad things are going to happen here. Tonight we will meet and I shall explain more."

***

Ted was having drinks with the Clarks when a messenger was shown in.

"Excuse me, sir," he addressed George. "Looks like a regular riot is going on out there at the quarry. Some men have been killed."

"Damn!" George pushed back his chair. "This could be bad. I'll go see what the British Consul advises. Did you see anything when you were out there, Ted?"

Ted said, "No, I saw a bunch of tribesmen milling around, but that was all."

George and Ted rode over to the Consulate. They found dozens of other worried expatriates. Nick Jenkins, the Consul, got the crowd settled so he could address them.

"Gentlemen, shortly after noon today a gang of Moroccans out at the quarry disabled the supply train, putting rocks on the tracks to derail it. They hauled the engineer out of the car and beat him to death. The same fate befell at least ten other Europeans working on that train. Their bodies have been found badly mangled and left for the vultures on the rocks of the quarry. May God have mercy on their souls." He bowed his head for a silent moment of prayer.

The men stirred angrily. Mutters were heard, "This is war, then!"

"How dare they attack Europeans!"

Ted asked, "What's being done to protect the city?"

Jenkins replied, "I'm about to go off now to talk to *Qaid* Ben Bouzid, our governor. He'll have to call out the militia and try to stop this violence."

"What about the other men still out there at the quarry?" someone said.

"We, that is the Consuls, have requested the militia to escort them into town, where they'll be safe," Jenkins said.

"Fat lot of good that will do," a merchant near Ted said. "The militia are a motley lot and couldn't hit a target at ten feet, from what I've seen of them."

"They're all we've got, gentlemen. I think the best thing the rest of you can do for the moment is to return to your homes, be sure they are as secure as possible, and get your own weapons into order in case they're needed."

The crowd dispersed.

The situation in the streets was tense with large crowds of Moroccans muttering insults at the foreigners. As Ted rode alongside George Clark, a small figure approached his horse. It was the same boy who had contacted him this morning. Leaning down, Ted questioned the boy with a glance.

"Please, my lord, can you come with me?"

***

Tariq told Ted about the attack that had taken place at the quarry and acknowledged what Ted already suspected. Tariq's men had provoked the tribesmen, stirring up their anger over the past week and encouraging them to take action.

"We must start defending ourselves, *ya* Ted. The French are searching for a chance to take over. Allah forbid that we just open our gates for them."

"You know that I don't necessarily agree with you, Tariq," Ted said. "But thank you for the story."

"Just promise me that you will not publish it for a few days," Tariq said.

"I can do that. But now what do you think will happen?"

"We will have war. And I am going to do my best to provoke it. This will be long and can not be avoided. So I choose to go on the attack. I want the international public to know that the French are taking us against our will, that they are a power much stronger and more sophisticated than we are, but that we are resisting. Can you tell that story?"

Ted said, "I'll try to be even-handed, not take sides, *ya* Tariq. You know that's my role. Just keep me informed and, for God's sake, take care of yourself, my brother. I wouldn't want to answer to Lili if something should happen to you now!"

Tariq clapped him on the shoulder and gave him a brief smile that lit up his whole face.

Ted got up to go.

Tariq said, "In a few days Farid will bring you to me. Be careful that you are not followed. Now, go with God."

Ted paused. "*Ya* Tariq, there is something I must tell you. Meriam had a brilliant flashback to Taza and says she is positive Kassim led those soldiers to her house and incited that attack."

Tariq's eyes flashed. "It only confirms what we have suspected. But I am sorry, my brother, for your sake. I think we may see Kassim soon and have our chance for vengeance."

***

The Europeans got ready for action, buying up whatever provisions were in the stores, bringing out and cleaning guns, counting their ammunition. George Clark sent his wife out of the city in one of many small caravans leaving the gates. The Moroccans stood around in large groups, moving only reluctantly when a horseman or carriage approached, spitting as it passed. Some threw rocks and small pebbles. Ted stayed with the Consul, trying to get as much information as he could.

"If *Qaid* Bouzid's the best we have to defend us," Jenkins said to Ted quietly, "then God help us. His soldiers didn't even have bullets for their guns! When we sent the troops out to get the rest of the Europeans at the quarry, we had to wait two hours while someone went to customs and got the bullets unlocked. What a country!"

***

Ted rode out again with Farid, this time to a small settlement of workers located near the beach on the southern side of the city. There was a cluster of *nowellas*, straw houses that had been erected to provide shelter for the workers' families. He arrived slightly before the time Tariq had indicated and sat with several of Tariq's men outside one of the huts. Suddenly he noticed a small group of horsemen riding fast toward them.

391

Ted stood up to get a better look. To his shock, he saw that Kassim was at the head of the group.

He turned to warn the men with him, but it was too late. Jumping down from his horse, Kassim pointed a finger accusingly at him and commanded, "This is the ring-leader of the trouble makers. Kill him."

Ted ducked behind one of the houses. He felt a bullet strike his shoulder and sat down abruptly. Through a daze he thought to himself, "That bastard has finally won."

But something else was happening. Tariq and his men appeared and even in his weakened state, Ted could see that they vastly outnumbered Kassim. The men surrounded Kassim's group. Tariq commanded, "Seize that man, take him to our camp and await further instructions from me."

His men dragged Kassim from his horse. Tariq's men fired on the others from their horses, and many of Kassim's men fell; the others turned and fled. In minutes they had all disappeared, and Tariq was bending over Ted. "My brother, are you badly hurt?"

"I don't think it'll kill me," Ted said, "but it sure as hell hurts!" He took his hand away from the wound, and blood gushed forward.

Tariq assisted him to remount his horse, and he and Farid led him through the back roads, along the beach, by the half-built jetty, and finally to the door of the Clarks. "You will be all right, Ted. God keep you. When all this is over, I will see you again, *insh'allah*. Please give this to Lili, my brother." Tariq briefly grazed Ted's hand, tucking a piece of paper into it. He touched his own heart and rode off. Somehow Ted dismounted and gained the entrance of the house, where George Clark got him into bed and called a doctor.

As he lay in bed over the next week listening to what was

happening, Ted had a million questions. What had happened to Kassim? How had Kassim known he was there, in the first place? Had Tariq known Kassim was in the vicinity? What would Tariq and his men do to him? He hoped it would be harsh; he knew Tariq could be brutal if provoked. He wondered if Tariq would simply execute Kassim. He certainly had sufficient cause, Ted thought, and he had to admit he wouldn't care.

Ted used the time in bed to begin assembling his report. He drafted an article that he asked George to get out through the telegraph office.

JULY 31: Recently several incidents have rocked Casablanca and set the scene for a potential explosion. Casablanca is a new town, five hundred kilometers south of Tangier, population composed mostly of foreign representatives of trading concerns and their estimated 10,000 protégés.

A week ago local Arab inhabitants complained about a small train, built to bring construction materials to a new jetty that would facilitate unloading of larger ships. The train passed through a cemetery, issuing loud whistles that the tribesmen claimed were disrespectful to their dead. Their complaints to the Compagnie Marocaine, funding the jetty, fell on deaf ears. Yesterday the Muslims took matters into their own hands, placing rocks along the tracks to disable the train. They then attacked the French and Algerian workers, murdering most of them, mutilating their bodies and leaving them exposed along the road and in the quarry.

This tragedy is the result of rising ill will among

the population, caused in large part by the arrival of French customs officers. The Moroccans accuse them of collecting not only the port taxes, but also of appropriating the bulk of contributions made to the local religious shrines.

Barring other immediate means of protection, the community has sought refuge in the French Consulate. *Moulay* al Amin, uncle to the young Sultan of Morocco, Abdel Aziz, arrived in town yesterday and convinced all the Arab tribesmen to meet with him outside the city gates, which he promptly shut, locking them out.

The situation is grave, although for the moment all is calm in the city.

***

In Tangier Lili read Ted's article to Matt and Amelia. They were in the garden talking to Amelia as she puttered around among her roses, clipping off dead heads and keeping up a steady litany of complaints about the aphids.

Amelia continued to prune until halfway through the story, when its full gravity struck her. Then she dropped her shears and looked up in shock. "My God, Matt, it sounds dreadful! And Ted is right in the thick of it. He shouldn't have gone down there. This is just too dangerous. Oh dear, Matthew. Can we find out anything more?" She was wringing her hands by now, the aphids totally forgotten.

"Now honey, don't fret," Matt said. "I'll get Regnault or St. Aulaire on the telephone and see what they can tell us. They must be in the know, since it's the French Consulate where all the foreign community has gathered. You just come inside, my dear. Lili will fix you a nice cup of tea." He took her arm and led Amelia gently into the house.

A few minutes later, Matt joined them on the porch. "This is darn serious. I knew something like this would happen. Wasn't I just saying so the other night."

"What, Matthew?" Amelia couldn't restrain herself. "What did Regnault have to say?"

"Oh, sorry, my dear. Well, he said that he had the news from another ship that just come up from Casablanca, but of course, he'd be mighty grateful to see Ted's article. I'll run it over there in a minute."

"Yes, Papa," Lili intervened gently. "That's a good idea. But what else is happening?"

"St. Aulaire's sent a battleship down from here. The Galilee. Maybe you noticed it sitting in the harbor? He's given it strict orders not to do anything, but just to show we mean business. He's to make it clear that the French won't put up with any further loss of life. How's he going to send that message without doing anything, I'd like to know?"

Matt continued, "Just between us, not for general publication, you understand, St. Aulaire has called for reinforcements from Paris, and another battle ship is on the way to Casablanca. Should be there in a day or so, I believe. It'll have troops and be equipped for a real battle. The Du Chayla is its name."

"But this is terrible!" Amelia said. "Ted's caught in the middle of this situation which sounds quite dangerous. Isn't there anything we can do?"

Lili was quieter, but she shared Amelia's concerns. She was sure Tariq was there, too.

The whole city of Tangier waited, aware of at least the

broad outlines of the situation, if not all the political details. Lili tried to go about her work at the clinic, relieved that Kassim seemed to have disappeared for the moment. Alice told her he'd gone down to Casablanca and confided that she was a bit worried about him. Immediately, Lili's anxieties increased.

Resolutely, she refused to think about Tariq. By now sure that her pregnancy was not imagined, Lili had decided to keep this fact to herself. She knew what Tariq was doing was important and feared to distract his focus by announcing this information, even if there had been a way to do so. She was proud to be carrying Tariq's baby and one way or the other she could manage this by herself for the moment.

Amelia and Matt grasped at any bit of news their friends might have, besieging the French Legation for bulletins. News began to filter back. There had been a bloodbath. The Galilee did not wait for the Du Chayla as instructed, but had landed its untrained men, who panicked and started shooting at random. This triggered large scale retaliation by the Arabs, who went berserk, and simply ignored the bullets, clubbing people to death, looting in the streets.

***

Regnault announced that the French had restored order in Casablanca. Almost everyone in the city was dead; bodies were piled in heaps, just a handful of survivors. Despite their best efforts, Matt and Amelia couldn't get news of Ted. There were few first-hand witnesses and the rumors never mentioned his name. Just as Lili was beginning to fear for Amelia, who had worked herself into a state, they received a telegram from Ted. It was brief:

I'm fine. Don't worry. Wounded slightly but nothing serious. Plan return Tangier first week September.

Everyone except Lili relaxed. It had been a long time since she had heard from Tariq. She shared her fears with Mohammed, who had obediently dogged her steps since the day he arrived, but if he had news, he loyally refused to divulge anything about Tariq's whereabouts.

***

Ted returned, pale and weak, but full of stories about the siege, the state of war that now existed, the difficulties he had in leaving Casablanca, which he had finally achieved by ship, it being too unstable in the countryside to risk travel by land.

"This looks like the beginning of the end," he told the family. "French troops are increasing daily in the city, and a commander's been posted. I think we're in for it now." Soon after his arrival, Ted found private time with Lili and was able to tell her as much as he knew about Tariq.

"I'm so worried, Ted," Lili said. "Why haven't I heard anything? It's been three months."

Ted started. "Oh, I have this note from Tariq. I should have given it to you earlier, but it completely slipped my mind."

She leaned forward and Tariq's silver ring, which she wore around her neck, slipped from her bodice, catching Ted's eye.

"What's that?" he said.

"This is actually Tariq's and my wedding ring," she said. "We plan to marry formally as soon as Tariq gets back, but in the meantime he wanted me to have this." She unfolded the note and read eagerly:

My heart, you know why I can not be with you right now, but I am thinking about you daily. Lili, leave Morocco as soon as possible. Go to Paris to wait for me. There are enemies here, one of whom you know well. Take Mohammed and go to Paris, to Meriam. I will meet you there when I can, *insh'allah*.

***

Tariq turned Kassim over to his men with instructions. "Take care of this son of sin. I want him to live to regret the harm he has done to my friends." He did not stay to see what would befall Kassim as he had received an urgent note from Madani al-Glaoui, urging him to come and join him in Marrakesh. He was to bring as many of his men as possible.

To avoid arousing undue attention Tariq and five hundred men, all trained by him in Egypt, split into groups of five or six, taking slightly different routes south. Tariq kept Hassan by his side; he had grown fond of the young boy, who was quickly becoming a man under his guidance. On the sixth day, they arrived at the Glaoui's mountain fortress outside Marrakesh. Tariq's men trickled in little by little until all were assembled by midday.

Madani al Glaoui strode out into his sunny tiled courtyard, his arms open wide in welcome. "*Ahlen*. It is good that you are here. Much is happening right now and you must be a part of it."

Tariq wanted to ask him more, but the Glaoui strode off to meet a new group of arriving horsemen. Everywhere he looked, Tariq saw groups of men, all armed with expensive, up-to-date weapons. A servant showed him to his quarters and pointed out where his men were housed in an outlying building.

That night Tariq joined the Glaoui and his guests for dinner in his huge outside court. It was August, and the stone paved courtyard, covered by bright red and black woven rugs, had a pleasant breeze, compared to the heat of the plains he had passed through. Tariq sat at a table with T'Hami al Glaoui, Madani's brother, and five other Berber *sheikhs*. Tariq looked around; there were at least ten clusters of people grouped around small tables. Cushions had been placed for them to sit on, and brass kettles on glowing braziers added to the light of a full moon.

T'Hami nodded in greeting. "We are glad to see you back in Morocco, my brother."

Tariq smiled. "I felt there were things I could do to help my country here."

"Yes, we have heard of these 'things'," the younger Glaoui said. "Much still needs to be done. Your work has helped by bringing the French out into the open. Now we can do battle with them."

Another chieftain had been following the conversation and said, "Our lord Abdel Aziz is not capable of leading such an effort. Would you agree?" He stared at Tariq, waiting for his answer.

Tariq's answer was quick, "By Allah, I have thought about this constantly since I left Fez. I love our Sultan, but yes, I am sorry to say that he is too much dominated by his advisors. One cannot trust that he will stay constant in his views. His new Prime Minister, Omar Tazi, is a great friend of the French."

The man grunted in agreement. "We do not want the French in Morocco."

A sizzling roast lamb was delivered to the table and the

men fell to eating. Tariq was left to reflect on this discussion. It was true that he was disillusioned with Abdel Aziz. His leader had shown himself to be fickle, even to those like himself and Mehdi, who had been his closest friends. Abdel Aziz did not have the steel inside himself to fend off the French. Without this, Tariq thought, all his efforts would come to nothing, since the Sultan's ultimate support could not be counted on. He wondered what was brewing at the Glaoui palace.

***

Madani al Glaoui invited his guests to a gazelle hunt. Looking from his window that morning Tariq saw a hundred or so horsemen approach the fortress. He stared out, shielding his eyes from the sun, to see if he could identify the rider in their midst. *Moulay* (prince) Hafid, he thought, in surprise. What would he be doing here? This older brother of Abdel Aziz had been passed over as leader of the country. Tariq had never liked him very much and suspected many did not, as he had a reputation for perversion. Perhaps this was why his father had selected the younger brother, Abdel Aziz to be sultan. Or maybe Ba Ahmed had wanted it because Aziz could more easily be manipulated by the courtiers. *Moulay* Hafid had been named Governor of Marrakesh by his brother, and had proven to be corrupt and greedy. Tariq had heard rumors that Madani al-Glaoui had been supporting the prince for some time, and his arrival here with such a large troop of soldiers seemed to bear this out.

The hunt was a huge success. Tariq found himself enjoying the chase. It was fun to forget Morocco's problems for a while and give in to the excitement of the moment, trying his skill against the silvery gazelles, trying to calculate their speed and where to place his bullet to catch them in mid-leap. Afterwards as the large party feasted on the sixty or more animals they had shot, he noticed Madani al Glaoui in close conference with *Moulay* Hafid, who had agreed to stay on a few more days.

***

They met in Marrakesh, at *Moulay* Hafid's palace, along with the group of tribal leaders and others who had gathered with the Glaoui. The men were seated on the brocade cushions lining the room, talking quietly among themselves and sipping tea, all equally curious about what had brought them together. Then one of the prince's men stood up and addressed the group. "Gentlemen, I wish to read you some of the correspondence we have been receiving about *Sidna* Abdel Aziz's actions, which are leading to the sale of our beloved country to the infidels."

A hush fell over the room and for the next half hour, the secretary read aloud from many letters complaining of the Sultan's extravagances, the debt he had accumulated with France, the French incursion into Casablanca. All had as a common theme that Abdel Aziz was not competent to protect their country and many begged *Moulay* Hafid to take over the leadership from his brother.

The men sat in silence. They already had Abdel Aziz and Bou Hamara, still pretending to have a claim to the throne. What would they do with a third contender?

Madani al-Glaoui rose to his feet. "My lords, I put it to you that *Moulay* Abdel Aziz has failed in his duty to protect Morocco from the infidel. It is time to let his brother, *Moulay* Hafid, who represents a united south, as shown by your presence today, take his place. *Moulay* Abdel Aziz is no more than a shadow of a Sultan."

People shifted uncomfortably in their seats and muttered to their neighbors. Then one *qaid* stood up and said, "We do

401

not have this authority. Only the *ulema* in Fez have the right to elect the Sultan."

Now that the unthinkable had been raised, no one knew what to do next.

Madani made a motion to his men, standing nearby in the courtyard, and on cue they turned toward *Moulay* Hafid and shouted, "Long live our Lord," the salute traditionally given to the Sultan. As if it had been planned, the call to prayer rang out seconds later, and everyone rose to go to the mosque. From somewhere, the Glaoui put his hands on a long crimson parasol, duplicate of that used by the Sultan, and raised it over the head of *Moulay* Hafid.

Tariq thought, that's it then. It had become *a fait accompli*.

With the election of *Moulay* Hafid as Sultan in the South, Tariq became optimistic. Maybe with a better leader they could drive out the French. He also worried for Lili, though, since he'd had no news of her since he saw Ted a month ago in Casablanca. Had she had followed his request and left Morocco? He knew he would not be able to protect her from Kassim as long as he was down in Marrakesh. He decided to send Hassan to Tangier to make sure Lili had gone, even though he knew it would take at least a month for the young boy to make the round trip.

***

Lili read and reread Tariq's note. Amelia and Matt would have to understand why she wanted to go to Paris. That night as they gathered for their afternoon drinks, she steeled herself and began.

"Mama and Papa, I have to talk to you. Ted already knows some of this, but now I must bring you into my secret."

Both parents put down their drinks.

Lili realized she was wringing her hands, and put them in her lap. "Tariq came back to Morocco some time ago. This must remain completely confidential within our family, as there are good reasons why people should not know this."

Matt nodded. Amelia was looking apprehensive.

"Tariq and I love each other. I think we both have for a long time, but by the time we realized this, we were both married to others, so there was nothing to be done."

Lili thought both her parents relaxed slightly. "When I met him again in July, I realized fate had given me a second chance. You remember that weekend I said I had gone to Gibraltar with friends?"

They nodded.

"Actually, I was with Tariq. He is so wonderful, Mama. I knew we were meant for each other. I'm so grateful that things worked out this way." Lili was getting tearful. "We married secretly then; he gave me this ring." She pulled it out of her dress. "And now, the best news of all; I'm pregnant! I'm so thrilled, and I hope you will be, too." She looked at them both a little fearfully, hoping they would share her joy and not condemn her for such unconventional behavior.

Amelia went over to Lili and kissed her. "My dear, some things are destiny. I think you and Tariq fall into that category. The test of time has run its course, and clearly you two are meant for each other."

Matt was a little more gruff. "Well, I don't like the fact that he can't be with you right now, especially with you expecting."

"I wish he could be here, too. And I'm worried about him. Ted told me he was in the thick of things in Casablanca. It... well, it frightens me." Lili's eyes filled with tears again. Then she straightened up. "But Tariq is strong and brave. And he wants the best for Morocco. I'm proud that he's willing to fight to get it."

Ted agreed. "He knows what he's doing. I wouldn't worry too much. He's a trained soldier and can take care of himself."

"Yes," Lili said, "he can. I keep reminding myself of that. But he has sent me this note and told me we are in danger here. I must go to Paris, to Meriam, and wait for him there."

"Why?" Matt said. "Darned if I see why you have to go running off to Paris."

Ted said, "We can't get into all the reasons. But he's right. Tariq has enemies. It's best to follow his advice."

Matt sat thinking, puffing on his cigar. Lili could tell he wasn't happy about all of this. Then he looked up, "Well, he's your husband, and if that's what he wants, I guess you'd better do it."

"Maybe we should all go," Amelia said. "It's awfully grim here right now and probably it will get worse. Why don't we shut up the house and all go spend a few months up there? It would be great fun."

Lili's heart soared. With her whole family around her and Meriam nearby, the wait for Tariq would be easier.

Lili made arrangements with Alice Watson at the clinic, promising that she would come back and continue to work in her clinic. Alice admitted she was distracted these days because Kassim had been in a terrible accident in Casablanca and was taking a long time to recover. She confided, in strictest confidence, that he had been wounded in his groin, emasculated, in fact.

"For a while, my dear, we weren't sure he would make it. But now he seems to be recovering. What a tragedy, though, poor boy."

Lili shuddered. She knew Tariq could be ruthless, but this was a severe punishment. Of course, she acknowledged, he deserved it and this was the Arab way.

***

It was time to force a direct challenge between the two princes. Tariq was leading the unruly army, which had grown to forty thousand men with the deserters from Fez, as well as with tribal recruits. His core was the four hundred men he had trained personally in Cairo. He put Hassan, who had returned from Tangier, in charge of this squad, since he thought it would be good experience for the young man, and these troops, in fact, needed little guidance.

They marched north from Marrakesh, skirting the area around Casablanca, where the French had settled in, making passage almost impossible. Their destination was Fez, where Abdel Aziz was still holding court. After two weeks' march, a scout rushed into Tariq's tent where he was sitting with Hassan having a glass of tea. "*Ya sidi*," the scout gasped, "*Sidna* Abdel Aziz's army is not more than a day's march from us."

Tariq poured him some tea. "He must know *Moulay* Hafid has declared himself Sultan."

"He has many troops, my lord, and cannons. And I talked to one of his soldiers, who is a cousin of mine and wants to desert. He told me they have many machine guns. The French are with them, maybe ten advisors. They have long tubes they see through, and machines they use to signal messages to distant parts of the army."

"May Allah protect us," Tariq said. "They seem much stronger than we are." He turned to Hassan. "Go and see if *Moulay* Hafid will meet with us. We need to discuss this."

In a half hour they were seated in the older prince's tent,

where the scout repeated his information to *Moulay* Hafid and Madani al-Glaoui. Hafid looked more and more dejected as the scout enumerated the superior number of men, arms and advisors controlled by Abdel Aziz. When he had finished his report, the three men sat without saying anything for several minutes. Then Prince Hafid broke the silence, "We shall capitulate. *Si* Madani, you shall carry the white flag and go to Aziz. Try to negotiate good terms for us."

Tariq was stunned. How could he give up without a fight? He tried to argue with the prince, but soon saw that the older man, unused to warfare, did not want to face useless bloodshed. And, Tariq suspected, he was also loathe to harm his younger brother, despite wanting to wrest the leadership from him.

Madani reluctantly agreed to carry the truce flag, but Tariq resolved to make a last ditch effort, regardless of Hafid's orders. The following day, as the Glaoui rode out slowly toward Abdel Aziz's camp, Tariq led his core squad, armed with the best equipment they had and made up of his most accurate sharpshooters, toward the Sultan's camp. They crouched behind an embankment, where Tariq could see Abdel Aziz and some of his advisors watching from a peak. He signaled his men to stay low until he gave them the go-ahead. He looked at Abdel Aziz, despair in his heart. Had he come so far, and now turned against his own ruler, just to end in ignominy? And worse yet, to let the French take over without a battle? As he watched the ruler, he saw Walter Harris next to him, loyal to the end, he guessed. Maybe they had a hand or two of bridge in the evenings when the war talk was over. It looked like there were enough French there for three tables. Abdel Aziz was always one to provide for his own comforts. Undoubtedly the women of his harem were there, too.

He noticed a column of soldiers wheel away from the

camp. Quickly, he signaled his men to be ready. "Let them come as close as you can, before you shoot, my warriors," he instructed. They waited, and then, at his arm motion, fired at the column. To Tariq's amazement, the column stopped in disarray, and almost immediately turned back. "Now, men," Tariq shouted. "They are retreating. Do not let them get back to camp. Follow them. Every one up." His men rose from their crouched positions and started running after them, some finding their horses quickly. They fired barrage after barrage of shots, many finding their marks. Abdel Aziz's men started going down. Tariq saw the twenty-five year old ruler, who had been watching the spectacle much as he watched his beloved fireworks turn and flee the scene, bullets flying past him. Tariq, on his black charger, pursued with his men, and saw that no shots actually hit the Sultan, although his cloak was shredded.

Tariq shouted, "Abdel Aziz and his men are retreating! Don't let them gain any ground. Someone find *Si* Madani and tell him to stop. We are victorious."

A distance from the royal camp, Tariq stopped his troops. They sat in amazement and watched as slaves disbanded the camp, soldiers and servants running in every direction. His soldiers were pillaging. How could they have defeated this well-equipped army that outnumbered them so greatly? He shook his head in disbelief, as Madani al-Glaoui rode up to him. "Thanks to Allah. Our cause is just and he has smiled on us today," he said to the Glaoui.

"*Al Hamdu lillah*, praise be to Allah," the Glaoui responded. "It is good that I rode so slowly. Thanks to Allah that we did not surrender. His ways are mysterious, indeed." The two men, both incredulous at such an easy rout, fell into each other's arms, pounding each other on the back.

***

Tariq and his men returned to the area around Casablanca to lead the fight against the French. The tribes had kept a nine-month siege against the French army that had invaded the town, but in March General Lyautey was sent to replace the weak commander. The fighting became more intense, although Tariq, with his expertise in guerilla warfare and agile horsemen was able to evade the formal battle squares of the French, and inflict serious damage.

In May, 1908 *Moulay* Hafid was formally declared Sultan in Fez.

***

The Shields family rented a comfortable apartment in Paris near the Ben Simons and settled in for the winter season. Lili was grateful to have Amelia and Matt around her. They had accepted the news of her secret marriage and pregnancy with an aplomb she would never have predicted and she sensed that they felt she had made the right choice, even if her timing left something to be desired. She couldn't help reflecting that nothing in her family's life had gone the conventional route, no matter how hard they had all tried. Meriam was estranged from Ted with an illegitimate child, and now she, too, was only informally married to a man who already had one wife and might never return. But she just couldn't worry about all those things. She was cushioned by a loving family and realized she always had been; they had helped a defenseless Moroccan orphan come to full maturity. Lili realized now that she had always struggled to find her identity. When she was younger, she had wanted desperately to become a European, to fit in with Matt and Amelia and the Western community. But slowly she had been drawn more and more to her Moroccan background. Tariq had pointed out to her, that long-ago day at Ted's wedding, that she was not an American, not really. At that time she hadn't wanted to accept it. So she had married Arthur and had pretended to be a conventional American wife. But it had never worked. In Fez, she had begun sloughing the European accoutrements, the clothes, the furnishings. Maybe circumstances had forced her into this to some extent. She admitted they had certainly played a strong role. Tariq had always been there, reminding her of her Moroccan heritage, drawing her toward him. It had been a difficult transition, she thought, and maybe she wouldn't have chosen if it hadn't been for him. But now the past was behind her. Lili knew she could be herself and no longer had to pretend to a background she didn't have. Her only fear was that, having found happiness with Tariq, he wouldn't return to fulfill her destiny.

The first few months Lili was in Paris, she constantly looked for Tariq in the crowds, always expecting to find him striding toward her with his quick smile. But as time went by, no news came and he did not appear. Although Mohammed continually reassured her that he was positive things were all right, as her pregnancy progressed, Lili became increasingly dispirited. The lack of any news seemed to her to confirm that Tariq was dead. The Paris newspapers were full of reports about the fighting in Morocco; she knew her husband was deeply involved in these battles and it was hard to convince herself he hadn't been hurt. She tried to reconcile herself to the fact that Tariq might be dead, telling herself that their love had been a wonderful thing and giving thanks for the fact that Tariq had left a part of himself with her.

In March, Lili delivered a beautiful boy whom she named Amir. She poured her love and affections into the baby, refusing to think anymore about Tariq, walling away her memories of him, determined only to think about the future. She was so proud. Finally, a child.

Then, one day in May, as she was sitting in Luxembourg Gardens, gently rocking the baby carriage, she felt someone behind her. She bent protectively over the carriage, checking to see if Amir was all right. Then a gentle hand on her shoulder melted away all the fears of the past months. She turned around to see Tariq, standing gazing fondly at the baby.

***

Sherif Raisuni, after a brief spell as a German protégé, became allied with *Moulay* Hafid. When the new Sultan offered him governorship of the entire northern region of Morocco, he renounced his agreement with the Germans, as *Moulay* Hafid explained he could not have a foreigner ruling part of his kingdom.

***

In summer of 1909 *Moulay* Hafid's troops captured Bou Hamara, who had lost much of his following as he became more and more closely allied with the Spanish. The Pretender was put into a small cage and tortured by *Moulay* Hafid for six weeks. He was then fed to the Sultan's lions.

***

In July 1912 *Moulay* Hafid signed a document with General Lyautey agreeing to abdicate in favor of his brother, *Moulay* Youssef, who assumed command of a Protectorate under the rule of France.